CURSE

CURSE

Andrew Neiderman

severn House

This first hardcover edition published in Great Britain 2004 by
SEVERN HOUSE PUBLISHERS LTD of
9–15 High Street, Sutton, Surrey SM1 1DF,
by arrangement with Simon & Schuster UK Ltd.

British Library Cataloguing in Publication Data

Neiderman, Andrew
    Curse
    1.   Witches - Unites States - Fiction
    2.   Suspense fiction
    I.   Title
    813.5'4 [F]

    ISBN 0-7278-6074-7

Printed and bound in Great Britain by
MPG Books Ltd., Bodmin, Cornwall.

For Robin Rue
Who seized the moment and kept the flag flying high

Curse

Prologue

Even without the mystical ceremony, burial at night was enough to unnerve the mourners. They clutched the black candles tightly in their right hands as if their holding firmly onto the light kept them from falling into the newly dug grave they surrounded. The pungent odor of freshly uncovered damp earth filled their nostrils, but no one coughed or as much as cleared his throat.

They had been instructed to hold their candles at least six inches above their heads. Most had their arms stiffly extended, their bodies trembling like the bodies of subway riders clinging to their straps while the train jets into the night. Looking at each other, they saw how the small flames dripped yellow light over their faces and how their eyes glittered like those of the curious nocturnal creatures hovering in the shadows.

The candles flickered in the cool late September New York Catskill Mountain evening, but not one was extinguished. Anna Young had lit them while reciting some ancient incantation and that seemed to help each defy the wind. No one present questioned her power to do just that.

All those who were paying their final respects to Gussie Young felt they had benefitted from Anna's mother's spiritual gifts and were now benefitting from Anna's. Some were here out of a sense of obligation; some out of fear that what they had been given would be taken away if they weren't here.

Standing in the old cemetery about a mile out of Sandburg proper, the mourners were surrounded by hickory, oak, and birch trees and wild berry bushes. It was a pristine, ancient place where the thick forest was dark even in the middle of the afternoon. The closest home was Melvin Bedik's, a retired poultry and egg farmer, about midway between the cemetery and town.

The mourners closed the gaps between them, trying to touch, trying to feel secure and protected. They continued to cling tightly to their candles and stared at Anna, wondering what would take place next in this strange yet fascinating burial service, while off to the side the gravediggers waited uneasily for her command to lower her mother's coffin and make her an eternal citizen of this graveyard, the oldest in Sandburg, a hamlet in the town of Fallsburg. In New York state the communities were collected into townships and the townships into counties.

The cemetery had recently been added to the Fallsburg township's list of historical properties as a way to at least keep the graves and stones under the umbrella of the township's maintenance. The church that had once supported it was long gone, and with its demise went anyone to administer care. The sanctuary itself had become a shell that had gone up in flames when a drunken homeless man had wandered into it and fallen asleep with a cigarette that had slipped from his fingers and ignited the dry wood. Reverend Carter, the Episcopalian minister, actually was heard to say, "What better place for him to die than there, cupped in God's hand?"

Anna stood at the foot of her mother's grave. Her eyes were shut so tightly her eyelids looked like they had been stuck together since birth. Her head was back and she held her arms out to the side in crucifix fashion. In her right hand she clutched what the mourners knew to be strands of her dead mother's gray hair, which the eighty-four-year-old Gussie Young had worn long and straight, nearly down to her wing bones. In her left hand, Anna held a silver chalice. Some of the village children claimed they saw her drink a witch's brew from it when there was a full moon.

Everyone at the grave site had heard all of Anna's chants, even the ones that were nearly whispered, but no one could make any sense out of them. The language was gibberish, yet melodic. Of course, they had anticipated something like this and nothing traditional. No one had expected the presence of any clergyman at the funeral, not with the way they all were condemning Anna and her mother for what they characterized as the Black Arts.

Anna stopped her chant and tilted the chalice to pour what the mourners thought was either wine or blood over the strands of hair which she immediately dropped into the grave. Then she turned to the gravediggers and nodded.

Mesmerized by her actions, they jumped to lower the coffin. They were both eager to do what had to be done and then leave. Anna watched, her hands pressed against her bosom. After the coffin settled at the bottom, she turned to the mourners.

"My mother should not have died," she declared. "Despite her age, it was not her time. You all know she had much work to complete. He who caused this is here among you and you know who he is and where he is. I will not leave you until he is gone. This was what I have promised my mother and what I promise you."

Anna looked down at the coffin.

"My mother will not leave you either."

She smiled at them.

"You all know this is true," she said.

No one spoke, but some nodded. When the first shovelful of dirt hit the coffin, a large crow screeched and flew over their heads. The gravediggers paused and gazed at each other as if they were deciding whether or not to throw down their shovels and run for their lives. Then they looked at Anna and quickly resumed.

Anna nodded at the mourners, signaling the end. She turned back to the grave to watch the coffin being covered, and the mourners began their departing, each touching her arm or embracing her, speaking soft words of commiseration and then stepping away from the old cemetery and into their cars, snuffing out their candles one at a time.

The cars pulled away quietly, no one leaving too fast, some even keeping their headlights off until they were a bit down the road. They looked like they had simply materialized out of the shadows, old black souls fleeing their entombment.

Anna remained until her mother's grave was filled and the gravediggers had left. Then she knelt over it in the thick darkness. She put her palms down on the cold, fresh earth and raised her head to look up at the cloudy black sky.

It was as if something rose out of the grave into her arms and through her body. Her eyes were suddenly electric.

"I hear, Mother," she said. "And I swear he will not live to harm another."

One

Whoever said that April was the cruelest month wasn't thinking of upstate New York, Ralph Baxter thought. There was nothing cruel about seeing the ground thaw and the buds sprout on the tree branches. And there was certainly nothing cruel about the warmer air, the bluer sky, the birds returning, and the cold shadows retreating to wherever the hell dark things dwelt. He stood on his large front porch and took a deep breath. He was seventy-four and widowed for three years. Five years before Jennie's death, he and she had terminated the Cherrywood Lodge, his family's old farmhouse that had been converted into a tourist rooming house twenty-eight years ago.

It was a long time to be in the hospitality business, he thought, and laughed at what he imagined his grandfather would have said had he lived to see his cornfields turned into a couple of tennis and handball courts, a baseball field, and a swimming pool. The pool had long since gone to disrepair, the cement cracking, the paint nearly completely faded and gone. Weeds grew profusely where the baseball infield once was.

During the heyday of the New York Catskill resort years, his guests would play in tournaments against the guests of other rooming houses and small hotels. They had great picnics with barbecued hamburgers and chicken, fresh corn on the cob, and a salad made with the vegetables from his own gardens. Their clientele was comprised from nice New York City families. The grounds were alive with children and noise. Jennie was like everyone's grandmother. Guests got used to calling him Pop and her Mother Baxter. Despite what his grandfather would say, running a tourist house was a lot easier than farming and, for quite a few years, a lot more profitable, Ralph thought. It gave them enough for a comfortable retirement, but not enough to keep up a property this size.

Now, of course, it was too much house for just him. He had shut down most of it, confining the heat to just the kitchen, small parlor, and one bedroom. The lobby was too big to keep warm in the winter. Paneling peeled, window casings expanded and contracted, the old rugs were worn thin, and the furniture, never really used anymore, looked like rejects from even the thrift stores. It pained him to see the property degenerate, but there wasn't much he could do. Tourists were long gone. Even the memory of them dwindled and was lost in the darkness of the forest that surrounded his home and property, shadows and voices drifting in the wind. Occasionally, something would creak and echo in the house and he would lift his eyes expecting to see a group of New Yorkers walking down the hallway, laughing, their faces tan and robust, children trailing behind them, giggling and shouting, their voices tinkling like cans tied to the back bumper of a car for Just Marrieds.

But there was no one there, no one's voice or laugh to hear but his own.

He dug out his pocket watch and checked the time. Henry Deutch was late. Unusual for that man to be late, he thought. From what he knew about the man, he worked like a Swiss timepiece: efficient, coldly methodical. Ralph didn't like him. The only reason he was interested in Henry's arrival was his curiosity as to what in hell that man wanted from him. He couldn't recall passing more than a handful of words between them all these years.

As if thinking about him produced him, Henry Deutch's Mercedes came around the bend, up from Sandburg. The old road wasn't traveled much anymore and the county rarely came by to clean or maintain it. The dust spiraled behind the car. From this perspective, it looked like the vehicle was on fire. Deutch pulled up the driveway and stopped. He seemed to wait for the dust to settle before stepping out.

"Sorry I'm late," he said without much remorse in his voice. One could easily see from his expression that he didn't think it mattered very much to a man like Ralph Baxter. What else did he have to do with his time but to wait for busier, more productive men?

"That's all right; that's all right," Ralph said. He extended his hand when Henry reached the porch. It was a quick, perfunctory greeting. Deutch already looked preoccupied, nervous, even tense. "How you been, Henry?"

"I've been better. Maybe you heard about my problem in town," he added, and looked up expectantly, perhaps searching for a face bathed in sympathy.

Ralph shook his head slowly.

"No sir. Don't get into town as much as I usta. What's goin' on?"

"It's that damn seamstress, the madwoman some people believe has supernatural powers . . . Anna Young."

Ralph nodded.

"Yeah, I hear a lot about her. Heard she cured Simon Karachek's arthritis."

"Ridiculous. All of them, idiots, paying good money for her hocus-pocus."

"I wouldn't disregard all that out of hand, Henry. I remember when my father usta bring old lady Nussbaum up here to bless the soil with her charms. Rarely had a bad crop, too. 'Course, you probably don't remember her. I was barely five or six and you weren't even here yet. Railroad was just gettin' to be a big thing up here then and of course, later it would encourage all those city people to come up here for summer holidays. They published a magazine called *Summer Homes*. Why, I can remember—"

"Right," Henry interrupted. "I don't remember any of that and the railroad's gone so why waste time talking about it?"

Ralph could see how Henry's impatience made him fidgety, that and whatever was going on in the village.

"Um. How's Anna Young a problem for you?"

"She's been harassing me," he said, his face reddening with the effort. "I've had to get the law on her, not that it does much good."

"That so? Now that you mention it, I do recall something about you having her and her mother evicted nearly a year ago. That was a bit of a mess, wasn't it?" Baxter asked with a twinkle in his eye. He knew the story, but pretended to be vague about it.

Conniving old fox, Henry thought, just like the rest of them.

"I had no lease with them. I was kind enough to give them a place to start, but I had to get them out of there."

"Why?"

"Why? Because they were both crazy, spooking people, especially prospective new tenants, that's why. How would you like someone smelling up your home with that stinky incense and burning candles in the windows while chanting gibberish all night?"

"Yeah, I remember it better now. That eviction was quite a mess, quite a mess, and didn't the old lady die soon after?"

"How's that my fault?"

"I guess the turmoil was too much for her. Stress can kill, Henry," Baxter said almost gleefully.

"A man should have a right to do what he wants with his own property, shouldn't he?" Henry practically screamed. His face looked like it was swelling as well as turning another shade of crimson.

Ain't he a time bomb, Ralph thought, but he enjoyed seeing Henry disturbed. He thought about his uncle Charlie, his father's brother, who was good at putting little digs and scratches into people, infuriating them with remarks and expressions just for the pleasure of seeing how easy it was to rile them up.

"I've got no argument with that, Henry," Baxter said. "However, there are some people you just don't want to cross. They have some sort of power."

"Nonsense," Henry Deutch said, but not with as much enthusiasm as he had before. Ralph wondered how much about Anna Young Henry didn't believe or didn't want to believe and how much he couldn't help believe. A woman like that could keep you up nights, for sure, he thought.

Deutch looked around.

"It's so dry out here, you can taste the dust in the air."

"Oh? Would you like something cold to drink? I got some lemonade I just made."

"No," Henry said sharply. "I'm not here long." He gazed about. "This place is sinking so fast, it won't be worth tearing down," he muttered.

"Tearin' down? Who'd want to do that? This is a historical property, Henry. My great-grandfather built the main part of this house in the early 1800s. The rest was completed before the turn of the century. We still got the field stone foundation. That there's a workin' well, one of the best around," he said, pointing to the well in the front. "Water's delicious. Upstairs, I got a lot of the antiques, including oil lamps. Some of those antique dealers would piss in their pants from excitement, they ever came around here."

"Yeah, well, that's not going to happen. I come to make an offer on the place, Ralph," Henry said quickly, and wiped his face with his handkerchief.

"An offer?"

"I know you're struggling with the payments for all the improvements you mortgaged years ago," Henry said.

"I'm not struggling with them."

"I have it on good authority that you've missed some payments and been late. Someone could swoop in and buy up your debt," Henry threatened. "Bank would be glad to dump you."

"Is that right?"

"What you're paying every month doesn't leave you all that much for your retirement. What do you want with this big shack anyway?"

"Shack?"

"You don't need all this. You don't use most of it. It's like hanging onto a sinking ship or something. Fact is, I bet it's a fire trap by now. Looks like the building's dry enough to blow away," Henry commented. "Someone tells the insurance company to take another look at it, they'll drop you like a hot coal. Someone could do that, too, Ralph," he added, his eyes dark and determined.

Ralph looked at it as if he'd never noticed.

"I've lived here all my life, Henry. My wife gave birth to one of my boys in this house. She's buried up there in the family cemetery along with my parents and grandparents," he said, nodding at the small hill to his right. "I wouldn't sell this place."

"What do you think your boys are going to do with it after you're gone, Ralph? They'll give it away. Neither of them live around here, right?"

"That's not important now. What's important is what I want," Ralph said. "You just said a man has a right to do what he wants with his own property."

"Well, I came up here to give you an opportunity few will give you. I'm willing to put down fifty-five thousand for this wreck," Henry said. "Get someone to invest it properly for you and it will provide you with some nice retirement income and you can live in a decent apartment."

"Apartment?"

"Sure. I could even rent you one of mine at a discount as part of the deal. How's that sound?"

"Pretty disgusting," Ralph said with a laugh.

"Well, that's my offer and it's final," Henry said.

"What would you want with this property anyway?" Ralph asked, still smiling.

"I have a developer I might talk into subdividing and building here. It's a gamble, but I think I can make it happen," Henry said. From the way he said it, Ralph sensed it wasn't such a gamble. They had probably already analyzed the property and its potential.

"Oh, no," Ralph said, gazing over the overgrown fields. "I couldn't stand to see this property cut up like that."

"I'm not going to take this crappy ride up here again,"

Henry said. "When you get some sense in your head, you'll have to call me, but I wouldn't wait too long. You'll miss your chance, your last chance," he said, heavy with threat. "There are other properties that will fit my needs."

"Then you should go seek them pronto," Ralph said. "You're looking at a man who doesn't change his mind about the important things."

"Too bad." Henry started toward his car.

"What made you think I'd even consider it?" Ralph asked, more out of curiosity than anything else.

Henry paused and gazed around.

"I guess I thought if I lived in a graveyard, I'd want to get the hell out."

"Graveyard?" Ralph gazed at his property. "I suppose to someone else it might be, but it's not that to me. No sir. To me, it's home."

Henry shook his head.

"I don't suppose you ever felt that way about a piece of property, did you, Henry?"

"Nope," Henry said, opening his car door.

"I don't suppose you felt that way about anything," Ralph muttered. He remained where he was, watching Henry Deutch drive away, the dust cloud lingering like a bad thought. Then he stepped down and walked up to the cemetery to confer with his loved ones and tell them about the most ridiculous thing that just happened. Even the dead would laugh.

Henry Deutch cursed under his breath most of the way down the side road. He had been so confident. Usually he got what he wanted when it came to property, especially old and useless property. Since that Anna Young had crossed paths with him during the past year, nothing he touched or thought to touch amounted to anything. If he was superstitious . . .

Ludicrous. And all those people in town who gave way to her were just buffoons. She was just a madwoman, that's all, who happened to be choking him like a chicken bone in his throat, he thought. In fact, he was positive he had heard her outside his window reciting some gibberish two nights ago. He went for his shot gun immediately. If she was on his property, he'd blow her head off, he thought, but there was no one there, or at least, she was gone by the time he came rushing out of the house. He had nearly stumbled and fallen on his face, too. He could have accidentally blown his own head off!

It raised the level of his ire as he recalled it all. Now, instead of heading back to Sandburg, he decided to drive into Centerville and go to the First National Bank. He knew they held the mortgage on Baxter's property. Those weren't idle threats he made back there. He had dealt with Sam Wuhl, the vice president, a number of times before, to their mutual satisfaction. This would be another instance of that, he thought. He intended to buy Baxter's loan from the bank, offer them a little more, and wait for his opportunity to foreclose. It was what he did, what he did best.

Just as he reached the corner and started accelerating into his left turn toward Centerville, however, feathers and blood exploded on Henry Deutch's vintage Mercedes windshield like cannon shot.

He hit his brakes as fast as he could and the car spun out of control on the macadam. It literally bounced over a rise in the road and the rear right wheel caught on the edge of the ditch, turning the car off the road. He held on as best he could and kept the entire vehicle from going over the side. It rumbled to a stop and he clutched his chest.

The angina raged. His first thought was to get out his nitroglycerin and put a pill under his tongue. As Doctor Bloom had explained, it should relax his heart muscle and get the blood there quickly. Recently, he had to take two, the second following the first after about three minutes. It wasn't that long ago that one worked rapidly and that was that. Now the doctor was telling him he was experiencing unstable angina.

No wonder, he had thought. Look at the hell I'm going through with that woman.

Henry waited nervously after taking the second pill. He tried to relax, sat back, and stared at the windshield. The bird's head had slammed into it so hard, some of it remained glued to the glass. The eyes peered in at him, maddening, furious, angry. A piece of the beak hung on some flesh and then began to slide along the stream of blood.

Slowly, so slowly he was closing in on taking a third pill this time, Henry's breathing returned to normal and his heart slowed to a safe rhythm. He reached over to turn on the windshield wipers and washer fluid. It moved the blood, feathers and parts of the bird's head to the side, but it just streaked the glass even more. Henry started the stalled engine again and tried to back the car out of the ditch. However, the wheels spun and then he heard a terrible grinding noise and took his foot off the accelerator.

What the hell now? he thought.

Fortuitously, George Echert was returning from giving someone roadside assistance. The mechanic had gone to boost a battery. He slowed the tow truck as he drew closer and came to a stop.

"Henry?"

"Yeah," Henry Deutch said, lowering his window.

"You all right?"

"Yeah."

"What the hell happened? Is that blood on the outside of your windshield?"

"A bird flew right into me."

George, forty, lean but muscular, with stringy black hair that reached the base of his neck, hopped out of his truck. He shook his head and smiled.

"Sure you weren't speeding along and caught it?"

"I never speed," Henry said.

"Birds don't usually do that," George said, nodding at the windshield.

"This one did."

George scratched his head and then shrugged.

"We got to get you out and make sure you didn't do any damage to the axle. I'll pull up and tack you on from behind. Unless you want to wait for Triple A."

"I don't belong. Get me outta here."

"Okay. Jesus," George said, looking at the windshield again. "A bird just flew into your windshield, huh? Just committed suicide?"

"I told you that's what happened," Henry snapped.

Echert shook his head and then turned to him. Henry could hear the words coming.

"It's spooky."

"Don't even start that stuff," Henry warned, but deep down, he was beginning to wonder.

Two

The tiny bell above the shop door tinkled and Anna looked up from the pants she was taking in for Stuart Levy. The fifty-year-old owner of the Sandburg Gravel Company had taken his doctor's advice and lost fifteen pounds. The successful dieting had produced five suits and ten pairs of slacks for Anna to alter. A little less than a year ago, she had let out a dozen pairs of pants for Stuart who had gained the weight. Some people, especially Tilly Zorankin, who owned and operated the village's fish and vegetable store with her daughter Lily, claimed Anna made people lose and gain weight to create income for herself. Tilly wasn't complaining. She was just trying to show she knew all about those things.

With a soft, graceful motion, Anna brushed the strands of her raven black hair away from her forehead and turned to greet Joyce Slayton, who closed the door softly behind her, gazing out at the street as she did so. The forty-eight-year-old widow looked worried, her wide forehead wrinkling under her recently colored light brown bangs.

Joyce had lost her husband two years ago from congestive heart failure. She had a married son who had produced two beautiful grandchildren, a boy and a girl, and a thirty-year-old unmarried daughter, Lois, who lived in Los Angeles and worked for a television producer. Doug had left her comfortable, but not wealthy, although she always looked elegant and well-to-do. She had to watch her budget and the house seemed to constantly need something, whether it be plumbing or roofing. She despised the idea of ever having to ask her children for anything. Dependancy was the last stage in the journey toward the great beyond.

I'm still a very attractive woman, she thought. My life is nowhere near over.

Joyce stared at Anna for a long moment.

"Do you have it?" Anna asked her.

Joyce nodded. It was obvious that she was having difficulty. Maybe she had spoken with Reverend Carter, Anna thought. Maybe he had frightened her with talk of hell as he had some of Anna's other clients.

Joyce looked down and then glanced again at the street before stepping forward, looking a little more determined.

Anna Young put the slacks aside and turned to fully face her. Anna's age was a mystery to everyone. In fact, everything about her was cloaked in an enigma. She had come to Sandburg a little more than two years ago with her mother, who established the tailor shop in Deutch's building. Her mother looked so much older than Anna that there was a theory Anna wasn't her true daughter. She was either a younger sister's child or some adopted child. Yet there were strong enough physical resemblances to challenge the latter theory. Others who believed in the mystical, fostered the idea that Gussie Young had even greater powers and became pregnant when she was in her mid-fifties. She died when she was eighty-four, but Anna did not look much older than a woman in her late twenties, early thirties at most, most of the time.

That was what made predicting her age so difficult. She seemed to have the uncanny ability to look older or younger some days. It wasn't how she dressed. Usually she wore a loose fitting long skirt and a pearl button, frilly collared, and frilly sleeved blouse. She never wore any makeup, not even lipstick, and yet her lips were a rich ruby, especially on dark days, rainy days, and always at night.

The mystery of her age had its home in her eyes. They twinkled with youth and vitality, but they gazed into the faces of her customers and clients with a wisdom that filled these people with awe and respect, or at least a healthy amount of credibility. It was nearly impossible to talk with her on a one-on-one basis and not come away feeling you had experienced something extraordinary, something beyond reality.

Anna had classical beauty features: high and prominent cheekbones, a full, perfectly shaped mouth, and a neck that was just the right length to turn gracefully into her inviting shoulders. Sometimes her collarbone was visible, the thin gold chain with her gold pentacle lying so softly and yet so firmly against her skin it looked burned into her. Although the blouses she wore were loose, it was not difficult to see she was a full-bosomed woman whose breasts held their shape and moved tightly along with a turn of her shoulders and waist. She wore no bra and when she stepped into the daylight with the sun behind her, the silhouette of her bosom was clear enough to turn men's heads and make women envious.

And yet, she had no romantic relationships, no beau, no lover of her own. However, there was nothing about her that suggested frustration or any sort of longing. A more contented looking woman could not be found. Her Mona Lisa smile of peace added to the mystery and helped to stir the stories, the rumors, and create the aura that Anna needed in order to capture her clients, win their faith, and work her deeds. For some time now, area clergymen had begun to take notice, and most, like Reverend Carter, Rabbi Balk, and Father McDermott were beginning to feel threatened, some preaching outright warnings against Anna's spiritualism that to them was either bogus or heathen.

"What's wrong, Mrs. Slayton?" Anna asked when Joyce still held back. "Don't you want to do this? It's very important that you do it out of your own will."

"Yes, I do. It's just that . . ."

"Just that what, Mrs. Slayton?"

Joyce looked reluctant to say.

"We must have no distrust between us, Mrs. Slayton."

"I can't help feeling like it's cheating. I mean, what about afterward? Will he still love me, care for me?" she blurted.

"Oh," Anna said, laughing to herself. So Joyce Slayton's hesitation wasn't born from some religious predilection after all. She was merely worried about the future. "Of course, he will, Mrs. Slayton, otherwise, what would be the point?" she replied with a soft smile.

Joyce Slayton nodded, her turquoise eyes darkening as the determination began to build.

"All right," she concluded. She stepped closer, opened her purse, and produced a recent head shot of herself. Her fingers trembling, she handed it to Anna who looked at it for a moment, nodded, and then rose.

"I'll just be a moment," Anna said, and went through the beaded curtain at the rear of her shop. When she returned, she had an antique mirror in her hands, the frame of which was made of a rich dark mahogany with what looked like tiny hands embossed around the glass.

"It's very pretty," Joyce said.

"Yes," Anna said, turning the mirror over. "It's more than a hundred years old."

"Is it really?"

Anna nodded. She opened a drawer in her desk and produced a small knife. Carefully, she brought the edge of the blade to the backing and pried enough of it away to slip Joyce's picture inside. Then she found some glue in her drawer and repaired the backing neatly.

"Now what?" Joyce asked quickly, holding her breath.

"Step into the changing room, please," Anna said. She opened the door of the small cubicle. One wall was a mirror. She hung the antique mirror on the hook of the door and turned to Joyce.

"What do I do?"

"You must disrobe and stand before the mirror for at least ten minutes."

"Just stand there?"

"And think of Mr. Gardner. Think of nothing else. Picture him. Conjure him. See his face in the mirror. Focus, fixate, put all your mental powers into it, Mrs. Slayton. You must see him in the glass."

Joyce hesitated.

"If you don't believe in this; if you don't do it with a full heart, Mrs. Slayton, it won't work," Anna said.

Joyce Slayton took a breath. She had reason to come here; she had reason to believe. She had seen what Anna Young had done for Mildred Thompson's mousey looking daughter. Two months ago she had married handsome Clark Potter, a young real estate agent, and everyone was amazed. Everyone but Anna Young and Mildred Thompson, that is.

"I understand," Joyce said, and went into the dressing room. The other walls were a pale yellow and the floor was covered in a cheap linoleum. There was the strange aroma of some exotic incense, but there was no smoke, no evidence of anything burning.

"I'll keep time for you," Anna said before closing the door. "Good fortune, Mrs. Slayton."

Anna closed the door and returned to her sewing machine. She worked quietly. The small grandfather clock on the shelf by the door ticked. When ten full minutes had passed, Anna put down the garment and knocked on the door.

"You can get dressed now, Mrs. Slayton," she said.

Moments later, Joyce Slayton emerged. She looked flushed, her eyes full of excitement. Anna smiled.

"You did it, didn't you?"

"Yes, I did. I felt almost as though he was really there, as if it was a window and not a mirror."

Anna nodded.

"That's right, Mrs. Slayton. It would feel that way."

"Now what?" Joyce asked, her eyes glittering with excitement.

"Now, you must give him the mirror. Every time he looks at it, he will see you and his heart will begin to unfold and be vulnerable to your charms."

"How long will it take?" Joyce asked breathlessly. She felt as if she had been running miles.

"I have seen it take no longer than a few days and I have seen it take as long as a month or more," Anna said. "If he puts the mirror in a prominent place and he looks into it more often, it will work faster."

"And he'll love me forever? I mean, even if he doesn't look into this mirror?" Joyce asked.

"It's like a mold being made," Anna explained. "You will become part of him, embedded in his heart."

Joyce nodded as if it was all scientific. She looked at the mirror and then at Anna.

"Oh. How much do I owe you?"

"As I told you, it's a hundred and fifty dollars, Mrs. Slayton," Anna said. "A hundred for the mirror and fifty for the ritual."

Joyce smiled. A bargain if it worked, she thought. She took out the bills and handed them to Anna.

"Thank you, Mrs. Slayton, and good fortune to you," Anna said.

Joyce moved to the front door quickly and then stopped.

"Oh, do I have to wrap it in anything special?" she asked.

"No. You don't have to wrap it at all, but if you do, be sure he unwraps it in your presence," Anna instructed. Joyce nodded, absorbing the information as if she were being told something by her internist, and then left the shop.

Jonathan Gardner was the best catch in Sandburg, Joyce Slayton thought as she stood on the sidewalk watching the light traffic. She had gone out with a few men since Doug's death, but most of them were looking to marry her for the little money she had, she thought. Jonathan Gardner was independently wealthy, inheriting his father's fuel oil company. He had married when he was very young and lost his wife to a Greyhound bus driver, a man much more handsome and passionate, and Jonathan had remained a bachelor ever since.

He was the butt of jokes, people claiming his young wife was far too hot and sexy for him. He couldn't satisfy her and not even his money was enough to keep her within his bedsheets. There were jokes about his sexual failure, but Joyce was convinced he'd make a good husband and a good life for her. She wasn't a young woman anymore. Yes, she was still attractive, but she couldn't compete with twenty- and thirty-year-olds, and so many men her age were fantasizing and marrying women too young in order to keep the illusion of youth for themselves.

Jonathan Gardner had taken her out three times, but the dates were so far apart, she was never sure there would be another, and he hadn't been very aggressive. She was the one who had kissed him good night. His one bad experience had turned him into a very shy man and at the rate their relationship was developing, they would spend their honeymoon in some adult residence. Maybe she was silly going to Anna Young. Should I believe or not? Was I a fool? Am I so desperate that I would do the silliest things?

Her children would be absolutely embarrassed. They'd be afraid to show their faces in this town.

Maybe Reverend Carter was right about Anna. Maybe it was sinful and she would be punished for it. Maybe he wasn't right and she would be rewarded.

She walked quickly to her car, not glancing left or right for fear that someone would see her and ask her what she had been doing in Anna's shop. Somehow they would see in her face that she hadn't gone to have something tailored.

Except her own future.

I'm so foolish, she thought, but she certainly held on tightly to the mirror.

Three

Henry Deutch froze on the narrow, chipped sidewalk that led to the rotting wooden steps of his front porch. Weeds grew unabated through the cracks in the squares of concrete below him. There was an air of decay and degeneration about the entire single-story gray Queen Anne–style structure. The wooden cladding was chipped and faded; the window casings cried out for touching up and the roof looked like it could be blown off by a moderately strong northerly wind.

Henry hadn't invested a nickel into the house since his wife had died. She had been the one who had insisted on maintenance and improvements after Henry had acquired the home in a bank foreclosure, which was the way he proudly acquired most of his real estate. He hovered over bankruptcies like some economic buzzard, swooping in at the right moment of near death. That was why he was the hamlet's biggest landlord, the owner of four of the main buildings. The economic downturn at the death of the resort economy gave him the opportunities.

When George Echert had offered him a ride home after towing him back to Sandburg, Henry had declined, choosing instead to walk proudly through the village, past all his commercial properties, his head high, his stride firm and arrogant. It wasn't more than a third of a mile at most to his house and the doctor had advised him to walk more and keep his troubled heart muscle as strong as possible.

Sitting in Echert's tow truck cab as he dragged the Mercedes through the village was humiliating enough, Henry thought. He could see the way people came to their windows and stopped their conversations to gape and smile.

But now . . . this!

He stood in a downpour of rage as he looked at his home.

It was all part of some coordinated new effort she was mounting against him. She had stepped it up so that there wasn't much time between each of her horrendous actions. He could barely catch his breath before she was throwing those bones and curses at him again.

Now he fumed as he stared at the vacant eye sockets of what he felt certain was a dead cat's skull centered on the top step. For a long moment, he didn't move. He and the skull contemplated each other and then Henry took some deep breaths, reminding himself to stay calm while he searched the nearby woods for a thick stick. When he spotted one sufficiently long enough to make him feel he'd be at a safe distance, he seized it and stepped slowly toward the porch, the stick out like a knight's lance. He wasn't going to touch that thing if he could help it. Maybe there was some poison on it that would get into his body through the pores in his skin, some witch's concoction. Why take a chance?

He caught the tip of it in the skull's open jaw and lifted. The stick snapped rather than move the skull. How in hell could an old cat's skull be so heavy? he wondered. Maybe it was nailed or glued there with one of those super cements. Anna Young was capable of that.

And then, whether he imagined it or not, he thought he heard the hiss of a cat. It shot through him like a jolt of electricity as he spun in a circle looking for it. He saw none, but he dropped the remainder of the stick he was clutching like a club now.

A sharp pain shot through his chest, making him feel as if one of Anna Young's sewing needles was being stabbed into his heart. He had been told that she'd created a doll in his image and, like a voodoo queen, jabbed it in the chest with pins she first had held over a candle flame. His chest did feel hot.

He stood there for a moment gasping and gazing at the skull. I'm not going to put up with this another damn minute, he concluded, not another damn second! She's out to kill me.

He turned and marched back into Sandburg proper, heading for Kayfields Bar and Grill.

It was five-fifteen on a Tuesday. Munsen Donald would be playing gin rummy with the other good-for-nothings in the rear of the local restaurant, he thought. Munsen was the town of Fallsburg's policeman assigned to Sandburg. The Catskill Mountains township had several hamlets within it, each with a town policeman. Many taxpayers believed the police department was one of the local government's vestigial organs. They were convinced the town should turn over its policing authority and responsibilities entirely to the county sheriff and save the expense. Henry was one of them, but as long as there was a police force, he was determined to make use of it and get his tax dollar's worth.

A half dozen teenagers sat on and stood around a large black late model Pontiac in front of one of Henry's build-

ings as he marched back down Main Street. The car radio
was blasting, its sub woofer thumping so loud it sent earth-
quake like rumbles along the macadam. When they saw
him taking his vigorous, angry steps, they smiled and
laughed. He glared back at them, recognizing three as children of tenants, but that only made them laugh harder. It
put more fury into his gait.

Little bastards, he thought. All of them.

Everyone in Kayfields turned when Henry jerked open
the door and entered, permitting the screen door to slam
behind him. It snapped like a fly swatter. The air was still.
No one moved.

"Afternoon, Henry," Roy Kayfield said. He was a tall,
thin man in his early forties with premature balding sweet
potato red hair. He had inherited the restaurant from his
father. Managing the restaurant had always been all that he
did and all that he cared to do. At the moment, dressed in
jeans and a light cotton plaid flannel shirt, he was sitting at
the bar, reading the New York Post. "I saw you had trouble
with your car. Serious?"

Henry ignored him and looked directly at Munsen.

"I need our policeman."

"Oh?"

"What's up, Henry?" Munsen asked, the right corner of
his lips tucking into his cheek. He held his fanned cards up
and out like a shield in his thick fingered left hand.
Whenever he made a fist, it looked like a mallet.

The others gazed from Henry to him and back to Henry
as if they were watching two gunslingers about to duel.

Before Henry could respond, Tony Monato stepped out
of the kitchen where he was finishing his cleaning, and
wiped his hands on his apron. His hair was out over his
ears, the front in a limp wave. His face was spotted with red
blotches, which always occurred when he drank alcohol,

even a beer. The part Filipino, part Italian thirty-four-year-old short-order cook grimaced at the sight of Henry Deutch.

"Kitchen's closed," he growled out of his smoker's throat. "Lunch's long over and we don't do no dinner anymore."

"I'm not here to eat," Henry retorted, pressing his lips at the right corner to clearly indicate he never would be. "I need Munsen."

"And I asked you, what's up?" Munsen said.

"She's at it again," Henry said.

No one spoke. Roy closed the paper and spun on his stool to look at Munsen. Tony grunted and then backed into the kitchen as if this was to be a very private conversation or at least one of which he wanted no part.

"She do something to your car, Henry?" Roy asked quickly.

"No, damn it. She had nothing to do with that," Henry snapped at him, stamping his right foot simultaneously.

"Just asking," Roy said, holding up his hands. He smiled at the others behind Henry's back.

"I need you to come up to the house right now and see what she's done," Henry continued, directing himself to Munsen. "I want this to be the end of it."

"Shit," Munsen said. "Wouldn't you know it? Just when I have a great hand."

He threw his cards down and rose.

"What is it this time?"

"Cat's skull," Henry said. "On my top front step. I think she mighta glued it there."

"Cat's skull? No kiddin'," Phil Katz said. The fifty-five-year-old village baker's eyes widened, lifting his bushy eyebrows toward the deep folds in his forehead. He was barrel-chested and had bloated forearms resembling Popeye the

Sailor Man's. The sleeves of his light blue cotton shirt were rolled back to his elbows.

"What's that mean, cat's skull?" Charlie Trustman asked Dennis Rotterman, as if the town's only barber was an expert on the subject. Usually, he did have an opinion on any subject, but he wasn't going to offer any on this.

"Who the hell knows?" he said. "You think I read up on this stuff?"

"You would if she was doing it to you," Henry said, nodding. At sixty-one, Henry Deutch still maintained a full head of dark brown hair and posture so firm one could imagine a steel rod down the center of his spine. Despite his having been in a car accident earlier and frightened at his house, the widower looked as cold, hard, and determined now as he appeared to most of his tenants.

"Ruth was going to look up some of this stuff for me next time she went to work," Charlie Trustman said. "Monday, probably." He looked pensive, calm, thoughtful. His wife had just retired from teaching, but was doing part-time work at the county library. Charlie had been the business manager for one of the county's biggest and most successful auto dealerships and now was retired himself. He was a small man, gentle and very sedate. His matter-of-fact demeanor fired up Henry's rage.

"Well?" he demanded, glaring directly at Munsen Donald.

Munsen reached for his hat and adjusted the belt that held his revolver. He was at least twenty-five pounds overweight for his five-foot-eleven frame, carrying most of the excess in his stomach and love handles. Now in his mid-forties, he had once been a star athlete for the high school before going into the military. He was married with two teenage daughters. He walked to the door and turned when he reached it. His cronies stared. He looked at Roy and then back at them before letting his smile settle in his soft cheeks like strawberries into whip cream.

"I'll be back," he said in his best Arnold Schwarzenegger imitation.

Everyone but Henry Deutch laughed.

"What happened to your car, Henry?" he asked when they stepped outside.

"I had a little accident. Went into a ditch. It's being checked out," Henry said, choosing to avoid the details. "It's in Echert's garage."

"Oh, too bad. All right, get in the patrol car and let's get up to your house," Munsen said.

He got into his patrol car and waited for Henry to do the same. Then, wagging his head in disgust, he turned the key in his ignition and drove off. His heart wasn't in this. He almost hoped it was all true: that Anna had some supernatural powers and she would eventually make Henry disappear. He, along with just about everyone else, didn't care for him.

The town looked quiet by this time of the day, not so much asleep as it was relaxed. Even the buildings seemed to lean as if dozing. Munsen felt safe here, content and as satisfied as a well-fed cat, speaking of cats. Getting up to work in the morning was like lowering himself into a tepid bath. Everyone who mattered knew him. He was homegrown with family lineage that went back to the days before the railroad, which itself was long gone. He considered himself more than just the neighborhood policeman. He not only knew why a light was on in a building, but usually who left it on.

All of the buildings except for the relatively new post office were turn-of-the-century vintage, especially the four owned by Henry Deutch. He did little to change or maintain them. He wouldn't whitewash or repair until he was literally up against the wall, whenever the county or the township's building departments and inspectors threatened to take him to court for permitting things to get unsightly or unsafe. Most of his apartment tenants were low middle-class families who had little choice but to put up with his small rent increases and lack of maintenance. Recently, he had evicted a couple with a five-year-old child, the Dixons. Munsen hated to have been a part of that, not that he was fond of Lester Dixon. He considered Lester poor white trash, but Munsen felt sorry for Lois Dixon and her daughter Mary.

"I'm not the county welfare department," Henry Deutch had told him.

When he was a teenager, the village was always alive and busy, Munsen thought sadly as they passed the boarded up stores and white-washed windows. He recalled how store owners kept their businesses open until at least nine, and the luncheonettes, soda fountains, and small restaurants remained open until at least eleven on weekdays.

With the slow demise of the Catskill resort season, the population diminished and underwent some significant character changes. Gone was the sense of community, the feeling that everyone was part of something. There were actually people living here now that Munsen didn't know very well, new families, transients, welfare recipients. The old timers were dying off. More stores were closing.

Some day, the whole village will fold up, he thought sadly.

There was always talk of some miracle reviving the area. The latest hope was legalized gambling. The dream was it would revive the old hotels and bring the crowds that were herded to Atlantic City up here instead, and with that would come new jobs, more population, a bigger tax base, more investment, new buildings, improvements in roads and services.

Reverend Carter and Father McDermott both preached that putting your dreams and hopes into something as evil as gambling was inviting the devil. However, even those who agreed felt desperate and saw no other way. It gave Munsen a sense of impending doom sometimes: the feeling that evil was like some oozing putrescence seeping in from every direction, invading even the most righteous, corrupting the children.

It was probably why the most skeptical of citizens didn't laugh at Henry Deutch's fear of Anna Young and her curses. If there was ever a place to serve as a proper battleground between the forces of good and evil, it was Sandburg.

Munsen pulled into Henry Deutch's driveway and got out, Henry right beside him. They both stared at the front of the house.

"Where is it?" Munsen asked.

"It was right there," Deutch said, pointing at the porch, "on that top step."

"Cat's skull? You sure?"

"Yes."

Munsen walked forward to the porch and searched.

"There's nothing here, Henry. Doesn't look like anything was glued down either," Munsen added, kneeling to look closer at the steps.

"It was there. I saw it. I know what I saw. She probably saw me leave to get you and took it off," he added.

"There's nothing here," Munsen repeated.

"I can see that, damn it. Damn her!"

"You want me to wait while you check inside?"

"No," Henry said, "but you can go ask her about it," he practically ordered as he approached. He dug into his jacket pocket and found his house keys. "You better do something about her, Munsen. I'm not going to put up with this forever."

"I have to have something, Henry, some reason to go bother her," Munsen said.

"Bother her? Jeezes. You're worried about bothering her? She's a kook and so was her mother, only worse. As long as they were in my building, I couldn't rent out the other store spaces. They spooked everybody. She makes this town look stupid, makes us all look foolish, even you, Mr. Policeman."

Munsen smirked. Anna Young and her mother weren't what kept anyone from renting Henry's apartments. It was their condition: the rusted bathroom fixtures, the rat droppings, the weak and dangerous stairways, and cracked windows. If a refrigerator broke, he would procrastinate in getting it repaired, hoping the tenant would eventually take care of it. People had to be desperate to put their families in Henry's buildings, Munsen thought.

"You've got to do more!" Henry insisted.

"She's a citizen too, Henry, with rights just like you."

"She's a nutcase. That's what she is. She shouldn't be out in population. She should be locked up somewhere. Don't I deserve protection? I'm a businessman paying taxes in this township, helping to pay your damn salary, Munsen. And I'm not well. I nearly had a heart attack today. Twice!" he added, and then pressed his lips together tightly, realizing he was giving Anna credit for the suicidal bird.

"I gotta have something to complain about," Munsen insisted. "Even if there was a cat's skull here, Henry, how do we know for sure she put it there? Kids mighta done it for a joke."

"What about those other times, the bones, the feathers she puts in my path or scatters on the road in front of the house, that time she was out here standing with a candle in the middle of a circle she drew on the street in the middle of the night to spook me, and . . . and those idiotic voodoo type dolls she's supposed to have, the mumbo-jumbo she recites in my face . . . what about all that, huh?"

"What are we going to charge her with, Henry, littering? And I never seen her putting needles into dolls, Henry. That's just a bunch of gossip. You can't arrest anyone for having a doll anyway, can you? We couldn't arrest her mother when she put it in their store window, remember?"

Henry winced at the memory. People from surrounding communities had actually driven to Sandburg to see the doll in the window. It only threw oil on the fire and made him angrier.

"You know she's been hauntin' me, Munsen. You know I ain't lying about it," Henry said, his eyes small and fixed with a cold, steely glint.

"All right. All right. I'll talk to her," he added, just to end it.

"You'd better," Deutch threatened. "Or I'm going to go over your head and make a formal complaint about how this is all being handled."

"Right," Munsen said.

It was easy to understand why the man's only child, his son Wolf, didn't come around often, Munsen thought. If I had a father like him, I'd pretend to be an orphan.

He headed back to his car. Deutch opened his door and entered the house, muttering loud enough for Munsen to hear him repeat his threats.

Munsen continued standing there a few moments, searching the late afternoon shadows. Was Henry right? Was Anna Young out there, lingering, watching? As if Henry Deutch's cat skull had come back to life and found the rest of its body, a dark gray cat suddenly appeared,

glanced at him and then sauntered around to a small opening in the bushes to disappear.

Predators, Munsen thought, cats were real good predators. You could leave your cat for days and it wouldn't
starve, but leave your dog and it would either chew up
everyone's garbage or die. Munsen wondered if that was
the reason witches had business with cats.

Witches? Damn, he thought, that Deutch is getting me
crazy. He got into his patrol car and drove back to
Kayfields. For a moment he hovered at the corner, thinking. Then he shook his head and made a left turn. He
drove the five or six hundred yards to the small building
where Anna Young now had her tailor shop. She lived in
an apartment above it since she and her mother had been
evicted from Henry Deutch's property.

Munsen couldn't help feeling sorry for Anna Young.
On this end of town, there were no street lights. The
building was even older than Henry Deutch's building
and smaller. Next to it was an abandoned building that
the county was moving toward having torn down. The
only lively spot was Katz's bakery across the street, but
only during the daytime.

This late in the day with the sun falling behind the
mountains, the shop itself was so dark, the window on the
door looked metallic. He remained there a moment and
then he saw Anna's silhouette move across the thin cotton
curtain in the upstairs window. There was no mistaking
that woman's beautiful body. She was home. She wasn't up
at Henry Deutch's terrorizing the man.

Should he speak to her anyway? He looked again at the
dark shop. Here he was, a grown man, over two hundred
and ten pounds, almost six feet tall, with a model 10.38
strapped to his waist, and he actually had a pang of fear just
with the thought of facing her with her face masked in

darkness, her body outlined against the rear light, her eyes unchecked, looking into his.

"This is crazy," he muttered, throwing his car into drive. "Deutch is just imagining things and I have nothing to confront her with."

He spun the patrol car around and headed back to his card game. As he pulled away, the curtain parted.

Anna Young gazed down at his departing vehicle. She thought she saw the shadow shape itself into her mother's form and then slide across the walk to enter another shadow on the street. Her mother's spirit was impatient, Anna thought. She could not rest in peace.

"It won't be much longer now, Mama," she whispered. "Not much longer."

She smiled and closed the curtain.

Four

Wolf Deutch coasted into his father's driveway, turned off the jeep's engine and just sat there staring at his father's house almost as if he expected his mother to come to the door as she often did when she knew he was on his way. He knew she was always sitting at the front window, anticipating.

No one can ever love you as much as your mother, he thought. He missed her so badly he actually hated coming here knowing she wasn't going to be here and that he wouldn't be hearing her voice, feeling her kiss on his cheek, her small frame hugging him. The laughter and joy in her eyes filled him with such warmth and hope that nothing disappointing in his life mattered. It was truly like a rebirth, a renewal each time.

He hated visiting her grave. Each time he looked at that tombstone, he reaffirmed her death. Once, he had considered never going to the grave and pretending she was still alive, imagining a phone call, even a visit. Growing up, though, meant the death of make-believe. Reality had a way of hammering dreams back into their little boxes.

He'd be the first to admit that he was his mother's boy, spoiled and coddled by her. He looked so much like his mother that someone could make the argument he had been cloned, not born. He had his mother's blue eyes, not his father's gray, he had his mother's thin lemon yellow hair, and his mother's sharp, straight nose. He only resembled his father when he lost his temper. Then his mouth tightened in the right corner with the same wry twist and his forehead wrinkled with a similar scowl.

Wolf was taller than his father and much leaner in build. Most of his life, he looked downright fragile. He was never good in sports, often sickly. His father called him lazy, but his mother was quick to come to his defense.

He did have those habitual sleepy eyelids, drooping. He walked as if his bones rattled, and answered people with a slight hesitation, suggesting it took him twice as long as it did for anyone else to formulate a thought and get it into his tongue. He had never been more than a mediocre student at best, and when he graduated high school, he never expected to go to college. With some extra help from his high school teachers, he managed to get into the state university at New Paltz, but after one semester, he dropped out.

Only, he didn't come home. He met a rather plain looking waitress named Barbara Loukis who was four years older than him, and they got married secretly. Wolf and Barbara had a plan. They wanted to buy a pool hall and tavern restaurant in New Paltz and cater to the college crowd. Henry thought the idea was ridiculous. Where did Wolf come to think he could run a business with some waitress?

However, Rose convinced Henry to give them enough money for the down payment and they purchased the place. They actually did well enough to buy a small home, but their future was obviously limited. They were constantly on the lookout for something more, some way to grow.

Wolf and Barbara had no children, and two years before Rose died, their business began to fail. Henry wanted Wolf to sell, but in the meantime, Rose funneled money to him and Barbara took on a part-time job as a counter girl in Rasklein's pharmacy, one of the few pharmacies in the area able to compete against the chains.

From time to time, Wolf managed to get his father to loan him more money, but it was getting harder and harder to get him to do that. His father wanted him to do something else and kept telling him it was simply poor business sense to throw good money after bad.

He hated not being able to bring better news to him. Despite their differences, he couldn't help but wish for his father's respect, for the day he would drop that tag of *lazy*, and nod and say, "Okay, now I can see where you inherited some of my blood, too."

Nothing had happened to change his picture yet and so they rarely spoke on the phone these days. Wolf and Barbara hadn't visited his father for months in fact, but when he heard that his father had suffered a car accident, he decided to visit and discuss a new, rather exciting idea with him.

Wolf and a new prospective partner had come up with a plan to turn the pool hall and tavern into a microbrew pub. Microbrew pubs were the rage, and theirs would be the first in the area. His father would have to see the value of that, he thought.

Wolf stepped out of his Wrangler Jeep and brushed down his jacket and pants. He checked his hair in the mirror, realizing it was far too long to please his father. At least he had it brushed down neatly, he thought. He had shaved, too, removing the small goatee. The only thing he regretted was his worn boots. They were beyond redemption, but Wolf was never one to worry much about his appearance. He knew his father wouldn't expect miracles on that score.

Taking a deep breath, he headed for the house. Something caught his eye on the front step and he paused. It looked like . . . like excrement. He approached slowly and then leaned over to smell, pulling back sharply when the redolent, nauseating odor hit him. He nearly vomited, turned and gagged for a moment before sidestepping the mess and rushing up to the front door. He pushed the button, waiting and looking back fearfully at the small pile of stool as if he expected it might follow him into the house.

"Who's there?" he heard his father bark in a deep, gruff voice.

"It's me, Dad. Wolf."

A door chain was undone and then a bolt before the door was opened and Wolf faced his father, who was in a faded brown robe and slippers, his hair wild, his face flushed.

"What's going on?" Wolf asked immediately

"What are you doing here?" he asked, without stepping back to let his son into the house. The expression on his father's face actually frightened him. He looked like he had seen a ghost.

"I came to see how you were. After you told me you had the accident—"

"I'm fine," Henry said. Only then did he start to turn away to make room for Wolf to enter. Wolf hesitated, glancing back at the steps. "Well? What are you standing there like that for? What is it?"

"Some animal took a shit on your front stoop," Wolf said.

"What?" Henry pushed him aside roughly and stepped out. "Bitch," he said. "This time I have her," he cried, his face full of glee. "She's desecrating my property."

"Who?" Wolf asked.

Henry glared at him, but didn't respond. Instead, he marched through the living room to his phone and dialed 911. The dispatcher was annoyed that it wasn't an emergency, but transferred him to the central police station where another dispatcher promised to send Munsen immediately.

"He's no damn good!" Henry shouted. "Send someone else."

"Munsen is the policeman on duty in Sandburg," the dispatcher replied calmly. "Do you want him to come by or not?"

"Send him," Henry muttered, and slammed the receiver so hard on the cradle the table shook.

"What the hell's goin' on, Dad?" Wolf asked.

"The witch," Henry said through his teeth.

"What?" Wolf stared at his father and waited.

"Dad?" Wolf continued.

Henry put up his hand to signal silence. Something he saw out of the corner of his right eye had caught his attention. He lowered his shoulders and practically tiptoed to the side window. Slowly, he opened the curtain a little farther. It looked like someone had drawn a cross in blood on the pane.

"This," Henry said, jabbing his finger at the glass, "is proof. She can't deny it. She's disfigured my window. That's a crime, ain't it? Well, ain't it?"

"Who, Dad?"

"I told you. That woman," Henry said, and sat himself back on the sofa quickly. He seemed to fall into it. For a moment he just stared and then he took a deep breath and rubbed his chest. He reached for his bottle of nitroglycerin and shook one out. "Getting low," he mumbled. "She's got me taking more and more of them. She and the druggist are in cahoots."

He closed his eyes as the medicine took effect and he soon felt some relief. Wolf stood watching and shaking his head.

"Have you been seeing your doctor, Dad? You sound like you're getting worse."

"What do you expect with her drivin' me mad? They think she made the bird fly into my car windshield. I know they do, and they're happy about it."

"Is that what you were saying on the phone? A bird flew into your windshield?"

"They all think she did it. Birds don't do that," he recited. "All of them, happy about it."

"All of who?"

"Them," Henry said, waving his hand toward the front of the house. "I know what they think of me, but I don't give a damn. None of them know the value of a dollar and how hard it is to make a good living. Most of them are just jealous."

He turned as if just realizing his son was there. His eyes narrowed suspiciously.

"What are you really here for, Wolf?"

"I told you," Wolf said. "I came to see how you are."

He had hoped for a good visit, maybe having lunch with him and then bringing up the microbrew pub, but his father looked maddened, beyond any sensible conversation.

"How I am? I'm sick from her."

"Who is the witch?" Wolf asked.

"That woman, that seamstress, the one who spits three times in front of me whenever I come across her in the street." His eyes brightened with paranoia. "Maybe someone has hired her to put curses on me and she relishes the work," Henry said, nodding. "That's why she won't stop. That could be. But who else? Who else beside her wants me dead?" he asked, his face in deep thought as he reviewed the long list of people he knew for a fact hated him.

"Dad?"

"Don't worry. I'll beat them. I always beat them," he declared.

For a long moment, Wolf simply contemplated his father. The elderly man seemed to wither with anger, his arms drawing tightly to his torso, his hands clenched like small claws, the long, hard yellow fingernails digging into his own palms. He used to look so big to me, Wolf thought. He's shrinking.

"What's the seamstress's name?" Wolf asked. "Do I know her?"

"How do I know if you know her? Did you ever take any interest in my business or my tenants?"

"She's your tenant?" Wolf asked in the tone of someone astounded that a tenant would torment her landlord.

"Not anymore. I threw her and her crazy mother out a little less than a year ago. Her name is Anna Young."

"Anna Young?" Wolf shook his head.

"She came here after you decided to become a big business man in New Paltz with that waitress." Henry paused and smirked. "Where is she now? Why didn't she come along to see how I am?"

Wolf hesitated. It was nearly impossible to deny Barbara's distaste for his father. Whenever his father spoke to her, he was always condescending, gazing at her with suspicious eyes that, if they were lips, would be firing off one ridiculous accusation after another, the least of which was why marry my son if not for his money?

"Is she sleeping with someone else? She's finally run off, is that it?"

"No. She had to work today, cover the place while I came down here to see you."

"Work," Henry spit. He paused and glared up at his son. Then his eyes returned to narrow slits of suspicion. "You drove all this way to see how I am?"

"You said you ran off the road. You sounded hysterical. I didn't understand about this bird . . . how's the car?"

"How's the car? How's the car? So you came to find out how the car is?"

"No, I just . . . I was just curious. I know how much you care about the car," Wolf said. His eyes shifted from side to side like someone who was searching for an avenue of escape.

"It's being checked out. That thief of a mechanic will find something, I'm sure, and if he doesn't, he'll make something wrong and charge me for it," Henry said.

"Not everyone's dishonest, Dad," Wolf said softly.

Henry looked up at him again and nodded emphatically.

"You know about people? You and your twenty-nine years know about people? Everyone is out to make a dollar for himself any way he can, believe me."

He paused again.

"You look disgusting. Do you know that? You look ten pounds too light and you wear your hair like some hobo. This is the way that woman takes care of you? When was the last time she washed those pants, and look at those boots . . . for god sakes, it's good your mother's not alive. She'd find a way to blame me. What happened to your wonderful living you were making?"

Wolf was about to use that as an opening, but Henry rose to his feet quickly and charged at the door.

"He's here. The idiot comes driving in with his lights going," he said, pointing out the window where the patrol car with its bubble light was visible.

As Munsen Donald began to get out, Henry opened the door and shouted.

"Go on. Step on the evidence. It's on my stoop," he cried.

Munsen stopped on the sidewalk and gazed at the pile of excrement.

"Evidence?"

"Who do you think put it there? It must mean something, part of some witchcraft."

"You called me up here to see a pile of shit on your steps?" Munsen asked, incredulous. He put his hands on his hips, but stopped grimacing when he saw Wolf come up behind Henry Deutch. "Any animal could have done that, Henry. A cat, a dog. Maybe even a raccoon."

"On a step? You're a country man. You ever see an animal like that shit on a step?"

"Yes, Henry, I have," Munsen said quietly.

"All right," Henry said, smiling. "Fine. Forget the shit. Come on," he beckoned, starting down the steps and carefully avoiding the mess.

"Now what?" Munsen asked.

"Dad, let him just go look."

"He doesn't look. He doesn't want to see, but this time, he'll see," Henry said.

Wolf shook his head and followed the two around the corner of the house. Henry paused and nodded at the window.

"What the hell . . ." Munsen drew closer.

"It's blood I bet," Henry declared, almost with pride. "She drew that in blood from some animal she butchered performing one of her rituals. Just go and check her fingerprints and you have her."

Munsen practically touched the cross with his nose.

"Maybe it is blood," he said. "Jesus."

"Right, Jesus. She drew a cross, which I suppose she thinks will intimidate me. It's like those KKK people burning a cross on someone's lawn," he added, his eyes wild and excited. "That's worse than anything," he said, smiling. He looked so happy he finally had something solid. "Now it will finally end," he said. "That's my property and she's marred it," he said as he jabbed his finger at the window. "I want her arrested. I'm pressing charges. Go on. Put her in handcuffs and cart her off to jail. You can do that much, right?"

"Yeah, but first we have to confirm she's done this, Henry; otherwise, she could sue you for false arrest. You want that?" Munsen asked.

"He's right, Dad," Wolf said.

"I know he's right." Henry thought a moment. "We'll get fingerprints taken. That'll be good proof, won't it? Well?" he asked Munsen.

"This doesn't look like it was put on with a finger, Henry," Munsen said, studying the red cross. "It looks dabbed or smeared with a stick. There are no prints in it, no skin lines. Look for yourself," he said, stepping back.

Henry shook his head, stepped closer, and then stepped back.

"She must have touched the window. I want an investigation. I demand protection."

"He deserves protection," Wolf said, "especially if he's being harassed. He's not well."

"All right," Munsen said. "I'll go question her and I'll call this in and have the chief send over a detective."

"Good," Henry said. He clapped his hands. "Good."

Wolf and Munsen watched him start back toward the front door.

"What's been going on here?" Wolf asked.

"Don't you know about this feud your father supposedly has with Anna Young?"

"He never told me. You know I live forty miles away."

"Well, your father's got this feud going with a woman in town who people think has supernatural powers. He claims she's been putting curses on him. He's taking it all too seriously. Half the time he imagines things," Munsen declared.

"Well, that's not in his imagination," Wolf said, nodding at the red cross on the window. "Someone did that."

"Yeah. Trouble is though, I suspect some of the town kids are starting to have fun with him. I'll see what I can do," Munsen added, and lumbered back to his vehicle. He sat and radioed the station, explaining the situation and asking the chief to send Phil Coleman to gather whatever he could forensically. Then he started his car and backed out to go question Anna Young.

Wolf returned to the house.

"I heard him call it in, Dad. They're going to send a detective," Wolf said.

Henry was back in his chair, staring at the floor.

"My grandmother used to tell me about the evil eye," he said. "They believed in that stuff, you know."

"But you don't believe in that crap, do you, Dad?" Wolf asked.

Henry looked up at him by just lifting his eyes and keeping his head tilted toward the floor.

"What I don't believe in is her right to drive me crazy," he said.

"You shouldn't. Wow. What a bunch of crap."

"Get it off the step," Henry ordered.

"What?"

"The shit. Get it off my step and wash it down. They won't consider that any evidence anyway."

Wolf stared a moment and then reluctantly turned and went outside. In the back of his mind, he was thinking, if my mother were alive, none of this would be happening.

Henry settled in his chair, confident it would all soon come to an end.

Finally.

He would get her.

Munsen pulled up in front of Anna Young's shop. The shade on the door was down and it looked dark. Nevertheless, he went up and knocked. Light flickered against the inside of the shade. He peered through the small opening between the shade and the window frame.

"What the hell . . ." he muttered.

He saw Anna Young sitting at a small table across from Benny Sklar. The seventy-five-year-old man had recently lost his wife. Munsen had directed traffic during the funeral. Sklar had his nearly bald head down and his arms stretched across the table, the thin wrists and long hands emerging from the sleeves of his dark suit jacket to take Anna Young's hands. She was looking up at the ceiling, but her eyes were closed. She was talking. Between them a single tall white candle flickered.

Anna was wearing a loose-fitting blouse and a long skirt. Because of the way the light played on her blouse and the way she arched her back, Munsen could clearly see the outline of her bosom.

He stepped back, sucked in his stomach, and knocked a little harder. He waited and then knocked again, permitting his school ring to tap on the glass as well. Then he looked through the opening. Incredibly, neither of them had moved a muscle.

"Miss Young," he called, pressing his mouth close to the

door and the jamb. "It's Munsen Donald. I have to speak to you." He knocked again, this time rattling the door and the glass so hard, it nearly shattered. He waited. Nothing. He looked in and saw that they hadn't changed position. Anna was still talking toward the ceiling. Benny still had his head down, his hands in hers.

"Jesus," Munsen muttered. "What do I have to do to get their attention, fire off a round?"

He rattled the door handle, knocked, rattled it harder, and knocked again.

When he looked in this time, Anna's head was down. Benny let go of her hands and sat back. Munsen couldn't be sure, but it looked like the old guy was crying. Anna rose, walked around the table and put her arm around his shoulders. He held her hand and pressed his head against her.

"What the hell are they doin'?" Munsen muttered. He looked around the street. The loud knocking and rattling of the door handle had brought Phil Katz out of his bakery. He stood in his doorway with Tony Monato and two women Munsen recognized as tenants in Henry Deutch's building.

"What's happening, Munsen?" Tony called. "You want your fortune told?"

Katz and the women laughed.

"Yeah. I'd like to know how to get the hell out of this place," Munsen quipped, and turned back to the door.

He knocked so hard this time the whole door rattled against the hinges.

"Miss Young!"

Finally, she approached and opened the door. Benny stood behind her, wiping his eyes with his handkerchief.

"Yes, Mr. Donald?" she asked softly as if he had just knocked.

"What the hell's goin' on here?" Munsen demanded. He looked at Benny.

"It's not your business," Benny said. He pointed his long, bony right forefinger at him. "Don't go spreadin' stories."

"What stories? What the hell . . . what's that smell?"

"It's yew, an herb, Mr. Donald." She smiled at Benny. "It helps us to reach beyond."

"Huh? Look, Miss Young," Munsen said, stepping back because the scent was so strong, "someone drew a cross on one of Henry Deutch's windows in his house. It looks like it was drawn with blood. You know anything about that?"

When Munsen looked at her, he couldn't help but be glued to her dark eyes. They seemed to suck out his aggression, relax him, even make him feel ashamed for creating such a ruckus. There was a softness there, a softness and an understanding he could feel deep in his heart, calming him against his will. He wanted to be a firm, intimidating policeman, but she stopped him, even making him feel naked, vulnerable, young.

"Blood on his window? Good for him. Good," Benny said. "It couldn't happen to a nicer person."

"Well, Miss Young? Mr. Deutch thinks you have something to do with it. I've called for forensics, a detective will be there shortly and search for fingerprints. Whose might he find?" Munsen asked softly.

"Most likely, the Devil's," Anna Young replied.

Benny Sklar laughed.

"That's right; that's exactly right. You go tell the bastard that."

"Look Benny, this is police business. It's serious," he said. Then he turned back to Anna. "If there's any evidence you were there, Miss Young, he's going to ask me to arrest you."

"I wasn't there," she said, "but I am there."

"What?" Munsen scratched his head. What the hell was he supposed to do now? "What do you mean you're there now? You're here," he cried, his frustration making his stomach bubble.

"She means she put a curse on the bastard," Benny said. "That's what she means."

"Miss Young, did you go up there and draw a cross on Henry Deutch's window? If you own up to it, I might be able to settle things down, but if you don't, and we find out you did . . ."

"Henry Deutch drew that cross himself," she said. "That's what you'll discover."

Munsen considered.

Henry might have done that. He might be trying to get me to believe she's doing it all. He's capable of that kind of deceit, he thought.

"I've asked you to stay away from him," Munsen said in a voice of some retreat.

Anna Young simply stared, those eyes searching his face. He had to look away. The crowd had grown in front of Katz's bake shop.

"I'm going up there to meet the detective," he muttered. "I hope I'm not coming back here," he added with as much of a tone of warning as he could muster. He needed a Tums or a Gas-X and soon, he thought.

"You're always welcome," Anna Young said.

Benny nodded. Munsen watched as the old man took a twenty-dollar bill from his fold and handed it to her.

"Thank you, Anna," he said, and stepped out.

She held the door open a moment and then closed it, pulling up the shade so that she stood there looking out at Munsen for a moment. Her body was close to the glass, the tips of her breasts nearly touching it. It aroused him and this was not the time to feel sexual, he thought.

He turned away and started for his vehicle. Benny paused on the sidewalk.

"What the hell were you two doin' in there, Benny? I could see you through the window. Huh?" Benny Sklar stepped closer to him.

"You want me to tell you?"

"What the hell you think I asked for?" Munsen snapped. He was getting a headache, too.

"I was talking to Martha," Benny said.

"Martha? You mean . . . you mean, Martha, your wife?"

"I'm not interested in any other Martha," Benny said dryly.

"How the hell were you talking to Martha, Benny? She just died, didn't she?" Munsen stated.

"Through Anna," Benny said. "Through Anna you can reach the dead," he added, turned, and walked off with as quick a gait as Munsen had ever seen him have. He looked like someone who had been rejuvenated.

Tony Monato crossed the street and looked after Benny, too.

"What's happening, Munsen?" he asked.

Munsen told him.

"The two of them aren't going to kill each other," he added, "they'll kill me."

Tony nodded, his eyes dark, as if he agreed.

Five

"This is what you brought me down here for?" Philip Coleman asked Munsen. He was about Munsen's height, but in better shape with a slimmer waist and harder upper body. He looked like an FBI agent: short hair, jacket and tie, firm and businesslike. The two of them gazed at the cross painted in red on the window.

"It's a crazy situation, gotten out of hand, Phil. Henry Deutch is Sandburg's biggest landlord. He had this woman and her mother evicted when he refused to give them a lease on their tailor shop and they tried to resist. The old lady attempted to keep Deutch away by putting some kind of a magic doll in the window."

"Magic doll? You're shittin' me."

"Deutch got a court order and I had to serve the damn papers!"

"So? That's why you get paid the big bucks."

"Yeah. Very funny. The woman's mother had a stroke and a heart attack and died soon afterward and the woman, Anna Young, blamed Deutch. She claims he was on the

Devil's side, trying to stop her and her mother from helping good overcome evil."

"As tailors? What were they sewing, vestments for the
church? Yarmulkes and prayer shawls?"

"No." Munsen looked away, rubbed his stomach, and
took off his hat. "Not their work as seamstresses. Some people here believe Anna and her mother were good witches.
They still think that's what Anna is."

"Good witches? What the hell is that?"

"This guy in town, Charles Trustman, had his wife do
research on it at the library. They call them white witches,
sort of good voodoo doctors or somethin'. People believe in
it," Munsen stressed, while Phil scowled. "They went to
her mother and now they go to Anna for remedies to help
with their children and their husbands and wives, to help
her get curses off them or put curses on their enemies, to
get people to fall in love, even, I recently found out, to talk
to their dead."

Coleman stared.

"Is this some fuckin' joke, Munsen, because if it is—"

"Look, I gotta lot of older people here and I gotta lot of
people who are superstitious, man. More and more people
believe in this stuff nowadays. It's not much different from
those thousands of people who come up here to have that
guru touch them with a peacock feather and bless their
eternal spirits, is it?" he asked.

Munsen was referring to a transcendental meditation
organization that had bought out one of the bigger hotels
and turned it into an ashram. Many residents were upset
because that property and others the quasi-religious organization had purchased were taken off the tax rolls and everyone else had to pick up the burden.

"Munsen," Coleman began, letting his shoulders sink,
"do you know how high the pile of work is on my desk?

People talk about doing away with the township's police department, but we don't lack for things to do."

"I know, I know," Munsen said quickly, his hands up. "But Deutch wants to press charges against her. He says she's harassing him, leaving all sorts of black magic on and around his house, like this red cross on the window. He's really starting to believe she can hurt him, I think, and he wants her to stop."

Coleman stared at him again.

"He believes she can hurt him by painting crosses on his window and sticking dolls in his face?"

"Well, he's had a stroke of bad luck lately, I gotta admit. His oil burner blew in the house. One of his buildings was nearly lost in a fire, and I found out from George Echert that earlier this week, a bird flew into Deutch's car windshield and drove him into a ditch."

"What sort of black magic?" Coleman asked as if he was impressed.

"I don't know . . . dead animals' parts, weird drawings in the sand, circles or shapes with sticks and bones. The day of his car accident, he claimed she had left the skull of a cat on his porch steps, but when I got up here, there was nothing."

"So he's crazier than she is. What's the problem?"

"I don't know what the hell to do, man. I came up here today and there was a pile of dog shit on his step and this," he said, gesturing at the window. "If she's doing it, I guess it is a form of harassment, ain't it? The guy's got a heart problem, too, and even though no one loses any sleep over the bastard, he is the hamlet's biggest tax payer, Phil. What am I supposed to do?" Munsen whined. "I can't just ignore him forever. He wants you to tie Anna Young to this and then he'll have her arrested. We got to do something, don't we?"

"All right, all right. Jesus, what a job this is getting to be. Witches and curses," Coleman mumbled, and began his examination of the window.

Munsen retreated to his car. He saw Wolf emerge from the house and go over to watch Coleman. After a while he sauntered over to Munsen.

"I have my father resting comfortably, but this is a very bad situation. You've got to end it. He's not a well man."

"I'm doing what I can," Munsen said sullenly. "You don't go and arrest people without some sort of evidence or witnesses to a crime."

"I swear, if something happens to him because of that woman, I'll sue the police department."

"Get in line," Munsen muttered.

Wolf turned as Coleman approached.

"First, it's paint, not blood. It was put on with a stick. I found it off to the side," he said, holding up a stick in a plastic bag. "I powdered the window and the frame for prints, but there's nothing there."

"No fingerprints? There has to be some prints," Wolf said. "Someone touched that window some time. I know that much," he said, nodding his head at Munsen. Munsen looked at Coleman.

"He's right, only there aren't any prints, man. Someone must have wiped it clean."

"Ha! See," Wolf cried. "My father's not nuts. Who would wipe a window clean?"

"Look, Mr. . . ."

"Deutch."

"Deutch," Coleman said. "We're in the business of gathering evidence to give to the district attorney who then decides if she wants to seek an indictment for a crime based on what we have given her. It has to be enough to justify the time and expense, and at least present the possibility there would be a conviction. The fact that I can't find any discernable fingerprints on that window is not any sort of evidence. It's actually the absence of evidence. I'll have our people send this stick to the lab to see if there's anything we can use. Otherwise, don't go making any rash statements. People can sue you for that kind of thing," Coleman warned.

"Did you tell him what this woman has been doing to my father?" Wolf asked Munsen.

"I told him all I know and what your father told me," Munsen replied in a tired voice. "And what I heard people gossip. You heard him. That's not evidence."

"If something happens to him, someone's going to pay," Wolf vowed, turned, and marched back into the house.

"Well?" Munsen asked Coleman. "You see what's going on here, what I have to deal with?"

The detective shrugged.

"I told you. That's why you're getting paid these big wages, Munsen. Just grin and bear it," he said. Munsen watched him get into his car. He nodded and backed out.

For a moment the hamlet's policeman stood gazing at Deutch's house. Then he got into his patrol car and drove off as he tossed antacid drops into his mouth.

Inside, Wolf told his father what the detective had said.

"They don't believe you, Dad," he concluded. "It's not serious to them."

Henry nodded.

"No prints on the windows . . . paint, not blood, huh? I'll get her yet," he vowed. "She'll do something she can't hide and I'll nail her."

"You're letting her drive you out of your mind, Dad. You should see yourself."

"I'm letting her? Letting her?" His eyes were wide and bulging like large marbles.

"You want some tea, something to eat?" Wolf asked.

Henry gazed up at him.

"So how long do I wait before you tell me why you really came here, Wolf?" he asked.

"I told you, when I heard—"

"I'm tired. I need a nap. If you have anything to ask, ask it quickly," Henry ordered.

Wolf swallowed, his prominent Adam's apple bobbing. Then he sat on the sofa and began his pitch. Henry listened with his fingers around his chin. When Wolf was finished, Henry rose with great effort and turned. It looked like he was just going to walk off without a word.

"Dad?"

"First, the idea of getting into another restaurant is stupid, especially for you. From what you're telling me, you've failed at that already. This microbrew pub is just another gimmick and it's still in that little town. Go find a job and stop with the easy outs. Your mother spoiled you rotten. You need to know what it's like to struggle hard for a dollar. Then you'll be more careful about wasting my money."

"But Dad—"

"I'm tired. I gotta get some rest. If you leave, be sure the door is locked," Henry said, and shuffled off to the bedroom.

Wolf sat there staring after him until he heard the bedroom door close. Then he got up, poured himself a glass of water, drank it and left the glass in the sink without rinsing it. He checked the door lock and walked out, pausing on the steps as if he had come up with a new presentation and wanted to go back to talk to his father. Instead, he went around the side of the house and looked at the red cross painted on the glass. He stepped up to it and touched it, shook his head, and went to his jeep.

Moments later, he was gone.

As he had feared and anticipated, he had left empty-handed.

Dennis Rotterman brushed the hair off Stuart Levy's shoulders and stepped back to get the hand mirror so he could show him the back of his head. Levy studied the cut and nodded as Dennis explained.

"I think you always have to have it cut closer here, Stu. The way a head sweats, it just grows faster on the back. Now you look ten years younger."

"You're an artist, Dennis, a regular sculptor of heads," Stuart said.

Charles Trustman, sitting across from them, lowered the paper and smirked.

"What'dya fillin' his head with all those compliments? You think it's easy bein' around him as it is?"

Stuart laughed as he rose from the barber's chair. He pulled his pants up and patted his stomach.

"You look good, Stu. Stay on your diet this time," Dennis advised. "Goin' up and down with your weight like that ain't good for the heart."

"Now he's a doctor," Charles quipped.

Stuart Levy laughed, handed Dennis a twenty and told him to keep the change. Dennis brushed him down a little more as the phone rang.

"See you guys," Stuart Levy said, heading for the door.

Charles watched him leave and then turned to Rotterman as he put down the receiver.

"Guess who's decided it's time for a haircut?"

"Larry Spizer's son, the rock star?"

"No, Henry Deutch. He's on his way. I guess I'm still a bargain," Dennis said, laughing.

He grabbed his vacuum and cleaned the floor around the chair and then brushed it down.

"Got to get it looking good for Henry Deutch," he muttered, "or he'll have Munsen after me."

Charles laughed.

"When's he coming?"

"Half hour."

"Just enough time for me to beat your ass at another game of checkers," Charles said.

Henry Deutch had woken out of a terrible nightmare, sleeping later into the morning than usual. He imagined the nightmare had been caused by the sight of his disheveled looking son. In his dark dream, he saw his own hair growing and growing while he slept until it was down over his eyes and below his chin. He saw himself suck in some strands and begin to choke to death on it. That was when he woke, coughing and spitting. His chest felt as if the engine of his car had been placed on it.

His car, he thought, and immediately called George Echert. To Henry's surprise, Echert claimed there was no severe damage.

"I cleaned it up and greased it, Henry," he said. "Some bad scratches underneath, but you were lucky."

"Lucky?" He muttered some obscenities under his breath and told Echert he would be down soon to get the car.

That was when he looked into the mirror and decided that as long as he was going to the village, he might as well get a haircut, too. The nightmare was still flashing ugly images. He even had trouble drinking a glass of water, much less eating any breakfast.

He dressed and left the house after calling Rotterman for a haircut appointment even though he thought the price of a haircut was ridiculous these days. People were so caught up in their coiffures and their complexions, they were willing to pay outrageous prices for the simplest things. A haircut wasn't a haircut anymore. It was a styling. And barbers were hairstylists, not barbers. God forbid you called them barbers. All it meant to Henry was they would double what they charged for the same things.

When Rose was alive, she used to cut his hair. He even told her she should do it for other people and get paid.

"Just call yourself a stylist," he said. "I'll find an old barber's chair someplace and set it up in one of the rooms."

She just laughed at him. He was dead serious and she just laughed. Sometimes, Henry believed his wife thought he was one big joke, that everything he did or said was not real or not intended to sound and be what it was.

"Oh, come on, Henry, you really don't mean that," she would always say. It was embarrassing when he was trying to negotiate with someone or be stern with a tenant. No matter how often he asked her not to interfere, she would.

She was the only person who could dip deeply enough into the anemic well of compassion at the base of his soul and come up with enough of it to have him compromise or grant someone a little mercy. When she died, the little humanity he had seemed to have had died with her. He buried the best part of himself and he knew it. That made him even more bitter. The soft skin, the grace, and the beauty that had covered his anger was stripped off, leaving his nerves like bare wire. He was left growling at the world, spinning around with his fingers turned into knives, keeping the wolves, the buzzards, and the parasites at bay. It seemed to be the only purpose left to life.

Filling with some of that rage as he walked, he strutted through the village toward the garage, past his properties, mentally calculating the rent monies coming due at the end of this month. The barber shop was a walk of some distance, so he had plenty of time to think and he reminded himself again that Doctor Bloom had advised him to get in more exercise, but he wasn't much for exercise. He was never much of an athlete, never really caring about anything that didn't look to be in some way profitable.

George Echert would have quickly volunteered to pick up any other customer and bring him or her to the garage to get his or her car, but the mechanic knew Henry Deutch would aggravate him over the bill, even though it was more than fair. Why spend any more time or money on such a person? He didn't appreciate anything. He treated any merchant, service person, professional the same way with the same attitude which began with the assumption, "You're robbing me."

What about how he robbed, exploited, and squeezed people? The truth was that when George saw there was no serious damage to Henry's Mercedes, he moaned with disappointment. Why did the worst people have the best luck? If Anna was after him, why didn't she do a complete job?

After Henry had arrived, it was just as George had anticipated: he had to defend the charges.

"I towed her in, Henry. That's a standard price, and I spent time pulling things off and putting them back on. You wanted it properly checked out, didn't you?"

In the end, Henry Deutch paid, but he wrote out the check as if he was giving George his last few dollars, and even then, even as he was leaving, he turned to say, "If something's wrong, you'll fix it at no charge now since I'm taking your word for it."

"Take it to another mechanic if you doubt me, Henry," George muttered.

He had begun his day feeling good and now he wanted to drive the sledgehammer through metal. That man could tie your insides into knots in minutes, he thought as he watched him drive off. His gaze panned right and he saw Anna Young standing across the way. She started after Henry Deutch's car, walking with her head up, that posture firm, moving gracefully over the sidewalk, her long skirt rippling around her legs as she floated along like some spirit assigned to follow Henry Deutch to his grave.

George watched her until she disappeared around the corner. The breeze picked up, blew some debris over the streets and sidewalk, and then died down. A cloud moved over the sun draping the village in a blanket of gray for a few minutes. Some light traffic went by and then the sleepy village turned, stretched, and continued to chug along at its nearly somnambulist's pace.

Henry was no conversationalist. For a barber that was depressing, especially a loquacious man like Dennis Rotterman. Henry planted himself in the chair and stared ahead with a look that resembled an expression of defiance or challenge. Go on, he seemed to say, try to do a good job and see if I appreciate it.

Rotterman truly hated long moments of silence while he worked. Chatter didn't detract from his concentration. On the contrary, it helped him settle into his work with ease. He had to be loose, relaxed himself, to do a good job. He despised being mechanical. Henry's hair was like thin wire: dull, dead, and split at the ends. His scalp was scaly and dry, and he kept his neck tight, the folds of skin forming tight little crevices.

Fortunately, Charles Trustman had remained to finish the paper after their game of checkers.

"This all you have to do with your time now?" Henry asked him.

Charles lowered the paper and stared as if he was giving the question great thought.

"The day seems to pass quickly. I don't mind not having problems to solve, people to please, deadlines to meet, Henry. You shouldn't knock retirement. Making money has no point if you don't enjoy your life, if all you want to do is keep your nose to the grindstone."

Henry scowled.

"There's plenty of time to rest in the grave," he said.

Charles shrugged.

"To each his own, I guess. Whatever makes you happy."

"That's why this town is dying, why there's no economy here anymore. People are dead and buried here before they died. It's harder to make a good dollar. My properties are all losing value. No one wants to live here anymore except parasites sucking on the welfare tit."

Dennis Rotterman nodded at his friend as if to say "That takes care of you, Trustman."

Charles shook his head and went back to the newspaper. A deadly silence fell over the shop with only the click of the scissors and then the electric shaver offering any sound. When Rotterman finished, he brushed Henry down and Henry stood up and nodded at his image.

"That do it, Henry?" Rotterman asked.

"Fine. What's it cost?"

"Same as last time, Henry, fifteen dollars."

"Fifteen dollars," Henry said through tight lips.

"Need some money, Henry?" Charles Trustman asked, lowering the paper.

"No, not yet, but at the way prices are going up around here, it won't be long," Henry Deutch said, and reluctantly counted out the fifteen and put it into Dennis Rotterman's open palm. Then he brushed down the front of his shirt and marched to the door.

"See you again, Henry," Dennis called as he left.

Henry didn't respond.

Charles shook his head and the two laughed. As Dennis went for the vacuum cleaner, the door opened and Anna Young stepped in. Both men froze.

"I need something," she said.

"Sure, Anna. What can I get you?" Dennis Rotterman asked.

"Nothing. I'll get it myself," she said. She had a small cloth purse in her hand. She opened it and then she knelt down and carefully plucked some of Henry Deutch's cut strands off the floor. She put them into the cloth purse, pulled the draw string tight, gazed at the two men, and then left as quickly as she entered.

"Jeezes," Dennis said.

Charles Trustman shook his head.

"What the hell's all that about?" Dennis asked.

"Damnedest thing I ever saw," Charles said. He looked at Dennis.

"Henry Deutch better watch his ass," Dennis said.

Charles Trustman nodded. He rose and went to the window to gaze out after Anna, but she was already gone. Dennis joined him and then they looked at each other.

It was as if the two of them had dreamed it.

Six

Anna Young stood naked over her bathtub. A light mist rose from the hot water. She opened the vial in her hands and poured the silvery contents into the water and then she closed the vial and placed it carefully on the shelf over the sink. She knelt at the tub and put her head against the top of it for a long, meditative moment. That done, she raised her head and, with her eyes closed, began.

"Lord, God, I beg of thee. Bless and sanctify this water so it shall wash away any evil from my spirit and purify my soul before I do what I am to do."

That said, she stood and slowly stepped into the tub. A small twitch in her lips revealed how hot the water actually was, but she sucked in her breath and lowered herself until she was submerged to her waist. Then she lay back and again, ever so slowly, sunk her upper torso under the water until it lapped over her breasts and reached the nape of her neck. She closed her eyes and baptized herself. After a second or two, she brought her head out of the water and sat upright. Her skin was crimson from the heat. She took another deep breath and then she stepped out of the tub, wrapped a towel around herself, and began to dry her hair.

A little less than an hour later, Anna emerged from her shop, closing the door softly behind her. In her left hand, she carried a small garden spade. The clouds that had been blocking the sun earlier in the day had passed on to the west, and a deep path of unencumbered blue loomed above and before her. She had tied her hair back and wore one of her pearl buttoned blouses and a long, maroon skirt. Without any hesitation, she started toward the cemetery where her mother waited in her coffin.

The cemetery was walking distance from the village along a wooded road that crossed a small bridge over a brook. Anna had made the trek often enough since her mother's burial, enjoying the birds, the sound of the crystal clear spring water, and the cool shade of the sprawling maple, hickory, and oak trees. Today, however, she walked with vigor and determination, noticing nothing in nature and covering the quarter mile or so in half her usual time. She never turned to look right or left and she never looked back. She didn't even gaze at the few automobiles that passed her by. The drivers looked her way with interest, and one, Melvin Bedik on his way to town, even honked his horn and waved. The sixty-four-year-old man had gone to see Anna two months earlier at the insistence of his wife, Toby, who claimed Anna could do something about his lumbago. She had helped relieve Simon Karachek of some nearly debilitating arthritis through the use of herbal medicine and some mystical chants, hadn't she?

Melvin was feeling better. It might be, as his doctor had claimed, only mental, but what difference did it make as long as it brought relief? he asked. Doctor Fernhoff shrugged and smiled.

"More people are turning to faith healers and spiritual gurus these days than ever," he had to admit. "Some under the guise of so-called holistic medicine, prescribing herbs and meditation. It's so old, it's new."

Anna didn't acknowledge Melvin's honking. She resembled someone in a hypnotic state at this point and Melvin wasn't going to do anything more to shake her out of it. He watched her for another moment in his rearview mirror, caught sight of the small garden spade in her left hand, and then drove on wondering, what was she up to? Everyone was curious about Anna. She was truly fascinating, he thought. He enjoyed fantasizing about her, imagining she had the capability of turning sex into something extraordinary, too.

When Anna reached the cemetery, she climbed the small hill quickly and stopped at her mother's grave. Gussie Young's granite tombstone was simple, with only her name and dates engraved. After a number of rains and the damage of sunlight, it looked as if it had been there almost as long as some of the others.

For a moment Anna gazed at the stone and smiled softly as if her mother's face appeared in it as well as her name and dates.

"Hello, Mama," she whispered. "I have come as I had promised. It is time," she said, and lowered herself to her knees in front of the tomb.

She began to dig a small hole. When that was done, she lit a match and held it in the hole for a few seconds. After that, she reached for the cloth bag on her side, opened it, and carefully extracted the strands of Henry Deutch's hair. She put them into the hole, sprinkled crushed dandelion after it to call forth the spirits, and covered it quickly.

"Do with him what you will, what you must," she said.

She meditated a moment, stood, and then started down the hill, unbinding her hair as she walked and then shaking her head to let her hair fall freely about her shoulders. With the sunlight on her face, she looked radiant and energized. She walked back even faster and quickly went to work as soon as she had arrived in her shop. She worked with a soft smile on her face; she worked like someone who knew the future and knew it to be what she wanted it to be.

Munsen Donald couldn't hear the sports commentator talking about the Giant's new quarterback. Brooke and Crystal were fighting again. His daughters were too close in age and thus were competitors for the same boys at school. Both were pretty, with attractive little figures developing. Both, he thought gratefully, took more after Lisa than they did him. He had been afraid one or both would be big boned like he was and then have a tendency toward being heavy. Remarkably petite and close in size, they could share clothing, even shoes. He used to think that would make for good economics, but they were after each other's things so often that Lisa simply bought double of everything most of the time. Gone was the economics.

They sounded like cats in heat. He rose with great effort and lumbered up to the den door to shout at the stairway in his three-bedroom bi-level built on Lisa's parents' property just a mile out of the village on Post Hill Road.

"Will you two stop it before I come up there and give you something to really wail about!" he cried.

There was an instant of total silence and then the usual ping pong like exchange of accusations, blaming each other for getting him aroused. Lisa came out of the kitchen, wiping her hands on a dish towel. His wife had apricot hair, trimmed stylishly. With her small facial features and soft, rich complexion, she still looked as much like a teenager as his daughters.

"What's wrong?"

"I don't know. They're both having their time of the month, maybe," he said.

She pressed her slim lips together and sucked in the corners of her mouth with a grimace of disapproval.

"Somewhere obviously it was written that you men would use our menstrual cycle to explain away any of our problems and lay blame. I wish for one month you could know what it's like, Munsen. Then you wouldn't be so quick to make light of it. Maybe I should go to see Anna Young, and ask her to really lay down a curse."

"Oh brother, not you too," Munsen groaned. "I just wanted to get a few hours of relaxation watching the game. It's been a crummy week. Is that too much to ask?" he whined.

"Depends how you ask," she said, unrelenting. Lisa, all five feet two of her, could stand up to him anytime. That was actually one of the reasons he loved her.

"Okay, okay," he said as softly as he could manage, "would you please beg our lovely daughters to stop bickering so loudly so I can hear the television without raising the volume so high it shakes the house?"

Lisa smiled.

"You're such an idiot," she said, poked him in the stomach as she passed, and climbed the steps. He watched her wiggle her little behind and envisioned the two of them later, when the lights were out, the house was quiet, the girls were in dream land, and he could be a teenager himself again.

He started back into the den when the phone rang.

"Shit," he moaned, and took it in the kitchen.

"Munsen," he growled into the mouthpiece. It was

always the way he answered the phone now, half the time hoping whoever it was would just hang up.

"Nothing," he heard Philip Coleman say.

"What?"

"On that stick. No fingerprints. Whoever did it probably wore gloves. The paint's common enough to be bought anywhere so that won't lead to anything."

"Oh."

"Look, why don't you get the two of them together and have a nice talk and settle their problems. Small town cops are supposed to be close to their neighborhoods. Maybe ask the rabbi or priest to help, okay? That's my best advice."

"Thanks a lot, Philip. That's a terrific idea. The rabbi and the other clergy here think she's contaminating souls. They won't have anything to do with her."

"Just trying to be of help. It's why they pay me the big bucks," he said. "Have a nice day."

Munsen muttered under his breath and cradled the receiver. Henry Deutch wasn't going to like this. It would go on and on. He shook his head and then smelled the aroma of the turkey and opened the stove to take a peek at it roasting. It looked Thanksgiving good. His stomach rumbled in anticipation.

He closed the stove and thought about the phone call from Coleman. Maybe they'll kill each other and he'll be free of it, he thought.

It was a wish he would soon regret.

Henry Deutch drove back from Centerville full of himself. As he expected, Sam Wuhl was eager to do business at the First National Bank. He made him a generous offer knowing he would get it all back on the other end once he succeeded in wresting the property from Baxter. The process was in the works. Henry knew he was good at all this, and the truth was he actually enjoyed it. One of these days he'd own practically everything of any real value around here and they'd have to come to him to take their next breath.

He didn't really like the people in Sandburg or even in Centerville for that matter, but friends weren't important to him. He knew they didn't like him either and he knew how much it bothered them that he was so successful. It was a part of what motivated him to succeed. If they cared about him, they wouldn't be permitting that bitch to torment and harass him. They were all laughing at him behind his back, but soon enough, soon enough he'd be the one with the last laugh, he thought.

The sky had darkened considerably since he had left Sandburg. When he entered the village proper, the first drop splattered on his windshield. For a split second, he recalled that damn bird smashing its bones and blood into his window and sending him careening off the highway. "Birds don't do that," George Echert had remarked.

Henry slowed down at the center of the village. The traffic light had been changed into a blinking yellow, stop and go. There wasn't even enough traffic to justify that, he thought. As he started the turn to climb Post Hill Road, he saw that hateful woman standing in the doorway of one of his apartment buildings, the one in which she and her mother had occupied a store space and an apartment. The moment she saw him, she stepped out and shocked him by releasing a bird she had been holding within her cupped hands. It fluttered and then flew over his car. He actually ducked behind his wheel. He saw her spit three times, too. How the hell did she know when he was going to reach town? What did she do, stand there all day?

"Damn you, you crazy bitch!" he screamed, and hit the brakes. She stood there, defiant, gazing at him. Then she lifted her hand as if she was holding back the air between him and her and started to chant something. It irked and unnerved him. He was going to back up and let her have a piece of his mind, but he changed his mind and put his foot down hard on the accelerator, jerking forward, tires squealing.

Out of the corner of his eye, he caught some of the tenant children laughing and catcalling.

He was still mumbling to himself when he pulled into his driveway and got out of the automobile.

"Nearly caused another accident," he said, and stopped. What did he mean, "caused another?" There I go again, he thought. It's getting so I'm really starting to believe this garbage about her, too. He considered telephoning Munsen to tell him what she had just done. But what had she done? Released a bird? Spit in the street? Chanted in his direction? How could he call those things aggressive acts? They would all just laugh at him again.

Frustration made his heart pound. Fortunately he had refilled his nitro prescription just today, he thought. Gerson Smallwood, the pharmacist, tried to get him to take something other than the generic again, but he didn't do it regardless of the way he spoke about reliability. He just wanted to make more money off me, Henry decided, and was happy he had insisted on a new bottle, rather than just refilling the old one.

For what I pay for medical insurance and co-payments, I deserve new, he thought.

He stomped up his front steps to the door and entered. For a moment he just stood there, fuming. Then he calmed himself down enough to think about making himself some dinner. It was too good a day to let her spoil it, he thought. He had coveted Baxter's property for some time now, and now he could see the real possibility of having it. Rose would chide him, tell him he was working too hard.

"The cemetery is filled with rich people who thought they could be buried with their money, Henry," she would tell him.

It was at meal time when he missed Rose the most. It wasn't just that she prepared good breakfasts, lunches, and dinners for him. She was good company. They were so unalike, their conversations could be interesting. The truth was she not only amused him, she intrigued him. How could someone, anyone, have such an optimistic and positive view of things and people? Her name truly fit her. She was rosy in every way. No matter what happened, how much he was aggravated, she never joined him in ranting and raving. She never encouraged his swearing. She always looked for the bright side, the benefit, no matter how small or insignificant, and tried to get him to concentrate on that aspect. Eventually, he would calm down and sometimes, he would come to agree with her.

Now, he sat across from an empty chair and nodded at the space as if death had proved his central point. She was better than he was in everyone's eyes. She was the good one, the pleasant one, cheerful and bright, and she was the one death came to fetch first. Where was the great justice? Who protected the meek and the innocent? Go ask Hitler, he muttered to himself.

The world proved his point, not just Rose's death. What was morality? It was something the weak had invented to protect themselves from the strong. Good people aren't rewarded for their goodness and the bad aren't punished for their badness. People are rewarded for their cleverness, their ruthlessness, their own initiative. That was the only morality he understood.

He chewed his food with a vengeance. It was nearly taste-less, some leftover chicken and warmed over vegetables. He didn't know how to season things right, but he wasn't going to go and hire someone to cook for him. Not at the prices they got these days, although he once came close when one of his tenants offered to trade some rent payments for domes-tic work. He thought she would probably steal from him or maybe poison him, so he didn't agree to it.

He was too tired to wash his dinner dishes tonight. He put them into the sink and went to his account books for a few minutes to review his assets and accounts receivable. He liked to keep abreast of things just to check on his thief of an accountant. The numbers grew blurry quickly how-ever, and he gave it up after only a cursory view.

The rain that had started earlier grew heavier. He heard the drops building in intensity, tapping on the roof and against the windows with machine gun rapidity now. It was dark and dreary, a good day for the world to end, he thought. He always used to say that to Rose when it rained like this, and she would smile and say, no, it made every-thing smell fresh in the morning, fresh and clean, and it was better for sleeping.

How he wished she was beside him tonight, just to hear her breathing, just to know he wasn't really alone.

He paused on his way to the bedroom. The tapping seemed different. It came from the walls now and not just the roof and the windows. Was it that bitch doing some-thing else? He went to a window and peered into the dark-ness. His porch light had blown and he hadn't changed the bulb. It was impossible to make out anything, even the shapes of trees. The whole world looked like a black cur-tain, a shroud that had been cast over him and his house. Something glowed for a second. It looked like the eyes of a cat, maybe that damn skull again.

"If you're out there, I hope you get pneumonia, you bitch!" he screamed into the closed window.

All he heard was the tapping of the drops and an occasional whistle of wind as it whirled around the house and into the nearby woods. Then he distinctly heard the sound of knocking at his front door. He listened again and again he heard it. How could anyone be there? He hadn't heard anyone drive up or seen any headlights cutting through the darkness. Another knock. He approached the door slowly.

"Who's there?" he called.

There was nothing, no voice, no knocking.

He looked around a moment and then went to the closet and got his shotgun. He always kept it loaded. Carefully, he opened the front door, raising the shotgun to waist level as he did so. At first he saw nothing, and then there was a flash of lightning and he saw the chicken hanging from the porch rafter over the steps. It was bleeding freely, telling him it had just been slashed open. Some of the entrails were hanging out.

He slammed the door shut and quickly worked the locks in place.

His heart was pounding, but his moment of fear was quickly replaced with rage.

"Deny that!" he cried, and hurried to the phone. Once again he tapped out 911, but this time there was nothing. He played with the cradle of the phone trying to get a dial tone. There was none. The phone was out, either because of the lightning or because . . .

"Damn her to hell," he muttered.

He went to the window and waited for another streak of lightning. When it came, he saw nothing. It was raining too hard to go back out. Then he thought he heard something at the back door. Cocking the shotgun, he walked slowly to the rear of the house, his heart pounding harder with each step. At the door, he listened. He could hear the rain, but nothing else. He waited and then slowly reached for the door knob. He flipped the lock and then, after a moment, he pulled the door open quickly and pointed the shotgun at the entry way. No one, nothing, just the steady rain and the darkness.

"Bitch!" he screamed. "Tomorrow, I'll get you. Tomorrow ends it!"

He paused again to listen, heard nothing unusual, and then shut the door and locked it again. He would wait until morning, he thought, and then he would drag that no good-for-nothing cop up here again, and again, and again, until something was done.

Content with his plan, he shuffled toward his bedroom. He was tired and needed to sleep. He wasn't going to get sick over this. That was what she wanted, he thought. Before he undressed for bed, he checked every window and was shocked to discover that the window on the north side, the one that had been painted with the red cross, was unlocked. When had he done that? he wondered. Maybe it was something the police had done, he thought, and made sure it was locked now. Then he went into the bedroom and pulled his blanket down.

The sight of it drove a knife through his chest and ripped his heart.

A rat, its long tail curled up toward its horrible face, lay dead on his bed, its pale pink tongue extended. It looked like someone had twisted and broken its neck.

He gasped and stepped back. How did she . . . how could she . . .

My pills, he thought, and lunged for the bottle at the side of his bed. He opened it quickly and shoved one into his mouth, closing his eyes and waiting for the expected relief. Only this time his heart began to beat faster and faster. The pain that had started continued to move with electric fingers over his chest squeezing and squeezing until he couldn't manage a deep breath. Quickly, he shoved a second pill under his tongue. The expected relief didn't come. He leaned against the wall. He would take another. He was taking them too fast, but he couldn't stand the pain. It was truly like a vise being tightened on his chest.

Moments after the third pill, he saw the room spin and reached out to steady himself on a chair, only he put too much weight on it and it flipped backwards, taking him along with it to the floor, where he fell face forward, slamming his jaw, smashing his teeth, and rapping his nose.

He groaned, turned over, and looked up.

He thought he saw Rose standing there, smiling.

"It's just a little flop," she said. "Next time, you'll take more care. Accidents make us careful. They're little warnings to keep us from really hurting ourselves. Don't be upset. Be grateful. Come on, smile, Henry. That's it. Smile."

He died with a grimace on his lips.

It wasn't really a smile.

It was disgust.

Seven

Munsen enjoyed the silence at breakfast. Neither of his daughters woke up easily. In that regard they took after him entirely. Sometimes he thought the dead had an easier time rising up from the grave than he did from his bed. Both Brooke and Crystal pushed the clock to the last dying second before surrendering to getting up, showering, and dressing. They were sullen and sat with their eyes down as they ate their toast or cereal while Lisa flitted around the table as chipper and bright as a sparrow, reminding them of this or that. They moaned their replies in monosyllabic grunts until they were ready to leave, one following the other out the door, like two sleepwalkers, to make the school bus pickup, their complaints lingering behind them like car exhaust.

"I tell them to get to bed earlier, but they're up to all hours talking on the phone or watching television," Lisa explained as if she had been brought before a jury deciding her fate as a good mother. "You'd think they would have learned for themselves by now, but they're stubborn, Munsen. They're as stubborn as you are."

"Me?"

"You're the one who still holds on to that dirty habit of chewing tobacco. Don't deny it," she fired quickly. "I'm always finding pieces of cheap cigars in your pants pockets."

"It's better than smoking them," Munsen said.

"See?" Her eyes were as big and as bright as a movie marquee.

"Jeeze, how do I get the short end every morning?" he moaned.

"You didn't get the short end last night," she replied with a small smile.

He laughed and the phone rang.

"It starts," he said, rising. "Munsen," he growled into the receiver. Lisa laughed.

"Mr. Donald?"

"Yeah, who's this?"

"Wolf Deutch. Henry's son, Wolf," he added.

"Oh." Shit, Munsen thought. "What's up, Mr. Deutch?"

"Did you have some kind of a storm there last night?"

"Yeah, it rained some, why?"

"I can't reach my father on the phone. I tried last night and all this morning. Are the lines out?"

Munsen looked at Lisa and shook his head.

"If the lines were out, how could you be talking to me?"

"Exactly. I'm worried, Mr. Donald. I'm about forty miles away and I know Dad's been on edge lately with all that's been happening. I haven't seen him since I was there last week when he called you. Could you do me a favor and look in on him? Tell him to call me as soon as he can. Would you? I'd appreciate it."

"Sure. I'm about to go out. I'll stop by on the way to the fire station this morning."

The fire station was where Munsen had his pathetic little office with just enough room for a desk, two chairs, and two file cabinets. It wasn't until last year that he got the chief to buy him a fax machine.

"Thanks again and sorry to bother you."

"Right," Munsen said. He cradled the receiver. Lisa stared at him as he scratched his head. "Oh, that was Henry Deutch's son. Can't raise him on the phone and wants me to check it out."

She nodded.

"It's not easy living alone," she said. "I feel sorry for anyone who does, especially people along in their years."

"Yeah, well it's hard to feel sorry for Henry Deutch. Anything doing today?"

"I've got my regular gynecological checkup," Lisa said. "Three o'clock."

"Okay. I'll call you before I come home," he said, moving toward the garage. He hit the garage door opener button and the door let in the full impact of a bright, sunny day. It nearly blinded him for a moment.

He got into the patrol car and backed out slowly. The school bus had just arrived and his daughters were getting on, both leaning so far back as they stepped up that they looked like hooked fish putting up resistance. It brought a smile to his lips. The bus started away, turning down Clancy Lane to make another pickup. It gave him an open road and he gunned it, annoyed that he had to see Henry Deutch first thing in the morning.

Minutes later, he pulled up alongside Henry's Mercedes and got out. The crisp morning air was still cool enough to reveal his breath, but the moment he turned toward the house, he stopped breathing for a second.

The dangling chicken swayed gently in the breeze.

"What the hell . . ."

He plodded slowly toward the steps and paused to look up at the butchered bird. Its entrails were dried and exposed and there was a terrific stench. Anna Young had struck again, he thought. This would be the end all, for sure.

Leaning to stay as far away from it as he could, he sucked in his breath, and went up to the door. The button for the door chime was hanging on a wire, obviously not working. Munsen estimated Deutch to have a multimillionaire's net worth, yet look how the man lives, he thought. People like Henry Deutch would always be a mystery to Munsen, someone who had trouble not spending an extra dollar whenever he had one. All he could do was think of them as squirrels, hoarding money instead of acorns, expecting that inevitable rainy day. Trouble was, when the rainy day finally came, they were long dead and gone and their children or beneficiaries enjoyed the horde. Dumb bastards.

He rapped hard on the door and waited, gazing back at the chicken and shaking his head in disbelief. Maybe Henry didn't know it was out here or maybe he saw it and was afraid to come out. He rapped again and called out.

"Henry?" He waited, rapped again, harder. "Henry, it's Munsen Donald. Your son just phoned me. He's been unable to reach you and he's worried. Henry?"

He waited and then he tried the door. It was locked solid. Now curious himself, but concerned the man might have gone bonkers after this episode and could be waiting someplace with a shotgun, Munsen cautiously peeked in the window. The living room looked worn and grimy, but not disturbed.

"Damn it," he muttered, and went around the side of the house. He was able to look into a bedroom window. The curtain was open enough for him to get a view of the room. At first he saw nothing, and then he caught a glimpse of Henry Deutch's feet and part of his leg sticking out from the side of the bed. He was prone. "Shit," Munsen cried, and tapped the window. Those feet didn't move.

He ran around to the rear of the house. There was a smaller door that opened into the pantry and then the kitchen. It was locked as well, but it wasn't as substantial a door. He stepped back and hit it hard with his shoulder just the way he used to hit a bag in football practice. The door groaned at the locks. He hit it harder and it snapped right off its top hinge. The wood looked rotten from dampness and time. He then kicked it in and entered the house. In his imagination, he could hear Henry Deutch complaining and threatening a law suit afterward.

The moment he looked at him on the floor, however, he knew he wasn't going to yell at anyone or sue anyone anymore. The pasty complexion and dull glassy eyes spoke of death convincingly.

"Jesus," Munsen whispered. He knelt at Deutch's side, felt for a pulse and then rose slowly. That was when he first saw the dead rat. Along with the sight of it was the horrible stench from all this death. He nearly brought up his breakfast. "What the hell . . ."

He rushed to the phone. No dial tone, just as Wolf had said, Munsen thought. He went to the front door, undid all the locks and, stepping gingerly around the swinging dead chicken, hurried down the steps to his patrol car to radio the police station in South Fallsburg. After that, he opened the trunk and took out his yellow tape to close off the scene. It was an unattended death, requiring an autopsy and an investigation.

As soon as he had cordoned it off, he stepped back and shook his head. What a sight . . . the old house with a butchered chicken dangling, a dead man on the floor, and a rat in the bed. Munsen felt he had just fallen into someone else's nightmare. It wasn't that he hadn't seen dead people before. He had been the first on the scene of at least five fatal traffic accidents during his tenure as a policeman, and there was Bert Silverman's accidental death, falling from his house roof last spring and breaking his neck. But he suspected nothing that had occurred in the entire township, maybe the entire county, was as bizarre as all this.

He remembered the telephone and went around to the side of the house to look at the wires. They were cut clean through. Someone didn't want Henry reached or worse yet, didn't want Henry calling for help. Obviously, Anna, your curses and rituals needed something more, he thought and returned to his vehicle to wait.

Town of Fallsburg police chief Barry Marshall and Philip Coleman arrived before the coroner. The paramedics, who were really volunteer firemen, were already on the scene. They were standing by their ambulance waiting for instructions.

"Did you touch anything in there?" Coleman immediately demanded as he stepped out. He had a camera in hand.

"Just him to confirm he's dead and the phone," Munsen said. "I broke in the back door. I also checked the phone wires. They've been cut."

The chief stepped out slowly and put on his hat. He was a tall, hard looking man with dark skin and features chiseled into a face of granite. At forty-eight, Marshall's hair had turned nearly completely light gray, which emphasized his caramel complexion. Everyone believed he had some African or South American blood in him. He had come out of the military police into the local force, and had risen like boiling milk to the top position in the department. He spoke in a no-nonsense, clipped manner, a holdover from his military experience.

Munsen knew the chief was critical of his physical appearance. He had tried to put penalties on his policemen for being out of shape, overweight, but the town board had it bottled up in committee because they feared lawsuits from the policemen's union. They were waiting for the county to do it with the sheriff's department first.

"What the hell is that?" Marshall demanded, nodding at the chicken.

Munsen looked at Coleman and realized he had obviously not told the chief any details.

"There's a woman in town who has a vendetta against this man, Henry Deutch," Munsen began. "She thinks she has supernatural powers, a witch. It's probably part of some sort of curse. Like voodoo or something," he added, nodding at the dangling fowl.

Marshall stared into Munsen's face with barely an expression of interest.

"You know for a fact that this woman hung that dead chicken?" he asked.

"No, not for sure, but . . . Jesus, man," he said, turning to Coleman, "didn't you tell him anything?"

"What was I going to tell him? I came down here to take prints off a window on which someone drew a red cross? We got a lot of real stuff going down," Coleman said in vigorous defense of himself. "Did you read about the drug bust yesterday, for example?"

"There's a dead rat on Deutch's bed, too," Munsen mumbled.

"What was that?" Marshall demanded.

Munsen described the death scene.

"I think the old man pulled his cover down, saw the rat

and dropped dead. If he tried to get help, he couldn't because someone cut the wires, too. I just told Phil."

The chief turned to Coleman, who needed only the look to get started. He hurried into the house.

"Better fill me in on everything here," Marshall told Munsen. He looked up at the dangling chicken and Munsen began the story. Midway, without comment, the chief started for the house. Just as they had reached the steps, the coroner pulled up. Marshall turned to greet him.

If the county supervisors had called central casting, they couldn't have gotten anyone who would have fit the part of county coroner better than Doctor Lawrence Battan. Barely five feet four, balding, light brown hair, with large brown eyes behind what looked like microscope lenses for glasses, and soft, feminine dark cherry lips that sometimes took on the purplish color of the lips of the corpses he examined, Battan moved and talked with a nervous energy that spooked everyone else on the crime scene. When he spoke to someone, he concentrated on his face with such intensity, the individual thought Battan was looking for signs of some impending fatal illness. He was dry, pallid, seemingly devoid of emotion, and always reeking of some chemical odor.

But he was good, efficient, and very self-confident.

"What do we have?" he asked.

Marshall turned to Munsen for the response.

"Henry Deutch, in his early sixties, dead on the floor in his bedroom. No signs of any struggle or anything. The doors were all locked from the inside. I know he had some serious heart problems."

"How do you know?" Battan snapped back at him like a cross-examiner in a courtroom. Munsen glanced at the chief. Battan had his face up, those eyes sweeping over Munsen's visage.

"His son told me. It's common knowledge. This is a small town," he blurted.

Battan smirked, looked at the chief, and headed into the house, just glancing at the chicken as if he had seen dozens of them dangling like that on people's front porches.

"And you confronted this woman on a few occasions regarding Deutch's complaints?" Marshall asked Munsen, as if their previous conversation had been kept dangling in the air between them.

"Yes, sir. She denied coming up here and doing these things, but she talks in a strange way."

"Strange way?"

"She says no and yet yes. I can't exactly explain it."

"Did you make a report each time?"

"Well, not exactly," Munsen said.

"What does that mean?"

"I mean, I have the dates, times, and incidents down, but I didn't file anything formal."

"Okay, let's see what we have here first," Marshall said, and started up the steps, pausing to inspect the chicken. Coleman emerged.

"No signs of any trauma as far as I can see, but we better wait for the medical report."

"You check the windows?"

"All batted down tight. From what Munsen tells me about the doors, I don't think anyone got in, hurt him in any way, and got out of there. Everything's locked from the inside."

"Okay, but you better bag all this," Marshall said, nodding at the chicken and the rope that held it swinging.

"Drop it in the back of my car and I'll get it to the lab. And take a picture of those cut telephone wires."

"Right." He glanced at Munsen. "Maybe she poisoned him somehow," he suggested. "You've got some town, Munsen," he quipped, heading for the police vehicle.

Munsen glanced at Marshall and then wiped his forehead. Suddenly, it felt really warm. The cool crisp morning was gone and in its place was a sticky, confining bed of air that threatened to suffocate the whole village. It was as if the stench of death was leaking out the windows and doors of Deutch's house. There would be a lot of buzzing in this sleepy old town today, he thought, and remembered he had to phone Wolf Deutch.

"I'll go call the son," he told the chief.

"Just give it to Phil," the chief said. "He's the lead investigator now and he'll want to question him first."

Munsen nodded. Marshall never hesitated to put you in your place, he thought. He stood by and watched Coleman gather evidence until Doctor Battan and the chief emerged from the house. They told the paramedics to go into the house to get the body. Munsen approached tentatively, as if he was eavesdropping on a conversation not for his ears. The chief turned to him.

"Doctor Battan's preliminary suspicion leans toward what you described, a heart attack. He found some medications that support it, but we've got to wait for a complete autopsy, toxicology, etc., before making any statements. Coleman will call the physician on the pill bottle. For now, if anyone asks, just say it's under investigation."

"The son's on his way here," Phil Coleman announced as he approached the gathering. "When was the last time you saw this guy?" he asked Munsen.

"When I was here investigating the window with you."

They watched as the paramedics brought out the corpse and loaded it into the ambulance.

"Okay," Marshall said as Doctor Battan headed for his vehicle without any comment. "I'll put a call into the district attorney's office and let her know what we have. Phil, you're going to pay this witch a visit ASAP, I assume?"

Coleman nodded.

"Munsen will show me the way."

"Fine. Get back to me by four. Munsen will drive you wherever you have to be," he added firmly. "I'll bring Max Sussman down to watch the house." He turned to Munsen. "Hang out and protect the scene until he arrives."

"Right."

"When do you expect the son?" Marshall asked Phil.

"About an hour."

"Max will be here before that. Tell him not to let the son into the house until we get more from Battan. Everyone clear?"

"Right," Coleman said. Munsen just nodded. He was impressed with the activity, but he didn't see it leading anywhere.

"I'm sure the guy probably just dropped dead. He was so mean spirited, his heart probably revolted at the sight of the chicken and rat," he said.

"Maybe. Probably," Marshall replied. "But let's go by the book so we don't get accused of being what we are."

"What's that?" Munsen asked.

"A small town police force."

Phil laughed.

"I'll go bag the rat," he said. He looked at Munsen. "Wanna help?"

"Not me. That's why they pay you the big bucks," he countered.

Phil had to laugh, but stopped smiling when he headed back toward the scene of death.

After patrolman Sussman arrived to guard the scene, Munsen drove Coleman to Anna Young's tailor shop. By now, word of Deutch's death had threaded itself in and out of almost every doorway. A small crowd had gathered in front of Kayfields. Tony Monato stood at the center in his apron. He didn't have to be over the grill. All the customers had come out to see what was happening. They watched Munsen and Coleman go by on their way to Anna's.

She was already at work when they arrived. She looked up without surprise, giving Munsen the sense that she had been expecting them.

This morning she wore a light-blue pullover blouse that clung like cellophane to her firm breasts, clearly showing her nipples embossed against the thin cotton. Munsen had never noticed until now how dark skinned Anna was. Her arms were firmer than he had realized, too. Her long, rich-looking jet black hair lay softly on her shoulders. When she turned, her eyes were so bright and alive, they were practically luminous. She looks years younger, Munsen thought. Maybe she's been rejuvenated and invigorated by Henry's death, he thought.

She moved her legs, turning to face them. She was wearing another one of those long, flowery pattern skirts, but it fell snugly between her legs. He couldn't keep his gaze from following the lines to the insides of her thighs.

"Good morning," Anna said. She didn't smile so much as she tightened her lips with what looked to Munsen to be an amused thought.

"Good morning, Anna," Munsen began. "This is Detective Philip Coleman. He would like to ask you some questions."

She fixed her gaze on Coleman without a word. He glanced at Munsen and then cleared his throat.

"Er . . . I understand you weren't getting along with Mr. Henry Deutch," he said, and waited. She barely moved. "Is that so?" he added when it looked like she wouldn't comment.

"Weren't?" she replied, glancing at Munsen. "Mr. Deutch is an evil man. He is possessed by evil," she continued. "I can never get along with him."

"Were you on his property anytime during the last twenty-four hours?" Coleman followed.

"Do you mean his home or his real estate properties?" she countered.

"Home."

"No," she said.

"You didn't . . . er . . . hang a dead chicken on his front porch?"

She stared, blinked, and shook her head.

"And you weren't in his house?"

"I have always been there," she said.

"I thought you just said you weren't on his property."

"I have been inside him, haunting him, driving the evil out of him," she explained.

Now it was Coleman's turn to just stare for a moment. He straightened up.

"Did you put your feet on that man's residential property?" he demanded.

"No," she replied. She looked at Munsen. "What has happened now?"

"Henry Deutch is dead," Munsen told her. "I found him on his bedroom floor this morning, but I also found a dead rat in his bed and a butchered chicken dangling from his front porch rafter."

"You didn't find Henry Deutch dead today," Anna said.

"Yes, I did, Anna."

She shook her head and turned back to her work.

"Henry Deutch died long ago. He died with his wife," she said. "The spirit that inhabited his body died today," she clarified.

"What?" Coleman looked at Munsen, but Munsen just shrugged. "I want you to know, Miss Young," Philip Coleman said, "that an autopsy is being performed on Mr. Deutch. If there are any signs of foul play—"

"Of course there are signs of foul play," she said quickly, pausing to turn to him again. "There have been signs of foul play for quite some time now." She returned to her work. "My mother will rest in peace finally," she said in a whisper. "Rest in peace."

Philip Coleman raised his eyebrows and looked at Munsen.

"We might return to speak to you again, Miss Young," he told her.

"You are always welcome," she said.

"Let's go," he said, jerking his head toward the door.

Outside, he paused and looked back at Anna. She worked without hesitation, her concentration unbroken.

"That's one crazy woman," he said. "You really do have some weird town here, Munsen."

"Now you know why I tried to get something done earlier," Munsen said.

Coleman looked at Anna again.

"I don't know as you could have. I don't know as I could have. What a strange woman. She didn't seem a bit nervous. But," he said, heading for the car and smiling, "what a piece of ass. Hey, I'm a detective. I notice these things," he added with a laugh and got into the vehicle. "I don't expect this to amount to anything, Munsen, but keep an eye on her yourself. I know you'll enjoy it. As soon as we get some information and direction, we might come back to see her, which won't be so hard to do," he added.

Munsen smiled and nodded, and then stopped abruptly. He felt heat on the back of his neck and turned.

Anna was in her doorway, staring at him. He hoped she hadn't heard Coleman.

After what he had seen, he was unashamedly afraid of her.

Eight

Rabbi Hyman Balk lowered his copy of Jerome Mahler's book on Jews and mysticism, and turned to his wife, Sophie, when the buzzer sounded.

"You want I should get it?" she asked.

His fifty-four-year-old wife looked more than settled in her favorite mushy cushion, big armchair; she looked like she had sunken into it and might disappear entirely into the frame after a few more hours. Of course he didn't want her to get up to answer the door. What an effort it would take and she had worse arthritis than he did.

"It's them," he said. "I'll get it. I'll get it."

"Should I make some tea, serve sponge cake?"

"We'll see," he said, rising. "We'll see how long they stay."

"Maybe it's not them," she said as he walked toward the front door.

Paranoia was like an Eastern European plague, Rabbi Balk thought. Everyone is afraid to open his or her door these days, especially at night, and especially after what had happened to Henry Deutch. A shadow was no longer a shadow and a clunk was no longer a clunk. Someone was always lurking. He and Sophie had enough relatives in New York City who had been either mugged or attacked. The stories flew over the bridges and tunnels and up the New York Thruway like birds migrating north. If it happened there, it could happen here. Why not?

"Ask who it is first," she warned from the living room.

He waved his hand at her. She couldn't see it, but it was the same as him saying "Stop with the worrying."

He opened the door without hesitation to face Father McDermott and Reverend Carter. With their jacket collars up, standing in the dark corner of his portico, Rabbi Balk thought they looked like conspirators. Sometimes it was the way he felt about himself, despite what he believed in his heart and soul about this Anna Young.

"Are we too early?" Reverend Carter asked when Rabbi Balk hesitated.

"No, no. Who pays attention to time at my age?" Rabbi Balk said, and the two clergymen laughed.

"I understand exactly," Father McDermott said. "No matter how deep our faith in the hereafter, it's nice to postpone the visit for as long as the good Lord will permit."

They all chuckled as Rabbi Balk stepped back to permit them to enter his house.

The aromas of the evening meal lingered in the house. Sophie had made a good piece of brisket, baked the potatoes in the gravy, and served it all with a side of fresh green beans. Earlier, she had made her speciality: a bittersweet chocolate sponge cake with a strand of jam in the middle.

The rabbi's home was similar to most of the vintage houses in Sandburg. The ceilings were low, the walls covered with dark paneling. Despite her arthritis, Sophie still managed to keep it neat and clean. Even what was tired and worn still looked presentable.

"I'm glad you agreed we should meet," Reverend Carter said.

"Of course we should meet. Why shouldn't we meet?" Rabbi Balk asked, and nodded toward his small den-office on the right. "We'll sit in here," he said.

Father McDermott walked in first, pausing to look at the mezuzah on the door jamb.

"Now I hear," he said, "it's important how these are put on."

"It's important," Rabbi Balk said. "We have a prayer to recite before we affix it. *Barukh atah Adonai, Elohaynu, melekh ha-olam asher keed'shanu b'meetzvotav v'tzeevannu leek'boa mezuzah.* Then we put it on the right side as one enters a room, placing it at the beginning of the upper third of the doorpost, tilted at an angle, with the upper part of the mezuzah slanted inward toward the home and the lower part away from the home."

"For good luck?" Reverend Carter asked.

"No, no. It's not a charm," he said with his lips twisted indignantly. "It is a symbol marking the home as a Jewish home. For the Jew himself, it reminds him upon entering or leaving his household of the Divine Presence and His unity, and of his own duties to abide by all the laws and precepts set forth in the Torah. We kiss our fingers and touch it."

"So we genuflect and kiss the cross," Father McDermott said with a shrug. "Maybe someone could say we've got our own Bell, Book, and Candle, huh?"

Neither Rabbi Balk nor Reverend Carter responded.

"I didn't mean to compare what we do to what she does," Father McDermott added quickly.

"Of course not. She's a pagan," Rabbi Balk said. "Come,

sit, please," he added, gesturing at the sofa and chairs in front of the small dark cherrywood desk. The two clergymen sat on the sofa and the rabbi sat behind his desk.

"What I'm afraid of," Reverend Carter began, getting right to the point, "is turning her into some kind of hero, some cause that makes her more famous and brings all sorts of people here."

"We shouldn't be afraid of the challenge," Father McDermott said. "We have a responsibility to make the challenge, in fact."

"I'm not talking about not going forward," Reverend Carter said almost angrily. "I'm talking about how we go forward. It's most important we do this right."

"No one wants to do it wrong," Father McDermott retorted.

Rabbi Balk sat quietly, watching his theological competitors go at each other for a few moments. It was easy to see how it all could go wrong.

"Let's first find out where we all agree," he said. "She's turning good members of my congregation into pagans. They go to her and perform these rituals of idolatry, pray to spirits, burn incense, put icons on their walls, wear them around their necks. They talk to spirits which are no more than devils. And all in the name of becoming one with the so-called good energy. This is what I've been told is the New Age, a union of the spiritual inside yourself with some all encompassing power that if they treat right, will grant them their wishes, even if it means harm to someone else.

"They claim they talk to the dead through her. She tells them their beloved lost souls want them to do what she tells them to do. She takes advantage of their sorrow. She's done it with Benny Sklar. He never would miss a Sabbath service before this and he's refusing to pay his synagogue dues. I don't have to tell you he has been a big contributor."

"I've got similar stories with my parish," Father McDermott said.

"As do I with my congregation," Reverend Carter added glumly.

"She's poisoning their minds and their souls," Rabbi Balk said. "Good people, too, people you would never imagine being taken in by her smoke and mirrors."

"Have you ever spoken to her?" Father McDermott asked Rabbi Balk. He fixed his eyes on him, obviously very interested in not only the answer, but how the rabbi gave it.

Rabbi Balk nodded slowly, pensively.

"Yes. She's never been nasty or unpleasant to me, but she looks and listens to me as if . . ."

"Yes?"

"She's humoring me, as if she knows more than I do, or something that I don't know which will make me feel like a fool someday."

"Exactly," Father McDermott said, nodding and looking at Reverend Carter.

"I haven't actually spoken to the woman. I didn't want to legitimize her in any way, but I have looked at her and found her gazing at me with that sort of smirk on her face, condescending. Dangerous woman," he added, "dangerous."

They were all quiet for a moment, each gazing expectantly at the other as if to see who would move this conversation toward its intended resolution.

"She killed that man," Reverend Carter was the first to charge.

"It was as if she had driven a knife in his heart," Father McDermott agreed.

"I don't doubt it," Rabbi Balk offered, "but this isn't Salem. This isn't the days of the witch trials. We can't expect the courts to do anything," he said. "You could excommunicate her; I could excommunicate her, but to get her charged with what she should be charged with . . ."

"That's exactly what we must do," Reverend Carter said.

"How?"

They all thought.

"We should talk to the district attorney, make sure she looks into every aspect of this and maybe finds a legal way that is not like the Salem witch trials, a legal way to hold her accountable for her actions," Father McDermott said.

"If the government goes after her, we can go after her and not look like we're doing it for any selfish or personal reasons," Reverend Carter said.

"And maybe it won't be a three-ring circus that way," Rabbi Balk added, nodding.

"We won't talk about evil spirits, about paganism," Father McDermott suggested. "We'll talk about responsibility and we'll keep it as down to earth as we can."

"Down to earth? That's a good way to put it," Rabbi Balk said with a smile.

"But let's not lie to ourselves," Reverend Carter said.

"What do you mean?" the rabbi asked.

"Let's three admit here to each other what we really believe."

They were all quiet.

"We have different thoughts about the Devil," the rabbi said.

"But not about evil as a force in the world with which we must all do battle," Reverend Carter said. "Isn't that so?"

The rabbi nodded.

"In a sense, yes. We believe that everyone is born with two impulses: Yetzer Hatov, a force for good; and Yetzer Hara, a force for evil. Thus we have a dual nature, capable of sin but not doomed to it. Yetzer Hara is more prevalent in children until they reach thirteen. Who is a hero? He who conquers his own evil impulses or turns them into good.

"If she gets my people to stray from the law and worship idols, she will make Yetzer Hara more of a force in their lives. And this is what I'm afraid she is doing," he concluded.

"And if she gets my people to forget their vows and turn from God to the Devil, she will be sending them to hell," Reverend Carter insisted. "We believe the Devil is among us, just waiting for opportunity, opportunity she'll give him."

"She's evil," the rabbi agreed.

The two looked at Father McDermott.

"She's possessed by Satan," he said. "You know my church believes that's possible, but for now," he added with a smile, "you're the only ones I'll tell."

The rabbi nodded.

"So?" his wife said from the doorway.

They all turned.

"She made a wonderful sponge cake tonight," the rabbi said. "Smeared with bittersweet chocolate icing and some jelly in the center."

"Don't mind if I do," Reverend Carter said quickly.

"One of my favorite cakes," Father McDermott said.

The rabbi nodded at his wife who went off to prepare the tea.

"If we could all only agree about everything else as quickly," Father McDermott said.

"There wouldn't be any Anna Youngs," Reverend Carter added.

They laughed.

The rabbi smiled.

Somehow, he thought, even then, there still would be.

* * *

Phil Coleman sat in front of district attorney Paula Richards' desk and watched her peruse the investigation report. As she read she fingered the beaded string that held her glasses around her neck when she wasn't wearing them. Phil thought she looked like she was working a Rosary. Ms. Richards, as she insisted on being called despite the fact that she was married to Edmond Scott, a very successful CPA, had been given the preliminaries and then the detailed autopsy. Coleman was somewhat perplexed about being called in on what he thought was pretty much an open and shut matter, despite the cut telephone wires. As Munsen Donald had sensibly suggested, that could have easily been the work of mischievous teenagers. He had caught them doing similar things.

Richards always hoisted her rather firm, athletic shoulders when she read something intensely. To Coleman, she looked like she was getting ready to pounce. Her strawberry blond hair was stylishly cut at the nape of her neck. She always had that not-a-hair-out-of-place look. He expected she even went to bed that way. It was funny. Although she was nowhere near the type of woman he would pursue, Coleman couldn't help fantasizing about her. It was as if he imagined that even sexually, she was efficient, productive, and successful.

"Trust me," he imagined she would say, "and you'll get the most out of it."

At thirty-nine, Paula Richards was one of the county's most prominent and promising female politicians. Despite her take-no-prisoners demeanor in court and on the job, when she was out in public or on the campaign trail, she was personable, warm, and elegant. She always looked like she was really not doing something political. Rather, she was involved in a social event.

Smartly attractive with a smile highlighted by gem quality turquoise blue eyes that dazzled her male constituents, Paula Richards had a way of flashing her grin, disarming her opponents, and then fixing her face with a mature, serious look that could be intimidating. In court, she was a relentless cross-examiner, turning a question with small or subtle syntactical changes that often ambushed a witness and put just the right twist on the responses and facts. Nearly five feet eleven, she religiously maintained her trim figure, and she was as conscious of fashion as she was of the law codes she was sworn to enforce. She prepared for trial with as much concern for her coiffure, her complexion, her clothes as a movie star preparing for a shoot.

Indeed, she often viewed her professional life as similar to theater. The courtroom, she was heard to say, has replaced theater in America. "We're on television more. Our work is scrutinized and witnessed more, and we deal with human drama with just as many characters and subplots as a typical Hollywood film. Appearance means a lot to a jury. If you are confident, you'll be convincing," she lectured her assistants.

Some of the older attorneys, the pillars of the old boy's club, claimed she was more show than substance. She did have a remarkable success record in prosecutions, but a large part of the reason was her wise selection of cases to try and cases to settle. No one would question her ability when it came to those decisions. Phil Coleman was about to be one of the first.

He shifted in his seat and gazed at the awards, certifi-cates, and photographs decorating Paula Richards' office walls. All of the pictures had Paula in them, of course. All of them were taken with either celebrities or important political figures. What was absent from the wall were pictures of Paula and her husband. There was only one small photo of the two of them taken at some political affair, but the picture was relegated to the far right corner of her desk and usually blocked by a pile of files. It was one of the photographs that had been used in ads for her last campaign, the ads that were intended to stress her familial qualities even though she had no children.

Paula turned to the final page in the report. The diamond-and-gold wedding ring caught the shaft of light from her desk lamp and glittered. After a moment more of reading, she sat back and looked pensive, her gaze fixed on the office ceiling. Coleman hinged his eyebrows in expectation as Paula pressed the tips of her fingers together and lowered her chin.

"This is a murder one case," she declared with her typical godlike pronouncement.

"What?"

"We're going after the witch."

"Excuse me?"

"What we have here is a clear pattern of intent to do harm, a knowledge that the acts undertaken would do harm and result in a fatal result. Foreseeability. It was premeditated, planned, and plotted for a harmful purpose.

"I believe we can show that if it wasn't for her actions, including cutting the telephone wires, this fatal result would not have occurred. This victim was literally frightened to death and unable to get help. Anna Young knew what would happen if she continued her nasty behavior and yet she continued, deliberately seeking out the result. What we have is an intent to kill with malice aforethought, if I ever saw it," she continued.

Coleman shook his head.

"I think she's just bonkers. She believes she has supernatural powers."

"From what I'm reading here, she's not the only one in the village who does," Paula Richards said.

She glanced at her calendar. Coleman noted how she gazed at the months and he began to surmise what was on the district attorney's mind. Maybe the rumors were true about Richards. She was going to run for Congress and was wondering how to fit in this prosecution. What did she expect this would do for her campaign?

"You're going to prosecute someone for being a witch?" he asked incredulously.

"No, not exactly. What she believes about herself isn't the point. Look," Paula said, leaning forward on her elbows, "someone uses psychological weapons, techniques to drive another person into suicide. Isn't that criminal? Shouldn't we prosecute? This is, it seems to me, even clearer."

"Why?"

"Suppose you knew someone had a bad heart and you got them into a situation where he was fleeing out of fear. You kept after him. You kept him running until he had a heart attack. You watched him drop and then you walked away. Willful. Consistent behavior for an intent to do harm. Planned." Paula Richards lifted her hands. "See?"

"Yeah, I suppose. I'm not a lawyer."

"I'm not asking you to be. I want you to go back there. Canvass the village. Get me witnesses who will testify to her intention to do Deutch harm. I want a more detailed record of what she actually did as well as when. Get Donald to write up his notes into formal reports. See about proving her responsibility for some of these or all of these bizarre actions . . . the curses, the bones . . . stuff that harassed him. See if you can tie her to the chicken and the rat somehow. Also, how much detail did she have about Deutch's condition? Find out about that. There's a real investigation to do here, Phil. This isn't funny."

Paula Richards tapped the report with her fingers.

"From what I read here, her answers were deliberately cryptic. I think she's avoiding legal responsibility. She might be smarter than you all think.

"Get me some of this by Friday, and I'll seek an indictment and we'll make a formal charge."

"Okay," Philips said, rising. "You're the district attorney."

"I'll talk to the chief. Get the son's testimony. I have some other ideas based on some interesting precedents. Bring forensics back up there. I want a more thorough examination. See if you can tie her to that house, around it, inside, anything that puts her at the scene. You know what I'm looking for," Paula Richards said, rising.

"Yeah, I think," Coleman said.

Paula gave him one of those famous smiles.

"Relax. If she puts a curse on you, I'll find another witch to get it removed."

"What if she curses you?" Coleman asked.

Paula shrugged.

"She'll have to get in line."

She walked Phil Coleman to her door. She was not a touchy-feely person and rarely put her arm around anyone or even held a hand. Of course, on the campaign trail, she hugged and kissed and shook hands when it was called for.

"This could be a very significant case, Phil. I want to get into some new territory. It's going to bring the spotlights down on all of us, so play it close to the book, okay? Substantiate as much as possible, get me a minimum of two witnesses for every incident where possible."

"I understand," Phil said. He thought he understood only too well.

"Call me any time with anything. I'm making this a priority," Paula added.

After Phil Coleman left, Paula returned to her desk and

then picked up the report. She smiled at it and pressed the intercom button on her phone.

"Melissa, get me Fred Horning," she told her secretary. Then she sat back. Horning, the state Republican party boss, had been after her all week to declare her candidacy. She knew they were sensitive to the need to have more female candidates. It wasn't exactly why she wanted them to want her, but maybe it was time to do so. She envisioned national headlines with this case. Of course, she wouldn't try her as a witch, but that was surely the way the newspapers would handle it. Paula could easily see herself on *60 Minutes*, defining a whole new area of criminal activity. People would call her innovative, brilliant, potentially a candidate for higher and higher office. Who knew where it could end?

Only the shadow, she muttered, or the witch.

She laughed and picked up the receiver when she was buzzed.

"I have Mr. Horning on the line."

"Okay, and as soon as I'm off, call Reverend Carter in Sandburg," she instructed, then she pressed the lit button.

"Freddy," she sang, "how are you doing?"

"You know how I'm doing, Paula. What's up?"

Paula Richards turned her chair and gazed up at her picture with George Bush at a fund raiser.

"I have come to a decision," she said, "a decision I believe you will like." She laughed. "A decision, I have come to the conclusion, that will be good for the party."

Father Vince McDermott sat in the rocker on the rear porch, an add-on to the rectory built for him by Billy Connor two years ago. It was just big enough for the rocker and one other chair, but it was meant to be his private meditative place anyway. Even a priest needed an escape.

Perhaps it was odd for a priest to seek some place other than the church itself to do his own introspection, but he could never flee from the feeling that the church was his place of work, the sanctuary to which his parishioners came for their needs and therefore where he dispensed advice to others.

There were those in the community who rarely attended church, who were Catholics only on the most solemn of occasions. Rabbi Balk had a term for his people who were this way. He called them Shabbus Jews. Some he saw only on the Jewish High Holy days. Regular churchgoers, whether they be of his faith or another, Father McDermott thought, were rapidly becoming the exception and not the rule. Sometimes, when he confronted one of his wandering flock, she would tell him she makes her peace with God out there, in nature, in the biggest church of all, God's very creation. Never mind this concept of a holy temple, and don't tell me about this where three are gathered in my name stuff. If God cares, he hears.

Sitting out here, looking at the forest and the Sandburg creek that rushed over rocks, polishing them into jewels under the midday sun, Father McDermott was tempted to agree, even though he knew it was blasphemy to even suggest he was unnecessary, that this whole sophisticated structure with its order of authority, its icons, and holy waters was beside the point.

He was only a man; he could have his moments of doubt, his skeptical times, his questions, too. He certainly had doubts about the complicated theology concerning the Devil and hell. So often during his theological studies, he would feel this incredulity that grown men, men of the twentieth century, subscribed to it all, even believed in demonic possession. He thought it made the church comical, another division of Hollywood, and gave credence to all those writers and producers of terror movies.

And yet, how was he to explain this Anna Young? How was he to emphasize just how dangerous she was? It wasn't only men who flocked to her side and became enamored. There were women of some reputation admiring her, and many of them were in his parish. For now, he had to put aside his doubts and think of her as his church would want her to be thought of: demonic.

She killed that man, he told himself. She as good as put a gun to his head.

He heard the telephone ringing and rose to go into the kitchen.

"Hello," he said. "Father McDermott."

"Vincent, it's Bob," Reverend Carter said.

"Oh. How are you?"

"The district attorney is going to pursue her," Bob Carter said quickly. "She's also eager to meet with us, and welcomes our support."

"We've got to be careful," Vincent McDermott warned. "My church has enough martyrs."

"Mine too, but more important, I don't intend to become one. We'll meet again before we visit with Paula Richards. You and I have to be sure Balk is with us all the way. It's better if this remains an interfaith effort and not just a private gripe."

"Why? Is the rabbi balking?" Vince McDermott said half in jest.

"I don't trust him completely," Bob Carter said. "You know how they can be."

Father Vincent McDermott nodded as if Bob Carter could see as well as hear.

"Yes, but they don't have a monopoly on retreat in the face of contention," Vince McDermott nearly boomed in his Sunday voice.

"I'll be right beside you throughout this whole nasty thing," Bob Carter promised. "I take pride in having gotten it started, being the most vocal about her."

"Pride?" Vincent McDermott half-kidded again. "Isn't that one of the deadly sins?"

"Not in this case, not for us," Reverend Carter insisted. "I'll be in touch. I'll call Balk now and tell him the good news."

"Okay," Vincent McDermott said, and hung up. He returned to his porch, sat and stared at the brook, its waters sparkling brighter under the unblocked sun.

Why is it, he wondered, that he felt like such a conspirator instead of a good soldier for God?

Joyce Slayton entered the shop and then leaned against the door as she closed it behind her. She stood there, her face beaming. Anna paused in her hemming of Gina Carnesi's black skirt, and then took the pin out from between her clenched teeth.

"Mrs. Slayton?"

Joyce held her smile. She stepped forward, almost dancing across the shop and simply extended her hand. The diamond engagement ring glittered. Anna nodded at it and then looked up at her.

"We're getting married!" Joyce cried. "It worked!"

Again, Anna nodded, barely cracking a smile. Joyce realized the news wasn't coming as any surprise.

"Oh, but you always expected this would happen, didn't you? Still, for me . . . I'm frightened Anna," she said, suddenly changing her expression. "I came here because I want you to tell me again that this is not some spell and that when the clock strikes twelve on some day looming in the future, it will end. He won't change his mind as if he woke up and realized what he had done, will he? Tell me."

"He loves you, Mrs. Slayton. It doesn't pop like a bubble. It's in his heart now, planted forever and ever," Anna said with confidence.

Joyce relaxed.

"You really can do these things. I can see that now. You really, really can."

"If you didn't think so from the start, Mrs. Slayton, why did you go through with it and pay me so much money?"

"I thought so from the start. I mean, I hoped so. I had tried everything else, it seemed. You must be so proud of what you can accomplish, Anna. You'll come to the wedding, of course. I'll want you there. Please."

"Yes, I'll come, Mrs. Slayton. If you invite me," she added with a twinkle in her eyes.

"Because we're going to have a real wedding, a church wedding with a big reception. He wants it more than I do. A grand ceremony makes it feel more like a marriage, don't you think?

"Oh," she said, quickly correcting herself, "but you haven't been married. Why not, Anna?" Joyce asked. She was so happy and full of energy, she couldn't stop herself from talking. "Wasn't there anyone you wanted, because I know now you could have had anyone, right?"

Anna's expression did soften for a moment as her eyes seemed to dim into a memory. She shook her head slowly.

"No, Mrs. Slayton. It's the story of the shoemaker without shoes. I can't help myself as much as I can help others. Any good psychic will tell you that he or she can't predict for himself or herself. But don't think of this as a mere casting of a spell. There has to be something with which to work. Mr. Gardner had the inclination. He wanted to love you. We only helped him along, Mrs. Slayton. You don't have to be anxious about it."

"Good. Good." She looked down and then at Anna again. "You have something else, Mrs. Slayton?"

"Everyone's talking about you and about what happened to Mr. Deutch. Did you do that, Anna? Did you hang a dead chicken on his porch and put a rat in his bed?"

Anna shook her head.

"Who else would have done such a thing?"

"He did it himself," Anna said.

Joyce grimaced.

"Himself? Why?"

"Evil begets evil," Anna said. "Don't concern yourself with it anymore, Mrs. Slayton. It's gone," Anna said with great confidence.

Joyce nodded. She thought a moment and then smiled.

"Thank you, Anna. I'll be sending you your invitation." She started out and then paused. "Oh. No one else knows about this, do they?"

"No," Anna said. "No one else."

"Good." Joyce smiled. "Good."

Anna watched her leave and then she sat back and closed her eyes.

Wasn't there anyone you wanted, Anna?

She permitted herself a small smile as she recalled. Her mother had come from Budapest, pregnant with her, to live with her sister Ethel in the Bronx. She claimed she had been raped and the man who had raped her was too powerful a bureaucrat to accuse. It was better simply to leave Hungary.

Aunt Ethel and Uncle John had a small supermarket on White Plains Road and some apartments they rented above. Her mother was given one, worked first in the supermarket, and then, at Ethel's insistence, John rented a shop for her so she could make a living as a seamstress. Very quickly, her powers became known and people began to come to her for readings, advice, herbal prescriptions and witchcraft as much as they came to have pants, dresses, blouses, and skirts altered. It created some conflict between her mother and Uncle John, but by then he, too, had come to believe in her mother's powers and eventually retreated. There was nothing more terrifying than the possibility of the evil eye, especially to a businessman who was enjoying success and knew there were so many who envied him. Gussie Young could protect him from all that.

Anna's mother told her that from the day Anna was born, she knew Anna had inherited the gifts and would be even a more powerful and talented spiritual woman. While other little girls her age were going over school work with their mothers, Anna was learning the secrets and the ways. It didn't take long for her classmates to look upon her as too different. Some of the girls, and even some of the boys, were actually afraid of her. She had a way of fixing her eyes on someone that made his or her very spine jitter.

She wasn't uncomfortable being a loner; indeed it seemed to fit her personality and her spiritual development more. When she was sixteen, however, she did develop a crush on a senior boy, Martin Court. The crush grew more and more intense until she was convinced it was love. She enjoyed simply watching him move through the hallways, laugh, and talk. His smile mesmerized her. It was like looking into the flame of a candle.

Not a night went by without her fantasizing, and when she was at school, she would do all she could to be in his presence, to be within the circle of his light. No matter what she did, however, he didn't take notice of her. He was too popular, a school athlete, a good student, the editor of the school paper. Girls buzzed around him like bees, circling, each hoping to sting him with her good looks and personality, and claim him for her own.

Anna wasn't emotionally or socially equipped to compete in this arena. Instead, she went home and practiced her ceremonies and craft. She cast her spells, wore her charms, waved her wand, expecting he would finally take notice of her one day, step out of the crowd, and with his eyes drawn to hers, take her hand and begin a conversation that would last a lifetime.

But nothing like that happened. When she asked her mother about it, her mother told her what she knew in her heart already.

"If what you want to do will only serve yourself, Anna, if it is self-centered and selfish, it will not happen. We are meant to help others. That is our blessing and, maybe, our curse. For us, what is to be will be, regardless of what we do or say, Anna.

"Look into the pool. When you fall in love with your own desires and touch your face, it will shatter into the ripples and be gone."

"Won't I ever fall in love, Mama, and have someone fall in love with me?"

Gussie Young wiped back the strands of hair that had fallen over Anna's forehead and smiled.

"I have tried many times to look into the future for you, Anna. I can't see for myself or for you. It's better that way. Life needs some surprises."

The longing she felt when she looked at Martin was painful enough to help her understand the turmoil others would experience when their hearts were frustrated. It gave her the motivation and desire to help them.

Finally, one time, one special time, she was standing alone outside the school when Martin Court came up behind her and said hello. He was looking at her with such interest, her heart began to pound. Had something she had done finally taken effect, regardless of what her mother thought? She wasn't prepared for this. She hadn't done anything special with her hair. She hadn't even put on any lipstick this morning and she wasn't wearing any of her nicer clothes.

"Hi," she said.

"You live above the supermarket near Wally's Garage, don't you?" he asked.

"Yes." He had more interest and he knew about her. Her heart beat faster with expectation.

"You're first-generation, born here?"

"That's right."

"You're the only one I know at the school like that. I bet you have a great family story. I was wondering if I could interview you and maybe even your mother for the school paper," he said.

"What?" She blinked rapidly. The vibrations she was feeling had instantly changed. A different sort of energy was coming from him.

"You know, a special interest piece. You're sort of a mystery to a lot of students and I thought—"

"No," she said quickly, stepped back, and shook her head. "I wouldn't like that and neither would my mother."

"I wouldn't take any cheap shots and you can look at any photographs of your mother and you beforehand, and—"

"No, no," she said, continuing to back away. The disappointment was like a small explosion in her heart, sending tiny electric shocks through her system.

He looked annoyed.

"Most of the kids here think you're a little weird, different. It would only help and—"

She stepped toward him this time, her eyes smaller.

"I am different," she said. She held his eyes in her own. He was unable to look away. "Do you understand? I do not want this."

"Yes," he said obediently. "I'm sorry. Yeah. Sure. Okay. Forget I even asked," he added, and backed away. He looked terrified.

She watched him hurry down the sidewalk, practically fleeing. It was as if a great hand had closed around the beautiful candle light and smothered the flame. She never felt as sorry for herself as much as she did in that moment.

At the time I would have traded all my powers for a chance to fall in love with someone like that, she thought, remembering. She sat there suddenly filled with nostalgia, reminiscing, recalling her earlier life: Uncle John's death, Aunt Ethel's retirement and sale of the market to go and live with her son in Jersey, and then her mother's decision to leave the city.

"We have work elsewhere," was all she would say. They traveled from place to place, doing their work until her mother would get the calling and decide it was time to move on.

What had brought them to Sandburg was strong. The day they entered the village, her mother had turned to her and said, "This is where I will die, Anna. We will go no farther. There is enough to do here."

Anna thought she had come to understand what had to be done, but as Mama had told her years ago, we cannot see our own futures. She was about to learn there was more, much more.

She sighed so deeply, it seemed to originate in her very soul. Then she returned to her work. She didn't look up at the sound of the doorbells when they entered. She finished her stitch first and lifted her eyes without surprise. A shadow had passed through the shop to warn her.

"Anna," Munsen Donald said, "I'm afraid we have to ask you to come to the police station for questioning concerning the death of Henry Deutch."

She looked at Philip Coleman and saw his reluctance. It brought a smile to her lips.

"Do you have an attorney?" he asked quietly.

"No," she said.

"Do you want to call anyone to help you find one?" he continued.

"No."

"You understand that you have the right to do so," he said, "and the right not to answer any questions without an attorney present?"

She nodded, folded the garment neatly, and put it aside as she stood.

"All right," she said. "I can go now."

"Isn't there anyone you want to call?" Munsen asked with a painful grimace.

She thought a moment and then smiled.

"I have already done that, Mr. Donald," she said.

It was as if he was a teenager again, playing in the snow, and one of his crazy friends had come up behind him and dropped a piece of an icicle down his back.

Coleman looked more confused than frightened, but Munsen shuddered, swallowed, and reached for the doorknob.

What the hell did she mean by that, he wondered, and feared for himself and his family.

Nine

"Members of the Jury," Judge Hoffman began, "have you reached a verdict?"

The foreman, a short, balding light-brown-haired man, rose. He pulled back his shoulders and pushed out his chest as if he thought he had to achieve a military presence.

"We have, Your Honor."

The bailiff took the slip of paper and brought it to the judge. He held his forefinger against the frame of his glasses as if he was steadying his eyes and read.

"Will the defendant please rise," he ordered.

Del Pearson stood up with his client Murray Pendeski, a burly six-foot-four-inch man with a shock of reddish brown hair. Pendeski pressed his thick lips together and glanced at Del who showed no signs of nervousness. Pendeski had been charged with armed robbery of a convenience store, but the clerk who was the only witness had contradicted himself a number of times on the stand, hadn't been wearing his prescription glasses at the time of the robbery, and had trouble speaking English well. It wasn't often that Del really believed in the innocence of his clients these days, but he did believe Pendeski had been wrongly accused.

The judge handed the verdict back to the bailiff who handed it to the foreman.

"What is your verdict?" the judge asked him.

"We find the defendant not guilty," he said.

There was no one in the courtroom but Pendeski's girlfriend. She jumped up quickly and the two hugged. Del began to put away his papers and close his briefcase.

"You did a great job, thanks," Pendeski told him. They shook hands. "Everyone was telling me I wouldn't get representation worth a shit from a public defender, but you proved them wrong, Mr. Pearson."

"The prosecutor never proved his case," Del said humbly. "Someone on their side didn't do his homework or you wouldn't have been charged."

"I'm just glad you did," Pendeski replied. He put his arm around his girlfriend and they started up the aisle.

Milt Rosen, the assistant district attorney, looked about as disappointed as a passenger who had missed his flight and minutes later had heard it had crashed on takeoff. He had little passion for his stream of felony cases, most of which were nickel and dime robberies, the common cold of criminal activity these days, and most of which fell to him. Most were victimless crimes, many covered by insurance, and most investigated and prosecuted without any more than an inch of press in the local newspaper. There were no plots for John Grisham novels in his briefcase, Del thought.

"Thanks for making my job easier," he told Milt.

Milt didn't smile as much as he bunched his cheeks into little puffs of soft skin and flesh. It made his dull brown eyes smaller.

"I didn't want to go to trial with this, but Richards thought I needed the experience."

"Nice reason to prosecute an innocent man," Del said.

"Welcome to the American judicial system," Milt replied, and walked up the aisle briskly, looking more like the victor than the defeated.

Del glanced at his watch and decided that instead of returning directly to the office, he would take advantage of the opportunity and buy Jackie her birthday present. There was a bracelet of rubies with matching earrings that she had coveted in Henkle's Jewelry store in the Middletown mall. They had paused on their way to the movie theater and she had spotted it in the store window. It was priced way above his budget at $2,800, but he was feeling reckless, especially when it came to putting a smile on Jackie's face these days. After two years of trying, and he did mean trying, she still hadn't become pregnant. The doctors had no scientific explanation. There was nothing wrong with him and nothing wrong with her. It was just one of those things. It would happen. Who could live with that? It trailed alongside them like some invisible black curse that really made itself heard and felt whenever they saw another couple, sometimes people much older than they were, pushing a stroller.

Outside the Monticello, New York, courthouse, gray clouds rolled in from the west, threatening rain. Del realized he might be returning in a downpour. Sometimes coming up what locals simply called the Wurtsboro hill was difficult in inclement weather. It put some hesitation into his steps, but, determined, he plodded on and got into his late-model Taurus. Moments later he was on his way toward Middletown, New York, about thirty-five miles away. He would skip lunch, buy the jewelry, and be back at the legal aid office to file his papers before the end of the day. The bureaucratic monster that ate legal paper work could wait a minute, couldn't it?

He was more than halfway there when his cellular went off.

"Pearson," he said, and grimaced in anticipation. Hopefully, it was just Jackie checking on him.

It wasn't.

"Mr. Douglas is looking for you, Del," Marge Anderson told him. "You've got a qualifying new client waiting on you at the police station in South Fallsburg."

"Great. What's the case?"

"They have a grand jury indictment, murder one," she replied. "The arraignment is scheduled for later today and the court has issued an order for a public defender."

"Murder one? Really?" This would be his first murder case, first capital crime. "Who's the accused?"

There was a moment of hesitation.

"Marge?"

"A witch," she said, and then laughed.

"Pardon me?"

"Her name is Anna Young. She's accused of killing a man named Henry Deutch in Sandburg."

"Did you say *witch?*"

"Just get to the station, Mr. Pearson, and you'll learn it all first hand." He heard her laugh again before she cradled the receiver.

He looked for the closest turn around on the highway, found it and headed northwest toward the closest South Fallsburg exit.

Del Pearson had graduated NYU Law and married his high school sweetheart the year after. It was one of those circles of destiny things. He and Jackie Brooks had ended their romantic relationship almost immediately into the first semester of his freshman college year. Jackie's father

Judson Brooks had been president of the Sullivan National Bank for as long as Del could remember. Del's in-laws lived in South Fallsburg on the lake and had one of the prettiest and most expensive homes, clad in fieldstone and bordered by two very valuable acres, which Judson and his wife Pamela still owned. There was an unwritten promise that when Del and Jackie were ready, they would build their own home on one of those valuable acres.

Jackie's brother Carlton was supposed to build on the other, but Carlton Brooks had been killed in a brutal automobile accident when a tractor trailer barreled down the Kiamesha hill between South Fallsburg and Monticello and the driver lost control. The truck literally drove over Carlton's Mazda RX-7. Fortunately, Carlton was alone, returning from dropping off his date in Monticello.

At Carlton's funeral, Del renewed his relationship with Jackie. She had gone to Bennington in Vermont to pursue a liberal arts degree, someday to pursue a career in journalism. But those ambitions, which were not very passionate to start with, seemed to die along with her brother.

Carlton Brooks was a brilliant student, a handsome dirty blond, six-foot-two-inch man who had his father's stocky athletic build and was everyone's vote for the one who was sure to succeed. He had begun a premedical program at Columbia. His death was one of those tragedies that made people pause and wonder whether there was any logic at work in the world, whether good really did exist, or more to the point, whether there was a God who really cared about good and evil.

The befuddled minister could only say, "God's ways are mysterious and beyond our understanding."

Any objective observer would have palpably felt the disgust and disappointment in the church that day. Words never seemed more inadequate as a means of communication. It was better to let your eyes do all the talking, Del had thought, and when he gazed at Jackie, the love that had gone into remission exploded with more passion than before. He wanted only to hold her for the rest of both their lives.

Del had just taken the position at the legal aid office a month before. While other graduates had gone off to clerk at prestigious law firms, he had decided to build his experience as a trial attorney. He had always wanted to defend, and had favored underdogs all his life, whether it be a prize-fighter, a baseball or basketball team, a football team, or a dance contestant. Maybe it was because of his own humble background and his own battle to get a piece of that pie usually reserved for the privileged. He had seen too many illustrations underlying the premise that justice is not really blind. It can be unequal when the plaintiff or the defendant is someone with means. Talent was expensive and those who could afford it got the best.

He admitted he was still in his idealistic stage: optimistic, full of the belief he could make a difference. Whatever the reason, he chose the public defender's office and he took particular pleasure in winning, more pleasure, he thought, than he would have taken had he earned a big retainer.

Now, of course, the big question was when would he and Jackie be able to afford that house waiting to be built on the choice acre? Wasn't it time to collect the big money and become part of the power structure? No question, Jackie thought so, and definitely no question, his in-laws agreed.

When he mused about it all now, he wondered if the real reason why he parted company with Jackie after high school wasn't because he didn't want to have her parents looking over his shoulder, measuring him, and giving him that look of judgement that said, "Our daughter could have done better."

Here they were now waiting to learn they would soon have a grandchild, and that hadn't come and might never come, and according to his in-laws, he was still piddling away, defending the underprivileged, wasting his talents, dreaming, chasing windmills instead of a new Mercedes.

Del wasn't surprised to see a newspaper reporter at the station, but he was surprised to see three and a reporter from every radio station as well. Who had put out the leads this fast and why? What the hell had Marge Anderson meant when she had said "witch"?

One of the reporters, Clifford Grayson from the *Times Herald Record,* knew him from previous courtroom proceedings. Del didn't like the man, didn't like his cynical view of everything. He always began from the negative standpoint, doubting, looking for ulterior motives. In Grayson's eyes, everyone was guilty of something, even defense attorneys. It almost didn't matter what the charge was.

"Are you taking the witch murder case, Del?" he asked quickly.

"I don't know what you mean by *witch*. I don't even know if there is a case to take," Del said.

"Oh, there's a case," Grayson said, lifting his eyebrows and smiling. "Maybe too big for you to handle."

"So? I won't handle it," Del said without breaking stride or changing his expression.

He entered the station and approached the dispatcher. She was a short, plump, poorly dyed-blond woman with a large bosom that put strain on the gold buttons of her uniform blouse. Her name was Rhonda Gerson and he liked her sense of humor. To Rhonda the entire county was one over-the-top sitcom.

"I'm here for Anna Young," he told her.

"Double, double, toil and trouble," she said.

"Come again?"

"The witches in *Macbeth*. What kind of an English student were you?"

"Oh." He grimaced with surprise. "Since when do you quote *Macbeth*, Rhonda?"

She leaned over the desk.

"Someone else was mumbling it. I picked it up," she confessed. She nodded toward the closed door on her right. "They got her in there. They talked to her for more than two hours after they picked her up and she signed something," Rhonda added, raising her eyebrows.

"Oh?"

Del turned just as Phil Coleman came sauntering toward him.

"I have a new client?" Del asked.

Phil laughed.

"Yeah, you have a new client. How come you didn't know? She knew you were coming," he said.

"What?"

"Just a few minutes ago, she stopped talking, turned to me and said in a deep, dark voice, 'Del vill be here soon.'" Coleman looked at Rhonda and they both laughed.

"Has everyone gone nuts here?"

"Just joining the club," Phil said. He stepped back and swept his hand across as he bowed.

"Mr. Court-Appointed Attorney, she's all yours now," he said.

"What exactly is the charge?" Del asked.

"Just an hour ago, the district attorney had her indicted for murder one. She and the grand jury say there is a clear, premeditated plan of murder. She knew what she was doing; she knew it would be harmful, and she pursued a definite plan," he recited.

"I hear you took a statement?"

"Sort of," Coleman said. "I have a copy all ready for you."

"You advised her of her legal rights beforehand, I assume," he followed.

"Does a bear shit in the woods?"

Del followed him to his desk and Coleman handed him a sheet. Del read it and then looked up at Coleman.

"She didn't do it, but she said she was responsible?"

"You read just like I do."

"What did the D.A. present to the grand jury, Phil?"

Coleman turned to a fat file on his desk.

"For starters: proof of Henry Deutch's serious medical problems, evidence of her aggravating actions and testimony from about a dozen reliable citizens confirming her actions, all of whom are convinced she did it too; only . . ." He switched over to whisper, "They think she did it through black magic."

"And the district attorney? Surely, she's not subscribing to that?"

"No, Ms. Richards believes that she used sophisticated psychological techniques. She may act whammy, but our district attorney is of the opinion Anna Young is a very smart lady and she convinced the grand jury of the same."

"We both know how hard it is to convince the grand jury if the district attorney wants them convinced. You know she could get them to indict a potted plant," Del said with a smirk. "What was the weapon?"

Del stared at him, waiting.

"Phil, how did she supposedly kill him?"

"Specifically," Phil said, "the state is going to claim she frightened him to death with a butchered chicken and a dead rat."

"Come again?"

"The district attorney says she knew of his heart condition and she pursued a course of action designed to bring about his coronary. It's all in the report. His telephone wires were cut. He couldn't call for help. Richards says there's precedent and she says she's going to convict her."

Del smirked and narrowed his eyes.

"Whom does she think she's kidding?"

"Twelve angry jurors," Phil replied. "Right this way, counselor. Your client awaits your expertise."

Del opened the door and Anna turned from the conference room table to look at him. For a moment he was caught up in her eyes. He moved off them and ran his own gaze down her face and body, impressed with her beauty. She wore no makeup, but there was a glow and a brightness in her face. Then he realized where he was and why, and stepped into the room.

"Anna Young?"

"Yes," she said.

"I'm Del Pearson from legal aid. You qualified and the court has assigned me to help in your defense."

She smiled softly.

"I thought so," she said. "You have an entirely different aura from the others here."

"Aura?"

She nodded. He thought a moment and then remembered the papers in his hands.

"Before you were interviewed by the police, were you told you had the right to remain silent until you were in the company of an attorney?"

"Yes."

"I read your statement. What's this all about?" he asked, putting his briefcase on the table.

"Good and evil," she replied. "Isn't everything?"

"Are you the evil?" he countered.

She stared at him a moment as if she was deciding whether or not to tell him where to get off, but then, her lips quivered and stretched into a different sort of smile, more sexy and feminine, the sort of smile that could break his heart. He settled into his chair and looked at her, waiting for a reply.

"No," she said, "but I am involved forever in a struggle with it."

He glanced at a blank pad and then wrote her name at the top of the page.

"You live in Sandburg?"

"I have a modest tailor shop there and live above the shop in a small one bedroom apartment, yes," she said.

"By yourself?" he asked. It was his subtle way of asking if she had a lover.

"I am never by myself, but I am alone," she replied.

"Then why aren't you by yourself?" he asked.

"I am in the company of angels," she told him with a warm smile.

He looked at her as if he expected a lot more explanation.

"Company of angels?" He wrote it down. "Now, then, what do you think you have told the police?" he asked, tapping the copy of her statement.

"Only the truth," she said.

He looked up at her again, and again she was smiling softly at him.

Is this woman bonkers? he thought.

"Apparently the district attorney's office has enough evidence, testimony, to convince the grand jury to hand down an indictment for a charge of murder one. You understand that's happened, correct?"

"Yes," she said. "I expected no less."

"Really?"

He read some of her statement.

"You told them that you destroyed the evil in Henry Deutch, that you used your spiritual powers to do this?"

"Yes," she said.

"You didn't elaborate on that. What spiritual powers?"

"There are prescribed ways to keep evil at bay and to do battle with it," she explained. "Do you really want to know about all the details?"

"It might help me understand what's going on here," he said softly. He felt as if he had been cast into some production from the theater of the absurd. "How do you begin this battle with evil?"

She stared at him a moment as if she was deciding on his sincerity and then she nodded.

"My first act was to create a sacred circle around myself to protect myself from the evil force once I knew it was in the village and had possessed Henry Deutch."

"A sacred circle?"

"Yes. The circle is the symbol of unity, oneness, a single line that has no beginning and no end."

"I see. What kind of a circle is this? I mean, do you draw it in paint, ink, blood, what?"

She smiled.

"You're humoring me, Mr. Pearson. That's all right," she added before he could respond. "Actually, how the circle is drawn is very important. It must be drawn in a clockwise manner to perform feats of good. The sun goes from east to west, from right to left. If you go in the opposite direction, you go against nature and therefore go against good. I draw mine in charcoal dust, but you can draw them with a sword or a knife if properly blessed."

"And as long as you are standing inside this circle?"

"I'm protected and can perform my rituals," she replied.

"Is this circle in your house?"

"I draw it wherever I need it," she said.

Del started to smile and then, out of the corner of his eye, he gazed to his right and down and saw that a circle had been drawn around the conference table in what looked like charcoal. For a moment he couldn't speak. It was as if he had lost his voice. A surge of warm air shot through his lungs and into his throat. He looked at Anna.

She smiled.

"Yes," she said. "You're safe. For the moment."

He nodded, glanced at his notepad, and then rose slowly. "I'll be right back," he said.

Taking pains not to step on the line drawn around the table, he left the conference room. When he closed the door behind him, he took a deep breath and wiped his face with his handkerchief. Phil Coleman turned from talking with one of the patrolmen and looked at him. They started toward each other.

"What's up, counselor?" Phil asked quickly. "You're out of there pretty quickly."

"You guys can't be serious about all this? That woman really believes she can perform magical acts. She drew a circle of protection around herself in there, for crissakes!"

Phil shrugged.

"You read what she wrote. She admits to wanting the guy dead. She'll admit to practically all those acts of psychological terror. Richards thinks she has a good case. We've got an ongoing investigation and expect to provide even more support for a conviction."

"She's not in her right mind."

"Which one, the district attorney or the witch, or both?" Coleman quipped.

"Maybe both, but my client especially."

"She looks pretty healthy to me," Phil said with a wide licentious smile.

"I'm not talking about that."

"You noticed, huh?"

"Come on, Phil. I don't know whether to burst into hysterical laughter or have her sent directly for a psychiatric."

"Go talk to Richards."

"I will. This is ridiculous," Del insisted. "You're actually going to have her arraigned for frightening a man to death?"

"In about two hours," Phil replied, glancing at his watch. "Better think about the plea."

"The O.J. trial didn't do enough to destroy the public's confidence in the American judicial system, huh? Richards has to add this."

"I'm just a working stiff," Phil said, but without any obvious enthusiasm. "It's not my business to make any other comments, but suffice it to say there are a lot of factors at work."

"Factors?"

"Religious and otherwise. You'll see," he added cryptically.

Del shook his head, thought a moment, and then returned to the conference room. Anna Young still looked cool and relaxed. He closed the door and sat across from her again. He continued to peruse the statement she had given.

"You admit to wanting . . ." He read from the statement. " 'The evil nature in Henry Deutch dead.' "

"Yes."

"You said you were responsible for that death, but specifically," he paused and grimaced, "you deny hanging a butchered chicken on his porch, putting a dead rat in his bed, and cutting his telephone wires?"

"That's so. I didn't do those things."

"But you've done other things?" He looked at the paper.

"Pronounced curses, seeded the ground he walked on with things that you brought out of your ceremonies? Cast the evil eye at him?"

"Yes."

"Who do you think you are?" he asked her.

"I am who I am meant to be," she said.

"And who's that?"

"Whom do you see? Some see themselves. Some see who they would like to be. Some see who they were. Some see who they must be."

"Do you realize they want to try you for murder one and they have restored the death penalty in this state?" he asked.

"I'll tell you whom I see," she said in response.

He sat back.

"Okay, tell me anything."

"I see the man who will not let that happen," she said.

He stared into those eyes.

She was right.

That's who he was.

Ten

"You can't go into a courtroom and say you admit that you deliberately caused the death of the evil in Henry Deutch," Del told Anna. "You can't admit to murdering someone's nature and not the man if the man was pronounced dead at the scene and expect to be exonerated and thanked, no matter what kind of a miserable bastard you thought the guy was."

"But I didn't say that," she said.

"In this statement you practically admit that you made his heart burst, that you deliberately sought to do that," Del reminded her. "If someone's heart bursts, he's dead."

"Henry Deutch caused his own death long ago when he sold himself to evil. Yes, I destroyed that evil that was in him, but you must think of his body as an empty vessel filled with this evil nature. Henry Deutch died long ago when the balance between good and evil in him was destroyed," she explained. "We are all basically born with those forces in balance, but things we do, things we permit to happen to us often upset the balance, and evil has more influence on our actions.

"Clergy like Reverend Carter in my village often talk about Original Sin, Adam and Eve's sin, staining the souls of all who came after and therefore the need to be born again, to redeem oneself. I'm not so different in what I believe and in what I do, but the Devil is clever and has learned to divide and conquer. The more religions there are, the less powerful each becomes against him. Men suffer from pride, and pride puts them into competition, and the Devil laughs at the wars, the prejudices, the hate crimes, especially those in the name of one form of God or another. Do you know that at this moment more people are killing each other over who has the religious truth than anything else?

"We've got to cast off everything and anything that keeps us from seeing each other's spirit.

"You're a man who believes in much of what I am saying," she added.

He did, but that wasn't the problem at the moment. Anna Young did impress him. She was well-spoken, eloquent, and commanding. There was something about her, some charismatic quality. He felt stupid asking the next question, but he had to get it down.

"Are you a witch?"

"I practice what is known as the Old Religion. *Witchcraft* means 'craft of the wise ones.' Its practices can be found in Stone Age paintings. Even modern medicine can trace its origins to herbal medications we employed and still employ."

"So you are saying you are a witch?"

"Witchcraft is nothing more than a nature religion, Mr. Pearson. We believe in God, but a God who is like the

Trinity. There aren't different gods; there are merely aspects of the one God. We see God in the woods, the sun, in grain, everywhere."

"I thought a witch was a bad person."

"No, no. Real witches don't commit evil acts. We believe in the Wiccan Rede, which is *If it harms none, do what you will.* There is also what we call the Three-Fold Law, which states that whatever you do comes back to you three times over, so you can see we don't want to do evil."

"But if you cause a man's death, isn't that evil?"

"I didn't cause the death of a man. I caused the death of an evil force," she insisted.

"Okay, okay," Del said. He took a deep breath and closed his eyes, keeping the lid on his frustration. Then he opened his eyes and spoke slowly as if he was talking to a child. "For simplicity's sake today, let's just have you plead not guilty when the charges are read aloud and the judge asks you what do you plead, understand? You have a much larger agenda than will fit into this proceeding.

"I'll make a motion to have the case thrown out in a preliminary hearing before trial. Just don't get into all this stuff about demons and spirits possessing the body of Henry Deutch."

"They did," she insisted.

"Right, but the judge isn't interested in that."

"He should be, if he's a judge," she said.

Del shook his head and smiled.

"What?"

"I'm having trouble accepting all this," he said, and quickly added, "and not only what you're telling me. I can't believe our illustrious district attorney wants to put the state into this scene, this circus."

"Perhaps it's not her doing," she said.

"Excuse me?"

"Perhaps there are other forces at work, forces beyond her control."

He stared at her a moment. Her eyes were so intently on him, he actually felt a surge of electric warmth in his neck and face. He felt like she could see right into his deepest memories and certainly could read his thoughts.

"Other forces," he finally muttered.

"Yes, Mr. Pearson."

"Meaning these demons, evil spirits," he said, twirling his hand in the air as if they were hovering around them.

"Exactly. Isn't it about time the courtroom became the battleground between good and evil, and not merely a fencing lesson between legal experts?" she asked. "People no longer believe that justice can be found there. This is your big opportunity to restore their faith, Mr. Pearson."

He laughed, but she didn't crack a smile and he realized she truly believed everything she said.

He spent the rest of his time with her explaining the arraignment process. He told her he wasn't sure what was going to happen when it came to bail, however she didn't look the least bit worried about any of it. Either she really does know more than I do, he thought, or she's absolutely off the wall.

A little less than an hour later, he entered the courthouse in Monticello. Again there were members of the local press, but he also noticed now that radio stations and newspaper reporters from Middletown were present as well. This thing was beginning to build, to have a life of its own. He had seen similar things happen, but for what he thought were much bigger stories.

Consequently, there was an explosive, charged atmosphere about the courtroom, something he was unaccustomed to seeing when he defended a client. Reporters and onlookers were straining their necks to get a good look at

Anna, treating her already as if she were a national celebrity. He was even more surprised to discover a group of Sandburg residents present, residents who were there to support her and told her so.

There was another small commotion at the door when Paula Richards entered the courtroom. She was going to be present herself and obviously therefore be the lead investigator and prosecutor. Milt Rosen stood beside her looking almost as confused and amazed by all this as Del was.

Has everyone gone mad here? Del wondered. Anna Young looked at him with a small smile on her lips as if she had been proven right: this was going to be a great battle between the forces of evil and good. Paula Richards quickly introduced herself to Del. They had met only briefly at a social occasion, and it was evident in her face that she didn't recall him.

"Isn't this a little overkill?" Del asked. "Indictment for murder one? You'd have enough trouble proving manslaughter."

Paula Richards' smile was so oily Del expected to see grease drip from her lips at any moment.

"After you have a chance to consider all the evidence, you will come to another conclusion, I'm sure," she replied.

Her confidence irked him. It wasn't only her condescending tone; it was as if she commanded the future, laid out the sequence of events that he would soon discover and obediently follow. No wonder some referred to her as the Ice Lady. She looked like she could freeze an opponent on the spot and dance her will around him.

Del gazed past her at Milt Rosen who quickly looked down at his notepad.

"Right," Del said, and gave her a mock salute. Her eyes

widened with surprise. He glanced at Anna. She looked as relaxed and as cool and confident as she had looked at the police station. "However, it may not be the alternative conclusion you expect."

Paula laughed as if he was the innocent and naive one, and then she returned to her desk where she opened her briefcase and began to take out her paperwork, still shaking her head and smiling.

Judge Landers entered the courtroom looking like he had a bad case of indigestion. He was normally cranky as it was, Del thought, recalling all the different occasions he had been in Landers' court. The judge was in his early sixties, but looked more like a man in his early seventies, his face wrinkled and red, with bushy gray eyebrows and a nose that came to a sharp point and looked even sharper and more pointy whenever he was annoyed with a lawyer's objection or comment.

"What do I have here?" he muttered aloud as if he really only first became aware of what case he had when he sat for the first time behind the bench. He looked at Paula.

"Paula Richards, Your Honor, on behalf of the State of New York."

"Del Pearson, representing the accused, Your Honor," Del said quickly.

The judge ignored him and continued to look at Paula Richards. She knew what he wanted. He was a formal man.

"And Milt Rosen, assistant district attorney, on behalf of the state, Your Honor," she said.

"He can and will speak for himself?" the judge threw back at her.

"Yes, Your Honor, I'm sorry." Paula looked at Milt.

"Milt Rosen, assistant district attorney, Your Honor."

"Very well, let's get on with it," Landers commanded. "*The State of New York vs. Anna Young.* Ms. Richards?"

Paula began to read the charges in a slow, but dramatic manner, lifting her voice as she reached the words *with malice aforethought*. When she was finished, there was a hush in the courtroom. All eyes were on Anna as observers were asking themselves: could she really have done all that?

"Anna Young," Landers said, turning to her, "do you understand the charges being made against you?"

Anna fixed her eyes on Landers.

"Yes, I do," she said firmly.

He nodded.

"You should understand that in the eyes of the court you remain innocent until the state proves you guilty beyond a reasonable doubt. You have the right to plead guilty or not guilty, and the right to a trial when you will hear the state's evidence against you and you can, through your attorney, cross-examine witnesses and present witnesses and evidence of your own. You can testify on your own behalf or remain silent. Do you understand all of this?"

"Yes, I do," she said.

"How do you plead?"

She gazed into Del's eyes and then smiled.

"Not guilty of those charges, Your Honor," she replied, emphasizing *those charges*.

Del released his trapped, hot breath. Who knew what she would say?

Paula Richards opposed the granting of bail. She argued that Anna had no firm ties to the community and was capable of flight. Del talked about her tailor shop and her clean record.

"By her own statements, Your Honor," Paula countered, "the defendant admits that she can be drawn to pursue evil anywhere at any time. Who knows when she'll get the calling?" she added with a smirk that put smiles on some of the reporters' faces.

Judge Landers raised his bushy eyebrows and glared down at Paula with a tight smile on his own lips.

"Next thing we'll hear about is a broom," he muttered. There was a titter in the crowd of observers. Then he turned to Del and Anna and granted bail, but at one hundred thousand dollars. Del tried to get it reduced, but the judge was adamant. After all, the state was asking for murder one.

Before Del could say another word, he felt someone tap him on the shoulder and turned to look at Jonathan Gardner. Joyce Slayton stood right behind him.

"Excuse me," Jonathan said, "but don't worry about making the bail. We're going to take care of that."

"We?" Del asked.

Jonathan nodded toward the small group of Sandburg citizens. Del gazed at them and then looked at Anna. She wore a soft smile, but her eyes were electric.

"We have our allies," she said.

He nodded and then looked from her to Paula Richards. She seemed pleased with the turn of events, even the fact that some citizens would pool funds and put up the bail. It was as if everything supported her effort to convict.

For his own part, Del was beginning to feel like someone swept along in a wild current. Turning and trying to fight against it was futile. It was easier to just let it carry him off, but to what end? The only one who seemed to know and not be afraid was Anna Young herself.

By the time Del arrived at his home, a modest ranch-style house he and Jackie rented outside of Monticello, the Witch Murder Trial, as the media had quickly anointed it, was the leading headline on all the local news shows and had even begun to tickle the interest of statewide and national news organizations. His name was merely attached as the public defender assigned to the case. There was nothing more said about him, but Paula Richards was taking interviews, beginning her public relations campaign, which really amounted to trying Anna Young in the press.

"A subtle murder weapon is still a murder weapon," she declared. "The state will prove that but for the defendant's actions, Henry Deutch would not have died when he died. We will show that his death was clearly a result of her premeditated, well thought out, and planned activities. Psychological warfare," she added. "Our government recognizes the potential. We have people in our employ who possess the ability to do such harm in precisely similar ways. I'll be explaining all that in court when we present the case."

"Then you don't believe she used supernatural powers?" a reporter asked her.

Paula Richards laughed.

"No, no, no. That's what she wants us to believe so we'll laugh and disregard what she carefully, with malice aforethought, planned in a meticulous manner to do."

"She's not a nutcase?" the reporter pursued.

"On the contrary," Paula Richards said. On television she would look directly in the camera when she added, "She is the first to claim she knows the difference between right and wrong. She's an expert when it comes to evil. Just ask her."

Del listened to the end of the news story he had tuned to on his car radio and then turned off the car engine and stepped onto the driveway. The rain had come and gone and left behind a fresh clean scent that made the newly cut grass redolent. In the distance the mountains were clear and the blue sky that was turning darker promised an evening of sharp, bright stars. Despite the maddening pace of his day, he felt energized. Was it just the change in the weather? There was something about Anna Young's eyes, something about her soft, knowing smile that filled him with new vitality, or was that all just his imagination?

He lingered so long outside, gazing at the moving clouds uncovering more and more dark blue, that Jackie, who had heard him drive up, opened the front door to see what was wrong. When she saw how he was just standing there, gazing at the distant mountains, she wore a confused smile on her pretty face. She had a dark complexion, rich with small features, almost too perfect to be natural.

Del often looked at his wife and thought plastic surgeons should have her face on their walls as the touchstone for how a nose and lips should be shaped. At five feet ten, Jackie had a model's lithe figure, with long legs and gently sloping shoulders. Whenever she was dressed in a formal gown, with her light brown hair brushed so it lay softly, just reaching her shoulders, Jackie always drew appreciative looks and put pauses in conversations as she entered a room. There wasn't always a lightness to her walk and her gestures, but there was always style and grace. She was the kind of woman who never seemed taken by surprise, who could turn a dark moment into a light one with a glance, a movement of her hands, or the sound of her voice. Del Pearson felt really lucky. Everything else in his life would surely fall into place because Jackie Brooks was destined to have married a successful man and, she had married him.

"Del?"

"Hi, babe."

"What's going on?"

"You haven't heard?"

Jackie was wearing jeans and had her old blouse tied at the bottom instead of buttoned. There was a streak of white paint on her left cheek. She brought the paint brush up for him to see.

"Been doing the trim in the guest room," she replied, "and listening to the CD. Something happen? Oh, what about your robbery case today?"

"Went well," he said, approaching. "Acquitted." He paused in front of her. "But that's not it, that's not hardly it. I got a new case almost immediately."

"You going to keep me standing here in suspense or what?"

"Or what," he said. He smiled and leaned forward to kiss her.

She gazed into his silly smile.

"What?"

"They're calling it the Witch Murder Trial. I'm defending a witch, but fear not, she's supposedly a good witch and will do no evil."

"Huh?"

"You heard me," he said, moving past her and into their house. He walked into the living room and flopped into his fat cushioned easy chair, dropping his arms over the sides and then bringing his hands back to loosen his tie. She stood in the hallway gazing in at him.

"It's on all the news programs," he began. "Woman in Sandburg harassed her old landlord who suffered from heart problems until she drove him into a heart attack doing such things as planting dead bones in his path, maybe hanging a dead chicken on his porch, and putting a dead rat in his bed, although she adamantly denies that. It wouldn't be witchlike. No one liked the guy, Henry Deutch, a modern day Simon Legree. Court appointed her an attorney because she lives in and works in an almost barter system in Sandburg, making a very small amount of money, and yours truly drew the short straw. You should have seen the arraignment. It's already a circus. People from Sandburg came to support her and put up her bail, a hundred thousand dollars!"

"The district attorney is prosecuting a witch? What is this, Salem?"

He laughed.

"No, not exactly. She is prosecuting her for maliciously, knowingly, consistently, harassing Deutch with psychological warfare until she killed him. The indictment reads like a psychological thriller. She had motive, she claims, because Deutch had her and her mother evicted from his building and her mother suffered a stroke and heart attack as a result. She blamed Deutch. Correction, according to Anna Young she blamed the evil demon that had possessed Deutch and she set out to destroy the demon. In the process, she assisted Deutch's heart disease and quickened his departure from this life. She had intent to kill with malice aforethought. Therefore, murder one.

"My client," he continued, "does not deny any of this, by the way. She is rather proud of it. After all, she succeeded in killing the demon. She even gave a statement claiming to have done so. I had her plead innocent by convincing her she didn't kill Deutch; she killed the demon. Something like that."

Jackie held her look of amazement.

"Da, da, da, da," Del sang as if he were on *The Twilight Zone.*

She widened her smile.

"What's going to happen?" she asked.

"Oh, I think it will all go away once the district attorney realizes how difficult it would be to prove such a charge. All I have to do is subpoena Deutch's physician, for chrissakes. I'll make a motion for dismissal at a pretrial hearing."

She nodded, thoughtful. He looked up at her as if some heavy cloud between them had disappeared and left her standing there, sharp and cool and very inviting. She had seen that look in his eyes before, lustful, so hot it was almost pure lechery. As always, it aroused her, beginning with a tiny but electric sensation at the base of her stomach that traveled out in wider and wider circles until it reached the base of her throat, brought a crimson tint to her cheeks, and filled her eyes with a wild laughter.

He rose and approached her, his hands going right to the place where she had tied her blouse.

"Forgive my perfunctory greeting," he said, untying it. He kissed her softly and then harder while his hands slipped in and around her waist, moving up quickly to her breasts. Her moan opened the gates of his own passion even wider. He felt like he was about to gallop.

Impatient, he brought his lips to the top of her collarbone and down between her breasts and then he went to his knees and undid her jeans, sliding them down and kissing the insides of her thighs.

"Del . . ." she muttered, but in seconds he had her stepping out of her panties, too.

He lifted her and carried her to the sofa, where he threw off his clothes and then proceeded to make love to her with more aggression and drive than ever. It took her breath away. Afterward, they held tightly to each other as if they thought one or the other might dissipate from the unbridled passion.

"Wow," she finally said. "Is this what a crazy new case does to you?" She laughed. "Maybe your client has put a spell on you," she added.

He laughed, too.

"Was it good or evil?" he asked.

She twirled some strands of his hair in her forefinger and then kissed the tip of his nose.

"Well, this is an unscientific opinion, but from my perspective, counselor, it was very good."

Munsen Donald stood next to Aaron Baer and looked at the four flat tires on his pickup truck. The pale red vehicle leaned to the left because of the slope of his driveway. Baer combed the fingers of his right hand through his long, straggly dull brassy-colored hair and turned to Munsen.

"Can you believe this shit?"

"No nails or nothing?" Munsen asked.

"No. They let out the air. I got up, came out to go to work, and this," he said, pointing at the truck as if it was the truck's fault. "Now I lost a day's work."

"I can run you over to the building site, Aaron."

"That isn't the point. I can get over there sometime, but what about the truck? I don't have an electric air pump for these tires and now I gotta call Echert and pay for the service call."

"You have any ideas who might have done it?" Munsen asked him.

Aaron Baer folded his arms across his stomach and looked toward the village.

"Dogs didn't even bark. They always bark when someone comes on my property. They barked when you drove up, didn't they?"

Munsen nodded, lifted his cap, wiped his head, and looked at the two Dobermans prancing nervously back and forth behind their fenced-in area. They growled and whined.

"Hell, a frog don't hop on this property without them announcing it."

"So what are you telling me, Aaron?" Munsen asked. He didn't have the patience for a game of Twenty Questions.

The twenty-eight-year-old freelance carpenter looked toward the woods and shook his head.

"I don't believe in that crap about Anna Young. I told a few people yesterday down at Kayfields when I stopped for a beer after work. I guess I got into a little argument about her with Tony Monato. I called her some names. Look how she wiggles her rear when she parades through the village!" he cried. "She got a bunch of old men creaming in their pants."

"What are you saying, Aaron? Tony Monato did this?"

"No way. He wouldn't have the guts. I'd smear him from one side of the village to the next."

"So?"

Munsen didn't want to say it, ask it, or even hear it. He gazed at the small cottage Aaron Baer and his latest girlfriend inhabited. The property itself was part of what once was a beautiful farm Aaron's grandfather had owned and operated. Munsen could remember coming up here to steal ears of corn on the cob. Ray Baer knew it had almost become a village tradition to pilfer some of his corn, but he was old fashioned enough to consider it a compliment and smart enough to realize it put a premium on his crop. Once Ray passed on, his son and daughter sold off the property, with Aaron keeping only this cottage and about five acres.

"Well, maybe she had somethin' to do with it," Aaron finally admitted. "They're all going to say so in town anyway once they find out, especially those fools who believe in her."

"Anna Young came up here and let the air out of your truck tires because you questioned her spiritual powers?" Munsen cross-examined with a tone of incredulity.

"I don't know as she actually done it. She had it done."

"Had it done? How?"

"Somehow. I don't know!" Baer cried, lifting his arms. Munsen smiled.

"Some kids probably pulled a prank on you, Aaron. You did things like this when you were younger."

"How did they get on my property and spend all that time doin' this without them dogs barking, Munsen?" he demanded, stabbing the air with his forefinger in the direction of the dogs.

"I don't know. They could have been real quiet about it, I guess. Maybe they did bark, but you didn't hear it, had the television too loud or something," he added.

"I didn't have any television going and even if I did, I always hear the dogs over it. We're not teenagers playing music that rocks the house. Dogs smell you, man. Come on, Munsen."

"Well, what do you want me to do, Aaron? Who should I go question?"

"I don't know," he said sullenly. "Shit."

"I'll take you to work," Munsen offered again, but Aaron Baer didn't look like he was interested in going to work. "Maybe you can do something for George, trade some work for him coming up here and getting your tires up."

"Forget it," Aaron snapped. "I don't know why I even called you. You're right. You can't do nothin' about it anyway."

"Well, I'm going to keep an eye out for vandalism, Aaron. It's good you called."

"Vandalism. Right. Thanks," he said, and stomped toward his front door.

Munsen walked around the truck, kneeled down to study the tires, convinced himself there were no nails, which meant of course that someone did it deliberately, and then headed for his patrol car. The radio was cracking. He opened the door, slid in and picked up the phone.

"Donald," he said.

"Munsen." Lisa's voice sounded so young, more like Brooke's or Crystal's. He could hear the tears in her eyes.

"What's wrong?" he immediately asked.

"My doctor called a few minutes ago. He wants me back. My Pap smear wasn't good."

"What?"

"I can't talk about this on the phone," she moaned.

"I'm on my way home," he said, and started the engine. His heart was pounding so hard by the time he pulled away from Aaron Baer's, he thought he might grow faint and lose control of the car. He nearly failed to negotiate the first turn, his tires squealing as they kicked up the gravel and slid toward the ditch. He got hold of himself, calmed himself, and drove more carefully.

All sorts of wild thoughts were circling his head, looking for an opening, an opportunity to settle in that place in his brain that stored fear.

She's doing this to us, he finally verbalized. She has the power. She did that to Aaron and now she's doing this to us because she's angry about my role in having her arrested. She's angry about my part in the investigation.

He recalled looking back at Anna Young when he and Phil Coleman first interrogated her. Her eyes were so dark and yet he felt the fire within. It had quickened his heartbeat then.

He could see Benny Sklar walking away and then stopping to tell him Anna spoke to the dead.

He wiped his forehead quickly. Bad Pap smear. What did that mean? Why hurt Lisa?

The look in Aaron Baer's eyes returned over the inside of his own eyelids like a television replay.

"I don't know as she actually done it. She had it done. Somehow. I don't know," he had said.

These weren't kids making these statements about Anna Young, going to see her, asking for her help, and then putting up her bail. These were respectable adults. And so many of them.

What's the world coming to? In the age of cyberspace, people believed in medieval magic?

Bad Pap smear.

Anna's face in the window.

She was angry. Somewhere in her small apartment, she performed one of those rituals, threw a curse out the window like a string of ribbon, and it got caught up in a wind of her making and carried the curse miles until it seeped into his home and wrapped itself around Lisa.

And punished him.

Please, God, no.

He accelerated, turning on his bubble light so the cars in front of him would move over.

With the siren only blaring in his heart, he hurried home, already thinking about ways he could placate Anna Young and get her to forgive him.

Was this the thinking of a rational man, an intelligent man? he asked himself.

What difference did it make now?

His wife could die.

Eleven

Del sat on the worn, imitation-leather chair in Doctor Bloom's waiting room and watched the mother sitting across from him comfort her five-year-old little girl, whose bout with the flu was making her very uncomfortable. Her throat ached, she was feverish, and her face was flushed. Despite that, the child occasionally glanced at him curiously from time to time, her gaze filled with some interest. Del realized that in her eyes he looked out of place. He evinced no symptoms of any illness and had no sick child or sick spouse with him. He carried a briefcase, wore a suit and tie, and smiled at her brightly. She could only stare numbly back.

"How's she doing?" he asked the woman.

"She's got a hundred and three and a pretty red throat," the woman replied with what Del thought was a response more colored by anger than concern. "It's her third cold this year."

"Oh," he said. He wasn't sure what that meant, but he decided not to offer any empty words like *I'm sure she'll be fine*. Instead, he asked if something wasn't going around in the schools. "I don't have any children, so I wouldn't know," he added.

The woman stroked her daughter's hair and shifted her more comfortably in her lap.

"Nothin's goin' around. I'm sure it's because we live in a basement," she replied, sending her words at him through her clenched teeth.

"Basement?"

He looked over at the receptionist's window. There wasn't any other patient waiting. It was just he, the mother, and her child. Del couldn't imagine what the doctor's lobby was like when there were a number of patients. It was so small and narrow it was almost claustrophobic. The receptionist had her face buried in a gossip magazine and had no interest in the conversations or the people in the waiting room.

"We needed some place fast and somethin' we could afford," the mother explained. Then she tightened her lips until there were little white dots in the corners of her mouth and added, "We were evicted from our home."

"Evicted?" Del turned back to her with new interest. "How did that happen?"

"My husband didn't pay the rent for nearly five months and the landlord got the law on us. They practically threw us out in the street, but my husband had a friend who had a basement apartment he was willing to rent, so we moved in. It's too damp. I keep telling Lester and he keeps sayin' he's lookin' for somethin' but he ain't found it yet," she continued. It was like Del had opened the floodgates by trying to make small talk and maybe cheer up the child.

"He don't get as much work as he usta," she continued. "He says it's because those meditation people is buying up the old properties and gettin' people to work for nothin'.

Lester usta work regular at one or the other hotels. He built some bungalows, too. He's a good carpenter, but lately he's been drinkin' too much."

"Maybe you should move to a different area where there's more work for your husband," Del suggested.

"That's what I keep tellin' him." She rocked her child. "Mary's missed a lot of school. She goes to morning kindergarten. I ain't one to be happy when someone has trouble, but the world's sure better off since Anna got rid of Henry Deutch," she added.

"Pardon me?" He actually held his breath a moment and waited. "I'm sorry, who?"

"Henry Deutch. He was our landlord and had us thrown out. It wasn't all that long after he had thrown out Anna and her mother." Her eyes grew small, dark. "I ain't ashamed of what I did, but I'm sorry Anna's bein' persecuted for it."

"Prosecuted," he corrected.

"Wha'cha say?"

"She's being prosecuted, indicted, accused of a crime. Persecution is something else."

She shrugged.

"Seems the same to me," she said.

He nodded, smiling. Maybe she was right.

"What do you mean, you're not ashamed of what you did? What did you do?"

"I asked her to get him," she admitted. "Even if you're poor as we are, you got to give somethin' that's valuable to you to make it a proper request. That's what Anna said, so I give her this cameo belonged to my mother. She didn't want to take it. She said it was too much, but I said it meant more to me for her to be able to do somethin' to that horrible man than keepin' some old jewelry. He knew we didn't have no place to go and how hard up Lester was for work, but he tells the court he ain't the welfare department. The rent was too high anyway for that place. We had roaches into everything and it wasn't cause I didn't keep it clean."

"So you asked Anna to do what?"

"Put a curse on him," she confessed proudly. She smiled. "And it worked."

He stared at her. The little girl moaned and she rocked her again. Finally, the door opened and the elderly lady who had been in with Doctor Bloom emerged. She started out looking sick and tired, but when she saw him sitting there, she looked interested and suddenly revived. He smiled at her.

"Don't get old," she warned him.

"I'll try not to, but the alternative isn't so good either," he said.

She nodded and left.

The receptionist opened the window.

"Mrs. Dixon, you can take Mary in now," she said. She glanced at Del and then went back to her magazine.

He sat back just as his cellular phone vibrated in his pocket.

"Pearson," he declared after he flipped it open.

"Del, Mark," Mark Carlson said quickly. Mark was another lawyer in the legal aid office. "Bill Marvin just called me from the sheriff's office. When they searched Anna Young's shop this morning, they found a sock they believe belonged to Henry Deutch. They've matched it with one at his house."

"A sock? What's that prove?"

"Could prove she was in his house and stole it. There's something about her telling people she has to have something of his in order to put a curse on him."

"Yeah, I just found out about that. Looks like I better read up on witchcraft."

"Someone's going to leak it to the press, I'm sure. Thought you oughta know."

"I'll get over to her place right after I speak with the doctor," he said. "Exactly where was this sock found?"

"On the floor in the back at the center of a circle drawn in what looks like someone's blood. Hope it's not Deutch's."

"This is really getting out of hand."

"Maybe. Maybe it's a way they can put her in his house. Maybe at the scene of the death."

"That's absolutely ridiculous," Del muttered. "What's Paula Richards going to claim anyway, the rat was the murder weapon? Jeezes."

"Just remember, if she went into his house to steal his sock, she lied when she told the police she'd never been in there. Thought you'd want to know."

"Yeah, right. Thanks. I'm about to speak to Deutch's physician. In an hour it'll all be over," he declared.

"You should have been brought up on a farm. Then you'd know what it means to be counting your chickens, partner," Mark kidded.

"Thanks for the age old rural wisdom. See you soon."

He closed the phone and looked toward the receptionist's window. She wasn't in sight now and the phone was ringing. Finally, it stopped.

Henry Deutch's sock in a circle? What the hell did it mean? He wondered. She had said she didn't put the rat there, but she hadn't exactly told him she had never been in that house, no matter what the police claim she told them. He realized he didn't ask her that question and she hadn't volunteered any more information than he had requested. He needed a more extensive interview with her, he decided, just to avoid any possible little surprises. Of course, if he didn't get this case aborted, he'd have to have more than one extensive interview.

A tiny feeling in his stomach, something akin to the trickle of ice water, began. What if he wasn't approaching this with a serious enough attitude? What if Mark was right: he was counting his chickens before they hatched? What if he was missing something that would cause it all to blow up in his face and make him look very foolish? Go get a good position with a private firm after that, he told himself.

A wave of heavy worry passed over him like a dark cloud. He sat back, pensive. Could Paula Richards have a reasonable case, an indictment that would hold up against the test of reasonable assumptions and logic after all? This defense might be a lot more involved than he first considered and he had to wonder on his client's behalf if he was capable of presenting an adequate defense against a charge of premeditated murder. After all, the risk was very serious.

He could be responsible for her death.

He shook off these doubts and laughed at himself for even thinking of them. Then he looked up at the door, hoping for Mrs. Dixon and her sick daughter to emerge soon. He was impatient now, anxious. Insecurity was the worst of all weaknesses for a lawyer. If you didn't speak with confidence, you permitted doubt to enter the mind of judges and juries. Maybe that was why so many attorneys he knew came off being so arrogant. They wore their self-confidence like badges bestowed on them at the passing of their law exams.

There was so much about this profession he hated, and yet so much about it he loved. Speaking for those who couldn't speak adequately for themselves was a privilege, and guaranteeing someone his or her protection under the law was a patriotic duty. Corny? Maybe, but it was what made his professional life comfortable. At least for now, he thought.

The door finally opened and Lois Dixon appeared, her daughter Mary now walking and holding her hand. Doctor Bloom stood behind them gazing out at him.

"I hope she feels better soon," he told Lois Dixon as they started by him.

She paused and looked at Del with the most intent expression in her eyes, an expression filled with determination and assurance.

"She will be," she said. "Everything will be better now."

He watched her walk her daughter out and then turned back to the doctor.

"Mr. Pearson?" he asked. He had Del's card in his hand and looked at it again.

The doctor was a stout, six footer with balding very light brown and gray hair, thinned to the point where his freckles and age spots were clearly visible on his scalp. His face was soft, his cheeks blown out a bit so that his mouth looked small. He focused his hazel eyes on Del just the way a doctor should look at someone, Del thought, scrutinizing, evaluating, searching for symptoms.

"Yes."

"You are Anna Young's attorney?"

"The court assigned an attorney. I'm with the public defender's office and she is my client, yes," Del said. "But I'd like to speak to you about Henry Deutch."

Doctor Bloom nodded and backed up a bit.

"Sophie, call Cohen's pharmacy and tell Howard it's all right to renew Mrs. Feinstein's prescription," he ordered.

Sophie put down her magazine and started to dial without comment.

"Come in," Doctor Bloom said.

He led him to a small office just past the examination room. It was cluttered with pharmaceutical samples and the desk was inundated with paperwork. There was another desk chair to the right. Doctor Bloom sat in his and indicated Del should take the other chair. He did so quickly.

"How can I help you?" he asked.

"I'm preparing a motion for a pretrial hearing. I know you've already been contacted by the district attorney concerning the death of Henry Deutch?"

"Yes, an assistant named Mr. Rosen was here and had a subpoena for Mr. Deutch's records."

"You know why they're charging Miss Young with murder?"

"I understand they're accusing her of driving him into a coronary, although I haven't been privy to the medical examiner's report. Was that the cause of death on the death certificate?"

Del opened his briefcase and pulled out some documents. He handed the medical examiner's report to the doctor who put on his thick framed reading glasses and read.

"Myocardial infarction. Heart attack," he said, nodding.

"You were treating him for angina, I understand," Del said.

"Yes, that's correct. He was initially diagnosed with what is called stable angina pectoris, to be more accurate," he continued. "In layman's terms that simply means chest pain caused by lack of oxygen to the heart muscle, usually a result of poor blood supply."

"And the cause of that is?"

"Normally, atherosclerosis, fat deposits on the walls of the arteries."

"You said you diagnosed him with stable angina. Was this still his condition last you knew?" Del asked.

The doctor raised his eyebrows.

"I'm not clear on what information I'm to reveal to you at this point, Mr. Pearson, although I'm sure for your defense, you can request a copy of Henry Deutch's records."

"The patient is dead, doctor. What difference will it make what you tell me now?"

"I'm aware of that, but there are so many legal issues these days, especially as regards to medicine, that I think I might have to confer with my attorney first."

"Doctor," Del said, not hiding his frustration. "I'm trying to cut this off at the start with a pretrial motion. The prosecution is claiming Anna Young, through a consistent and persistent design of activities, brought about the heart attack and subsequent death of Henry Deutch. There is something in criminal law known as the *but for causation.* But for the defendant's actions, the result would not have occurred. This is why I think I have a good opportunity to stop this insanity before it starts. In essence, how can someone cause another person's death by frightening him or her to death?"

The doctor took off his glasses and wiped the lenses.

"Well," he began, after he put them on again, "I'm not going to get into the legal arena. I have enough to do in the medical, but you should know that stress is a factor and anything that causes a jolt of adrenalin into the body can be the cause of trouble. Now, as to whether or not what your client did was in effect like a bullet, and Henry Deutch would have had a heart attack that day at that time, I'm certainly not prepared to say, but I can see someone arguing it's a little like slow arsenic poison, building it up until it proves fatal."

"But you did say he had stable angina," Del pursued.

Bloom didn't smile as much as he smirked.

"Serves me right for being so damn pedantic. Yes, that was the initial diagnosis, but recently that condition degenerated to unstable angina. Before you ask, I'll tell you that as far as I could tell, Henry Deutch wasn't a smoker and he took his medication when he needed it. He never called to say it wasn't working. If a patient with angina experiences chest pain for more than fifteen minutes after taking at least three tablets, he needs immediate medical attention."

"What distinguishes stable from unstable?" Del asked.

"In unstable angina the chest pain may occur at rest, or there may be an increase in the severity, frequency, or duration of the pain, with chest pain occurring at lower levels of activity."

"And Henry Deutch had those symptoms?"

Doctor Bloom hesitated again and then straightened up in his chair and put on his glasses.

"I suppose it's your nature, but you make me feel as if I'm already on the witness stand."

"How recent was his last visit?" Del pursued, ignoring the doctor's feelings. "That's not much for you to reveal without the presence of an attorney," Del added a little angrily.

"Just a moment," the doctor said, rising.

Del sat there, feeling more frustrated. He was hoping the doctor would laugh at the murder one indictment and give him statements that would clearly undermine Paula Richards' case, but everyone was so worried about covering his legal rear end these days, and now he was learning that Deutch's condition had recently degenerated. What would that mean for the case? Would Paula Richards be able to tie the degeneration to Anna Young's behavior, coordinate medical evaluations with incidents?

After a minute, Doctor Bloom returned with his appointment book in hand. "Three weeks before he passed away," he replied to Del's question.

"What was your evaluation then?"

The doctor hesitated.

"I will get it all from the D.A.'s office, and if they don't subpoena you as a witness, I will. We can avoid so much if you'll help me now," he added, practically pleading.

"I saw no dramatic change on this last visit," the doctor replied, "one way or the other. I'd still diagnose him with unstable angina."

"Does that mean he could have had a heart attack at any time?" Del asked.

"I suppose any cardiologist would agree. You want a black and white answer and it's not possible. Medicine isn't that exact."

That was still not quite the response Del hoped for. He wanted to hear a clear and unequivocal declaration that Henry's condition was stable enough not to be fatally influenced by the sight of a dead rat in his bed. It would support a more natural cause for events.

"The district attorney thinks it is." Del thought a moment. "After your preliminary diagnosis, Henry Deutch never went to a cardiologist?"

"Henry wasn't a cooperative patient. He told me specialists are only regular doctors who want to charge more. He was a piece of work," he said, shaking his head.

"So then how can you be sure he didn't do things to aggravate his condition and took his medicine properly?" Del pounced.

The doctor nodded.

"This is why I think I'd better wait before talking about it any further, Mr. Pearson."

"Henry Deutch wasn't on Viagra by any chance, was he?" Del asked, half in jest. There was good evidence that taking it with nitroglycerin could be fatal.

"Hardly. I don't think that aspect of his life interested him anymore. If ever," the doctor muttered.

"Did he have any other physical problems? Hypertension perhaps?" Del asked, ignoring him.

"If he did," Doctor Bloom said, "you don't help your client. Deliberately doing something that will raise the blood pressure of someone who already has a blood pressure problem is not very nice."

"Did he?" Del pursued.

"I'd better check with my attorney before I say any more or show you anything I have," the doctor replied.

Del nodded. He had the impression hypertension was also in the mix.

"I'll have to talk to you again after I see your complete medical records. I'll give you notice so you can have your attorney present if you wish," he told him and rose. He thought a moment and then glanced toward the lobby before turning back to Doctor Bloom.

"Your receptionist work for you long?"

"Couple of years," he said. "Nice girl, local girl. She got married recently. Her name is Sophie Potter, married Clark Potter. Potter real estate." The doctor saw the way Del was looking toward the receptionist's office and smirked. "She wouldn't go gossiping about anyone's medical problems," he said firmly. "I made that clear when I hired her."

Del nodded.

The doctor's face softened.

"Of course, she knows who Anna Young is. Everyone in this town knows her. I've got a number of patients who go to her for one reason or another, and I must say," he added, "most have had some significant improvement in their conditions."

Del started to smile.

"I've been in this health business a long time, Mr. Pearson, too long to ridicule or discredit anything out of hand. That, I'm afraid, goes for what can cause heart attacks as well as prevent them," he added.

Del said no more. The longer this conversation lasted, the worse the digressions and possibilities seemed to be.

He thanked him and left.

Anyone who saw him leave the doctor's office and looked at his face would understandably conclude he had come as a patient.

Munsen sat awkwardly on the sofa in Lisa's gynecologist's office lobby. He twirled his hat in his hand nervously and stared down at the black and white checkered tiles. They were about an inch wide and he had spent the first fifteen minutes or so counting them to keep his mind from traveling along any dark roads. A woman in her late twenties at most sat across from him sifting through magazines, apparently not finding anything that grabbed her interest. Once in a while, she looked at him, but she seemed afraid of conversation. Finally, more for himself than for her, he smiled.

"How far along are you?" he asked.

"Six and a half months. I already know it's a boy," she said.

"You wanted to do that, find out?"

"Sure. We got to plan the room and tell people what to buy for gifts," she replied as if he had asked the dumbest question on the face of the earth.

He nodded.

Someday, he thought, there won't be any mysteries left, no surprises. We'll all be psychics, Anna Youngs created by medical science.

"You guys want a boy?"

She smirked.

"Don't all men want boys?"

"We have two girls," he said. "As long as they're healthy kids, feel blessed," he advised.

"Billy wanted a boy," she muttered, and looked at the magazine.

When the door to the examination room opened, he felt his heart do a flip in his chest. The doctor had his arm around Lisa's shoulders. He smiled out at Munsen and nodded at her. Munsen nearly leaped to his feet as she crossed the lobby. His eyes were filled with questions, but she chose to leave the office before speaking. As they walked toward the elevator, he wondered if she would ever speak.

"Well, what did he tell you?" he finally asked.

"I took another Pap test and we'll see," she said. "Sometimes there are false positives."

"Well, what were his feelings? I mean . . ."

"He just wants me to stay calm and wait and see. If there's something there, he thinks we probably caught it in time anyway," she replied.

"Oh."

She looked at him when the elevator door opened.

"Probably," she emphasized.

He tried to swallow, couldn't, and just nodded.

"I need to stop at the supermarket on the way home," she told him as soon as they got into the car.

"Right," he said.

He glanced at her. She looked stronger, but cold as if all her emotions had been frozen for the time being. Keep life running as usual. Don't assume the worst and don't dwell on the tension, he heard himself advise himself.

"I don't want the girls to know about this, Munsen," she said suddenly. "They'll make me more nervous worrying."

"They're going to want to know what's going on," he pointed out.

"I'll tell them something. Just don't mope about and look like you look right now," she ordered.

He smiled.

"Okay. It's going to be all right," he promised.

She was silent.

"I'll get some chicken cutlets," she said after a while. "I can do something fast with them."

"We could go out to eat," he suggested.

"I'd rather keep busy," she said.

"Right."

Fortunately, when they arrived at home the girls were bursting with school news. Brooke had been told she was being inducted in the honor society and Crystal had been asked to the spring dance by the boy she had hoped would ask her. The conversation at dinner was dominated by their new clothing needs. It was one time Munsen was glad to see them absorbed in themselves as teenagers were wont to be.

Afterward, he left to make his rounds and check on any messages at the office. There weren't any. The village looked as quiet as usual, despite the heavy publicity that had begun. He hesitated when he drove up to Kayfields. He could see from the parked cars that there were more people there than usual, probably to discuss the big events. He drove by and cruised slowly past Anna's shop. He saw there was some light inside and from the way it flickered, he knew it was coming from a candle.

Slowly, he turned the vehicle and drove up to the front of the shop. For a long moment, he sat there staring at the dark entryway and the flickering illumination on the glass. Was Benny Sklar in there speaking to his dead wife again? he wondered.

As if it took form from the very shadows lying in the entryway, Anna's silhouette appeared in the door window. His first impulse was to drive off quickly because he was a little embarrassed about spying on her, but she opened the door and stepped out. It was too late. She knew he was there. She looked like she was beckoning him. He turned off the engine and got out of the car.

The street was so quiet tonight, he thought as he went around the front of the vehicle. The air seemed so still. It was truly as if the small village was in the eye of a storm.

"Evening, Anna," he said. "I'm just doing a routine check of store fronts," he said.

She stepped toward him. Without streetlights, it was nearly impossible to see the detail in her face, but there was enough dim illumination from the night sky to reveal something of a skeptical smile on her lips.

"You're troubled," she declared.

"It's a nasty business all around," he offered. "The village is going to get a lot of undesired attention."

"It's not the village, Mr. Donald. What is it that troubles you?"

How could she know that?

He hesitated, looked around and then took a deep breath. This was insane. What if someone overheard him?

"My wife got a bad scare today," he said. "A test didn't come out good. We have to wait on more tests."

She nodded.

"They were angry at you," she said.

"Who?"

"The spirits who lived within Mr. Deutch. You didn't do what he hoped you would. Their anger spilled over you and it entered your home."

She reached behind her neck. She wore a chain with a tiny tube on it. The tube had a silvery top.

"Give her this to wear," she said.

"Huh?"

"It will protect her," Anna said. "It is filled with salt my mother prepared for me many years ago. Salt like this will ward off the evil eye, Mr. Donald. Salt is the symbol of life and purification."

She held it out, but he didn't take it.

"It's my gift to you, Mr. Donald. You are caught in a whirlwind not of your own making. Take it and protect your loved one," she said. It sounded like an official order from the chief of police.

He took it in his hand and turned it around in his thick fingers. Lisa would never wear this, he thought.

"Tell your wife it's a gift from me," Anna said, "and she will wear it," she added with confidence. He looked up quickly. Can she actually read my thoughts? he had to wonder.

"This will all end soon, Mr. Donald," she promised him. "But it will not be over."

"Huh?"

"It's only one battle in an everlasting war," she explained. "Good fortune," she said, and went back into her shop.

He looked through the door window and watched her return to her table and her candle.

Would Lisa wear this?

Would it help?

He glanced around like a thief afraid someone had seen him take something. Then he shoved the chain and the tube into his pocket and returned to his car. He looked back at the shop before pulling away. The candle had gone out.

When he reached the center of the village, he hesitated. If he went into Kayfields, he would be there for hours, he thought.

The chain seemed to grow warm in his pocket. Was that his imagination?

He accelerated, turning up the hill and toward home.

He practiced his arguments.

What harm can it do to wear it? No one has to know. Who knows about these things?

Lisa was cleaning out the food pantry when he arrived. The girls were upstairs on their telephones. He knew Lisa was just trying to make work now. She looked a bit wild when she gazed up at him, her head disheveled, her eyes glassy, and her face flushed. Maybe not a good time to bring this up, he thought.

"You're back early," she said.

"Yeah," he said.

"What is it, Munsen?" she asked. They had lived too long as one for her not to sense when something raged within him.

"I was doing my rounds," he began. She stood up to listen and he told her what had happened.

Then he took out the chain and held it out. She plucked it from his palm, gazed into his face, and without hesitation put it around her neck.

If it worked, he thought, he'd make sure no harm came to that woman.

Somehow.

He'd make sure.

Twelve

By the time Del drove into Sandburg, it was a little after 8 P.M. He had tried to call Anna Young and discovered to his chagrin that she didn't have a phone. Who in this day and age of pagers and cell phones, not to mention radio phones, lived without a house telephone? What, did she communicate telepathically with people? He laughed to himself. Maybe she was the one who had put the idea in his head to go see her and find out about this sock, among other things. That's the next thing district attorney Richards will be telling the press: she killed Henry Deutch with powerful thoughts.

Del wasn't sure who should be psychologically evaluated, Anna Young or Paula Richards. Having Anna psychologically examined was certainly a consideration in his preliminary plans of defense. A woman who stands in the streets with a bag of chicken bones and drops them in someone's path, mumbling some mumbo-jumbo is seriously to be indicted for murder one? C'mon. She is seriously to be indicted for being off the wall.

Every once in a while, he would have to stop and ask himself if he was really doing the things he was doing with this case. Was all this actually happening? He was beginning to understand how ordinary people could be carried along in a wave of hysteria and madness. Sometimes events had a life of their own, a power inherent in themselves, and men of reason and logic were swept aside. Surely Judge Landers, who would preside over the hearing before trial, would be wondering what he was doing there, too. I hope, Del thought, and then imagined how the judges today probably often wondered how a specific set of events had brought them into the courtroom.

Jackie's phone call late in the afternoon rang his first alarm bell in regard to all that.

"Dad called before and wanted to know what was going on. He said some of his friends are calling and asking and making jokes about witches," Jackie told him.

"Tell him to ask the district attorney," Del responded, feeling himself growing a little testy already. "I'm not in charge of the insanity. My job is not to act; it's to react. I'm a defense attorney."

"Exactly. Dad wanted to know if there could actually be a trial and if there was, would you be the only one from the office who would be defending a witch in court?" she pursued.

"Of course, but, I'm working on stopping it as early as I can, Jackie."

"What if you can't?" she asked.

"I don't know right now, Jackie. In this business you take everything a step at a time," he replied.

"That's not what you tell me, Del. You're always preaching about being prepared for contingencies and how that's the difference between a successful attorney and an unsuccessful one," she continued.

He took a deep breath.

"Can we talk about this later? Between everything else Douglas is throwing my way and this, I have a stack of paperwork that would choke an elephant, much less a horse."

"Okay. I'm just asking," she said as if the questions were meant to be innocuous.

"Nobody just asks anything," he said. It just slipped out, but he could almost feel her tense up on the other end.

"I do, Del. I'm not like most people you know. I don't come to everything with an agenda," she said, "and if there is an agenda, it's usually entitled 'What's Good for Del Pearson.'"

"I'm sorry. I'm just . . . crazy with this at the moment."

"I know," she said sadly, "and it hasn't even started."

"Maybe it won't," he offered weakly, although he was never one to avoid a battle, especially one in which a giant was about to squash a pigmy. He knew it was because of who he was and how he had been raised.

His father had been in the air force and trained as an airplane mechanic, but he didn't especially like the work, so when he left the service, he didn't move into a job for a commercial airline as most of his buddies did. Instead, he returned to the Catskills where he was raised and decided he would open a television and appliance store in Monticello, transferring his knowledge and skill with electronics into what he believed would eventually become the next retail electronics franchise. He called his first store Rube's Tubes, which everyone thought was catchy and clever. Unfortunately, there would be only one store and that would fail once the bigger discount chains established themselves closer to the community and eventually anchored malls in the county. He couldn't compete. David and Goliath.

Not allowing himself to be discouraged, Reuben Pearson dove into a crash course in computer science and transferred his energies again into what he believed would become a chain: Chip Off the Old Block. For a while it looked like he had a chance. He was busy training and setting up people with their PC's, but the problem was most of them were buying their PC's from city discounters and catalogue companies. His inventory languished, became outdated and obsolete, and his investment began to wither away.

Del watched his father's optimism and enthusiasm diminish away as well. Slowly, like a crystal sinking in mud, his father's almost beatific rich and bright smile of hope wilted and sank into a face of bleak realization. He ended up working as a service technician for IBM, performing warranty and other work in an area that unfortunately covered nearly eighty miles in every direction. It put him on the road all week.

"Successful little guys are the exception, Del, not the rule," his father concluded, but in the same breath, turned to him, and smiling, said, "You be the exception for our family, son."

It all made him a little more class conscious and a lot more tolerant of the weaker, less fortunate. This was why he was destined to champion underdogs. It was just his nature, and Anna Young certainly fit the description: a woman alone, barely earning a living as a seamstress in this modern age, living in one of the dying Catskill resort villages, and targeted by the rich and powerful county office of prosecution, headed by its politically ambitious district attorney.

Madness.

Rube's Tubes.

Chip Off the Old Block.

Into the village of Sandburg he rode like Robin Hood, Zorro, the Cisco Kid, a David with his little public defender's slingshot, ready to turn to face the Goliath of the state's prosecution office.

It had been a while since he had been to Sandburg. His memories of it actually were anchored in a time when it, like most of the Catskill resort area, was a rather booming, busy little hamlet, almost a neighborhood in New York City during the summer months because of its traffic and bloated population residing in the surrounding small hotels and bungalow colonies. He slowed to nearly a crawl as he approached the center of the town. The main street was dark and deserted. There was actually a dog sprawled in the center of the road, barely concerned about his advancing headlights. The macadam was still warm from the day's sunshine and made for a very comfortable bed, something not easily relinquished. Not until he was within ten yards of it, did it rise with great effort and walk itself to the right, glancing his way as if still skeptical that he would actually want to continue into this community.

The bordered up store fronts, dark windows, and broken signs filled him with a sense of doom. It occurred to him that this might very well be a good place for witchcraft. Lost and troubled dead souls would be welcomed in a village that in itself was lost in time, the buildings resembling tombstones, the empty, untrodden sidewalks rambling off like sentences that no longer had grammatical integrity or any meaning and purpose.

A streetlight at the center flickered, making shadows jump and turn this way and that in a macabre choreography. The brightest light came from the bar and grill, where the longest line of parked cars was located. Del had Anna's address. All he had to do was remain on the main drag and look for her shop on the left, but he nearly missed it because of the lack of street lighting in her vicinity. He stopped, saw the small illumination in the window of her shop, and then made a U-turn and pulled alongside the broken, uneven curb.

Just as he turned off the ignition, his cellular vibrated in his jacket pocket.

"Hello?"

"Del, I heard your message on the answering machine. What about dinner?" Jackie asked.

"Oh. I had a sub at Donovan's Cellar about five so I'm fine."

"What are you doing? It's late."

"I've got to check out some facts with my client," he said. "It shouldn't take long, but I didn't want to have you wait and eat so late, honey."

"I can wait. I had a late lunch, too. Don't forget we're going to dinner with my parents tomorrow night. Daddy made reservations at Antonio's."

"He should have a seat with his name on it by now," Del said.

"You always love the food there, Del."

"I know. I'm just kidding," he said, but what he was really thinking about was all of his father-in-law's and mother-in-law's friends who were bound to come to the table and ask about the case. It was becoming notorious. There was already talk of New York City stations sending up reporters and a rumor that *60 Minutes* might send up Lesley Stahl.

He looked at his watch.

"I'll be home in an hour," he promised, "but don't do anything special. Something light is all I'll need."

"All right," she said, but she sounded far off, small, and very worried.

"It's okay. It's going to be fine," he said, not knowing what he meant himself.

"Be careful," she concluded.

He laughed to himself and folded the flip-top phone. Then he looked around. What evil spirit was lurking in those shadows, Del Pearson? he asked himself and shook his head as he stepped out and went to Anna Young's door. He was surprised to see that the only light in the shop was coming from a single, tall white candle burning brightly at the center of the table in the rear. At first he didn't see Anna. After he tapped gently on the window, she rose from behind the table on the floor where she had been on her knees. She put each of her hands through the candle flame once as if washing them in fire and then she brought her hands to her face and held her palms against her cheeks. All the while she looked in his direction, but her eyes were distant and without any recognition or awareness of his presence.

She was wearing a white blouse buttoned to the base of her throat and a dark blue skirt. Her hair was down, some strands over her shoulders and some in front, almost to the crest of her bosom. In the candle light her face appeared slightly yellow and her eyes larger. He stared at her a moment longer and then he tapped on the glass again. She turned as if she was speaking to someone behind her and then she walked toward the door.

"Good evening, Mr. Pearson," she said as soon as she had opened it and stepped back.

"I tried to phone you, but you don't have any listing," he explained. She just nodded with a small smile on her full, ruby lips. Now that she was closer, he saw that her face was far from pale. It was flush. She looked like she had been running and her eyes were absolutely electric. He almost forgot why he had come.

"Please, come in," she finally said when he hadn't moved.

"Oh. Yes. I hope it's not a bad time," he said.

"It is a bad time," she replied, "but it will soon be good."

He started to laugh, but just shook his head instead.

"I have a few questions to ask you in preparation for the hearing before trial," he said.

"Let's go upstairs where we will be a little more comfortable," she suggested, and led him through the shop to the stairway in the rear. He followed, his eyes fixed on the movement of her thighs and rear as she ascended the narrow steps ahead of him.

Her upstairs apartment was very small. The steps led into the living room. He saw that the bathroom was to the left and the apartment itself was one of those railroad configurations where you had to walk through the kitchen to one bedroom to get to the next. The living room decor was simple, almost stark. There was a glass table in front of the settee and two matching cushioned chairs, one on the right and one on the left. A painting of an intriguing looking woman was on the wall behind the settee.

The woman depicted wore a shawl and looked like her head was lowered in some prayer, yet her eyes were looking up. The way the artist had configured the picture, those eyes were what drew the most attention. Something about it was lifelike, almost like a photo that had been painted over.

"Is that someone special?" he asked, nodding at the picture.

"Yes. That's my mother. That picture was done many many years ago in Budapest," Anna said with a soft smile. "It was said that the man who painted it was so drained from the intensity of his attention on her and the power of her eyes that he had to take six months to recuperate." She laughed. "A good myth," she said. "Legends, fables, exaggerations help give us validity, my mother used to say. 'Don't deny them. Just don't verify them.' Like anyone, we need publicity," she added and laughed again. "Can I get you something, some chamomile tea, perhaps?"

"No, I'm fine," he said, placing his briefcase on the table and sitting in the chair on his left.

"My tea will help you sleep better and you'll need your rest and strength, Mr. Pearson," she pursued.

"Okay," he said, smiling. "Thanks."

She went into the kitchen. He rose and looked about some more, eventually wandering to the door of the bedroom. He saw the sword mounted above the bed.

"Is that a sword in there above your bed?" he called to her.

"Yes." She stepped out of the kitchen. "It's an athame. It was my mother's."

"Athame?"

"A ceremonial knife. I can cast a circle with it, direct power, and defend myself in the spiritual world. It is associated with the East and it is the element of Fire. There are four, as you know," she said, and plucked the pentacle from the depth of her cleavage and held it up. "The pentacle symbolizes it all."

"What exactly is a pentacle?" he asked.

"A symbol of unity that represents unity and harmony in Nature, how everything is connected. The star within the pentacle represents the different aspects of the universe with its different points. Since the star is five-pointed," she said, holding it up from her chest, "it represents the four elements of earth, air, fire, and water as well as akasha, the fifth element, the spirit or energy behind everything."

He drew closer to look at it in more detail. She continued to hold it up.

"The circle around the pentacle represents the oneness, not a circle and a star, not five triangles and a pentagon, but a pentacle, one thing," she said.

He stared at it. It seemed to glitter and hold him fixed. He blinked when he heard the teapot whistle. How long had he been staring, for crissakes? He blanched and looked up at her dark eyes. She smiled.

"The tea," she said.

He felt a soft, pleasant warmth in him even without the hot liquid, but when she brought it and he sipped, he did sense his body relax.

She sat across from him on the settee.

"So, let us talk," she said.

"Right." He had almost forgotten why he had come. "I was informed earlier that your premises were searched and they found a sock that supposedly belonged to Henry Deutch. Is that so?"

"Yes. It was still in its wrapping on the floor about where you're sitting."

"In one of your circles?"

"Of course," she said.

"You said, 'wrapping'?"

"How it came," she said.

"What do you mean, how it came?"

She smiled.

"Sometimes, most often in fact, things I say are merely what they are. Nothing cryptic, Mr. Pearson. The sock was sent to me."

"Sent to you? So the wrapping was postmarked?" he asked hopefully.

"No. The package was left at my door."

"Oh." That was disappointing. He thought he had an argument against it being circumstantial proof she had been in or around Henry Deutch's property.

"Someone concerned knew that I needed something of his at the time, something close to him. An article of clothing is perfect."

"Perfect? For what?"

"For what had to be done to defeat the evil in him, Mr. Pearson."

"What exactly had to be done?"

"I had to find ways to penetrate the wall around him and at the same time strengthen the wall around myself and others who were vulnerable until I had destroyed him," Anna explained in a tone of voice so matter-of-fact Del thought they could be discussing how she hemmed a skirt.

"So when you say 'him' do you mean Henry Deutch or someone else?" Del asked.

She smiled.

"You've been doing some research, I see."

"Not really. I merely read some of the things you've been quoted as saying to people in the town as well as to the police," Del replied.

She nodded.

"To answer your question, I have to explain a little about good and evil, Mr. Pearson. There are those who hold that we are all doomed to sin. As I told you when we met at the police station, some of the clergymen in this village believe that. They teach that we have all inherited evil and that it is inevitable we will commit evil acts, but what we must do is embrace redemption, accept their truths, and follow their rules and we will find forgiveness and paradise. What the devil will do is get us to keep sinning and never seek redemption. Then he will win our souls.

"Others believe we are born with the tendency to do evil and the tendency to do good and that doing evil is not inevitable, but something we do by choice. Here, we are not simply tempted to commit evil acts that are in us from birth, but we are convinced to choose them. If we resist and do good deeds, we have a promising afterlife.

"Whatever religious doctrine you choose, Mr. Pearson, you admit that in the end, the acts you commit and your attitude toward them will determine who you ultimately are.

"Once, there was a Henry Deutch who was vulnerable to sin, but who resisted because there was still an element of good in him. Perhaps because of his wife, because after her death he became more vulnerable and not only chose to commit more evil, but never felt a need to redeem himself and lost all compassion for his victims. This was a different Henry Deutch, one, shall we say, who was contaminated. He was who I had to destroy because he became a vessel, a device, a home for pure evil to reside among us. Does that help you understand?"

"I'm still not quite clear on why you had or have this responsibility," Del said.

She shook her head.

"That, Mr. Pearson, is the most intriguing question of all. My mother used to tell me that just as people could inherit a strong evil impulse, they could inherit a strong good. Ours was passed down through centuries and we are who we are because of it and not solely by choice. I suppose, in a way, the same was true for Henry Deutch. I could, and have been tempted at times, to give up this battle and be, as some might say, ordinary, but it is my particular destiny that if I did, I would have been defeated by evil and that's too great a responsibility for me to assume. For Henry Deutch, giving up the evil impulse was too much as well and so he and I were caught here, two adversaries on a great battlefield of neither's making.

"Now, my battle goes on to be fought in another arena and you have been chosen to carry my banner."

"Why have I been chosen?" Del asked.

"I do not know yet, but I know you have. Are you left- or right-handed?"

"Right."

"Let me see your left hand," she said after a moment.

"Huh?"

"Please."

He offered his hand and she turned it palm up and ran the tips of her fingers over the lines. Then she closed her eyes for a moment.

"What?" he asked impatiently.

"This is the art of chiromancy, from the Greek words for hand and divination," she said.

"You're going to read my palm?"

"In a sense of the word, yes," she said with a small smile. Her eyes were dazzling. He felt the warmth move through her fingers into his hand and up his arm to his heart, which began to pound a little faster, a little harder. He started to pull away. "Don't be afraid," she said, holding on. "I will tell you nothing you don't already know in your own heart to be true, but it will help me understand you."

She looked at his palm and he relaxed.

"Our hands are a very expressive part of our bodies and of course, the most utilitarian part. I look at your left hand because it has suffered less wear and tear and is therefore more easily understood and revealing.

"You have a long hand," she said, smiling. "It indicates someone inclined to spend more time perfecting his actions rather than simply concluding."

"I'd like to simply conclude all this," he offered.

"Yes, but you won't choose the absolutely easiest way out. You're too responsible, too caring. You want to do it right.

"This rise here at the base of your thumb is known as

the Mount of Venus. Yours is smooth, full. It suggests you are a warm, loving person, even quite sexual," she added, but without a smile.

His heart was actually thumping like a teenager on the threshold of some exciting first love experience.

"My wife might agree," he said, almost in a whisper. She nodded and felt along other rises in his palm.

"This," she said, moving toward his index finger, "is the mount called inner Mars. You are a good combatant, Mr. Pearson, yet the mount of Jupiter tells me you are not overly ambitious and prideful."

"Another thing my wife will attest to, and complain about," he added.

This time she did smile and nod.

"Every palmist stresses the lines in a person's hand. How deep they are. How long and how many there are. Your line of life," she said, tracing the line around the base of the ball of his thumb, "is deep. You are a man of great energy and the wideness of the curve tells me you have an active nature. You are a sportsman?"

"I play racquetball almost every morning and workout twice a week in a gym," he admitted.

"Your head line is deep. Your thoughts are deep. Your heart line suggests great conjugal joy, great affection."

"Okay," Del said. "Everyone wants to know something about the future though."

She nodded and looked at his hand and smiled.

"You see these three lines at your wrist. This is known as a Royal Bracelet and it's a strong indication you will have a long life.

"In short," she said, still holding onto his hand, "I see clearly that you are the man for the job."

He laughed. She held his hand for an additional beat and then she released it and sat back.

"Well," he said. He loosened his tie. "Let's talk about this procedure, hearing before trial. I know the judge, Judge Landers. He's a no-nonsense, cut-to-the-chase man who will not tolerate grandstanding, motions made for public relations, etc., which is all good for us.

"I am going to argue that under none of the facts presented could the state prove beyond a reasonable doubt that you specifically caused the death of Henry Deutch. It is in effect a frivolous use of the indictment power.

"The district attorney has charged you with first degree homicide. She has to show that you had premeditated intent to do malicious harm to Henry Deutch. Since the modus operandi here is supposedly your well thought out plan to aggravate Henry Deutch's heart problems, it presupposes that you knew all about them. You, along with other inhabitants of Sandburg, could have an informal hearsay knowledge that he had something wrong with him, but to presuppose that your knowledge was so detailed as to give you an opportunity to exploit it—"

"It was," she said coldly, almost proudly.

"Pardon me?"

"I did know about his cardiac problem and in detail."

"How?"

"A client of mine works for his doctor," she said. "Sophie Potter. I performed a love ritual for her and in return, she gave me what I needed to know. Good for good," she added.

He stared at her and realized not only was this a terrible realization for his argument, but worse, Anna Young had no deception in her. She would admit to every detail. No one would support district attorney Paula Richards' case better than Anna Young herself, the one accused. He had to remind himself continually that in her way of thinking, she had performed a good service and justified herself and her purpose for being.

What sort of a defense could he mount against all that? She had motive: her mother's death. She had a plan of action: all those rituals, symbols, chants, and maybe dead chickens and a dead rat. She had intent and she wouldn't deny any of it. In fact, she wanted it known.

What was left for him to prove was that what she had done couldn't have brought about Henry Deutch's death, and after spending only a little while with her, he was beginning to have grave doubts himself that she wasn't capable of it.

"I hope you're right about my hand," he said.

"Pardon?" She smiled.

"I'll need to be a good combatant and a man of great energy," he replied.

She leaned forward and reached for his hand again. He let her look at his palm. She closed her eyes and then she nodded to herself and opened them.

"In the end," she said, "we will both get what we want."

Thirteen

Antonio's was just outside of Monticello on Route 42 toward Port Jervis. It was a restaurant that had been converted from a turn-of-the-century Queen Anne–style two-story house set off the road on six beautiful acres of lawn, gardens, and ponds. The wood cladding had been replaced with aluminum, as were the Wedgwood blue shutters. Because the rooms were so large, Antonio left the interior walls essentially intact. The separated dining areas gave people a sense of privacy and importance, and the beautiful, hand-carved mahogany balustrade and stairway gently curved to an upstairs that was now solely used for catered events.

As was usually the case when he was to meet his in-laws anywhere, Del found they had arrived before them and were waiting at the table. Judson Brooks was truly a fanatic about being on schedule, even when that applied to recreational and social activities. Time was always money and a wasted minute was a wasted dollar.

"Good," he declared with regal authority the moment

Del and Jackie appeared in the dinning area that over-
looked the largest pond. From the tone of his voice, anyone
would have thought he had serious doubts they would
appear.

"We're not that late, Daddy," Jackie said quickly. "It's
only five after seven."

"Seven-ten."

"We've been here nearly twenty minutes because he
gets me here so early," Pamela Brooks complained.

Judson's habitually red cheeks blanched brighter and
his lime green eyes turned stone cold. Somewhere early on
in the formation of his personality, Del's father-in-law had
developed a hair-trigger sensitivity even to the slightest,
most inconsequential criticism. Del wondered if it wasn't
part of a strategy because anyone who had business with
Judson Brooks knew that if he reacted so aggressively to a
negative remark about small things, he would be an
absolute nuclear antagonist when and if he were challenged on serious matters. Be prepared if you wanted to
argue with Judson Brooks. That was the admonition practically engraved on the wall behind his desk in the bank.

"You look very nice, dear," Pamela said, turning her
shoulders so that she couldn't see her husband's indignant
glare even out of the corner of her eyes.

Jackie's mother was still a very attractive woman, who,
despite her lack of exercise, was able to hold onto her svelte
figure. She was always accused of having plastic surgery
because her youthful appearance never changed from her
rich, smooth complexion to her perfectly straight nose and
soft, full lips. Sometimes people mistook Jackie and her
mother for sisters.

Jackie and Del sat.

"You look like you need a drink," Judson told Del.

Judson had the most scrutinizing and intimidating gaze,

Del thought. He couldn't imagine a marine drill instructor with a better ability to fixate going nose to nose. It was certainly a large part of what made Judson Brooks formidable in any one-to-one situation. He practically radiated strength. Burly, thick-shouldered, and barrel-chested, he was as physically intimidating as he was psychologically. He had been a halfback in college and loved pointing to the picture of himself on the office wall and saying, "Those were the days when I could convince with just a pair of shoulders."

"I could use a drink, yes," Del admitted, and ordered a vodka and tonic as soon as the waiter approached. Jackie had her usual glass of Chardonnay.

Antonio's was one of those upscale restaurants where no pressure was put on the customers. No maitre d' hovered over the table using all his or her power of suggestion to get people to pay their bill so another party could be seated. The waiters were instructed not to bring the menus to the tables until the customers requested them. Dining was an event here. Conversation over cocktails was truly respected and even encouraged, and when it came to getting the entree, everyone was to expect a longer wait because most everything was cooked and baked on request. If someone was unable to relax here, he or she was probably unable to relax period.

Del really was hoping to do just that. He did feel as if all of his organs were stretched tight, his heartbeat echoing in his bones. He forced a smile for his mother-in-law.

"Poor Del," she said, shaking her head. "Thrown into such a bizarre mess. Stress plays such havoc with your nerves, with everything, I'm sure. I wish you didn't have so much pressure on you all the time," she added, the underlying and subtle suggestion about his failure to impregnate Jackie clearly implied.

"That's the danger of being a public servant. You don't have the freedom to choose your battles," Judson said. "Even with a law degree and honors, you're still a bureaucrat."

Here we go, Del thought, with not even a fair chance to get settled into position. It was as if he and his in-laws had a single, continuous conversation interrupted when they parted, but resumed immediately as soon as they met again.

"If we all chose our clients on the basis of what was only good for us, Dad, few defendants would get their constitutional right to a fair and proper defense," Del replied. He glanced at Judson and then he quickly looked around the room. He recognized Dan Ackerman, the new town of Liberty supervisor, who was gazing his way and talking with a smile to the other people at the table. They glanced at him as well, but no one had yet approached their table.

"You're a young man on the way up," Judson insisted. "You've got to be concerned about that. You don't have the luxury some of these fat, secure lawyers have. You've always got to consider the downside, Del. As a banker—"

"Dad, do we have to talk business now? This is such a great place. Let's just relax," Jackie softly suggested. "Okay?"

His women always tiptoed around him, Del thought. What comes first: fear, respect, or love?

"I'm not talking business. I'm just making conversation. We can talk about substantial things without it being a bore, Jackie."

The waiter brought their drinks. Del nearly gulped half of his.

"You know, I've been talking on and off with Arnold Sacks," Judson continued. "He's had his eye on Del for some time now. They've got a spot opening up soon in his

firm and what an opportunity that could be. Why Michael
Geary was just telling me yesterday that Sacks, Levits and
Aster are actually getting most of their clients out of New
York City and Long Island these days. You want to be part
of something that's got growth potential. When I first
started in banking, my father's best advice to me was look
for a bank that has legs. What he meant was don't get into
something that has a limited future. If the company grows,
you grow too; if it doesn't, you don't."

"I'm hungry, Judson," Pamela said softly.

"So get the waiter to bring the menus. I don't suppose
you read the editorial in the *Record* today," he continued,
directing himself solely to Del.

"Didn't get a chance to look at the paper."

"Del didn't get home until an hour ago actually," Jackie
said.

"Where have you been? It's Saturday," Pamela asked as
if they were all Orthodox Jews and he had violated the
Sabbath.

"Del was in New York," Jackie said before Del could
reply.

"New York? Today?"

"What for?" Judson practically demanded.

Del sipped his drink and looked down for a moment.
Maybe this was good, he thought. Maybe this was the ulti-
mate challenge and if he could make his in-laws see, he
could make anyone see.

"A college buddy of mine, Alan Gordon, has a younger
brother in premed at Columbia. He's specializing in cardi-
ology and he arranged for me to see one of the most highly
respected cardiologists in the northeast, Doctor Warren
Childs."

"Why?" Judson asked. He was leaning forward on his
elbows now. He looked capable of leaping over the table.

"The district attorney is seeking to prove that my client was capable of deliberately causing someone to have a fatal heart attack by doing things most people today consider laughable. They could be annoying, but lethal? Hardly."

"It has to be shocking to find a dead rat in your bed, Del," Pamela said. "I think I could have a heart attack too."

"Especially if you already have a heart problem," Judson added pointedly.

"They haven't produced any evidence proving she did that," Del said.

"Well, we all know the story whether we want to or not, thanks to the media. She was doing similar things for some time. Who else would have done it, for crissakes?" Judson cried.

"I don't know. The point is that even if she did, it's still quite a stretch to say that was the sole reason for Henry Deutch's death at that moment. I was able to show Doctor Childs Henry Deutch's most recent EKG results, and in his opinion, Deutch's heart muscle was still relatively healthy. He thinks Doctor Bloom's diagnosis of unstable angina was probably correct, but, and here's the good part for us, the dosage of nitroglycerin was probably insufficient, which would certainly contribute to Henry Deutch's heart attack."

"Probably? What kind of an expert is that?" Judson asked.

"As good as any they'll have. Doctor Childs was confident enough on the basis of what we have that he was willing to so stipulate and, if necessary, be a defense witness. It would certainly add the element of reasonable doubt. I'll just have to convince the court to give me the money."

"Money?" Pamela asked quickly.

"Expert witnesses are paid for their time," Del said.

"Then you mean to continue full steam ahead with this?" Judson asked.

"It's what I'm paid to do," Del replied.

Judson reached into his jacket pocket and produced the news clipping.

"Here's what you missed," he said, handing it to Del. Jackie looked over his shoulder and read the headline.

THE ULTIMATE EXCUSE—ABUSE UNDER ATTACK

California had its O.J. defenders, and now we have our witch defenders. Harassing someone to death because you think he's the Devil is okay if you're a white witch.

"I never said anything like this. This is disgusting," Del said, reading on. "It belongs in the *Enquirer* or the *Star*, not in a legitimate newspaper. If you follow this logic anyway, we should stone the woman on the basis of accusations alone."

"The point is no one is taking her defense seriously. She's a nutcase. Have her committed, if you want, but don't try to defend someone who thinks she's killing the Devil or something. Few people beside some kooks in that town care about her or see her as someone doing good. Pamela's right. Most people will believe you can be frightened to death. Paula Richards is going to be able to make a good case, even if you bring in your experts, Del. Clergymen, legal scholars, important people think Paula Richards is right in another sense: this spiritual, psychic twisting and turning of the mind, confusing and ruining good people has got to come to an end. Everyone is sensitive to cults and their leaders these days. We need to get back on track with family values."

"She's not a cult leader, Dad."

"That's not what I hear. She's turned some of those people into crackpots, mumbling chants, wearing chicken feet on their wrists or around their necks. She's just like the others. Charlatans, all of them."

"She can't be both," Del said.

"What?"

"If she's a charlatan, she can't have the power to kill someone with her rituals."

"What do you mean, Del?" Jackie asked suddenly, too interested to put it aside. "You're going to prove she doesn't have any supernatural powers? Is that your strategy?"

"No. That's not even the point."

"You don't really believe she has any, do you?" Pamela asked.

Del stared a moment.

"I don't know," he said. "I haven't really thought about it. I've just been concentrating on the medical-legal aspects."

"You don't know?" Judson repeated, his eyebrows lifting.

Del was silent.

"I'm hungry," Pamela said.

"Waiter," Judson snapped. Then he sat back. "All I want to say and I won't say another word, is you better think about your future, too. You might be more on trial than that woman," he concluded.

"In more ways than we know," Del muttered. "In more ways than we know."

Only Jackie heard and she suddenly looked troubled, very troubled.

Tony Monato stepped out the rear door of Kayfields and lit a cigarette. The short order cook stood there for a moment, gazing into the darkness as if he was looking at something specific and not merely running lines of thought across his inner eyes. The scratching sounds on his right spun him around in time to see the large rat slither through the spilled garbage and then under the broken slab of fence between Kayfields and the abandoned supermarket in one of what had been Henry Deutch's buildings.

"Son of a bitch," Tony muttered. He turned the can upright again and slammed the lid down.

Some of those rats were as big as ground hogs, he thought. If they could be harnessed, they'd pull down the damn building. Maybe now that Henry was gone, something serious would be done with the big shack, he concluded. Then he turned and walked around the building to the main street.

He paused and looked up and down the street, content that it was deserted. When he started to walk, he seemed to prefer the shadows. He headed toward the old school house. The sky was overcast. Without any moonlight or starlight there was only the weak streetlights here and there, but he appeared to fear even that and avoided all illumination.

In fact, when an automobile approached the village, Tony paused and leaned back deeper into the shadows to watch it pass. He recognized the driver to be Gina Carnesi from the way she held her body tense and upright, leaning over the steering wheel as if she were driving over broken glass. Some people are terrified the instant they get behind the wheel, he thought. They're the ones who cause most accidents.

After she passed, Tony continued, tossing his cigarette in the air and watching it explode in tiny sparks on the macadam. He walked with determination, mumbling to himself, his words running together until they sounded more like a chant.

"I deserve more. If it wasn't for me . . . more. I deserve more."

He crossed the street then quickly went behind Tilly Zorankin's fruit and vegetable store to follow a path through the overgrowth made by children years ago when the Sandburg elementary school was still functioning. It had long since been incorporated into a centralized district and the building vacated, most of the windows now shattered dark holes that looked like empty eye sockets.

It was Tony's idea to meet here. No one but children were on the property during the day and no one was anywhere near it at night. It was safe, no chance of being seen, no way to tie him to what had happened. He crossed quickly over what had once been the playground, his chantlike mumbling running down like some CD player losing battery power.

He paused and gazed around and behind himself to be sure there was no one unexpectedly nearby. The remnants of a swing set and a seesaw were still there: pipes and boards, but nothing else. The stillness made him feel more solemn and certainly more aware of his own heavy breathing.

Slowly now, he continued forward, his worn sneakers crunching gravel as he plodded along. When he reached his spot just behind the building, he waited for a sign, the flash of a cigarette lighter or a candle, something to indicate that the rendezvous was imminent. Silence and darkness unnerved him. He had hoped this would be fast and to the point and he could be quickly gone.

Tony didn't consider himself a superstitious man, but he fancied himself a careful man. You don't have to believe in spirits and all sorts of unnatural events, but you can have a healthy respect for the possibilities, he always thought. Why go under a ladder if you didn't have to, for example?

He turned to look to his left and then his right. His eyes were accustomed to the darkness now. He could distinguish among the shadows and realized when one was moving toward him. Good, he thought. Let's get this going and over with. He was eager to retreat to his small one bedroom apartment over the restaurant, pour himself a congratulatory two fingers of bourbon, and put his feet up on the hassock in front of the television set. He'd be on his way to the Phillippines sooner than he thought. Lately, seeing his mother's relatives was more important than ever.

He reached into his pocket and pulled out his cigarette lighter and another cigarette, which he lit quickly. He had barely taken a puff when he began to speak, the smoke following his words as if they were on fire as they left his lips.

"The way I see it," he said, "is what I did is worth more, especially now. And don't tell me anything about being greedy or about being like him," he added quickly. "I'm not greedy. I'm not here to ask for a whole lot, just twice as much is all. It's worth that."

He waited for some response. The silence sent a trickle of icy fear down the back of his neck.

"A lotta people are comin' around here askin' questions these days, lots of questions. I ain't said nothin' to nobody . . . yet, but I gotta look after myself, too. I might have to take a short vacation until this is all over, right? You see that, right? That cost money, money I don't have. It's better for you if I go. Right?

"Well?"

Where it came from, he didn't know. It was like a long, silvery finger that poked him in the diaphragm and then drew a line up to his heart. The line turned red. He gazed at it in absolute shock. Then he looked up once before the world slipped from under his feet and sent him flying back. All the shadows were merged into a solid wall of darkness.

"Huh?" he said as if someone had spoken.

Before he hit ground, he was dead. His fingers held onto the cigarette which burned his skin and began to singe it until it went out. Darkness seemed to pounce over him then, and in a moment even the shadow was gone.

Munsen Donald closed the door to his small office in the firehouse and quickly got into his patrol car. He carried his emotional fatigue like a lump of lead in his stomach, lumbering, shoulders slouched, his head down. He groaned like a man twenty years older when he sat and adjusted his legs before starting the engine. Then he took a deep breath and headed out to make his one final sweep of the village before returning home to where he knew Lisa worked hard at finding distractions to keep herself from thinking. He knew that every once in a while she would finger the charm Anna had given him to give to her.

Part of his fatigue resulted from his regret in having to put together a report for the district attorney, listing and describing all the occasions when Henry Deutch called him to complain about things Anna Young allegedly had done. Anna didn't deny much of it when he had confronted her. Yes, she had thrown curses at him as he drove by. Yes, she had dropped chicken bones and eyes of newts on Henry's street. Yes, that was she who had stood in a circle she had drawn on the macadam outside his house one night months ago holding a candle and performing some incantation. Munsen told Henry there was no law against her being in the street.

Much of this was common knowledge. He couldn't, even if he wanted to, keep it from the district attorney, but somehow, Munsen knew that Anna understood and even didn't care. He drove on.

As his headlights swept the street before him, he caught sight of someone moving quickly over the sidewalk, crossing the street a little past Kayfields and then continuing east. George Echert's black Labrador mix lifted his head and rose from his stoop in front of the garage to look at the pedestrian. The dog stared a moment and then lowered his head without barking a comment.

Whoever it was apparently was no stranger to the dog, Munsen thought, or else had a way with animals. It reminded him of Aaron Baer's Dobermans. He continued to cruise slowly behind the dark figure. As the figure moved under the last streetlight on the main drag, he realized it was Anna Young wearing a black hooded rain coat. Something glittered in her hand. She paused to glance his way and then she entered her shop and was gone. He slowed to a stop. She didn't put on a light. Moments later, a light went on upstairs. What the hell had she been up to now? he wondered. He stared at the window a moment before making a U-turn and heading up the hill toward home.

Sad, he thought. It's sad that the only sign of life in the streets was this solitary woman returning from one of her mysterious trips into the darkness. Even the half dozen or so teenagers who often hung out around their automobiles, talking and listening to music were absent. Nervous parents had reined them in, he concluded. He couldn't imagine even contemplating Sandburg was dangerous, not his Sandburg, not this sleepy little place with its lifelong residents and wonderful resort history.

Where's it all leading?

What have we become?

He sped up. The lights of his home never looked as warm and welcoming as they did tonight. He couldn't wait to have Lisa in his arms, to hold her and make her feel that he would wrap his strength around her forever and ever and keep her from harm.

All he had to do was convince himself he could.

Fourteen

Like a large, round rubber bullet, the racquet-ball whizzed by Del's head, nearly trimming two inches off his hair. Michael Burke lowered his arms and slumped in disgust and disappointment. The sixty-seven-year-old semi-retired attorney had a remarkably slim, tight six-foot-two-inch body and a robust complexion. His shock of gray hair was as full and as thick as a man half his age. Aside from some deep lines in his forehead, especially when he grimaced, and some thin and slight web feet at the corners of his eyes, he offered little hint to anyone who wanted to guess his true age.

Adding flash to Michael's hold on youth, were his Paul Newman blue eyes. Other than when he was disgusted, his posture was true and straight, with a firmness that radiated strength and self-assurance. His second wife was twenty years younger, but no one doubted his ability to keep her satisfied. Vigorous, handsome, and very distinguished, Michael's name had often been bantered about as a potential political candidate, but he had never succumbed to that temptation.

"Where are you? She didn't put a spell on you or anything, did she?" Michael joked.

"Maybe she did," Del said. "Sorry."

"It's dangerous to play racquetball with half a racquet," Michael said. "C'mon. I'm okay with it. I broke a sweat. Let's have a mineral water," he suggested, and the two left the court for the small refreshment area in the club. They sat and ordered their waters.

"The secret," Michael said, "is leaving your baggage outside. Otherwise, you never relax, and you want to know something, Del, you don't do as good a job for your client. You know that adage about watched water never boils? Lay off and you'll think better."

"I'm beginning to fear that I'm way out of my league here, Michael," Del said. "My wife and my in-laws want me to find a graceful exit."

"Why?"

"They believe I'll look foolish defending her. They think it will put a stigma on my reputation."

Michael thought a moment and nodded.

"It's a funny profession. Most of the time, I'd say that wasn't so, Del, but I guess no one can look at Johnnie Cochran or Alan Dershowitz these days and not think of O.J. as well. Since most people think he was guilty, they have somewhat negative views of his lawyers, but, on the other hand, if you're in trouble with the police, you might want to hire them for just that reason."

"So what will I get when I go into private practice, all the supernatural defendants? Whose next, Dracula?" Del asked.

Michael laughed.

"Maybe. Hey, there might be a whole market for that out there, especially these days. When are you doing your pretrial motion?"

"I'm not. I've withdrawn it."

"What?"

"I learned late yesterday that the district attorney's investigator interviewed Sophie Potter, the receptionist at Henry Deutch's doctor's office. She admitted to having given Anna Young the medical details concerning Henry's condition, something Anna told me as well, and proudly."

"So she was very familiar with everything and it could be shown she knew what she was doing might be harmful, even lethal. Is that it?"

"Exactly," Del said. "Foreseeability. If I go through with the pretrial motion, I'll just give Paula Richards another opportunity to drive another nail into her legal coffin. Landers isn't going to dismiss the case now anyway."

"So it looks like you'll be in court."

"It does."

"There is another avenue to explore," Michael said.

Del nodded and then anticipated Michael's next suggestion.

"Anna Young is a bright woman, Michael. I'm not confident about having success going for diminished capability. I'm even afraid to suggest a psychiatrist to her. As far as I know, she might think psychiatry is an evil art."

"There have been many times when I would have agreed, especially as regards forensic psychiatry used by aggressive prosecutors and even totally unprincipled defense attorneys." Michael shook his head. "This is turning out to be quite a high-profile case. Some of my contacts in New York were asking me about it yesterday."

"Tell me about it. I've been avoiding a conversation with Lesley Stahl."

"Really?"

"Yesterday the clergy started to go on the offensive, too. They interviewed Father McDermott on the post-morning show on local television and he talked about the responsibility that goes with influencing people spiritually. With the way the community feels about that meditation group buying up all the big tax payers in the township and the loss of parishioners, the flight from organized religion, this is becoming much bigger than a woman's vendetta against the man she thinks was responsible for her mother's death."

"Which is a major irony for you, Del. Anna Young's mother had what, a stroke and a heart attack as a result of their aggravation? She believed or believes that's what caused her mother's death, so she turns around and fights fire with fire."

"I'm losing hope for a sympathetic jury. I'll never put her on the stand," Del said.

"You sure? She won't force it?"

He thought and nodded.

"I don't know."

"It's bad to go into court with these many unanswered questions, and you know there are so many other ways for Paula Richards to get the details into the case. What do you have at the moment, Del?"

"My big witness is a specialist in New York. He'll testify that Deutch wasn't put on sufficient nitroglycerin which might introduce the element of reasonable doubt."

"Um. Are you familiar with *People v. Kane* (213 NY 260)? There, the Appellate Court held that even though improper medical assistance may have contributed to a death, a defendant whose assault had also been a cause of the death could be held criminally liable. In short, if a felonious assault is *operative* as a cause of death, the causal cooperation of erroneous surgical or medical treatment does not relieve the assailant from liability for the homicide. It is only where the death is solely attributable to the secondary agency, and not at all induced by the primary one, that its intervention constitutes a defense. So, if Paula Richards can show she caused the heart attack, whether the doctor had him covered enough or not, might not be of primary concern. Even with the proper dosage, a shock to his system like that could have done it. I'm sure Paula Richards will introduce the findings in *People v. Kane*."

Del felt himself sink in the seat.

"I didn't know about that case."

Michael nodded.

"But they haven't tied Anna to the chicken and the rat or the cut wires."

"Inference might be enough for this jury. There's another decision that Paula Richards is liable to bring into the mix: *People v. Mama LaBouche*."

"Mama?"

"She was a voodoo queen practicing her art in the South Bronx. Good place for it these days. Anyway, the court found that when a victim can be shown to sincerely believe that what black magic is being directed at him can be lethal, and he does suffer heart failure soon after the alleged black magic was performed to his knowledge, the voodoo queen could be held liable and was. Do you know whether or not Henry Deutch was literally afraid of Anna Young's powers or had reason to believe in their effect on him?"

Del shook his head.

"Richards might know that to be true which will support her charges and add to her proofs."

Del nodded. He felt overwhelmed.

"What would you do, Michael?"

"Maybe it's time to see Paula Richards about plea bargaining, do a vertical charge bargain and reduce it to manslaughter and end it before it gets nuts."

Del stared silently, thinking.

"If you want, drop over to my office later and I'll have the cases pulled for you to peruse."

"Thanks, Michael."

"If I were starting out, I'd think about bringing you in with me, Del. You have the hunger and the drive I once had. Just don't waste it."

"Right. All you wise older men have the same line. Like unwise younger ones know when they're wasting and when they're not."

Michael laughed and then paused as the waitress headed toward them.

"Mr. Pearson." She held a radio phone out to him. "You have a call."

"Oh. Thanks," he said, taking it. "Hello?"

"Del, it's Clifford Grayson, *Times Herald Record*."

"How the hell did you find out where I was?"

"It's what I do best. I'm a reporter, remember?"

"Yeah, look, I have no comment to make and—"

"Wait. I wanted to know what you thought about the second murder in Sandburg."

"Second murder?"

"You haven't heard? A short-order cook at the one and only restaurant was found by some kids this morning. Someone sliced him from the top of his stomach up, practically to his throat, from what I hear. You know, there hasn't been a murder in that town since 1881 when some farmer was assassinated by his wife's lover. And now, in the space of two months, there are two!"

"Sliced?"

"Yeah, like someone in a sword fight," Grayson said. "Any comment about evil in the town?"

"No. Thanks," Del said, and hung up.

"What?" Michael asked.

Del told him and then rose.

"Where you going?"

"Down to Sandburg to see what it's all about."

"Any way this victim can be tied to her?"

"The whole town was tied to her it seems."

"You know what someone's going to start spreading, Del," Michael warned, "that she sees the evil spreading and has to kill it in whomever it resides. Be careful," he added, but Del wasn't sure if he was warning him to be careful around Anna or around the press.

He hurried into the locker room. He decided he would even skip a shower. Time, suddenly, was growing more and more important.

Munsen stood by and watched as Coleman and two other detectives combed the murder scene at the old school grounds. Onlookers were kept nearly a thousand yards away. Tony Monato's body had just been removed and was on its way to the morgue. Munsen was beginning to feel he was playing a role in some movie. This couldn't be happening in Sandburg. Petty robberies and burglaries, homeless drunks causing a disturbance, teenagers making too much noise or speeding, some acts of vandalism here and there, an occasional domestic dispute, that was all this small village had known for over a hundred years. For that reason, many residents felt immune to the disease of truly violent crime. Bad crime was something to watch on the evening news and something that took place in much bigger, more urban communities. Some of these people still left their cars and homes unlocked, for crissakes.

Coleman sauntered back toward him. He looked at the crowd that had gathered in the street.

"How long you know this guy?" he asked.

"Tony? Jeeze, he must've lived here nearly fifteen, sixteen years."

"Had an apartment over the restaurant?"

"Yeah."

"We'll go up there in a little while. Nothing much here," he said, and smiled, "except this."

He opened his gloved hand. Munsen stared at the pentacle.

"What the hell is that?"

"You better start reading up on witchcraft, Munsen. Here you are living in a town with a major witch and you don't know what this is?"

"I've seen 'em, but—"

"It's called a pentacle. They use it for protection against evil spirits."

Munsen felt the blood draining from his face. He shook his head.

"You think she did that?" he asked, nodding at the murder scene.

"We'll check for prints and see if we can tie this to her, of course, but it's quite a coincidence, don't you think? We'll wait for the medical examiner to check under his finger nails, too. My guess is he put up a little resistance and maybe ripped this off his assailant. Hopefully he got some skin."

"Jesus," Munsen said. "I would never think her capable of that."

"She was possessed," Coleman said, widening his eyes with exaggeration, "and won't even remember doing it."

He put the pentacle in a plastic bag.

"We better go see her and ask her where she was last night," Coleman said.

"Last night?"

"Yeah, Munsen. Hello? This happened last night, remember?"

Munsen stared hard into Coleman's face.

"What?"

"I saw her in the street last night, going home about eleven. I had just completed my reports for Richards. She was dressed in a black raincoat and I thought I saw . . ."

"What?"

"Something glitter in her hands."

"Like a long knife?"

"I don't know."

"Shall we find out?" Phil said, gesturing in the direction of his vehicle. Munsen nodded.

They started toward the car.

"Do you know of any reason why she would go after him?" Phil asked.

"No. Matter of fact . . ." Munsen paused.

"What?"

"Just the opposite happened day before yesterday. Aaron Baer, a hotheaded plumber, had some words with Tony over Anna Young. Tony defended her when Aaron called her a cock tease and challenged the idea that she had any powers at all, except sexual. He even believed she had something to do with vandalizing his truck tires as a way of punishing him for criticizing her."

"Hmm. Well, none of this makes logical sense, Munsen. Let's go see her. That's about the only pleasure I've got with this case," he added.

They got into the car and turned around to head toward Anna Young's. Just as they pulled up to the curb, Del Pearson drove up behind them.

Phil froze as soon as he stepped out of his vehicle and saw him. He looked at Munsen. Then he turned to Del.

"I'm beginning to wonder if she doesn't have some sort of power, counselor. This is a bit too much of a coincidence."

"Maybe she does," Del quipped. He looked at Munsen and then the three of them headed for the tailor shop. Anna was already at the door.

"Hmm, expecting us?" Phil queried with a coy smile.

Anna opened her shop door and stood back as they entered. The heavy sweet smell of peppermint was in the air.

"Cooking something, Miss Young?" Phil immediately asked.

She glanced at Del before replying.

"Just my power to see the future, Mr. Coleman," she said. When she looked at Munsen, he immediately looked down.

"Yeah, well, we're here to test your power about the immediate past, like last night," Phil said.

"You don't have to answer any questions," Del quickly advised her.

"Yeah, well, if she doesn't, we'll have to think about taking her to the station for a more formal interview."

"I have never feared questions," Anna said, now fixing her eyes on Coleman's.

"Yeah, well, you were seen in the streets about 11 P.M. last night. Did you happen to be returning from killing evil in another person, namely Tony Monato?"

"Mr. Monato is dead?"

"Someone did a poor job of removing his appendix. Your psychic powers didn't tell you that before we arrived?" Phil pursued.

"I did sense an evil force here last night and went out to drive it from the village," she admitted.

"Oh?" Phil said, glancing at Munsen.

"Anna," Del said, "as your attorney, I'm advising you not to say any more at this time."

"It will be all right, Mr. Pearson," she said with that

quiet confidence again. "Yes, Mr. Coleman, I felt the presence and I went out to drive it away from the people I protect."

"And how do you do that?" Phil followed.

Anna smiled. Then she turned and walked to the rear of her shop, paused at the stairway and plucked something that had been placed against the wall at the foot of the stairs. When she turned, Del's shoulders dropped along with what felt like his heart in his chest. Munsen uttered a small moan and Phil said, "Jeezes."

Anna held her mother's sword. She came toward them. Phil Coleman actually stepped back in a defensive posture.

"This is an athame," Anna began. "It is used for directing my power and my defense in the spiritual world. Some use it like the traditional wand to cast protective circles. It belonged to my mother and carries great power," she insisted.

Coleman was speechless a moment. Then, seeing how she remained back and kept the sword down, he regained his composure.

"Did you use that on Tony Monato?"

"No. It's not to be used as a physical weapon anyway."

"Did Tony Monato have the evil in him?" Coleman continued, using the tone of voice of a psychotherapist, soft, urging her to be forthcoming.

"I cannot say. I haven't seen him closely enough."

"I'm going to have to take that," Coleman said, nodding at the sword. "I will have to have tests run."

"Tests?" She smiled.

"Not to determine if it has supernatural powers, Miss Young, I assure you. Del," he continued, "I have good reason to arrest her."

"We'll surrender the sword," Del replied in a tired, defeated voice. "Anna?"

"It will be returned soon after?" she asked.

"Unless it's an exhibit in a courtroom, yes," Phil said.

She nodded and extended the handle toward him.

Coleman reached into his pocket quickly and produced a handkerchief. He held the very edge of the handle only and nodded at Munsen.

"Get the door," he ordered. Munsen jumped to do it and they took the sword out and put it carefully in Coleman's car trunk. Anna stood beside Del and watched them through the doorway. As soon as they had done so, Coleman returned to the door of the shop. He reached into his pocket and produced the plastic bag containing the pentacle.

"Is this yours?" he asked, holding it up.

Anna smiled and shook her head. She plucked her own from between her breasts and held it out to show him.

"You could have more than one," Phil said.

"I do, but mine are all heirlooms, Mr. Coleman, with significant spiritual histories. That is some cheap imitation, something you might buy in a souvenir shop."

"How can you tell that so quickly?"

She put her hand up, the palm facing the bag, and moved it back and forth.

"There's nothing there," she said. "No energy at all."

"Huh?" Coleman turned to Del. "Man, I'm beginning to feel sorry for you, and I never feel sorry for defense attorneys. We'll be back," he told Anna, and turned back to his vehicle, Munsen trailing behind.

Del closed the door and turned to her.

"I want you to tell me everything about last night, Anna."

"Very well, I will," she said, nodding. "Let's go have some tea."

"Forget the tea. Let's just talk."

"No, you need the tea, Mr. Pearson. I can feel the turmoil raging inside you. Please."

"All right," he said reluctantly. "We'll have tea."

He followed her up the stairs and sat in the living room staring up at the picture of her mother as Anna put up water. His cellular vibrated and he lifted it quickly out of his pocket.

"Pearson."

"Mr. Pearson, I have Mr. Douglas for you," Marge Anderson said.

"Fine."

"Del, where are you?" Norman Douglas asked immediately.

"I'm with my new client."

"Has she been arrested again?"

"No, not yet," Del said.

"The place is buzzing with this new wrinkle and we're being inundated with calls from the media, including the *New York Times*." Norman Douglas's excitement rang in his voice. "I've got a television crew from NBC in the outer office. They're looking for you and they've just heard about this second murder. I expect they'll be there shortly."

"Thanks for the warning. I'll do my best to avoid them all," Del pledged.

"Stay in touch. Things are breaking quickly here."

"Okay."

Del's sense of impending doom thickened and expanded. He rose and went to the nearest window facing the street. He had to go through Anna's bedroom to do so, but he didn't look at anything. He went right to the curtain and parted it to gaze out. There it was, starting. One crew had already set up cameras and a commentator was talking about the village. He saw some people on the street answering questions while reporters scribbled notes on pads. A

truck outfitted for a live remote cruised into the village and
pulled to the side.

"Something wrong?" Anna asked.

He glanced back at her and nodded at the window.

"You better come over here and look," he said.

She stood at his side and gazed out.

"The three-ring circus is going to become a ten-ring circus shortly. You won't be able to walk on those streets,
Anna."

She stared. He turned to look at her. Her profile was
extraordinary, her complexion suddenly, more like
alabaster, smooth and rich with just a slight tint of red at
the crest of her cheeks. Her blouse was open enough for
him to see her collar bone and just the hint of her cleavage
and the promise it made to his intrigued eyes. Now this
close to her, he could smell the strangest, yet most enticing
scent. Her full, perfectly shaped lips quivered. Then she
turned and smiled.

"It is nothing to fear, Mr. Pearson. It is more light and
light will drive back the darkness."

"Right," he said, shaking his head.

She kept those wonderful eyes penetrating his own.

"There was turmoil in you before this, but this is making it worse, stretching your spirit like a rubber band. Have
you never meditated?"

Del laughed.

"Scotch and soda, that's been my meditation."

"It's a Band-Aid," she said.

"Yeah, well let's talk about your problems first. Once
they're solved, we can turn to mine."

"We're intertwined now, Mr. Pearson. When spirits
cross paths like ours have, it is futile to treat one without
treating the other."

"Look, Anna . . ."

"You have nothing to fear from me."

"I'm not afraid."

"Yes, you are," she insisted. "Look," she said, nodding at the window, "what you will be facing out there. It's best to be prepared."

"How do you do that?" he asked.

She took his hand so subtly, he didn't realize it until she started out of the bedroom. He followed her to the living room, where she placed a candle in a holder on the coffee table. She lit it and then she folded her legs into a lotus sitting position, keeping her back perfectly straight.

"Do the same," she ordered. He hesitated. "Indulge me for ten minutes, Mr. Pearson. I wish to give you something."

"Well," he said, thinking that there was no one around at least. He got down on the floor and imitated her.

"Meditation is not thinking," she said. "It's not dreaming and it's not hypnotism. You want to remain aware of the here and the now, and stay conscious of the process. You will be aware, but you must eliminate the thought process which drains your energy. Meditation will transcend the thought process and allow you to relax and reduce stress."

"Yeah, I got a lecture this morning from a friend about relaxing. Almost lost my head to a racquetball." He gazed at the candle. "I know about meditation," Del said.

"But you have never permitted yourself the luxury of trying."

He shrugged.

"Like I said . . ."

"Concentrate on the candle flame. Put all the thoughts out of your mind, all the worries. Listen to your breathing," she said. Her voice was soothing. He did what she asked. Thoughts raged like streaks of lightning across his brow, but he fought them back and directed all his focus on the candle. She talked him deeper and deeper into it until his mind did clear. Had he hypnotized himself? He didn't know, but he was amazed at how much time had passed when she said, "That's good," rose, and put out the candle.

He blinked and watched her go to the kitchen where she retrieved two cups of tea and brought them back.

"How do you feel?" she asked.

He nodded.

"Fresh, lighter."

"It's a start," she said. "Many people refuse to try because they think it only has something to do with Far Eastern religions. It has everything to do with contacting something within us that is calm, rejuvenating. If you want to call it your soul, fine. There are those out there who have created other names, like the inner child, the oversoul, great spirit, whatever. For me it's a way to get deeper in touch with myself and from there, I can move into a more spiritual plane.

"I have gotten so I can meditate away distractions and stress instantly. My mother taught me how to do it a long time ago," she added, handing him his cup of tea. "There's some ivy in there," she said, "for protection and for healing."

He sipped it and smiled.

"Strange flavor." He took a deep breath.

"Okay," she said, "now we'll talk."

He set the cup down.

"Do you know anything about the death of Tony Monato?"

"Sometime before 10 P.M. last night, I was overtaken with the awareness of evil out there. I realized it wasn't coming from within the village so I went out to do what I could to keep it from entering. I didn't know until just a while ago that I had failed; that it had already come."

"Will your sword have anything on it that will implicate you in Tony's death, Anna?" he asked firmly.

"No," she said. "I never saw Tony Monato, but he has seen me."

"What does that mean?"

"I have felt his eyes on me," she said, "moving like two small marbles here," she said, running her fingers down over her breasts and to the small of her stomach, "and here, but I ignored it because there was something stronger to hold my energy and attention. I do not know why Tony was harmed, but yes, there was something evil swirling in him."

"Anna, it's important that you don't discuss these ideas with people, especially press people. They'll distort them and sensationalize them and make you look like something you're not. I have a lot of research to do and I'm not going to return to my office." He took out a pad and a pen. "Here is my cellular phone number."

"I have no phone."

"You can get to one, I'm sure," he said, "should you need me immediately."

"You will know when I know," she said.

"Anna."

"Leave the number," she relented with a smile. Then she stared at him with a more serious expression. "You have another problem, Mr. Pearson, something that doesn't involve me."

"All of us have problems," he said quickly.

"No, yours is something more. Let me look at your hand again."

"I haven't got time for this now, Anna. There's so much to do."

"It will get done," she assured him. "Indulge me."

He stuck out his hand and she held it softly in her left

hand while she ran her fingers over his palm, tracing the lines, her eyes closed. It gave him an opportunity to look at her directly, uninhibited, almost voyeuristically. He could see himself kissing those lips. The thought of it reminded him of himself as an adolescent, romanticizing and fantasizing about kissing Elaine Wilson, the prettiest girl in his seventh grade class. He imagined it would be so wonderful and so explosive, his whole body would tingle.

"You are trying to have a child and you have not succeeded," she suddenly said.

"What?" He pulled his hand away as if it was on a hot stove.

"It's tearing away at the fabric of your manhood," she continued. "This is the weight of your guilt and the cause of much of your turmoil."

"How can you . . . that's my private business, Anna," he said sharply. He rose. "I have to get back to work."

"I can help you," she said, looking up at him. Leaning forward, she revealed more of her wonderful bosom.

"Right now," he said, "We've got to concentrate on my helping you."

He started away, practically fleeing.

"Remember what I told you," she called after him. "We are now intertwined. One cannot be independent of the other or we will fail."

"I'll talk to you later," he said. "Stay away from those reporters."

He hurried down the stairs, through the shop, and out the front door into the pathway of a dozen cameras. He heard them clicking away. A light went on. He raised his arm and charged toward his car.

"Mr. Pearson. Is your client being charged with another murder?" he heard someone shout, and that was followed by a slew of questions, all merging. He unlocked his car door and practically lunged in, shoving the key into the ignition.

"No comment," he screamed at the mob of reporters and pulled away from the curb.

Their questions continued and fell behind like a ribbon of smoke drifting back, hovering, and then turning in another direction.

How in hell could she touch his hand and know his deepest pain? he wondered, and for the first time, he really considered the possibility that Anna Young had the power to have spiritually murdered Henry Deutch.

Fifteen

"Tony's been with me almost sixteen years now," Roy Kayfield said. "He started as a dishwasher and gradually, I taught him everything and he got better at it than I did," he added as he led Phil Coleman and Munsen through the rear of the restaurant to a side door. It opened on a small stairway.

"He always lived up here?" Phil asked, gazing up the tunnel-like stairway lit by a single, naked low wattage bulb that dangled like an afterthought.

"Not in the very beginning, but about six or seven months into it," Roy said, turning back. "I trusted him with the place and it was good to have someone here all the time. When we were really busy during the heyday of the Catskill resort period, Tony would keep the bar open until three. He was up at six prepping the kitchen the next morning. The guy ran on . . . I don't know . . . pure energy or something."

"Didn't he ever have a girlfriend or anything?" Phil continued as they started up the stairs.

"There was someone once, a chambermaid from the Pioneer Country Club in Greenfield Park. I used to think they might get married. Her name was Sally Jean or Sally Rae, something like that. It's so long ago now that I can't remember. She was kinda dumpy," he added, looking back, "but Tony and her got along enough to shack up once in a while. Then she suddenly disappeared. A lot of those hotel workers were transient in those days. You'd never know if they'd be to work."

"And after that?"

"Nothing, no one. He wasn't gay or anything," Roy quickly added.

"You know what they used to say, 'Only his hairdresser knows for sure,'" Phil quipped.

Roy and Munsen laughed as they all stepped up to the landing. There was no door to the apartment. You were just in Tony's bedroom.

"No kitchen up here. Just the bedroom and a bathroom. I guess it's not really much of an apartment. You didn't need a kitchen with what we got downstairs and there's a television down there, so Tony was comfortable. Jeeze, I can't believe he's actually dead, murdered."

"You have any ideas about it?" Philip Coleman asked as he perused the sloppily made double bed and the scratched and worn light maple dresser. One of the drawers was partly open with an undershirt hanging over the edge. On the night stand was an ashtray full of cigarette butts. A cross with a quite battered and chipped Jesus hung over the headboard.

On the dresser was an Olympus 35 millimeter with a telephoto lens and a wide-angle lens beside it. There was a packet of film as well.

"No. I can't think of anyone who'd want to do that to Tony. He'd get into an argument with someone once in a while, like he did with Aaron Baer the other day," Roy added, looking at Munsen who nodded, "but the next day, he'd be like there was never a word between them. That was his way. I never saw him hold a grudge or even complain all that much about people, except of course, Henry Deutch. Tony couldn't stand being near the man, but then again, few people could.

"When I told him Henry was found dead, Tony just nodded as if he had expected that a man with that much venom in him would just naturally poison himself one day."

"What do you think he was doing over at the school that late at night?" Phil asked.

Roy shook his head.

"Got me. Only places Tony ever went was down to the creek occasionally to fish or over to Centerville to see a cousin, Orlando Goya, a handyman at the Dew Drop Inn, but last I heard, Orlando went to New York. Tony was a loner. The only outside interest he had was photography. That's a pretty expensive camera and expensive lens," Roy said, nodding at the camera on the dresser. "Practically the only expensive thing he ever owned. He took some great nature pictures. There's a bunch in that carton," Roy said, nodding at a carton on the floor by the dresser. "He was hoping to sell some to a magazine. I know he was saving his money for a trip to Manila. He has family there and always said before he died, he wanted to visit. Too late now. Damn, it makes me sick. He's such a part of this place, it's just not going to seem the same . . . to anybody.

"I'll take care of the funeral and all, Munsen. Be sure the people who gotta know, know, okay?" Roy said.

"Yeah, we'll let you know about it," Phil said quickly.

He went over to the dresser and started to look through the drawers.

"What do you expect to find?"

"Anything," Phil said, "that might give us a lead. This is all his stuff? What's in here and that closet?"

"That's it. I gotta go back down and start on some of the menu. Thing like this will bring a crowd here tonight and they'll want to eat," Roy said. "Damn, I wish it was Tony making it for them."

He shook his head and started down the stairs.

"Go into the closet and check the pockets on every pair of pants and jacket," Phil told Munsen.

"Right."

The two worked silently, turning over clothes, sifting through garments. Phil was down to the last dresser drawer and had just lifted some underwear when he cried out.

"Jesus!"

"What?" Munsen said. Phil remained crouched over the drawer. He looked back and smiled.

"Take a gander," he said, and Munsen stepped over to look at the pictures of Anna Young.

They were pictures obviously taken through a window and in each of them, Anna was in one state of undress or another. One picture in particular was a rather clear shot of her drying her hair with a towel right after a shower.

"Huh?" Phil said.

Munsen looked like he had lost his breath. He studied the pictures a moment and then looked at Phil Coleman.

"Some kind of a stalker voyeur, maybe. Maybe she found out and that was why she did it. Evidence," he said with a wide smile and put all the pictures into a neat pile. He found a paper bag and ripped it to wrap the pictures.

"That's not much of a reason to slice someone from the navel to the throat, Phil," Munsen said.

"She don't need much. It's evil," he said, grimacing as if in pain. "Evil be in this town. Got to get it out." He laughed, shook his head, gazed around quickly, and then nodded at the stairway. "Let's go. I can't wait for forensics to get their paws on that sword and this pentacle," he said patting his pocket.

He bounced down the old wooden steps, invigorated by his discoveries. Munsen followed, sadly, lumbering, wishing he had taken his father's advice and stayed in the armed services.

Rather than return to his office where he knew the media lay in wait, Del had a courier bring over as much of the Rosario material the district attorney's office had at this stage. In *People v. Rosario*, 9 N.Y.2d 286 (N.Y. 1961), *cert. denied*, 368 U.S. 866 (1961), the court established the Rosario rule which required complete disclosure of all pre-trial statements of prosecution witnesses. Sitting in Michael's law library, Del began to peruse the interviews and easily began to see the case Paula Richards was structuring against Anna.

Most of the people Paula Richards would use as witnesses actually seemed eager and proud to reveal Anna's attitudes about Henry Deutch and actions directed toward destroying him. Del got the sense that they believed they were doing Anna some good service by supporting her claims of spiritual power and authority. People like Melvin Bedik and Gina Carnesi talked about Anna's medical powers, but also made clear that she felt threatened by Henry Deutch and whenever they were in her presence for treatment, she voiced her intention to rid the town of "this evil force." The term kept popping up.

There were a number of people who admitted to attending a occultlike funeral for Anna's mother where she was quoted by all present as vowing to destroy Henry

Deutch. The local barber and a retired businessman testified to Anna gathering up Henry's freshly cut hair and
rushing off to do "whatever she does with those sort of
things."

A number of people had witnessed Anna's throwing of
curses, scattering of bones, frog eyes, and the like in
Henry Deutch's path, and many had seen Henry's reac-
tions, his rage and irritation. They were more than eager
to describe his frenzied anger in detail, rejoicing in the
way his "eyes popped" and the way he "seemed to lose
breath, clutching that hollow hole where he was supposed to have a heart."

All of the official police visits to Henry's property were
dated and described. A quick comparison with Henry's
medical records and dates of doctor's visits supported Del's
fear that the theory these incidents might have caused further physical degeneration was indeed going to be a primary point in Paula Richards' case.

Paula Richards was clearly building the motive, the acts,
and premeditated malice aforethought arguments. As of
yet as far as Del knew, the district attorney didn't have concrete forensics to put Anna at the death scene, nor did she
clearly tie her in any way to the final acts of harassment,
which could arguably be described as the most severe, but
she had somehow found an expert in witchcraft who
attested to the use of butchered chickens and dead rats as a
way of delivering curses of death.

What was most disturbing, however, was an interview
with Deutch's son Wolf, who claimed his father was in a
"disheveled, maddened state of mind, babbling about the
power of the evil eye." Paula Richards could now make an
argument that Henry Deutch believed Anna's antics could
harm him and therefore, make her actions fit more easily
into the "but for" rule as established by the case precedent

Michael Burke had cited, a case Michael had set up for him to read.

Although she hadn't done it yet, it was clear that Paula Richards would be gathering specialists to testify to the probability of Anna causing Henry Deutch to suffer a fatal heart attack. The confident, flamboyant, and ambitious prosecutor was already giving more frequent interviews on television and in the newspapers, asserting her determination to lay blame and responsibility where it belonged, to establish what she characterized as the state's need to firmly determine that people could harm other people psychologically and emotionally, especially when the victims were weak and sickly, and therefore, the modus operandi was not some far-fetched theory, but as real and as deadly as a sharp knife in the heart.

These references to knives on the radio interviews and local television stations was obviously Paula Richards attempt to tie Anna to Tony Monato's death. It would, Del feared, have the effect of creating even more hysteria around her and would most certainly poison the jury pool.

Del realized he had to start interviewing some of these Sandburg residents himself and quickly. He decided to begin with Munsen Donald, the man who was on the scene for most of the alleged harassment. The problem now was how to move around that town without a trail of reporters and cameras behind him. He had no choice though.

After reading some of the cases Michael Burke had suggested, Del rose, intending to return to Sandburg, but his cellular vibrated and he stopped on the way out to answer. It was Jackie, and she sounded quite distraught.

"You've got to come home and get them out of here, Del," she practically screamed. "They've been ringing the doorbell all morning and the moment I opened the garage, they pounced around my car. I literally had to throw them out and then I closed the garage and didn't leave. I'm a prisoner in my own home!"

"Easy, honey, easy. What are you talking about?"

"These cameras and reporters. The phone rang so much, I just took it off the cradle. How did they get our number?"

"They have ways."

"I can't stand it anymore, Del."

"All right, all right. They're not permitted to be on our property."

"They're not. They're in the street, but it's the same thing."

"I'll see what I can do," he muttered.

"That's not the worst of it," she continued. "Dad called just a minute ago."

"What?"

"Reporters found out his relationship to you and they've gone to the bank to ask him questions. Stupid questions like do we believe in witchcraft? Someone even asked him if he would loan money to a witch? He's so angry, he can hardly talk on the phone. I never heard him like this. My mother just cries."

"I'm coming home," he promised. "I'm going to call the police first."

"I can't stand all this!"

"I know. Let me try to do something about it."

"There's only one thing to do about it," she said in a calmer, harder voice.

"I'll be home soon," he said, and shut her off.

Michael and his secretary were staring at him. Del hadn't realized how loudly he had been talking.

"Jackie," he said, shrugging. "Those reporters are camped on our front lawn."

"Legal aid attorneys aren't supposed to have all this attention, Del. You're going to make Johnnie Cochran jealous."

"Thanks a lot."

"Hey, I'm here if you need me," Michael said.

Del nodded and then went to the phone to call the sheriff's office. He got the sheriff himself, Sam Siegal, which was testimony to Del's new notoriety, something he would much rather not have.

"Mr. Pearson. How can I help you?"

Del quickly explained the situation.

"Well, they have a right to be on public streets, unless they're blocking traffic or something. I'll send two patrol cars over there and keep them off your property."

"Thanks, Sheriff."

"Del," Michael said as soon as Del hung up. "You should go right over to see Landers and get a gag order. All these press releases are prejudicing your client and making it impossible for her to get a fair trail in this venue."

"Right," Del said, chastising himself for not thinking of that. "Thanks, Michael."

He shot out of the office and for a moment actually stood in the parking lot next to his vehicle, unsure of where he should go first: home or to the judge's chambers? He owed his client a responsibility, but his wife was going bonkers. If only he could instantly meditate like Anna, he thought. Visualizing her trapped in her shop, waiting for some instructions from him, pushed him to decide to go first to the judge.

Maybe that was a mistake. Maybe that was something he would soon regret. Maybe, he was like a man possessed. There just wasn't enough time to decide and the longer he waited, the more difficult it would all be.

Unfortunately, he couldn't get in to see Judge Landers

as quickly as he would have liked. The judge was in the middle of a plea bargain negotiation and Del had to sit and wait for nearly an hour before the judge could see him.

Arthur Landers was crusty old school, formal and very firmly in control of his courtroom at all times. He once made an attorney leave and change his tie because the tie he was wearing was too loud. At five feet eight, sixty-three-year-old Arthur Landers seemed capable of intimidating the President of the United States. There was a courtroom joke about him arriving at Heaven's gates with Mother Theresa and Winston Churchill. God sat before them and asked Mother Theresa to tell him why she belonged in Heaven. "Because I've devoted my whole life to the sick and the poor," she said, and he nodded and let her in. He turned to Churchill, and Churchill said, "Because I gave my country the spirit to stand up to the worst evil ever, Nazi Germany." God nodded and let him in, and then he turned to Judge Landers and said, "What do you have to say?" Landers looked at God and said, "You're in my chair."

Landers sat behind his large dark mahogany desk and folded his hands as he leaned forward.

"What can I do for you, Mr. Pearson?"

Del quickly explained what was happening and why it would poison the jury pool and therefore prejudice his defense.

"I've been expecting you for days now," the Judge replied. "I didn't expect Richards to complain about your pretrial publicity."

"I know, Your Honor, but it's just gotten out of hand and—"

"I will issue the gag order immediately," he said.

"Thank you, Your Honor."

The judge sat back and nodded, almost smiling.

"I was expecting you to ask me to relieve you," he said with a twinkle in his cool, gray eyes.

"I guess I'm like Gary Cooper in *High Noon*," Del said. "It seems to me I've got to stay."

The judge did smile.

"One of my favorite movies." He glanced at the clock and then at Del. "Paula Richards is coming on the noon train."

"I'll be here," Del said, smiling, and left, somehow a little buoyed.

Munsen's beeper went off. He had returned to the scene of Tony Monato's death after Coleman shot off to get his evidence to the lab. One of the other detectives, Ted Davis, an African-American man in his late twenties, called him over to look at something about five yards from the site where Tony's body had been found.

"Didn't notice this before, but it sure is strange," he said. "What do you make of it?"

"What?"

Ted pointed to a circle drawn in the dirt.

"See this?"

Munsen swallowed what felt like a lump of lead and nodded.

"Yeah."

"Make any sense to you?"

"Yeah," he said in a tone of exhaustion. "It's something she does."

"Who, the witch?"

Munsen nodded.

"I'd better get a picture of this," Ted said excitedly.

Munsen shook his head and that was when the beeper buzzed. He glanced at it and realized it was his home number. The sight of it put a trickle of ice down his back and made his heart skip a beat.

"I gotta make a call," he muttered, and hurried back to the patrol car. When he got in, he took a deep breath and then called home. Lisa answered on the first ring.

"Munsen?"

"Yeah, babe," he said, holding his breath.

"It's good," she said. "It's good, Munsen. I'm okay. It's good."

"Christ Almighty," he cried, the tears streaming out of his eyes. "Thank God."

"I'm okay," she said, and laughed.

"I'm coming right home," he said. He had to hold her in his arms.

"I was hoping you would say that," she said, with another laugh trickling.

"On my way."

He started the engine, whipped the car around and shot off, swiping the tears away as he accelerated up the hill.

Anna, he thought. Thank you.

Sixteen

By the time Del arrived home, there were two Sullivan County Sheriff's Department patrol cars in front of the house. The officers were leaning against their vehicles, arms folded, and actually conversing casually with the reporters whose cars and trucks lined the road. As soon as Del started to turn into the driveway, the reporters and cameramen bolted toward him. He had to wait in his vehicle for the garage door to rise and the reporters swarmed over the driveway. Del stepped out. Questions were shouted at him. He held up his hand and turned to the deputies.

"Can you get these people off my property, please," he demanded.

As the deputies began to move them back, the reporters continued shouting questions, some designed obviously to inflame.

"Does your client belong to a satanic cult?"

"Has she harmed any children in the village?"

"Does she perform blood rituals?"

"Is it true she talks to the dead and was told to kill Henry Deutch?"

"Does she hear voices like the Son of Sam?"

Del held up his hands again and they all quieted down at the foot of his driveway.

"Judge Landers has issued a gag order. Neither I nor the district attorney's office is permitted to comment on this case. You're all wasting your time here," he added, got back into his car and drove into the garage. The door came down behind him. He caught his breath and then he got out and entered the house.

From the garage, the entrance to the house was directly through a small entryway and into the kitchen. Jackie wasn't there and there was a heavy silence greeting him. He paused, listened for a moment, and then continued through to the dining room and then into the hallway.

Jackie was sitting in the living room. She was so still, he almost didn't see her and was about to shout for her. All the shutters were drawn closed and there were no lamps on. She stared at the floor and looked like she hadn't heard him come home.

"Hey," he said.

She looked up slowly.

"Where were you? You said you were coming right over."

"I had to see the judge first," he said. "Partly to see if I could put a stop to all this," he added, gesturing toward the window. "I asked him to issue a gag order to prevent Paula Richards from conducting all these interviews that will in effect prejudice the jury."

"Prejudice the jury?" She turned slightly toward him. "That's what you were worrying about?"

"Yes," Del said. "If it continues, we couldn't find twelve people who weren't influenced, mostly by the most ridiculous assertions you can imagine. They're already asking questions about blood rituals and Satanic cults."

"How do you know it's not true?"

"What?"

"My mother's friend Peggy Schmitt, whose husband owns the Sandburg Sand and Gravel Company, told her this woman you're defending has been performing ritual sex abuse on the village children, tempting them first to come into her shop to see the magic room."

"What? Magic room?"

"She performs little tricks to tempt them in. Then she gets them to strip and she has them touch each other to see her do more tricks."

"My God! That is so outrageous and false. If there was any validity to it, don't you think some parent would have gone to the police by now?"

"Most people are afraid to get involved and would just tell their children to stay away. That's what Peggy Schmitt says."

"It's all a bunch of crap spread by people who have nothing better to do with their lives."

"How do you know for sure, Del? Plenty of times you've told me you couldn't be sure your clients were innocent, but you believed you had to defend them, that it was their constitutional right for you to assume their innocence and give them the best possible defense."

"This is different. I'm convinced she doesn't deserve to be charged with premeditated murder."

"Why?"

"This woman isn't evil, Jackie. She's . . ."

"What?"

"Overly zealous about good, if anything. Anyone who practices some offbeat spirituality is considered dangerous or Satanic these days. She's harmless, for crissakes, and for your mother's information—and I'm surprised you never pointed it out—a group of citizens from Sandburg were the ones who put up her bail money, remember?"

"The story about that is they're in her cult. She has them under a spell."

"Oh, God," he cried. "Do you know who these people are? Bakers, shopkeepers, a retired accountant, chicken farmers. What's she supposed to have done, turned the village into a bunch of zombies?"

"I'm just telling you what's going around. It's a fact that all those people who have helped her also have left their churches and their synagogue. The clergy themselves have been complaining about it. It's in today's paper and Reverend Carter was on the radio taking phone calls this morning."

He shook his head.

"You listened to that?"

"A little," she confessed.

"Totally ridiculous."

"Why are you so adamant and determined about this woman? Is there something you're not telling me, Del?"

"What's that supposed to mean, Jackie?" he demanded when she turned away.

"There have been other phone calls."

"What other phone calls?"

She shook her head. The tears were streaming down her cheeks now.

"Jackie?"

He went to her and sat beside her.

"What's going on? What other calls?"

She took a deep breath.

"Someone's been calling on and off all morning, warning me that you're . . . you're . . ."

"What?"

"Sleeping with that woman, that you've been put under one of her spells."

"That's so damn . . ."

"What?" she said, turning.

Of course he could deny it. He hadn't done it, but had it crossed his mind? Had he had a fleeting fantasy? It was as if someone had been spying on his subconscious.

"Plain vicious. There are people out there who revel in this kind of thing, Jackie. They enjoy tearing people apart because their own lives are so miserable."

"We've been hearing a lot about her promiscuity and not just from vicious crank callers, Del. Is it true that she parades about in clothes that are so thin, you can see everything? There are also stories about her seducing some of the older men."

"That's another ridiculous statement. What is your mother doing, reading all the garbage and listening to all the stupid gossip, Jackie?"

"She doesn't read garbage, Del, and it's not just coming from gossiping women. Respected businessmen have told similar things to my father."

"Oh. I should have expected that."

"Damn this case. Look what it's doing to all of us. Dad wants to talk to you after dinner," she added. It almost sounded like "The principal wants you to report to his office."

Del felt his face redden, the blood rising up his neck like milk boiling over.

"I hope it's not another lecture about the direction I'm taking professionally, Jackie. I've been polite and patient with him. You know that."

"He's only looking out for us, Del."

"And what am I doing, making chopped liver?" He rose as if he had sat on a hot seat.

She glared up at him. Even in the poorly lit room, he could see her eyes crystalizing with tears.

"We're fighting," she declared. She made it sound like a discovery she had just made. It nearly brought a smile to his lips, but he fought it back, deciding it wouldn't be politically smart.

"I don't want to, that's for damn sure. I've got enough of a war out there," he said, nodding at the window again.

"Can't you get off this case, Del?" she pleaded. "You've never defended anyone accused of murder anyway. You don't have the experience."

"Thanks for the vote of confidence."

"It's not that I don't think you're a good lawyer, Del. You're going to be a great one someday. Maybe this is all happening too fast. Dad says it's like a fighter taking on the champ after only some preliminary bouts."

"Oh, is that what he says? Paula Richards is supposed to be the champ and I'm some ham-and-egg lug?"

"You're deliberately misinterpreting everything."

"I am not. Look, Jackie, every criminal attorney who is presently defending someone accused of murder had to start with someone, had to do it without having done it before. What sort of a reason to excuse myself from this case is that for me to give to Judge Landers?"

"Dad can help with him, I'm sure," she said.

Now he really felt the heat rise. It threatened to take off the top of his head.

"The day I need to go to your father to help me with judges and clients and courtroom procedure is the day I quit being a lawyer," he said, clipping his words sharply.

"That's not what I meant and you know it," she fired back.

"I need a drink of something cold," he declared. Time out is what he really meant. He turned and quickly went to the kitchen, his heart feeling like it wanted to rap a hole through his breastbone and scream.

She didn't follow as he expected she might so they could start to work their way back.

I'm just wasting time here, he thought, wasting important time.

The phone started ringing. He stared at it.

"I'm not answering it anymore," she cried from the living room. "You talk to your public."

It continued to ring. Finally, he lifted the receiver.

"Yes?" he practically shouted into the mouthpiece.

"Mr. Pearson?" he heard a raspy voice say.

"Who is this?" There was silence. "Who the hell is this?"

"She killed Tony. Go to her mother's grave. You'll find a freshly dug up area right in front of the tombstone. Dig it up again. The knife she used is there. I'm telling you before I tell the police so you can get her to confess and cut a deal."

"Who is this?"

"A friend of the truth," he said, and there was a loud click and then silence.

"Hey?"

The phone felt hot in his hand. He cradled it and stared at the wall. Whoever it was spoke as if he were talking through a funnel.

"So?" Jackie said, coming to the doorway. "Another vicious crank caller?"

"Worse," he said. He turned and put his glass down on the counter. "I've got to go."

"Del," she called after him. He turned in the doorway. "Won't you think again about all this?"

"What if I did quit the case, Jackie? What happens next time when I'm asked to defend an unpopular or distasteful client? Do I check with your father first and see how it will affect the bank or with your mother to see what the women's associations are saying?"

"You're missing the point, Del."

He shook his head.

"I don't think so, Jackie. I think I fully understand the point and it's not pleasant. You think about all this once again, think about what you want us to be. Let's not lose that edge, those qualities that will make us something special. You wanted that, too."

She stared.

"I'm afraid, Del," she revealed.

"What?"

"There's something else going on out there," she said, gazing out the kitchen window as if something was floating near the house. "It frightens me."

Her voice cracked and her tears thickened in her eyes. He stepped forward to embrace her and kiss her softly.

"There's nothing else out there, Jackie. She's just some woman who was brought up to believe in a more spiritual world. She's offbeat, maybe even peculiar, but she's not the vicious, premeditated killer Paula Richards wants everyone to think she is. Besides, she's not what's important to Paula or her followers. She's a device, a stepping stone to lift Paula to higher political goals. And those clergymen who fear her have good reason. They're not providing the kind of spiritual guidance people need nowadays. They're just interested in protecting their safe little sanctuaries. So you see," he said, smiling, "I'm David out to slay the Goliath. You'll be proud of me," he promised, kissed her again, and hurried out.

She looked after him a moment.

"David had his Bathsheba," she muttered.

*   *   *

"Donald," Munsen said, but he didn't bellow into the receiver as usual. He was too full of joy to project any unpleasantness to anyone. He thought he could even be cordial and sweet to the dead Henry Deutch at this moment. He gazed at Lisa, who sat at the kitchen table holding her glass of champagne. She and he had toasted their good fortune. She looked so young to him, just the way she was when they were going together after he had left the army, fresh and innocent and so pretty she made his heart ache.

He listened, the smile disappearing.

"Okay. I'll meet you at the fire station. That's where my office is," he said. "I'll take you there."

"What's wrong?" Lisa asked.

"That was Anna Young's lawyer, Pearson. He received an anonymous phone call telling him where to find the weapon used to kill Tony Monato."

"Really?"

"It's supposedly buried in Anna's mother's grave plot."

"Oh."

"He wants me to take him there so if there is a knife, he can't be accused of deliberately mishandling evidence. As an officer of the court, he has to turn it over to the district attorney, just the way O.J.'s lawyers had to turn over that knife, remember?"

She nodded.

"You don't think she actually killed Tony Monato, do you, Munsen?"

"I gotta go," he said.

"Munsen? Why would she do that?"

"I don't know," he said, dropping his eyes toward the floor too quickly.

"Yes, you do," she returned before he could move another step. "What?"

He hesitated.

"Tell me," she demanded.

"Tony was a Peeping Tom with a camera. He took dirty pictures of her and she might have known it," he revealed. "Maybe that made him full of evil or something. I don't know. It's not my job."

Lisa nodded, saddened. She fingered the charm around her neck.

"I hope it's not true, Munsen," she said.

He gazed at her.

"Me neither," he said, smiled, and left to meet Del Pearson.

Munsen found the hamlet was still busy with far more traffic and pedestrians than normal, despite the judge's gag order. Looking for a new sound bite to open their articles and news reports with, reporters were now swooping down on every available citizen of Sandburg. Anyone who was actually an eyewitness to one of Anna's rituals was treated like gold.

As Munsen turned the corner to head toward the fire station, he saw a group surrounding Tilly Zorankin who was giving them a lecture on the power of the evil eye. With her Confederate gray hair hastily brushed down, hanging stringy and thin, and her face ridiculously over-made, she looked like some old witch herself, a fugitive from Halloween searching for a place to set down her broom.

The traffic, the noise, the people scurrying about gave Sandburg the circus atmosphere everyone had anticipated. However, some of the vendors and shopkeepers who still had viable businesses were smiling. Kayfields was, as Roy had predicted, packed. Some of his regulars like Charlie Trustman and Burt Connolly had donned aprons and were working behind the counter and working as waiters. There was a line of cars at Echert's gas pumps. George's lun-cheonette was sold out of newspapers hours ago and already out of some cigarette brands. Children and dogs were running through the streets, weaving in and out of the small clumps of people. The very air was electric, full of the static generated by the sounds and the sights.

It disgusted and disturbed Munsen Donald. To him it was like some unmanned fire horses bucking and twisting beyond control and whenever anything like that happened in his quiet little village, it filled him with anxiety. Something else that was terrible lingered and loomed in the background, encouraged by all this, ready to exacerbate and intensify the already explosive situation. How would it end?

Del Pearson arrived at the station soon after Munsen.

"If they see us riding through town," Munsen explained, "we'll have a caravan right on our tail. I got my car parked in the rear. You get into the rear seat and get down and I'll cruise by as if I'm just taking a routine ride."

"Fine," Del said, and did just as Munsen asked. He felt silly crouched below the window, but nothing that happened these days really surprised him anymore.

"Okay," Munsen said, announcing the all-clear, and Del sat up.

They were already outside the village. The midafternoon sun had fallen behind a wall of bruised clouds rolling out like a dirty white blanket from the northeast.

"Going to rain later," Munsen predicted.

The wind was already rustling the leaves and causing thinner branches to wag like forbidding fingers. The woods thickened as they continued, and Del felt as if he was descending into some netherworld inhabited by all the spirits and goblins Anna Young saw through either her special eyes or exceedingly paranoid orbs.

"How far is it?"

"Just another minute," Munsen said. He explained how old the cemetery was and what had happened to the church that had once administrated and cared for the graveyard.

"It figures she would bury her mother in such a cemetery," Del muttered.

"Well, the other cemeteries are run by the active churches and the synagogue here and they wouldn't have been exactly hospitable. Anna knew that."

"Were there many people at the funeral?"

"Don't know. It was held at night. I think only people who had something to do with her mother and her attended," Munsen explained as the cemetery came into view on Del's right.

"Burial at night. I read about it." He shook his head.

"I know," Munsen said, smiling. "She's something else."

He pulled in and stopped. Del and he got out and Munsen went to his trunk and took out a shovel. Then the two of them approached Gussie Young's tombstone and plot.

"You couldn't recognize the voice on the phone at all, huh?"

"No. Whoever it was disguised it."

"Man though?"

"I wouldn't swear to it," Del said. "It was too distorted."

"Sick bastards," Munsen said. "So anxious to do her harm."

Del gazed at him for a moment.

"You like her?"

Munsen glanced at him and looked away.

"I don't dislike her." He smiled. "I never liked Henry Deutch."

Del nodded and they stopped at the plot and gazed at the earth.

"Looks like something over here," Munsen said, tapping the earth on his left. An area did look recently turned over and smoothed clumsily. He and Del looked at each other and then Munsen put the spoon to the ground and his foot on the back of it. He pushed and began to dig around the area. It took only three small spoonfuls to reach the knife housed in what looked like ordinary kitchen plastic wrap. Munsen carefully extracted it from the ground and placed it on the ground before himself and Del.

"Blood," Munsen said, pointing to the long blade. "It looks like one of those replicas of old time knives, the kind you see for sale at Renaissance Fairs. Medieval. Something Anna would have, I suppose."

Del nodded glumly. The two of them continued to just stare at the knife as if they hoped it would disappear before their very eyes.

"This could wrap it up for her and you," Munsen muttered.

Del continued to nod and then stopped.

"Wrap," he said. "Yes, why?"

"Huh?" Munsen asked.

"Why would she wrap it in this stuff? Why not just bury it in the ground?"

"Who knows? She has all these very specific steps and ways she takes with all her mumbo-jumbo."

"Maybe," Del said. He looked at Munsen. "And maybe someone wanted to be sure the blood would be visible."

"Yeah, I guess it protects that, but it also protects the fingerprints," Munsen added pointedly. "It simply could be that she's not a professional killer. She would think first about her ritual procedures and not worry about incriminating evidence. Believe me," he added, "I didn't want to find this."

Del raised his eyebrows.

"Oh?"

"Causing Henry Deutch's death almost made sense," Munsen continued as he carefully palmed the knife in the wrapper. "I could practically forgive her for it. I had my suspicions about how much she was responsible for anyway. A few times when Deutch called me, I suspected he might have done things to put blame on her or get me to arrest her."

"Like what?"

"Paint a cross on his own window, claim there was a cat's skull on his steps, stuff like that. Maybe even he hung the chicken himself and put the rat in his own bed. Everything was locked in that house. I had to break the door in. He just had a heart attack when he least expected it. That's what I wanted to believe, but . . ."

"But?"

"But killing Tony is a whole other thing, no matter what he did to her."

Del nodded and gazed at the knife.

"Who could have called me and why?" Del mused.

Munsen shrugged.

"Maybe someone saw her, followed her here. Maybe she confided in one of those townspeople who think so much of her. Maybe she called you herself," he suggested.

"Huh?"

"You said you couldn't be sure if it was a man or a woman."

"Yeah, but why would she call me herself?"

"Maybe it's part of the ritual she's following or maybe it's a weird psychological thing. I've read about people who were so burdened by their conscience, they helped the police find evidence to convict them. I get all these police and detective periodicals and usually have time to read them in my office," he explained. "Who knows?"

Del stared at the tombstone and nodded softly.

"Can you get my shovel, please?" Munsen asked.

"Sure," Del said, following him. Munsen put the knife in the trunk, treating it as if it was a dozen eggs.

"What did you mean a while ago when you said, 'no matter what he did to her'?" Del asked. "Do you know of some reason for her to want to hurt Tony Monato?"

Munsen closed the trunk.

"Well, you're going to hear about it anyway so I guess it's no big deal coming from me. Phil Coleman and I searched Tony's apartment earlier today and discovered he had been taking dirty pictures of Anna Young through her window. Tony was an amateur photographer, usually taking mostly nature pictures. Roy Kayfield said he dreamed of selling them to magazines, but the pictures of Anna were a whole different thing. Phil thinks she found out and did him in because it was another evil act or something."

Del nodded, a deep sense of weighty fatigue coming over his body. He gazed around the cemetery. Long, deep shadows seemed to be oozing out of the surrounding woods, creeping over the tombs and plots as if taking possession of what was theirs. In moments Gussie Young's would be darkened as well. Munsen reached into the trunk and plucked his camera out of a corner pocket. He returned to the grave and took a picture of where the knife had been buried. Del got into the front passenger seat where he watched and waited.

"I'm going to drive this right over to the district attorney's office," Munsen said, getting into the car. "I'll be sure to tell them how you were responsible and cooperative."

"Okay," Del said. "Thanks for that."

"You going to go see her and ask her about all this?" Munsen asked as he started the engine.

"I'd better."

"Tell her . . . tell her I'm sorry about all this," Munsen offered.

Del smiled.

"Despite everything, she gets to people in this village somehow, doesn't she?"

"Yeah, I suppose," Munsen said, smiling back, "and it's not just because she's an attractive lady. She's special I think. I don't know. You get to a point where you wonder about everything," he added, sounding guilty about it.

"Nothing unhealthy about having an open mind," Del said.

Munsen nodded. He looked more pensive, more troubled.

"Something happen to make you think like this more?" Del asked.

Munsen was silent a moment, and then he shrugged and quickly told Del about Lisa and Anna and the charm.

"Could just be coincidence, of course, but it wasn't so much whether she had the power to do anything as it was that she wanted to do something, that she cared and tried to comfort me, understand?" Munsen asked.

"I think so," Del said. He sat back as they returned to the village.

Munsen let him out by his car.

"Good luck," he told him, and started off with the newly found incriminating evidence. Del quickly got into his own vehicle and drove to Anna's shop. Some of the reporters spotted him and started in his direction, but he waved them off and went to the shop door quickly.

Anna was sitting at her table in the rear and a stout man with thinning gray hair streaked with some stubborn dark brown strands stood talking to her. He wore a pair of coveralls and a thin long sleeve blue shirt as well as a pair of light brown boot shoes that were a little more than ankle high. They stopped talking as Del entered, both looking his way.

"I've got to talk to you, Anna," Del said. "Sorry to interrupt, but it has to be private."

"No problem. I'm just leaving," the man said. He smiled at Del. "Anna here cured my lumbago. Just wanted to stop by and wish her luck with all this nonsense. I know who you are, too. I was there and put up some money for the bail. Name's Bedik, Melvin Bedik," he said, extending his hand.

Del shook it and smiled.

"You don't let her down, Mr. Pearson. She's a treasure here and we don't want to lose her."

"I'll do my best," Del said.

"Yeah, well I expect that will do just fine," he said. "Good luck, Anna. I'll be by to see you again soon," he promised, and nodded at Del as he started out.

Del didn't speak until he was gone.

"I have some new information for you Anna, and I need you to tell me what you know about it," Del began.

Anna smiled softly as if she knew.

"Please, have a seat," she said, nodding at the chair across from her.

Del settled in it like he would never get up again. He took a deep breath and gazed at the three dozen eggs on the table.

"What's all this?"

"Mr. Bedik brought it. It's his way of showing his support and the way he pays me for helping him with his aches and pains," she said with a smile. "Old fashion barter system, but it carries something more with it than just payment for services rendered, Mr. Pearson. Money is impersonal. You hold a dollar today and tomorrow someone else does, but these eggs, these eggs represent more than payment. They are part of whom Mr. Bedik is and when he gives them, he gives something of himself, just as I try to do when I help him.

"Wouldn't it be a better world if it was all still run on a barter system?" she asked with playful eyes.

"Tough on bankers," Del quipped. "Can you imagine a large safe full of eggs and vegetables?"

She laughed and then her face quickly changed, her eyes dark and still.

"You have come here with a shadow around you," she said. "This is a cold shadow, a shadow from the land of the dead."

"Yes," he said, nearly breathless, almost anticipating that she would tell him all that he had come to tell her.

"Whatever brought you to that darkness is very, very evil, Mr. Pearson. Beware," she warned. It nearly made him laugh. She was worried more about him?

He began by telling her of the phone call, explaining his responsibility as an officer of the court, and then describing what he and Munsen had done and had found.

Instead of the look of concern and perhaps the inevitable confession he had expected, Anna Young smiled.

"What?" he asked, "could possibly make you happy about all I have told you, Anna?"

"He made a mistake," she said. "He violated the sanctity of my mother's grave, and when he opened the earth above her, he released her anger. It swirls about him."

"Who?" Del asked.

"Whoever carries it," she said cryptically.

Del shook his head.

"Anna, if that blood on that knife is tied to Tony Monato and your prints are found on that knife, you'll be convicted of both homicides. I have to know if I should go see the district attorney and work out the best arrangement for you," Del explained, almost pleading.

A distant look came into her eyes before she turned back to him.

"The other night, when I was returning, I touched him," she said.

"Who? Tony?"

"I could feel him nearby, hovering, so I turned and I put out my hand and I could see his shadow. I felt him go by. His cold wind grazed the tips of my fingers, but it wasn't enough for me to stop him. That was when I knew it was too late," she said. "Morning would reveal something ugly."

"You're not making any sense, Anna. I'm asking you a simple question. Did you bury that knife in your mother's plot?"

"No," she said.

"Did you use that knife to kill Tony Monato?"

She shook her head.

"Did you know that Tony Monato had been taking pictures of you when you were undressed, taking them through your bathroom and bedroom windows?"

Her eyes widened.

"So that was it," she said. "That's why I felt his eyes on me."

"In light of all I have told you, you have nothing else to tell me?"

She shook her head.

"All right," Del said, rising slowly, looking like a man who had aged years in minutes. "We'll have to wait to see what the results of the forensic tests reveal."

"We must talk about your turmoil, Mr. Pearson. I must help you," she said.

"Anna, you don't get it. I'm here to help you now. Forget about me."

"I can't help myself until I help you," she replied. "It is written in the wind that brought you here."

"Okay," he said, no longer having the patience for all this. "I gotta go. I have some work to do. Some work," he added with a laugh. He glanced again at the table. A cold thought raced across his brow and settled like a blemish on the clear face of his curiosity.

"This man, Bedik, he has a poultry farm?"

"Not really. He just keeps some for personal food. These are today's eggs. Please, take a dozen. I can't use them all," she said. "Here." She held out a carton. "Please," she insisted.

He took them.

"Anna," Del continued, speaking in a tone of voice he would use if he was speaking to a child, "if you wanted him to give you a chicken, a live chicken, would he?"

"Without hesitation," she said.

"That's what I thought," Del said, nodding. "That's what I feared."

He turned and started out.

"Don't be afraid," she called to him. "My mother's spirit has been disturbed."

He nodded.

"I'll be back when I have some more information, Anna, and we'll talk."

"And I'll be ready to help you," she promised. "If anyone asks about the eggs, Mr. Pearson. Tell them it's barter," she followed.

He looked back. She was smiling like a schoolgirl, rejuvenated, full of glee.

She might very well be unbalanced, he thought. Maybe he really could go for diminished responsibility. He would move for a psychiatric exam. No matter how it would make her feel, it would be irresponsible of him not to, he thought.

He paused outside when the first heavy drops splashed on his cheeks. The heavy rain was coming, rolling in on the back of thunder and lightning, clearing the streets of Sandburg, washing away the carnival.

At least for a little while.

Seventeen

"This just came from the prosecutor's office, Mr. Pearson," Marge Anderson said. She put the packet on his desk and he just stared at it. Everything could be over, he thought. A part of him wished it would. All of his problems with Jackie and his in-laws would be ended, as well as the media frenzy that had stolen his sense of proportion. He and his father-in-law had practically gotten into a hot argument, and Jackie couldn't be any cooler. The toll it was taking was too heavy. Anna, he thought, you read my palm wrong. I'd welcome an easy way out.

Marge Anderson lingered. Although she never called him anything else but Mr. Pearson, Del often felt her motherly concern. She hovered around him, making sure he had everything he needed for court, expediting materials and information whenever possible, and always warning him about taking care of his health, especially eating properly. She wasn't above leaving fruit on his desk or a health food store power bar when she knew he had missed a meal.

Marge was more aware than anyone of how the Anna

Young case had been wearing on him. She also knew what
the case had become in the community and elsewhere and
told him about some of the things people were saying,
especially clergy.

"You'd think it was seventeenth-century Salem,
Massachusetts," she complained, and after some urging
went on to tell him rumors being spread claiming that he
was victim to a spell Anna Young had cast over him and
that was why he was working so hard for her defense.

"Might be my in-laws spreading the rumors," he
quipped. She didn't smile. Maybe it was!

"You think that's the forensics you've been waiting for?"
she asked, impatient with his hesitation about opening the
package.

"Probably," he said, and tore open the envelope.

She watched him read. He flipped through the pages
and documents and then set them down.

"Good news and not so good news," he said. "There's
nothing on the sword to tie Anna Young to Tony's death
and there's nothing on the pentacle found at the crime
scene to tie it to Anna. The knife has Tony's blood, but
there are no fingerprints on the handle or the blade. It
looks wiped clean."

"That sounds like mostly good news," Marge said cautiously.

"Someone drew a circle in the vicinity of Tony's death,
which is something Anna Young does, the knife was buried
in her mother's plot, and she has admitted to putting
strands of Henry Deutch's hair in the grave as well for
some ritual, so it looks like something she does. With the
nasty pictures of her that Detective Coleman found, Paula
Richards has a possible motive. Along with Munsen
Donald's seeing her out and about around the time of the
murder, there is enough to keep her a suspect, of course,

and," he continued, tapping the package, "they're asking me to bring her in today at two for formal questioning in regard to Tony Monato's murder.

"Notice how Paula Richards first delivers all this as a preamble to her request," Del said, holding up the packet. "I know what she intends to do. She'll have her indicted for Tony's death right before the trial for Henry Deutch's death begins. That oughta seal it with the jury."

"What are you going to do first?" Marge asked.

"Meditate," he muttered.

"Pardon?"

"Nothing." His buzzer went off and he lifted the receiver. "Hello? I'll be right in," he said. "Norman wants to see me. Maybe he wants to take me off the case and take charge of it himself," Del said, rising.

Marge laughed. They both knew why.

At fifty-eight, Norman Douglas was content settling into his niche as a bureaucrat, with his responsibilities mainly centered on administration of the legal aid office. At least forty pounds overweight for his five-foot-ten-inch frame, Douglas had stereotypical jovial jowls and round, button blue eyes. He looked remarkably unscathed from years and years of public service. His skin was smooth, his dark brown head of hair still quite full and rich.

Long ago Norman had concluded that he was no Perry Mason. He was actually a shy man, conscious of his appearance whenever in court, slow, nonaggressive, with a thin, high-pitched voice that sounded too shrill when he tried to initiate some passion. He liked the idea that he was in control of more skillful and even more intelligent men and women. One-on-one meetings were his cup of tea. Even the occasional staff meetings were somewhat disconcerting, and this, after more than twenty years at the job.

"I wouldn't count on it, Mr. Pearson," Marge said as he started out.

"Not counting on that is about the only thing I feel I can count on these days, Marge."

He crossed the hallway to Norman Douglas's office, knocked, and entered.

The stout man was watering his plants in the window box and turned.

"Oh, Del. I have some good news for you." Douglas put down the watering can and went to his desk. He liked to be sitting behind it when he spoke to his staff. He wrapped himself in his furniture as if it all were part of some protective shield.

"Good news is just what I need, Norman. What?"

"The judge will permit the court to give you the money you need for the medical witness you want."

Douglas sat back, surprised at Del's lack of reaction.

"You don't seem too excited about it, Del. You know how hard it often is to get the court to finance a decent defense for someone who qualifies for public assistance. I think this is a direct result of your good efforts. You should be proud."

"No, I'm happy about it, Norman. I'm just very concerned about how the case is developing."

"Having some doubts yourself, are you?"

"Serious concerns," Del said, finally relaxing into a small smile.

"Um. Well, a plea before trial wouldn't be so terrible, if it comes to that," Norman Douglas said.

Del raised his eyebrows.

"Oh?"

"We're all feeling some pressure from various sectors of the community. My wife had a call from Father O'Brian. She's active in the church fund raisers, you know. Father

O'Brian and Father McDermott from Sandburg held some sort of a seminar on spiritualism and the church, and they were quite critical of Anna Young, without mentioning her by name of course."

"Yes, I've been hearing the same sort of rumblings from my father-in-law who is quite friendly with Reverend Carter from Sandburg. Whether she is actually guilty of committing a premeditated murder doesn't seem to be the issue as much as who she is and what she represents."

"Be careful, my young friend. You've got places to go and promises to keep."

"I know. I couldn't forget if I wanted to. Not with my father-in-law breathing down my back," Del said, and Norman Douglas laughed. It was a laugh without much sound, just a trembling in his jowls and a shudder in his shoulders.

"I'll go call Doctor Childs in New York and let him know I'll be calling him as an expert witness should the case go to trial," Del said. "Thanks."

"Good luck," Douglas called to him as he left.

Luck, Del thought. When the case first came up, he wondered if he wasn't lucky, if it wasn't a chance to do something significant quickly. More often than not, high profile cases should help an attorney. He thought he would stop Paula Richards at the gate and get credit for being smart and efficient. So much for luck.

Moments later he was in his vehicle and on his way to Sandburg to pick up Anna Young and bring her to the district attorney's office for questioning regarding the death of Tony Monato. He had no idea where it would lead.

Anna put a sign in the window to indicate she would be gone for two hours. She locked the door and headed toward the cemetery, carrying her tools and spiritual weapons in a cloth bag tied to her left wrist. It was warmer than usual for late spring. Weathermen and women were predicting a more humid, hotter summer than usual. Some people with pools at their homes had actually begun getting them up and ready because the evening temperatures weren't dropping as dramatically, and daytime temperatures were running in the low eighties. The warmer weather had accelerated plant and flower growth. The precipitation during early spring had been greater than the year before, making the forests even more plush. A number of Anna's regulars already had come to her for herbal hay fever remedies.

As usual when she walked along Church Road, she kept her focus fixed directly ahead, never turning to look at passing cars. Her straight, firm posture remained as perfect as ever, and her soft Madonna smile on her lips looked frozen forever. No one could tell that her heart was pounding because she was responding to a call from the beyond. Her mother had been whispering in her ear all morning.

It had begun like a soft breeze that gently raised and lowered its speed and intensity, and then soon metamorphosed into a melody her mother had brought with her from Hungary. That then turned into her name *Anna* being whispered repeatedly, and she knew she had to go to the grave.

Anna believed, as did her mother, that one's spirit resided there in the grave, but the spirit could travel when it was needed. Spiritually, one never left his or her loved ones. How much contact we really had with our dearly departed depended entirely on our own spirituality, our own ability to peel away the distractions and concentrate on the world beyond touch and smell and taste. A phone call from the dead began in one's own heart. It rang throughout your soul and you answered only if you had faith and trust.

For most of her journey, Anna felt as if she were floating. She heard nothing: no songbirds, no car tires, no voices. She saw only her mother's face growing stronger and larger as she drew closer and closer to the cemetery. At the entrance, she hesitated. The vibrations that lingered told her evil had been through here. It left its footsteps in the shadows. Despite the warm air, Anna shuddered with a chill. She drew out another athame, an eight-inch-long, two-sided, nonsharp knife, and drew small circles on her right and then on her left. She pointed it toward the east and then she made a cross in the air and continued to her mother's grave.

When she arrived, she immediately set herself to repairing the disturbed earth. An unwanted and corrupt thing had been embedded here and that had interrupted her mother's rest. Carefully, she cleared out the portion of polluted earth, using her athame, sweeping it all into a neat pile. When she was content that she had dug out all the ground that had been touched, she scooped it up with her small garden spade and scattered it in the wind, heaving it toward the east, crying "Be gone" with each throw. She knelt down and literally cleaned away every grain of dirt. Then she took out a red ribbon, kissed it, and placed it in the ground where the knife used to kill Tony Monato had been buried.

The evil eye had been here and had to be countered. Its presence could weigh heavily on her mother's spirit, and she had promised Del Pearson and predicted that her mother's spirit was going to offer protection.

Anna lowered her head and then raised her right hand, forming the *mano cornuto*, making the Devil's horns by holding down the two middle fingers with her thumb while sticking up the index and little finger. "Be gone!" she shouted, and then she spit three times into the hole.

After that, she rose and went to an untouched area of the cemetery and scooped up new earth, dropping it into her skirt between her legs. When she had a sufficient amount, she took hold of her hem and carried the new ground back to her mother's grave plot and used it to fill the cavity and cover the red ribbon. She smoothed the ground and pressed her palms to it, whispering another prayer. A sparrow landed on her mother's tombstone and gazed at her while it moved from side to side nervously. Anna held herself perfectly still. She knew why it had been called. She waited and then the sparrow flew off only inches above her and headed toward the village.

Anna was confident it carried her mother's spirit on its wings. She smiled, gave thanks, and rose to start back, first brushing down her skirt and then putting her tools and her athame back into her cloth bag.

The sparrow was long gone by the time she started back toward the village, but its speed and its direction filled her with some gloom.

"He is still here," she muttered. "He is still among us."

It quickened her steps.

There was much yet to do and someone new to protect.

Del was both disappointed and frustrated when he stepped up to the door of Anna's shop and saw the sign. Damn, he thought, why didn't she have a telephone? He had just assumed she'd be here. He glanced at his watch. If she had just left, it was going to be close. Maybe she had just gone upstairs, he thought and went to the left side of the building where there was a narrow alley between it and the deserted structure beside it. He walked in a few feet and looked up at the windows he was sure were windows in Anna's apartment. None of them were opened. Still, he cupped his hands and shouted her name.

He waited, shouted once more, and shook his head. Before he turned to go out front, he spotted what looked like a ladder resting against the rear of the deserted building. He went to it and looked up. This was probably what Tony Monato had used. He had gone up to that window in the deserted building, which was just about parallel to the windows in Anna's apartment, and set up his camera. Del wondered if the police had been here and checked it.

Curious himself, he started up the ladder. When he reached the top, he saw a blanket and some empty beer bottles. He crawled through the window and gazed around the otherwise empty room. It smelled musty and damp. Wallpaper was long faded and peeled. A rug had been ripped up, with some of the tacks still embedded in the floorboards. He saw some cigarette butts and a wrapper from some beef jerky.

Well, there was never any doubt Tony had done this, he thought. He turned and looked out the window. The buildings were close enough so that he could get a very clear view of her bedroom. She had no shades, just a curtain that was parted. For a moment he stared at her bed. Suddenly, as if someone flashed a picture on her wall, he saw her standing there completely naked, her back to him. She turned slowly and stood gazing back at him, a smile on her lips.

It gave him a jolt and he stepped back. Christ, what is she going to think of me? he worried, and quickly returned to the ladder and stepped down. He hurried through the alley and returned to the front door of the shop where he knocked harder. He'll explain. He was just checking out the situation because that was all part of the investigation. She'll understand he's not a perverted nutcase.

He knocked again and he peered through the door. She wasn't coming down. What could he do but wait, he thought.

He looked up and down the street. No one had taken notice of him. The only place that had some traffic and looked busy today in fact was the bar and grill. He decided to get something to drink and maybe a sandwich while he waited. When he got back into the car, he called Richards' office and informed them he might be a little late. The district attorney's secretary was not cordial about it after she delivered the message to Paula Richards.

"If you're not here by two-thirty," she said, "we will have to consider sending an officer."

"Sure, it's the public's money. Let's spend it," he shot back, and hung up before she could respond.

His hand was trembling. She saw him for sure, he thought. This is silly, he concluded. He'll explain it. She'll understand. He headed for Kayfields.

Practically everyone in the bar and grill appeared to know who he was. His picture had been in the paper and on local television, of course, but Del was still not used to the notoriety, nor did he welcome the looks and whispers. He took a bar stool and sat, noting how flushed his face looked in the mirror across from him. Roy Kayfield came over quickly.

"How's it going, Mr. Pearson?"

"It's going," Del said, and glanced at the menu.

"That's a bit ambitious," Roy said, nodding at it.

"What's quick?" Del asked.

"We've got a great meatloaf sandwich, the special of the day."

Del smiled.

"Sounds good to me. On whole wheat, if you have it."

Roy nodded and headed toward the kitchen while his new voluntary assistant, Charlie Trustman took position behind the bar.

"Can I get you something to drink, Mr. Pearson?"

"Sure. Let me have a soft drink, nothing diet," he added.

"Don't blame you. I hate those chemical tastes. My wife works over at the county library and reads up on this stuff," he continued as he poured Del's drink. "She says the chemicals can hurt you more than the calories." He placed the glass in front of Del and stepped back. "How's Anna holding up?"

"Better than me," Del said quickly, and Charlie laughed. Everyone around them had stopped talking and was hanging on every word.

"She's a strong woman," Charlie said. "Nothing seems to throw her off-kilter. Oh, I'm Charlie Trustman," Charlie said, offering his hand. Del shook it. "I guess I'll be seeing you in court."

"Oh?"

"The district attorney's people interviewed me because I was in Rotterman's barber shop the day Anna came in to get some of Henry Deutch's hair before Dennis could sweep it up. She said she would be calling me to be a court witness."

"That's right," Del said. "I remember seeing your name. I was going to talk to you about all that."

"I don't know what else I can say. Anna didn't say anything. Just asked if she could get something and did it. I didn't learn until later that she buried it in her mother's grave plot. Why'd she do that, Mr. Pearson? Was that part of a curse?"

"I don't know," Del said, smiling.

"My wife did some research on all this. She says in order to cast a spell, you've got to have something personal from the target so that's why I thought so."

Del nodded.

"My wife would be glad to talk to you if you need any of that information," Charlie continued. "We all like Anna and hope it works out for her. I don't believe she killed Tony Monato. Nobody here does, right fellas?"

Everyone grunted assent. Del gazed at the group.

"Why not?" Del asked them, playing the devil's advocate.

"Anna's got friends here, people she has helped," Charlie explained. "She never wished anyone but Henry Deutch any harm for as long as we all knew her, right fellas?"

There was a repeat of the grunts. Roy Kayfield returned with Del's sandwich and set it in front of him.

Del started to eat his sandwich. "Very good," he told Roy who smiled.

"Tony made it better," someone in the rear shouted. There was agreement and then a deep silence. "Poor bastard," he added. They all returned to whatever they had been doing before Del entered, but they all kept an eye on him as well. Just before he finished the sandwich, Munsen Donald entered. When he saw Del, he stopped and nodded.

"At least you get to eat in a good place these days," Munsen said.

Del laughed.

"Not bad," he said. "I recommend the special."

"Everything's a special here nowadays," Munsen said, sitting beside him. "Going over to see Anna?"

"Yes. I've got to bring her in for questioning," Del said softly.

Munsen nodded.

"She should just about be home," Munsen said.

"Pardon?"

"I passed her about five minutes ago on Church Road. I stopped to offer her a ride, but she wanted to walk. She had been out at the cemetery."

Del just stared.

"I told her about Lisa," Munsen continued. "She didn't want any thanks or anything nor did she seem at all surprised." Munsen shook his head, his eyes tearing.

"Are you sure she was just at the cemetery?" Del finally managed.

"Yeah. She was carrying something. She did say she had to repair her mother's grave plot. Don't ask," Munsen said. Then he took a closer look at Del. "Something wrong?"

"What? Oh. No. I've got to get her and get moving." He turned to Roy. "What do I owe you?"

Roy told him and Del paid quickly.

"Good luck," Roy shouted, but Del was already out the door. "There's a man in a hurry," he muttered to his customers. He looked at Munsen. "What's up with him?"

"I don't know," Munsen said, still looking after Del. "But there's something more than meets the eye."

"Tell us something we don't know," Roy said.

Munsen turned to him, thought a moment, and then remembered why he had come.

"Give me one of those specials," he said, and went to his table.

As Del drove back toward Anna's shop, he could indeed see her coming down Church Road toward town. He drew to a slow stop and watched her for a few moments. Then he looked back at the shop and the building beside it.

Never in his life before had his imagination been as vivid and as convincing.

Or had it been something more? How could he explain it? He would surely never tell a soul. He felt at once like someone caught with his hand in the cookie jar and also like someone who'd had a supernatural experience.

Maybe Jackie and her parents were right about his having to leave this case, but for reasons they could never imagine.

He surely couldn't when he first had begun.

But what about now?

He shook his head vigorously as if to scramble his thoughts and drive the creepy madness from taking hold.

I'm a lawyer.

I'm just here to give my client good representation.

That's what I do and that's what I will do. There's nothing else.

Most everyone would understand that.

Now, he had only to convince himself.

Eighteen

All throughout Del's explanation and description of the forensics reports he had received concerning the death of Tony Monato, Anna sat there in his car and stared ahead with no expression of either relief or concern. She couldn't have been more indifferent had she been listening to events that involved someone else, someone entirely unknown to her.

"Then they will return my mother's sword to me?" she asked when he concluded. It was as though she thought that was Del's main point.

"Yes, I expect so. But Anna, this isn't over for you. They want to question you today because you're still their prime suspect."

"I understand," she said, turning to smile at him. "It's not something I haven't expected."

Del nodded, smiling to himself. Even truly innocent people, people with alibis and relatively good defenses accused of crimes and brought to trial showed more worry these days. There were too many unpredictables, at least for people who couldn't see clearly into the future, he thought.

"The way this is going to work," Del continued, "is if they ask a question which will force you to be self-incriminating, I will object and advise you not to respond, or if they ask a question I think is ambiguous, I will object and so tell them. I always explain to my clients that they are in an adversarial position. This is not a little get-together in which everyone's purpose is to arrive at the truth and go home.

"There are either assistant district attorneys, investigators, or the district attorney herself who believe you to be a prime suspect in a homicide and want to reinforce that belief through your responses, hoping you will say something, reveal a fact that will incriminate you."

"I understand," she said.

"Do you?" Del pursued. Maybe now was the time to suggest the possibility of having her psychiatrically evaluated. "You do not want to deny that you destroyed what you saw as an evil spirit in the community, a spirit that happened to house itself in the body and soul of Henry Deutch. You say Henry Deutch, therefore, was dead before you even began to do battle, correct?"

"Yes," Anna said.

"The state, represented by the district attorney, doesn't see your actions in the same favorable light, Anna. They want to hold you responsible for the death of the body of Henry Deutch and they want to hold you responsible in the most criminally liable way, first degree homicide. You understand all that, correct?"

"I do, Mr. Pearson, even more than you imagine." Her eyes grew narrow and dark.

"I know, I know," Del said, "you also believe the evil spirit is now in the district attorney. She might not be too happy to hear that."

"Nevertheless, it is so," she said confidently.

Del couldn't help but smile when he imagined Anna stating her belief in front of Paula Richards.

"You have a certain, how should I say, *unique* interpretation of these events, Anna. Some people might find them unbalanced, at the least. The court, at my request, perhaps, might want to have someone speak to you about it, someone who is considered an expert in psychology, to determine how much you really understand about your own actions and about what's happening to you now. Would you be opposed to that?"

"Not if you're not," she replied. "I have faith in you and the forces that brought you to me."

"Right," he said. "Thanks for the vote of confidence."

"In time, you will have the same vote," she said, and he had to laugh.

"Good and evil are like two opposing winds sometimes, Mr. Pearson, and men who believe they can harness the two by strapping them down with laws and codes and legal procedures are often overwhelmed."

"That's for sure," Del said. He glanced at her, his gaze locked in hers as if those two dark eyes were armed with magnets that could hold his thoughts for as long as she wanted. A driver passing in the opposite lane leaned angrily on his horn because Del had drifted just a little too far to his left. He shifted his gaze quickly to the highway, but Anna's eyes had fished a memory out of his pool of remembrances.

He was only eleven and there was this class bully, Ernie Pedestro, who was big enough to be mistaken for a fifteen-year-old. One of Ernie's favorite acts of mischief was to ride his bike up to a smaller boy's and shove a stick in the spokes of the rear tire, thus sending the boy careening off the road, often into a ditch. Del had managed to avoid this fate, but never thought he was out of danger.

One afternoon he had the opportunity to sabotage Ernie's bike without being seen or caught doing so. He reached into his little tool pocket on the rear of his bike seat, and with a wrench he loosened Ernie's rear tire. It didn't come off until Ernie, going fast down a hill in pursuit of someone, bounced over a bump. Subsequently, Ernie was spilled and hit the pavement head first. Pedestro punctured his forehead and scalp, and streams of blood poured down his temples. He looked far worse than he was, but the sight of his bloodied face stopped traffic and he was rushed to the hospital. One of his gashes, required ten stitches, but he somehow had avoided a concussion.

The sabotage cured him of being mischievous on his bike, but on more than one occasion, when he looked at Del, Del couldn't help but let his eyes shift guiltily away. His conscience reared its head to haunt him with accusation and guilt. However, he could never deny the sense of satisfaction he enjoyed at the sight of Ernie clutching his head, screaming in pain, and crying.

Wasn't it true that when he looked at people, especially his classmates, he saw something of good in some and something of evil in others? Weren't there people he could never even imagine harming others and people he easily could imagine doing harm? Was it just that he never put it all into a framework as Anna and her mother and people like her had?

I wonder, he thought, if I had been shown to have been the one to hurt Ernie, would I have rationalized away my guilt by thinking I had struck a blow of good and a blow against evil? Surely my father would have lectured me and told me never to take the law into my own hands. But what's wrong with my hands if they are hands of good? Is law enforcement justified merely by a matter of numbers? It takes twelve people to decide someone should be punished. Sometimes it takes only one, a judge, who is admittedly educated and trained and supposedly objective and empowered by the state, but what if the choice is so clear and so right that anyone with a good heart, compassion, and a sense of what's right took action? And then, what about the forces of good that never go into action or get corrupted or distracted?

Yes, Anna, he thought, we might be deluding ourselves into believing we can harness the two winds.

He was so deep in all this thought, he didn't realize how far he had driven until the county buildings loomed ahead. He glanced at his clock. They'd be on time and hopefully there would be no members of the press.

It was a futile, vain, and foolish expectation. Either Paula Richards or someone from her office was leaking information like a punctured tire leaked its air. The gag rule was one of those legal pipe dreams these days. More often than not, trials were being conducted through television news sound bites and newspaper headlines. Anna might be right about another thing, Del thought, the justice system is sick with viruses born out of the deadliest of sins: vanity, pride, greed, and a pure lust for power.

The pack of reporters and cameramen came to life the moment Del and Anna emerged from his vehicle. They swooped down the steps like buzzards, pecking at them with questions.

"Is your client being arrested for Tony Monato's murder?"

"Does Monato's death have anything to do with the murder of Henry Deutch?"

"Anna, did you kill Tony Monato?"

"Del, are you here to plea bargain?"

Del paused at the door and turned to the clump of media people. They all grew quiet. For a moment they looked like starving children hoping for some charitable morsel to be tossed their way.

"I am amazed at how quickly you all learned about today's session with the district attorney in light of Judge Landers' gag order. Since I know I didn't tell you and I'm sure the district attorney's office wouldn't dare disobey the judge, I have to assume you are all clairvoyant, and if you are all so clairvoyant, you can easily answer your own questions."

There was a moment's pause and then a burst of laughter. Del smiled and escorted Anna to the district attorney's chambers where they were first greeted by Milt Rosen and then joined by Paula Richards herself in a conference room.

"Thanks for coming in promptly," Paula Richards began. She looked at Milt Rosen. "Did you offer them something to drink?"

"Oh. No, I—"

"That's fine," Del said, opening his briefcase and taking out a legal pad. "Anna?"

She shook her head, her eyes fixed on Paula Richards. The district attorney maintained that confident smile, but there was just a tiny twitter in her lips that indicated she wasn't all that comfortable under Anna's fixed scrutiny. Del had to smile to himself. She was glaring at Paula Richards as if she could see the devil himself behind Paula Richards' eyes.

The stenographer, a thin, balding, pale man who looked more like an undertaker, took his position and stared ahead as if he was alone. Del imagined that Paula Richards trained her people to be as inscrutable as possible. What she didn't want was someone to suggest that an answer was surprising, incriminating, revealing.

"Mr. Rosen will conduct most of this interview," Paula

Richards began. "I believe you two know each other well," she added, addressing Del.

"We've crossed swords here and there," Del replied, and Paula Richards laughed.

"Swords. Just an innocent reference, counselor?"

"Let's get on with this. We have to run a gambit outside thanks to someone feeding the press."

"Nothing like that came from my office," Paula Richards asserted.

"Of course not. It would be contempt of court, and who should hold up the court orders higher than the people's advocate?" Del countered.

Paula Richards' plastic smile began to darken and thin out as her lips tightened in the corners.

"Milt," she muttered.

Milt Rosen flipped a page on his pad, adjusted his glasses, and turned to Anna.

"Miss Young, were you acquainted with the deceased, Tony Monato?"

"Yes," Anna said. "I'm acquainted with everyone in Sandburg."

"When was the last time you saw or spoke with Mr. Monato?" Milt asked, gazing at his pad rather than Anna. Paula Richards, on the other hand, stared intently at her.

"I have never spoken with Mr. Monato," Anna said, "but I have often seen him."

"Did you see him the night of his death?"

"Yes," Anna replied without the slightest hesitation. "I saw him not long before his death."

Del felt his heart start to pound when Milt looked up and then glanced at Paula Richards. Anna wasn't listening to him. He had clearly instructed her not to volunteer information. Answer all the questions specifically, he had told her. But Anna had a deeper faith in the outcome. Was this going to make it all that much easier for Paula Richards? The district attorney grinned like someone who knew it was. That damn self-confidence sickened Del. More and more it was becoming personal, a need to wipe that grin off her face.

"Did you see him on the school grounds?" Milt Rosen quickly asked.

"No," Anna said. "I saw him in the shadows on the street. I had no idea where he was going," she said.

"So you followed him?" Paula Richards said.

"No," Anna said.

"But you knew he was going to the school grounds?" Milt asked.

"No."

"Did you go in the same direction?" Paula Richards demanded, impatient.

"Who's doing the questioning here?" Del demanded. "You're firing at her from both sides before she has a chance to think. You're making this into an inquisition."

"Like the Spanish Inquisition?" Paula Richards quipped. She smiled. "We'll slow it up. Sorry, Miss Young. Milt?"

"The question was did you go in the same direction as Mr. Monato on the night in question," Milt said.

"For a while," Anna said. "I thought I still had time to shut the door."

"Huh? What door?" Milt asked, glancing at Paula Richards.

"The doorway to the souls of my good people. I knew that evil was entering the village and I went to drive it back," she explained.

The two prosecutors simply stared a moment.

"Yes," Paula Richards said, "Detective Coleman told me a little of what you told him about the night in question.

You were out to fight or find evil. Exactly how do you do that, Miss Young?" Paula Richards asked.

Anna began to explain the purpose and power of an athame.

"The sword, right," Paula Richards said. Del could see the glee forming in Paula Richards' face. She nodded at Milt.

"Was this then another one of your athames?" Milt Rosen asked after he reached into his briefcase to produce the knife found buried in Gussie Young's grave site. It was in a plastic evidence bag.

"No," Anna said, smiling. "That is some cheap replica with no spiritual power for good."

"Is that right? And how do you know that?" Milt asked.

Anna held her hand out, palm toward the knife. She closed her eyes. The two prosecutors looked at Del who tried not to smile or react in any way. Finally, Anna shook her head.

"It has no positive energy," she said. "However, it was used to do evil."

"Are you saying you recognize this knife as the murder weapon?" Paula Richards asked quickly.

"She didn't say that," Del interposed. "Although she does know the results of lab tests on it."

"What did you say, Miss Young?"

"I said it was used for evil. His dark spirit is still on it," she added, and the two prosecutors looked at the weapon as if it was contaminated.

"Do you know or have any knowledge of how this knife ended up being buried in your mother's grave plot?" Milt Rosen asked.

"The evil one put it there," she said in a matter-of-fact tone as if it was the most obvious fact of all.

"The evil one. And who is this evil one?" Milt continued.

"I do not know the form he has taken yet, but I will know."

"That's nice. Be sure to tell us," Paula Richards quipped. She sat back and then nodded at Milt Rosen, who leaned down to pluck an envelope from his briefcase.

"Miss Young," he began as he opened it, "we understand that part of your rituals, as you call them, often involve the drawing of a circle. You've admitted to having done so in front of Mr. Deutch's home and you did so in the Fallsburg police station when you were first brought in for questioning about the death of Henry Deutch, is that correct?"

"Yes," Anna said.

Milt plucked a photo from the envelope and extended it to her and Del. He held it up for both of them to see.

"That's a photograph of a circle found at the Tony Monato murder scene. Did you draw that in the ground?"

"No," Anna said quickly.

"Is there another witch at work in Sandburg?" Paula Richards asked with a wry smile on her lips.

"Not that I know of," Anna said.

"So you guys don't stay in touch or stake out your own territories?"

It was obvious Paula was playing with her, but Anna didn't get angry. She smiled.

"You above all people in the community should know where evil resides and where something must be done to stop it," she said.

"Yes, I have it all on a map in my room. Milt," she said.

Rosen reached into the envelope.

"Miss Young, did you have any idea that Mr. Monato was spying on you, taking pictures of you we assume without your knowledge or permission?" Milt asked, sliding more pictures toward her and Del. He couldn't help but glance at them, but she didn't look down.

Del focused on one photograph because it bore remarkable resemblance to what he had imagined when he had gazed into Anna's bedroom window earlier.

"Must be a good camera, huh Counselor?" Paula Richards quipped.

Del looked up sharply and then at Anna. She stared at Paula Richards.

"Did you know about this, Miss Young?" Milt Rosen repeated.

"I felt his eyes on me, but I didn't understand why until Mr. Pearson revealed the reason," she replied.

"When you felt his eyes on you, did it make you angry?"

Anna thought a moment. Del watched her eyes shift from side to side as if she was reading from a chart held up in front of her.

"No," she finally replied. "It made me sad to know he was in such turmoil."

"Sad?"

She nodded.

Del looked away to hide his smile.

"You felt sorry for Tony Monato and not yourself even though you were the victim?" Paula Richards pursued with incredulity ringing in her voice. "Look at those photographs. He could show these pictures to people, maybe sell them and embarrass you."

"I am not embarrassed by my body, Ms. Richards. Are you embarrassed by yours?" Anna fired back. Paula Richards turned dark crimson.

Del couldn't keep the air from escaping his lips. He covered his mouth quickly.

"I certainly would be if someone took pictures of me in compromising positions, naked, and showed them to people."

"Would you be angry enough to kill a man for that?" Anna followed.

Richards' eyebrows nearly jumped off her head.

"We're here to question you, not me, Miss Young. Did you kill Tony Monato? Did you follow him to the school grounds and attack him with this knife?" she nearly shouted.

"No," Anna said. She leaned toward Paula Richards. "Do you have the feeling often that you are being followed, Ms. Richards?"

"What?" She looked angrily at Del and then turned back to Anna. "You were seen in the street about the time of his killing," Paula Richards continued more forcefully. "What were you really doing? None of the stores were open and you haven't said you visited with anyone."

"She's already explained why she was out," Del said.

"To stop evil from entering the town," Paula Richards muttered. "I know."

"It's what she set out to do," Del said casually. "It's what she does."

Paula Richards stared at him a moment and then nodded to herself and stood.

"Let's you and I have a short side bar, Del," Paula Richards said.

"Fine," Del said, rising.

Milt Rosen looked at both of them and then at Anna as if he was worried about remaining in the room alone with her.

"Maybe you can read Mr. Rosen's palm while we talk," Del suggested with an impish grin.

Milt Rosen instinctively closed his hands and sat back.

"Let's go into my office for a moment," Paula Richards suggested with a slight edge in her voice and led Del down the hallway.

"Please have a seat," she said once they entered. She moved behind her desk and Del sat in the black leather chair to the right. "You've seen what we have accumulated as evidence in the Deutch murder," Paula Richards began, and then she put her hand on a small stack of documents to her right. "These are letters I've received from citizens and members of the clergy who are concerned about the spiritual health of our community. They're not accusing her of actually being a witch as much as they are of being spiritually corrupt and corrupting others."

"Fortunately," Del said quickly, "we try our cases in a courtroom and not in the court of public opinion."

Paula Richards smiled and leaned back.

"You're a young man, Del. I don't mean to sound condescending or make myself out to be some kind of wise old judge, but it's naive to think that public opinion plays no role in that courtroom. We're all creatures of influence, formed by our various prejudices and schools of thought. How many people are Catholic or Jewish or Episcopalian because they actually made a conscious choice to be so and how many are what they are because that's what their parents and family are and that's how they've been raised?"

"Less and less," Del insisted. "Anna Young is not an evil person, and when people learn what she believes and what she does, that stack will diminish."

"Maybe. I'll get right to the point. I won't for a moment tolerate any argument that she is a kook, suffering diminished capacity. If you try to show her as such with some psychiatric evaluation, I'll get ten to contradict it. It's my firm belief that she knows exactly what she's doing and all this black magic stuff is just theater. I'll parade witness after witness who'll testify to the fact that they paid her, and paid her good money, to perform these feats of magic. She's out for a buck just like anyone else. Stopping evil from coming into the town," she said, shaking her head. "Give me a break. You think a jury is going to sit there and be impressed with any of that?"

"I guess we'll soon find out," Del said.

Paula Richards smirked.

"I don't have to offer you any deals, Del. I've got a pretty damn strong argument here," she said, patting another stack of documents. "This may look like I'm staking out virgin territory and making precedents . . . that's all good fodder for television talk shows, but I'm on solid ground. There are two rules of law which will make my case. One is foreseeability." She leaned forward, elbows on the desk. "If one knows of a particular, peculiar, or special sensitivity of another and uses that to their advantage or to the detriment of the other, liability can and will attach."

"I don't need the law lesson. I'm aware of that."

"Are you?"

"Yes. *People v. Kane.*"

Paula Richards widened her eyes, impressed.

"Let me save you some breath. The second issue becomes one of proximate causation," Del fired back as if they were already before the jury. "Let's cut to the chase," Del suggested.

"Let's."

"Can the magic be the proximate if not the but for cause of the homicide, if it is indeed a homicide? I know you have your medical experts to testify that it was, but that's where reasonable doubt will be nourished."

"You're wrong, Del. It's well documented," she said, patting the stack, "that strong beliefs and fears can cause change in someone's bio pathology. That's what I'll prove happened to Henry Deutch and she'll be shown beyond a reasonable doubt to be the but for."

"I don't think you've really asked me in here to argue the case."

"No, I called you in to make it clear to you that if you think her answers in there will support a plea of diminished capability, you're mistaken, and I called you in to offer you this onetime opportunity. I'll give you twenty-four hours. I'm willing to drop my request for the death penalty. Plead her guilty and we'll agree to life with parole after twenty-five years. I'm going to indict her for this second murder," she added threateningly.

Del closed his eyes and took a breath. The moment he did, he saw Anna looking at his palm and then looking up to tell him he wouldn't choose the absolutely easiest way out.

He leaned toward Paula Richards.

"Aren't you at least supposed to say I'm going to seek an indictment, Ms. Richards? There's still a grand jury in this state and we still have to pretend that the people do that," Del said, rising. "I have to return to my client. If you don't have any further questions, we'll be gone," he added, and started for the door. "Oh, I guess you don't have any further need for her mother's sword, correct?"

"I'm having a cut expert from New York compare it to the wound," Paula Richards said, her face stern, dark. "You're not listening to me, Del. I'll get my conviction. Twenty-four hours. I'm risking a lot just offering this to you."

Del looked back at her. Sitting back in her chair with such arrogance, she did look evil. Perhaps Anna wasn't so off the wall after all.

"Maybe you are," he said. "Maybe you're risking more than either of us can imagine."

Nineteen

Del was comparatively quiet during the trip back to Sandburg. Well into it, Anna turned to him and asked if he was troubled because of something she had said. The truth was he was wondering if the bravado he had exhibited in front of Paula Richards was really to Anna's advantage. He considered paying Michael Burke a visit to get his advice. Perhaps he should be in a negotiation to avoid trial.

"Well, you did say more than I would have liked."

"Perhaps more than they would have liked as well," she retorted.

He shook his head. How do I defend a client who won't back off her pride in destroying the victim? Simply put, do I go after the prosecution's case and risk a verdict or look for mitigation? "Suppose I got them to reduce the charges against you, Anna? Suppose they did what we call a vertical plea bargain and had them charge you with manslaughter?"

"I slaughtered no man," she said.

"Well, it's a legal term which makes the state's view of your offense less severe. We could argue that you contributed to Henry Deutch's demise, but you weren't solely responsible for it. It would result in much, much less of a sentence, perhaps carried out in a less severe penal institution with a quicker release date. We wouldn't be risking your life. Anna?"

She shook her head.

"I risk my life every day, Mr. Pearson. Doing it in a court of law is just moving to a different battlefield. The risk doesn't change." She looked forward. "He could be waiting for me right now, in some shadow, waiting and looking for an opening, an opportunity."

"Who, Anna?"

"His identity, his form is fluid, Mr. Pearson. That's his most significant power, the power to slip in and out of people, even animals."

"Do you ever wonder if he's slipped into me?" Del asked.

"When and if he does, I will know," she assured him.

He laughed.

When they arrived in Sandburg, she asked him to come into the shop with her.

"I must help you," she insisted, "or you will not be strong enough to help me."

"How do you intend on helping me?"

"I have put all my trust and faith in your decisions, your acts, Mr. Pearson. Do the same for me," she replied.

He thought for a moment.

"I've got a lot to do yet today, Anna, people to see, documents to study."

"You will do it all with cloudy eyes," she predicted. "We won't be that long," she promised.

Am I becoming as nutty as she is? he wondered when he

nodded and got out. He followed her into the shop. She turned and pulled the shade down on the door and led him through it to the rear.

"We're going upstairs?" he asked as she began to ascend.

"It will be all right," she replied.

"Look, Anna, it's late and—"

"Time is not really like water. It doesn't just flow by. We can, if we want, hold the second hand back or fill a minute with so much more thought and action, it becomes an hour. You will see and understand," she promised, turned, and continued up the steps.

He followed.

In the living room, she set a small dish on the table and filled it with some powder. Then she lit the powder and a thin spiral of smoke twirled up. She indicated that he should sit close to the table.

"On the floor?"

"As we have sat before," she said.

With some reluctance he did so and then he twitched his nose.

"What is that stuff?"

"A little leek, a little apple, and a little purple orchis," she replied.

"What is it supposed to do?"

"Strengthen your power for love," she replied.

He started to smile.

"When I held your hand the other day and read your lines, I saw something else. I saw that you have been in a combative mode for so long, you have lost your balance. There's a part of you that is angry about that and when you call on your essence, your spirit to reproduce itself, it cowers.

"Sometimes," she continued in her fortune teller guise, "you have doubts that you really want a child. You fear that

what you might create will not be the better part of yourself."

"Sounds like you're trying to be more of an amateur psychiatrist than a spiritual healer, Anna."

"They are not separate. Where is the soul, the spirit
housed within us? Is it here?" she asked, placing her palm
over her left breast, "or here?" she asked, touching her
forehead. "Perhaps it is in both places. If we separate parts
of ourselves and become blind to how one part of us
touches another, we diminish our power and our very
being."

"That sounds . . . wise and true."

"My mother taught me all I know," she said.

He looked up at the painting. Those eyes seemed
focused on him.

"I wish I had met her."

"You have," she said. "She has touched you and brought
you here. I believe that."

"Maybe," he said. "What now?"

She went into the kitchen and returned with a glass
filled with a light brown liquid.

"You must drink this," she said.

"What is it?" he asked, grimacing.

"You must drink it with trust or it will not work for you,
Mr. Pearson."

He hesitated.

"Would I do anything to harm my protector?" she asked.

He raised his right eyebrow.

"How do I know you don't think the evil is in me
because I suggested we plea bargain, Anna?"

"You had a moment of doubt, a weak moment, which
convinced me even more that I must help you first, Mr.
Pearson. It wasn't evil."

She held out the glass.

He took it slowly and then smelled it, but he didn't detect any discernable or unpleasant odor.

"What's this supposed to do?"

"Mend something in you," she said. "Heal. Make you stronger and complete."

"Can't you tell me what's in it?"

"It's an ancient recipe of herbs. Trust, Mr. Pearson," she said, fixing those magnetic eyes on him. "That is essential or it will not work."

He brought the glass to his lips, paused, and then tasted it quickly. It wasn't like anything he had ever tasted before, but it wasn't bitter.

"Just herbs?"

"An ancient recipe," she repeated a bit more cryptically.

"Okay, but after this I have to get going."

He downed the drink and handed her the glass. Then he started to rise and she put her hand on his shoulder.

"Wait, just a moment," she said, putting the glass on the table.

"Anna."

"Look at your watch," she commanded. He did so. "A moment is all I ask," she added, and sat across from him in the lotus position. The smoke seemed to thicken and become more like a veil between them. He couldn't help but close his eyes and when he opened them again, the room spun. He started to speak, but stopped when he thought she was rising slowly, levitating. He blinked and blinked and wiped his face, and then he closed his eyes and felt himself drifting as well.

Suddenly, he was falling through a dark place. The more he descended, the more he panicked until Jackie appeared, calling to him with her beautiful eyes, her soft lips. She reached for him and he took her hand. The descent stopped. She drew him closer to her and he kissed her. He held onto her and they both rolled over and over until they were on what seemed like a cloud. It was so soft, so inviting.

They made love gently, sweetly until they were both crying with pleasure. He kissed her tears and she kissed his. Afterward, they fell asleep in each other's arms.

He woke.

What a dream, he thought.

Anna wasn't there and the smoke barely rose from the dish. Confused, he looked around and then he stood up.

"Anna?"

He heard water running in the kitchen and he went to the doorway. She was just rinsing the glass she had given him.

"What happened?" he asked her.

She turned and smiled.

"How much time has gone by, Mr. Pearson?" she asked as a response.

He glanced at his watch. Maybe a minute, he realized.

"Not much," he said. "How can that be?"

"You were worried about time, but as you see you held it back."

"What was in that drink, Anna?"

"Shall I really tell you?"

"Please," he said.

"Besides some herbs, there is the heart of a dove, the liver of a sparrow, the womb of a swallow, the kidney of a hare, all put into a powder. My mother prepared it some time ago."

He stared at her.

"You're kidding?" he said.

She smiled.

"Good fortune, Mr. Pearson," she said.

"Huh?"

"What's done is done," she said, "and what will be will be."

"All right, Anna," he said, shaking his head, "If I don't end up in the hospital getting my stomach pumped, I'll be back tomorrow."

She nodded.

"I know you will be back," she said.

When he stepped out of the shop, he took a deep breath and gazed around the village. He smiled to himself, recalling his conversation with Judge Landers and the comparison he had made between himself and Gary Cooper in *High Noon*, claiming he had this deep sense of responsibility. With the reporters gone, the village looked like the village in *High Noon* just before the big gunfight. It had returned to its look of hibernation, vacant and deserted, but perhaps it was only each building, each telephone pole, every door frozen, waiting, its population holding its communal breath.

He drove out slowly, never before as impressed with the quiet and absence of movement. Truly, he thought as he sped up when he reached the outskirts, it had been like entering and leaving a dream.

Jackie was curled up on the sofa. She was gazing at the television screen, but she looked like she was gazing at her own thoughts and not the flicker of lights and images before her. For a long moment Del stood in the doorway and studied her. He didn't believe she was ignoring him. She was once again in too deep of thought or perhaps the television sound was a little too loud for her to have heard him come in.

She wore a pair of white shorts and a black tank top. She had kicked off her sneakers and pulled her feet under her legs. Her hair was pinned up, and for a moment she looked so young to him. He was thrown back to their high school days. In the beginning of their courtship, he couldn't help feeling her parents disapproval. Her mother was always such a social butterfly, getting her name in the papers as the member of this charity committee or that, and her father was always brushing shoulders with the movers and groovers in the community. Their home was rich and elegant, a castle compared to his own, and they drove luxury cars and went on European vacations and cruises. By the time she was a senior, Jackie had seen more than Del expected he would see in a lifetime.

Yet she never gave him the feeling she was slumming when she went with him. There was never anything snobby about Jackie. She was always sincere and sweet and always very popular. In the end, their breakup just after they had graduated high school was as much his doing as hers. Despite how his own parents pumped him up and despite his good grades and significant accomplishments, he had trouble shaking off that sense of inferiority. It was the degrees, becoming a member of the bar, that eventually gave him the confidence.

What was it Jackie had said when they began again, had that first dinner date? "Sometimes you've got to travel a wide circle to realize you were better off where you began. I've often thought of you, Del, thought of us, remembered times when I felt so content."

There it was, that circle again, he realized. Anna Young.

"Hi," he finally said.

Jackie turned slowly and looked up at him.

"You look tired," she said.

"Tough day, full of surprises and tension, but all I kept thinking toward the end was what I would come home to find."

"Oh?"

He approached her slowly and went to his knees so he could lay his head on her lap. She ran her hand through his hair.

"I don't want us to fight, Jackie. I'm sorry I haven't been more sympathetic about what you've been experiencing with the press, the calls, your parents. I can't stand this silence that's fallen between us."

"I told my parents to lay off," she said. He looked up. "I said, 'Dad, you had your chance to do the things you thought were right. Give Del his.'"

"You said that?"

She shrugged.

"I thought, what am I doing to us just when you need the most support? I don't know if your client is crazy, truly a witch, or just a conniving killer. If I do this with every client you have, we'll go nuts, and besides, why shouldn't I give you a chance to do what you do best?"

Del held his smile, his eyes full of impish delight. She raised her right hand.

"Honest."

"And your father?"

"He was silent and then he muttered something about going to a Kiwanis club meeting and gave the phone to my mother. As soon as she began to talk about it all again, I reminded her that she had a cardinal rule in our house: my father was to leave his work worries outside the door. I told her that's what I want too. I don't want you to have to relive your cases when you come home. I'm not saying I won't be willing to listen when you need a sounding board or even give you advice if you should ask, but I want us to have a life aside from all that, too, Del."

"Absolutely."

"I'm also thinking I should reconsider Howard Jaffee's offer to me to work at the radio station, creating those human interest pieces. I once had some ambition in that regard."

"Whatever you want, Jackie."

"When I get pregnant, I'll take a leave," she said. He smiled. "I've got a light dinner for us. And a nice Merlot to go along with it."

"Great. I'll take a fast shower," he said. He rose a little and leaned over to kiss her. She still had her eyes closed when their lips parted so he kissed her again on the tip of her nose and then he went to the bedroom. He was almost finished with the shower when the door to the stall opened and she stepped in, naked.

"I forgot to take a shower after my workout," she said with a lusty smile.

He laughed and she turned her back to him.

"Soap me up," she said.

He started to do so and reached around to cup her breasts and kiss her neck while the warm water beat over both of them. She turned and they kissed.

Their passion took them, still quite wet, out of the shower and onto the bed. She moaned about their soaking the comforter, but neither of them did much about it. Their lovemaking was more than just sex; it was a renewal, a thousand apologies, a reaffirmation of what they were to each other. It lasted longer, and just when it seemed to be coming to an end, it went on until they both turned away, pleasantly exhausted. Neither spoke for a few long moments.

It was almost like it had been in his dream at Anna's, he thought.

"Maybe we should have more fights," she joked. "Making up is more fun."

"Is that right? Are you trying to say something about my lovemaking before?"

"Let's see," she teased, "when was that?"

"Wise guy!"

He buried her in kisses and then they rose, put on robes, and went to eat their light dinner. Afterward, they sat on the sofa with her cradled in his arms. They started to watch a movie and then when both of them had trouble keeping their eyes open, they decided to go to bed. He really thought he would have a good night's sleep. She was asleep so fast, he was envious. Contrary to what he had hoped, the wonderful lovemaking, the food and wine, and the contentment that followed didn't relax him so that he could drift into an easeful repose. Instead, it freed him from some stress and permitted his mind to work overtime.

Something occurred to him, and he rose and went to his den-office where he sat perusing the depositions gathered by the prosecutor. He reviewed some of his own notes. As a result, he knew where he should go first in the morning.

She surprised him by appearing in the doorway.

"What are you doing? I woke up and reached over for you and you were gone."

"Couldn't sleep so I thought I'd make myself tired."

"Did it work?"

"I think so," he said, stretching and yawning. "Sorry."

"Just come back to bed, Del. What good will you do your client if you're walking around like a zombie? I thought you were going to try to relax one night."

"You're right."

He rose, put his arm around her waist, and followed her back to the bedroom.

"Del," she said, before she closed her eyes again, "just promise me one thing."

"Okay, I'll try."

"If this looks wrong, looks hopeless, take the easiest way out."

He smiled.

"If I can, I will," he promised.

"Why," she asked, "do I feel like that's a no?"

He laughed, kissed her softly, and lay back. In moments, they were both asleep.

He was up an hour before her in the morning, dressed, had some juice, coffee, and a slice of toast, which he barely ate. When he looked in on Jackie, he saw she was still in a deep sleep, so he left her a note.

> I had to get up with the chickens. Don't worry. I'll find another reason to fight so we can make up.
>
> Love,
> Del

He pinned it to his pillow and left for Sandburg.

A little more than forty minutes later, Del drove up to Melvin Bedik's. The house and property were right on the highway, and some of the chickens were visible from the road. They were kept in a small pen and henhouse just to the right of the house itself, which was a modest two-story Greek Revival with a porch supported by four rounded columns. The grounds and the house looked neat and well maintained, and indeed Del could hear the sound of a lawn mower when he got out. Melvin Bedik appeared on a rider. The moment he saw Del, he turned off the engine, hopped off, and started toward him.

"Morning. You're out working early," Melvin said with his hand out. They shook.

"Looking for that worm," Del said, and Melvin smiled and nodded. He gazed about.

"Mornings are the best times of the day around here, always were."

Del gazed at the obviously empty henhouses down left of the house.

"How long have you been out of the egg farming business?"

"Oh, about five years now. Usta be a big industry in this county. The corporate farmers slowly drove most of us little guys under. I got out in time, but"—he nodded at his chickens in the smaller henhouse—"as you can see, it's in the blood. My family was in the business forever. This house really goes back."

"Looks like it was impressive once," Del said, referring to the long henhouses.

"Oh yeah. We kept up with all the latest machinery. My eggs were laid, packed, and delivered to stores within thirty-six hours. We didn't have no antibiotics or hormones in our feed. Only wheat, maize, rye, barley, and oats."

Del stood there nodding, a soft smile on his face. Bedik studied him a moment.

"I know you didn't come up here to talk about the poultry and egg business, Mr. Pearson."

"No," Del said.

"Let's sit here," Bedik offered, indicating the chairs on the front porch.

Del followed him up the short wooden stairway and sat in the rocker. Melvin Bedik leaned on the railing to face him and folded his thick forearms under his chest.

"So?"

"I need an honest answer to a question, Mr. Bedik. I think you want me to do the best I can for Anna Young."

"You got that right. Yes, sir. Shoot."

"Did you give her one of your chickens for her to use in one of her rituals?"

Bedik stared.

"My brother who lives in Chicago told me it's possible someone who gave her something to use might be considered an accessory. He's not a lawyer. He's a stockbroker, but he's pretty smart."

Del nodded.

"The district attorney or one of her associates might pressure you with that to get you to tell them you gave Anna a chicken," Del told him.

"I haven't had much to do with legal things. Never been to court, never been sued or sued anyone. Oh, I had my business lawyer write some letters over the years, but nothing much more came of that, but my wife, she likes to watch them law shows on television. Lawyers are always telling their clients not to say any more than they have to."

"It's usually good advice," Del replied.

"I did not give Anna Young one of my chickens," he declared as if he was already on the witness stand.

Del nodded.

"Okay. Let's go one step further. Did you give or sell one of your chickens to anyone about the time of Henry Deutch's death?"

"Whew, that's a tough one to get out of," Melvin Bedik said, "when it's asked that way, I mean."

"Uh-huh. The district attorney is famous for her questioning of witnesses, Mr. Bedik. She won't be any less tough on you," Del warned.

Melvin Bedik reached into his rear pocket to get his red and black handkerchief. He wiped his face and then looked at the handkerchief as if he expected to see blood.

"I didn't sell it to him. He come up here and he asked me for one and he told me it was something he needed to do for Anna. I never asked her about it. I figured that was between her and him, and maybe it was even bad for me to ask. I mean, it might ruin her work or make her unhappy," he explained.

Del just stared, expectantly.

"I hope this doesn't put me in the middle of all this."

"I'll do what I can to help you as long as I know it all," Del said.

Bedik nodded.

"It was Tony Monato. He come up here that day. Next thing I know, he's been stabbed to death, but boy, I can't believe Anna done that."

Del nodded.

"Tell me exactly what he said."

"He just come up here and he stood around talking to me and he comes out with Anna's asked him to help her with Deutch. To do it, he says, he needs one of my chickens. He offered to pay for it, but I said if it's to help Anna, I'll gladly donate one. I put it in a sack for him and he left. That's it."

"And she never mentioned it to you, not even the time I saw you with her in her shop?"

"No sir, she didn't."

"Okay," Del said, standing.

"What happens now?"

"I'm not sure. Who else in this town has some chickens?"

"No one I know," Melvin said.

"Well, if Tony told someone where he got the chicken, the district attorney's people will be up here to see you and ask the same questions. Follow your brother's advice," Del added.

"Give them only what they ask for," he repeated as if it was his mantra.

"And be truthful, Mr. Bedik. People get into trouble when they wrongly assume telling the truth will get them in worse trouble."

"That's for sure," Melvin Bedik said. He followed Del to his car. "I guess it's looking bad for her, huh?"

Del held the door open and thought.

"It's not looking any better yet, but I've got a question rolling around in my head."

"Which is?"

"Why wouldn't Anna have asked you for the chicken herself? She told me if she had asked you for one, you would have gladly given one to her."

"That's true. Then you think Tony was lying?"

Del just stared a moment at the coop.

"We'll see," he finally said, and got into his car.

Bedik watched him drive off and then headed back to his riding mower. For a few moments, he just sat on it and thought. Then he shook his head and started the engine. It was all too complicated. Stick with the simple things, he told himself. Just cut the damn grass.

Del reviewed Anna's statements concerning Tony Monato. She claimed, he recalled, that she didn't speak to him. What did she mean, speak to him normally or speak to him spiritually? That was always what she either meant or, if he wanted to think of her as evil, what she used to cloak her deeds. Maybe Jackie wasn't so off, he thought. Maybe he was permitting Anna Young to charm him and not necessarily through some supernatural power. Perhaps Paula Richards was right about her: she was clever and knew how to hide behind the mystery. He hated doubting her like this. For some reason it made him feel so guilty, and he never ever felt guilty about doubting clients, especially some of the bottom of the barrel of humanity he had been forced to represent.

It has to be a good thing that it bothers my conscience, he concluded.

As he returned to the village, he slowed down, considered stopping at Anna's, but he spotted Phil Coleman and Munsen Donald standing in front of Kayfields Bar and Grill. They saw him and waved him over. He pulled up and rolled down his window.

Coleman sauntered over, his grin spreading over his face like butter melting on a hotcake.

"Now where you comin' from, Counselor? Wouldn't be the only one in the village who has chickens, would it?"

Del felt the heat rise up from his neck. Bedik would think he had sent them after him for sure.

"Why do you ask?"

"I've got a forensics team back up there in Monato's hovel," Coleman said, jerking his thumb at the building.

"Why?"

Coleman smiled at Munsen Donald who let his eyes shift downward.

"When I found those pictures, I thought I should check the camera and sure enough there was undeveloped film in it. Figured there might be more evidence," he added with a wide, lusty grin. "Painful to have to look at that stuff, but that's why I get paid the big wages. Anyway, what a surprise! Guess what we found instead."

"A picture of a dead rat in Henry Deutch's bed and maybe a picture of a dead chicken dangling from his front porch?"

Coleman's mouth fell open and Munsen looked up sharply.

"How the hell—"

"I'll save you the trouble of composing your suspicions.

Tony Monato did the dirty deeds and then tried to black-mail Anna Young, whom the district attorney will claim asked him to do them. He knew he would eventually pres-sure her for something more. That's why he captured the evidence on film with which to threaten her. Our district attorney will put all that forward as a motive for her killing him. It works better than the theory about Anna eliminat-ing evil wherever she sees it."

"Maybe you should be the prosecutor," Coleman said.

"It's an old debate trick . . . take your opponent's point of view in order to see the weaknesses in his argument."

"I don't know about any weaknesses. Tony certainly liked her enough, and I don't mean just those pictures. There's that account of him having an argument with Aaron Baer when Aaron criticized her," Munsen reminded him, but not with any glee.

"Maybe you better turn around and have another con-versation with your client," Phil Coleman suggested. "There are some witnesses now who will testify they saw Tony going over to her shop at night."

"To take those pictures," Del said. "He did it from the building next door. Go look for yourself."

"You've been there, huh?" Coleman said. He turned to Munsen. "We've got a real Perry Mason here." He looked at Del, his face grim, his eyes darkening. "Maybe she wanted him to do that. Maybe that was her way of bringing him into her dark, mysterious, and magical world," Phil Coleman half jested. "Stay tuned," he added, gazing back at Kayfields. "We might find something to make the rela-tionship even tighter."

"Thanks for the encouragement," Del said.

"Hey, I like the lady. So she's dangerous. Most pretty women are," Coleman quipped.

Del pressed his foot on the accelerator and pulled away.

His first thought was to run to his office and hide or go talk
to Michael Burke, but before he drove completely out of
town, he slowed down and tried to think clearly. It was better to go back, to talk to Anna, and to confront her with the
new information. Maybe what Jackie had wished for would
come true: he would take the easiest way out.

Twenty

"Can I offer anyone a cup of coffee, tea?" Paula Richards asked the three clergymen who had come to her office.

"Tea would be fine," Reverend Carter said.

"I don't want anything," Rabbi Balk said.

"Coffee, black," Father McDermott muttered.

Paula Richards nodded at her secretary who stood in the doorway and then she sat back in her chair.

"So, gentlemen, thanks for seeing me at such short notice," Paula Richards began, "but this is moving faster than I had expected and I wanted to lock up what I need from you."

"Of course," Reverend Carter said, smiling.

"I appreciate all of you coming and having interest in this thing, and I certainly appreciate your advice," Paula Richards added.

She had that magic in her eyes, that ability to turn on sincerity like a flashlight and direct it into the heart and soul of whomever she was placating, convincing, or trying to dominate. For a moment Father McDermott felt uncomfortable. What was that expression his father used to use: Don't kid a kidder. He wondered if the other two sensed how well they were being handled. The woman is a consummate politician. We all are; we have to be. It's our business.

It's also the Devil's business, he thought. It was just a passing thought, but it was like someone had truly plucked a string in his heart. The resulting vibration of conscience traveled through his very being and made him take a breath. Were they too involved? Was that constitutional admonition to keep church and state separate there for good reason? Would this end up biting them all in the ass?

"We're here willingly because we've all become somewhat concerned with the circus atmosphere surrounding this situation," Rabbi Balk said. "What we're afraid will happen," the rabbi continued, "is people won't take it as seriously as they should. They'll consider it a frivolous prosecution and we could all be swept up in that tabloid mentality."

Paula Richards was about to speak and reassure them, but paused when her secretary brought in the cups of coffee and tea. As soon as she left, Paula sat forward again, her hand on a stack of papers.

"Let me assure you all, there is nothing about this case that is frivolous. All of this documentation is about concrete, scientific evidence. It is my intention to show this woman for what she is, a charlatan exploiting people's fear of the unknown, the mysteries of life and death, to cover her own criminal activity.

"I want to further assure you that if I use the words *witch* or *spiritual*, it will be solely to point this out. There are serious issues of faith at stake here as well as legal justice. I won't permit this charlatan to achieve any validity and I hope to open the eyes of those who have been taken in by her antics. I'll need some expert religious testimony."

The three glanced at each other.

"So then you do intend to call one or all of us up as witnesses?" the rabbi asked.

"Well, yes," Paula Richards said, sitting back, "I would like to lay a foundation that involves the spiritual sickness she has engendered, and as you know, her lawyer could call anyone he thinks relates to her defense. He might, for example, call you up, Father McDermott, to get the church's view of the Devil, just to give some credence to Anna Young's views about evil and the Devil, especially if you are an adversarial witness."

"You know that he intends to do that?" Father McDermott quickly asked. Would his own skepticism about that matter be obvious under a lawyer's cross-examination? He could look foolish or he could look like a Catholic priest who had serious problems with his own theology.

"As of now, he hasn't indicated that in writing, but I have my sources and it seems it might be his intention. It will be in her best interest for him to give as much credibility and respect to what she does."

"Respect," Rabbi Balk practically spit.

"We've all spoken out in one way or another about this case," Father McDermott acknowledged. "I've given the church's view of those matters in interviews and, of course, in church," he said, practically whining.

The district attorney nodded.

"That's good, Father, but we would have to put some of that in a court record."

"I wouldn't want to drag the church into some sensational event that best belongs on the front page of the *National Enquirer*," Father McDermott warned.

"I won't let that happen," Paula Richards promised. "If there is any possibility of it happening, I will not drag you into it. On that you can rest assured."

The three smiled.

She stared at them a moment.

"Do any of you have anything else you can add to a presentation of evidence, any of you had any direct or significant contact with the accused woman? Witnessed anything I don't know of at the moment that would help me toward my goal?"

"Well, it's hard not to have seen her doing some ridiculous thing," Reverend Carter said. "It's a very small village."

Paula Richards nodded and pressed her fingers together in prayer fashion as she rested her elbows on the desk.

"Why don't we just talk a little about all that and let me see how it might help my prosecution. Keeping it all distinguished and respectable, of course."

"Of course," Reverend Carter said. He looked at his theological colleagues.

"We want only what's right for the spiritual health of our people," Rabbi Balk said.

"Then you've come to the right place," Paula Richards said. "Let's first explore this together and I'll be able to best judge how I can use your testimony." She pressed her buzzer and her secretary appeared in the doorway.

"Melissa," she said, "we're going to take some information we might use in depositions. I'd like you to take some notes."

She nodded, fetched a legal pad, and returned to the office, closing the door behind her. Then she sat to the left of the clergymen and held her pen poised.

"Who'd like to begin?" Paula Richards asked with a cold smile that strummed that cord of conscience in Father McDermott again.

"I saw her in the forest behind my church one night," Reverend Carter said. "She was with a group of people from the village and she was invoking some heathen spirit in a ritual of fire and smoke. I could hear the gibberish, the chanting, even screams!" he added with his eyes wide.

"I saw her walk in the wake of Henry Deutch's footsteps, scattering some powder and mumbling some silly incantation," Rabbi Balk revealed. "She was doing it right in front of children, too!"

They all looked at Father McDermott.

"There are men who have told me how she has used her sexual charms to draw them into her wicked circle where they blasphemed," he said. "She even tried to turn those charms on me!"

Paula Richards shook her head and looked very glum, but the excitement she felt was almost palpable. What wonderful witnesses she had, what testimony.

"I consider myself fortunate to be able to do the state's business and at the same time, strike a blow for family values, spiritual goodness, and the very souls of the people I serve."

The three clergymen seemed to be of one face, one of admiration, respect, and even a bit of relief.

This is really going to be something, Paula Richards thought.

Suddenly she felt invincible.

It was as if she was growing in her chair.

Anna was cutting some red velvet material when Del came to her door. She looked up and smiled, but she continued to work as if he was only another customer she would be with in a moment.

"I've just come from Melvin Bedik," he said.

"And something he has told you is troubling," she concluded. She finished snipping and set the material aside. Then she sat and looked up at him.

"I believe it can be convincingly established that it was Tony Monato who was either responsible for hanging that chicken and putting that rat in Deutch's bed or at least assisted someone in doing so."

He quickly explained why anyone would reach that conclusion.

"What the prosecution will now try to do is tie you closer to Tony and make it seem like he was doing something for you, something you asked him to do. It would help the district attorney to further her efforts to charge you with Tony's murder, too, and I know she would love to do just that before this trial commences."

Anna nodded.

"You told the district attorney and his assistant that you never spoke with Tony. If they come up with a witness who saw you do just that, it would be very, as you say, troubling, Anna. Did you ever have a conversation with him witnessed by anyone at any time that you can recall?"

"I have never spoken to him, but I have heard his voice," she said. She widened her eyes at his expression. "I wasn't dishonest. I did what you told me to do in this instance: I answered the question specifically and added no information when they asked."

Del smiled. Although he would do his best to prevent it and strongly advise against it, he envisioned Anna on the witness stand being cross-examined by Paula Richards. Even the well-acknowledged expert interrogator would have her hands full trying to trap this woman, he thought. How do you question someone who lives on two different levels, one physical and visible, and the other spiritual? It was almost as if she spoke two different languages.

"When you heard Tony's voice, what did you hear?" he asked.

"His pain and his loneliness. As I told you, I felt his eyes on me and when I did look his way, I saw the unbridled lust. Perhaps it frightened me so I avoided him."

"Was there anyway anything you might have done— signaled, somehow communicated to him, that you would like him to do such a thing as hang a chicken on that porch and put a dead rat in the man's bed? Maybe you said something to someone you knew would bring it back to Tony? Is that a possibility, Anna?"

She started to shake her head.

"Because you knew he admired you and perhaps would do what you wanted," Del added.

"Is this what you believe?"

"I have to ask these questions because they are very probably going to be asked in court, if not to you, to someone who might know, have been a go-between. Melvin Bedik gave Tony the chicken because Tony said he was going to do something for you. According to him, he never told you he gave Tony the chicken. Is that right?"

"Yes," she said, "but I sensed he had something to do with it."

"So why didn't you ask him?"

"I didn't want him to feel guilty," she said. "I saw no reason to put him into any pain," she added when Del looked unimpressed with her response. "You don't believe this?"

"I just don't want to be caught by any more surprises, Anna," he said.

"Every day I'm surprised by something," she replied, gazing at the material and spreading it out on her table. "You've got to use the surprises, read them. The truth is waiting to be discovered, anxious to be born in your eyes,

Mr. Pearson. Keep them wide open and willing to see."

"This isn't the time for word games, Anna."

She looked up at him, her face so tight and her eyes so intense, she suddenly looked like she had aged years in the moment. Wisdom changed her complexion, deepened her gaze.

"It never was," she said.

He took a deep breath, nodded, and stood.

"Okay," he said. "I'm off to prepare for trial. We've got a date and it's sooner than I expected."

"That's good. Oh," she said, putting the material aside and standing herself. "I have something for you."

"For me?"

She turned and went to her small desk in the back of the shop. She opened a drawer and then returned, holding her hand out and open. He looked down at the ring.

"What is this?"

"It's a gemstone, red garnet. It will protect you if you wear it, especially at night," she said.

He started to smile.

"What harm can it do to wear it?" she asked. "It's a pretty ring, is it not?"

"Yes, but . . ."

She took his right hand and slipped it over his pinky finger. It fit perfectly.

"How did you know my ring size?"

"It was here, waiting for you. The size was always there," she said.

He laughed and looked at it. It was very attractive.

"Okay," he said, "but I better start relying on some old fashion research and work, too. Talismans, spells, charms, and the like might not be enough, Anna."

"Whatever you must do, I am sure you will do," she said.

Nothing seemed to shake her confidence, nothing he

told her, nothing that was discovered. Either she was too far gone to understand or . . . she was right.

How he wished he was the one who could read a crystal ball, he thought, and left.

Edmund Scott's eyes popped open as if someone had snapped his fingers right in front of his face. For a moment he forgot where he was. It was like those times he found himself waking in a hotel room and forgetting he was on a business trip.

He glanced at the clock and saw it was nearly 2 A.M. He had to look to his right to see if Paula was beside him. She rarely touched him after they fell asleep. She liked her space, and having a king size bed was almost as necessary as having indoor plumbing.

She wasn't there and from the looks of it, she had yet to come to bed.

"What the hell . . ." he muttered, and sat up to listen. The house was deadly quiet.

Edmund had been taking a lot of ribbing these days, especially these past few weeks. There was no one with whom he was acquainted who didn't know he was married to the district attorney, and no one, perhaps throughout the state and even large parts of the country, who didn't know Paula was prosecuting a woman who claimed to be a witch or at least a spiritual woman.

The jokes were plentiful as were all the warnings about his crossing the path of a black cat or throwing salt over his shoulder. Some of his associates went so far as to send him good luck charms, and someone in his office, someone who wouldn't admit to it, had pinned a red handkerchief on his office door to ward off a curse.

Despite his being good-natured about it in the beginning, it had begun to wear a bit, and in truth, he wasn't one to disregard any form of belief. He could even remember the childhood chant about step on a crack and you'll break your mother's back. Would he be a liar and deny he avoided cracks, black cats, walking under ladders? Why take a chance, right? Just don't be obvious about it.

Now, he couldn't help worrying a bit. So many people were ascribing unusual spiritual powers to this woman. Was Paula risking some unseen wrath? Would bad luck befall them? It would be World War III for him to even suggest something like that, but he would have to be blind and deaf not to have seen the changes coming over his ambitious wife these days.

To him she seemed under some spell and very distracted. Most of the time when she returned home from work, she and he could be like any other man and wife, enjoy a dinner together, go to a show or a movie, take trips, in short be people. Lately, he felt as if she was looking right through him and barely heard him speak. When he had the courage to mention this to his partner of fifteen years, Albert Palmer thought a moment and said, "Maybe she's made you invisible to Paula."

What a curse that would be and yet, how often during their marriage had Edmund felt such a thing? The witch knew the weakness in their marriage and exploited it. That's what witches do, he thought and then chastised himself for being so ridiculous.

Where was she? What could she be doing this late?

He stood up, reached for his robe, and left the bedroom. He found Paula hovered over her desk, her hands pressed against her temples, her elbows down. For a moment he just stared at her. She was so still, almost as if she had been turned to stone in that position. Another curse?

"Paula!"

She looked up slowly. In the glow of the desk lamp, her eyes were like two dark blue neon bulbs.

"Are you all right? What are you doing still up? It's nearly two in the morning," he emphasized.

She held that cold, even frightening smile on her lips.

He waited.

"This is going to be brilliant, Edmund," she said. "I've been inspired."

"Inspired?" He started to smile himself and then stopped. "You mean like touched by God or something?"

"That's exactly what I mean," she said. "I've been preparing my opening statement. Take time off. Come to court. Watch me. You'll be so proud. I used to hope and pray I had been chosen for this role in life, and now I feel it's true."

Edmund nodded slowly.

I thought, his troubled mind pondered, that it was the witch lady who was supposed to be obsessed with herself.

Twenty-one

The advent of media circuses materializing seemingly overnight in front of courthouses was no longer an unusual or surprising event in America. Del had seen it often enough on television since the O.J. Simpson murder trial in Los Angeles, but there was still something surreal about seeing it here, in front of the courthouse that had become his everyday workplace. The frenzy created its own new frenzy, like some continually exploding gases in outer space. Local citizenry flocked to the stone steps and neoclassical facade as much to see the commentators and news personalities that had become celebrities in their own right, as they did to see Anna Young and the combatants, and the resultant size of the crowd fed the hunger of the media to feast on another notorious event.

There was Court T.V., of course, as well as CNN, the major networks, Fox, and even a crew from a Canadian television company. Surprisingly, the *New York Times* had decided to cover the trial, along with practically every tabloid. Photographers jostled each other for good position.

Del and Anna had no real opportunity for a secreted entrance. There was little choice but to walk the gambit and face the exploding flashbulbs and the waves of questions hurled at them from every direction. The half dozen or so sheriff's deputies looked vastly outnumbered and overwhelmed themselves, barely keeping the pathway open.

It was one of those perfect Catskill mountain early summer days with clouds splattered against the nearly turquoise sky as if they had been hurled like snowballs. It was in the mid-seventies, with a cool, northerly breeze. All of the greenery around the courthouse was plush and rich, colors vibrant. The director of photography of a feature film couldn't have asked for a better backdrop for his cameras.

As if she knew she was playing a role in some great morality play, Anna had chosen to wear all white. She had a lace shawl over her shoulders and her hair tied in the back with a white ribbon. Her ankle length skirt had just a touch of blue swirling through the material. Del thought she looked absolutely radiant, her dark eyes catching the sunlight as would black diamonds, her lips full and richly ruby. When he glanced at her to see her reaction to their welcoming throngs of press and spectators, he thought she was stimulated by the noise and turmoil. She wore that soft smile on her face, a smile that deepened and seemed capable of soothing the savage beasts that hungered for sound bites, unusual pictures, drama. When she first stepped out of the car in fact, the crowd pulled back on its own as if they all paused to take a deep breath before lunging forward, thrusting lenses toward them, prodding for a better angle, a closer shot.

Del shook his head and held onto Anna's arm as they climbed the steps to the front entrance.

"Are you a witch?"

"Did you curse the district attorney?"

"Did you kill Henry Deutch with a spell?"

"Do you drink the blood of bats?" someone screamed. That drew some laughter, even a wider smile from Anna.

At the top of the stairway, she suddenly turned, and she did it with such a slow and dramatic air, the crowd grew still. She tilted her head as if she was listening to something and then she looked out at them and said, "Beware of the voices in the wind."

For a moment all anyone could hear was the wind through the trees and the sound of cars passing on the street. Those seconds of silence were quickly followed with shouts.

"What she say?"

"What's that mean?"

"What voices?"

Del urged her into the courthouse. He shook his head as he walked along. The only encouraging thing this morning was the fact that the district attorney had not yet sought the indictment of Anna Young for the murder of Tony Monato. She didn't have enough evidence and cleverly realized that if she did indict Anna without it, he could make something of it in regards to this case. It might even have justified a motion to change venue because of the contamination of the jury pool. Still, he worried that Paula Richards had something up her sleeve, some second shoe to soon drop.

He took a deep breath. He was here and it was beginning. He was taking a journey he wasn't sure he could make, and had grave doubts he should have even started.

The courtroom itself barely held fifty spectators, but somehow nearly seventy had managed to squeeze into it, including Jackie and her mother. The overflow crowd heavily taxed the air-conditioning system, something Judge Landers obviously sensed the moment he entered. As soon as he sat, he mumbled to the bailiff, wondering aloud if they were violating some fire department ordinance with so many people in the courtroom. The bailiff wasn't sure if it was the judge's dry sense of humor or if that meant he should turn around and count heads.

"Let's get this started," Judge Landers said quickly, and looked to the district attorney. In contrast to Anna Young, Paula Richards wore a dark blue skirt suit. She had her hair styled and sprayed and wore some rouge, a little eyeliner and dark red lipstick.

When the judge spoke, Paula sprung up from her seat as if she had been foaming at the mouth in anticipation. She turned and fixed her gaze on the jury with such intensity, the twelve men and women looked immediately hypnotized. Someone coughed in the rear of the courtroom, a chair, shoved over the wooden floor, screeched, and then the stillness lingered like the moment before a clap of thunder.

"Ladies and gentlemen of the jury," Paula began as she came around her desk. She had her palms pressed together about waist high. "In many ways this is admittedly a unique case, an unusual case, but in more ways it is not. In the end you will see that it is truly a simple case because it is an obvious case in which one person, the accused, Anna Young, is beyond a reasonable doubt responsible for the death of another person, Henry Deutch. The state will prove that Anna Young deliberately planned actions with the intent to do fatal harm to Mr. Deutch and the state will clearly show she had motive, motive she admitted freely many times in many different ways.

"What will make this case unique is that the defendant, also by her own admission, is proud of what she has accomplished, and what will make this case unusual is exactly how Anna Young accomplished her premeditated murder of Henry Deutch. But the state will clearly show and support the characterization of her actions as deadly, deliberately deadly. About that, ladies and gentlemen, have no doubt."

She turned and looked at Del, nodding as she continued.

"The defense will, I'm sure, attempt to engender reasonable doubt in your minds because that will be the defense's only avenue of escape from a truth that will be obvious to you and will be substantiated factually and scientifically. The state will show all this in an organized, methodical manner and will take great pains to close that one avenue of escape so that justice will and can be served in this courtroom.

"This is a case that involves more than just the death of one man. The defendant will be shown to be a shrewd charlatan exploiting the fears and the sorrows and the frustrations of vulnerable people, turning them from the sanctity and spiritualism that has sustained them and their families for generations, in order to further her own mercenary and evil ways.

"When you find her guilty, as I know you will by the end of this trial, you will not only find her guilty of premeditated murder, murder in the first degree, but you will also find her guilty of manipulating the very souls of good people in the community. She did this in the hope of cloaking her evil act under the guise of something spiritual," Paula said, and glanced at Reverend Carter, Father McDermott, and Rabbi Balk who all sat together three rows back.

"The defense might try to enter evidence proving that
Anna Young is the high priestess of a so-called alternative
faith. He might even suggest freedom of religion entitles
her to distort and manipulate vulnerable people and even
drive Henry Deutch to his death, but," Paula Richards said,
smiling and shaking her head, "you will, I feel confident,
see through that phony doorway of escape as well.

"I want to clearly state this at the outset, ladies and gentlemen," she said, turning to face Anna. Slowly, she lifted
her right arm and pointed her long finger at her. "The state
is not, I repeat, not trying Anna Young for witchcraft. No,
indeed not. We are trying her, and we intend to convict
her, for knowingly harassing Henry Deutch to death, for
using effective psychological techniques, techniques she
knew would have a deadly effect on Henry Deutch's bio
pathology." She emphasized by stabbing the air with that
extended forefinger. Then she turned back to the jury.

"Her weapon might not have been a knife or a gun or a
club, but it was just as deadly and just as effective, believe
me." She smiled. "I wouldn't ask you to believe only me,
however. The state will provide expert opinion and clear
case histories to substantiate our claims."

She looked at Anna again.

"We will show that she knew Henry Deutch was weak
and sick. She knew that with a physician's details. We will
show how his illness intensified with each of her acts. In
short we will show how she pursued this man relentlessly
until she killed him."

She paused, looked thoughtful, and then put her hands
on the railing as she leaned toward the jury, panning each
and every face as she spoke.

"Think of him as being on a treadmill and having a
weak and sickly heart, and think of her as being the one
who could turn up the speed, turning it up every day until

she killed him, and then, to add insult to injury, claiming victory over her imaginary evil so she could exonerate herself in the eyes of the community, indeed even build their dependence and faith in her so that she could steal them from their faiths and turn herself into their savior.

"How many people in history," Paula said, smiling at them, "how many evil people in history," she repeated with deliberateness, "presented themselves to their people as their people's savior?" She paused to let the idea settle in their minds, and then she turned and stared at Anna Young in silence.

"Yes, this is a unique case," she said slowly, "an unusual case, but," she added, turning back to them, "in the end you will clearly see that it is nothing more than a simple murder after all and you will send a message that every charlatan will hear."

She took a deep breath, nodded, smiled, and returned to her seat.

Del felt a pair of steel marbles rolling around the base of his stomach. He took a deep breath and looked at Anna. She was facing forward, undaunted, her eyes fixed on the judge who sat hunched over his papers.

Instinctively, he gazed at Jackie. She gave him that smile of reassurance. Her mother looked absolutely terrified, however. It nearly made him laugh.

"Mr. Pearson," Judge Landers said. "You're up at bat."

"Thank you, Your Honor." Del rose.

"It's cases like this that make you wish prosecutors had to pay some of the court costs and fines for the time they can make people like you and me waste," he began, addressing the jury. He was surprised and encouraged by the smiles on the faces of some of the jury members. Even Judge Landers looked like he was letting his thin, rubber lips stretch.

He looked at Paula. She wasn't just glaring at him, she was sending darts from those eyes.

"The state is worried about us establishing reasonable doubt? Of course they are. Reasonable doubt is so obvious it practically calls out to us. At least give me a challenge," he added. Then he shook his head and strutted toward the jury.

"They don't want to try her for being a witch? Ladies and gentlemen of reasonable minds, if you don't believe in spells and curses, in voodoo and hoodoo, you can only find Anna Young not guilty, especially of premeditated murder. Murder?

"You will see that the medical examiner listed Henry Deutch's death as caused by myocardial infarction . . . a heart attack.

"You remember every time your own mother or father yelled at you and said if you don't stop, you'll give me a heart attack?" He smiled. "Mine sure did."

Some of the jury members nodded.

"Are we to believe that everyone in the cemetery who wasn't stabbed, poisoned, beaten, accidentally killed, or shot, was murdered? Find Anna Young guilty and you'll have to do that because someone is always aggravating someone. We're all under stress caused by someone else from time to time.

"Heck, I'm under it right now!" he cried, raising his arms. "The state's put me under it. If I dropped dead at this moment, can we blame the district attorney for bringing this case to trial and making me shout and argue like this?"

One of the men on the jury actually chuckled. There was a ripple of laughter in the audience, but the judge's hard gaze ended it quickly.

"All right, we're prepared to admit," Del continued, pacing toward the witness stand, stopping and turning to the jury, "that Anna Young did not like Henry Deutch, that she even blamed him for the death of her mother. It's a natural thing for her to feel. Shortly after he threw Anna and her mother into the street, she suffered a stroke and she died. Anna's human. She blames Henry Deutch.

"Oh, one more thing about Anna we'll admit. She is a witch," he said.

Even the judge couldn't stop the loud murmur with his gaze. He had to rap his gavel.

"We will, however, explain what a witch is and does, and why, to the dismay of the prosecution, it is even a recognized and protected religion.

"Who among you hasn't at one time or another wished ill would befall someone? If it did, would you be ready to stand trial? Anna simply has a more organized system of beliefs in regard to that.

"But remember this, ladies and gentlemen, she did not lay a hand on Mr. Deutch. She did not, and the state has not and will not be able to prove otherwise, enter Mr. Deutch's house. She did not put a dead chicken on his porch and a rat in his bed, which the state will contend through its expert witnesses, were catalysts responsible for Mr. Deutch's subsequent heart failure.

"So what did she do, scare him to death with her chants and her looks and her religious icons?

"We will bring in our expert witnesses too. Yes, stress can kill. Stress is more dangerous for a man or a woman with heart problems, but let us consider this . . . was Anna Young the only source of stress for Henry Deutch? What kind of a man was he? What aggravated him? If the barber charged him more than he thought was right for a haircut, should the barber be brought to trial?

"Henry Deutch was a landlord. Did some of his other tenants aggravate him that day, the day he died?

"And of course, maybe he would have had heart failure anyway at that moment. Maybe his time had come, simple and true.

"In short, ladies and gentlemen of the jury, you will hear the words *reasonable doubt* resonating in your minds at every stage of this trial and you will ask yourself, as I do, why are we here?"

He nodded at them, turned, and walked slowly back toward his table where Anna Young gazed up at him as if he, not her, was the one with magic.

Del's exaltation was short-lived. Paula Richards began to do what she had promised: build a logical and scientific case for the state. First, she established the motive. It wasn't hard because even the people from Sandburg who respected and admired Anna were more than willing to describe how much she hated Henry Deutch. It was obvious from their testimony that they disliked Henry as well. Sometimes, they sounded almost like co-conspirators, applauding her efforts to do him in. In particular, the description of Gussie Young's burial ceremony was mesmerizing. Anna's vow was emphasized, underlining her determination to rid the village of the evil. All who were there characterized it as a promise to them.

Through cross-examination, Del tried to show that the witnesses to Anna's vows did not literally understand her to mean she would kill Henry Deutch. Ironically, one of his best witnesses for this strategy turned out to be Father McDermott. Since much of what he was testifying to was secondhand, Del was able to object on the basis of hearsay. The judge sustained his objections, but in the end, Paula Richards got Father McDermott to repeat what he had actually overheard Anna say to someone in the streets of Sandburg.

"So you heard this with your own ears?" Paula asked.

The Catholic priest was firm in his affirmative response. Del wouldn't shake it. However, he had another intention.

"Father," he began instead, "will you explain to us what exactly happens when the Catholic church performs an exorcism."

Paula Richards was on her feet objecting.

"This is irrelevant, Your Honor."

"On the contrary, Your Honor, it's highly relevant. It's our contention that Anna Young was performing a ritual of exorcism and not a premeditated murder."

Judge Landers permitted the question and Richards suffered her first significant setback in the early going. The priest was obviously very uncomfortable when he was forced to answer. His voice dropped a few octaves and he squirmed in his seat.

"Exorcism is the ritual act of expelling demons, or evil spirits, from persons or from animals," he replied quickly, speaking like one who wanted to get something painful finished.

"How did this become part of the Catholic theology, Father? It sounds . . . pagan."

"Years and years ago, many sicknesses were believed caused by the activity of such spirits."

"I see. And there is a prescribed method of spiritual treatment?"

"The rites of exorcism have varied accordingly. Simple blessings may be given in order to remove persons or things from the presence or power of evil. One can say that in this sense, exorcism is a kind of prayer for healing, since evil and sin are often considered as the causes of sickness, disharmony, and death. The practice is regulated by canon law and must be authorized by a bishop, so it is hardly pagan," he added.

"I agree. It sounds harmless," Del said, smiling at the jury. "But I always thought it had more to do with the Devil. Doesn't it, Father?"

"In the strict meaning of exorcism, the level of possession is such that the personality of the person possessed is completely taken over by the personal presence of the Devil, yes."

"So you believe in a literal Devil walking the streets, visiting our homes?"

"Yes. The Devil exists. He is here to defeat God and to test our faith."

"Everyone's?"

"Yes."

"Even people who don't look to him, so to speak?"

"Cases of involuntary as well as voluntary possession have been claimed."

"So the evil spirits in some cases choose their victim without the victim's cooperation?"

"Yes," Father McDermott replied. His lips twisted in as if he wished he could smother the answers to death.

"And it takes a trained religious eye to see this or diagnose it, if you will?"

"Yes."

"I'm sure you are aware, Father, that exorcism is practiced in many religions throughout the world."

"I'm not that familiar with it, no," Father McDermott muttered, hoping that was the end.

Del raised his eyebrows.

"Well, any basic course in comparative religion would reveal it. In Islam it is called *da'wah*. Traditional Judaism," Del said, gazing back at Rabbi Balk, "has a large body of literature dealing with the exorcism of evil spirits called *dibbukim*. In Japan, Nichiren Buddhist monks perform exorcisms based on the teachings of the Lotus Sutra.

"Surely you remember that The New Testament records instances of exorcisms performed by Jesus. In one of the most dramatic of these, he expelled a legion of unclean spirits from a possessed man, which then entered into a herd of swine and he drove them into the sea. I believe that's Mark, chapter five, is it not, Father?"

"Yes," Father McDermott said, looking angrier and angrier.

"So, if the Catholic church does it and the Jewish and Islamic faiths have a place for it, and what Anna Young practices is her form of religion, can't we say she wasn't doing anything more or less than that?"

"Objection, Your Honor. This calls for pure speculation on the Father's part, especially in light of evidence he is totally unaware of."

"Sustained. Rephrase your question, Mr. Pearson."

"Thank you, Your Honor. From the limited knowledge you have of this situation, Father, from what you claim you heard yourself, wouldn't you at least admit that what Anna Young was doing was a ritual of exorcism?"

"I have absolutely no knowledge of Anna Young's rituals, what they involve or how she carries them out, so I can't say that, and I would never raise her activities to the level of a respectable faith like Catholicism or Judaism."

"So you just don't respect her religion?"

"I didn't say that. I . . ."

"What did you say?"

"The woman's a . . . pagan."

"What did you see her do that characterizes her as pagan?"

"I saw her draw circles in the air. I . . ."

"You mean make a design, like a cross?" Del asked, crossing the air between him and Father McDermott as would a priest offering a blessing.

The priest's face turned crimson.

"I will not sit here and permit you to compare—"

"No further questions, Your Honor," Del said, and turned his back on the priest.

When Del returned to his seat this time, he saw a look of growing respect in Paula Richards' face. She nodded as if to say "touché," but then she called up Benny Sklar.

"How long have you known Anna Young, Mr. Sklar?" Paula asked.

"A year maybe."

"And during this period, your wife passed away, I understand?"

"Yes, a few months ago."

"I understand you told people you communicated with your dead wife. Is that true, Mr. Sklar?"

Benny glared at Munsen Donald.

"Yes."

"You did this with the help of the defendant, Anna Young?"

"Yes."

"Did she come to you and offer her services in this regard or did you just ask her if she could do it?"

"I heard from someone else that she could do it, so I asked her and she offered to do it."

"For how much?"

"Twenty dollars."

"Twenty dollars," Paula Richards repeated with a short laugh. "Seems cheap enough for such a long-distance call."

The courtroom roared. Judge Landers rapped his gavel, but not with the same enthusiasm as before.

"You have heard Anna Young claim she put a curse or a spell on Henry Deutch, have you not?"

"Yeah, I heard her say that."

"And did you understand her to mean she was cursing the Devil in him or him?"

"I thought she meant he was the Devil."

"Himself? So she wanted to do away with Henry Deutch or make him a better person?"

"A better person? Never."

Paula nodded.

"Exactly," she said, and looked at Del. "She wanted to do away with Henry Deutch. Your witness."

"Mr. Sklar, did Anna Young ever say she wanted to kill Henry Deutch?"

Benny raised his arms.

"Kill, do away, what's the difference?"

"Did she say 'kill'?" Del demanded.

"I think she said 'get rid of him' once," he admitted.

"Which could mean drive out of town?" Del asked.

"Objection, Your Honor. Leading, speculation."

"Sustained."

Del thought a moment. He was violating the cardinal rule. Don't ask a question if you don't know the answer.

"No further questions, Your Honor."

Mark one up for Richards, he thought.

Before the trial adjourned for what would be a weekend hiatus, Paula Richards called Doctor Bloom to the stand to review Henry Deutch's heart condition. He explained the difference between stable and unstable angina. Paula Richards emphasized the dates of Deutch's doctor visits. Del knew why and what was coming.

Del cross-examined, getting Doctor Bloom to describe similar cases, many of which became more serious heart problems.

"If Henry Deutch didn't take his medicine properly, didn't follow a better diet, didn't exercise properly, he could have brought about his own demise, could he not, Doctor Bloom?"

Richards tried to object, calling it speculation.

"The witness is the state's own expert, Your Honor. Surely what he has to say is more than mere speculation."

"I'll allow it," Judge Landers said.

"Yes," Doctor Bloom said. "Of course."

"Thank you," Del said.

Paula Richards leaped to her feet.

"Recross, Your Honor. Doctor Bloom, did Henry Deutch ever mention Anna Young?"

"Yes."

"What did he say?"

The doctor looked at the jury.

"He said the woman was driving him to his grave."

"And he said this after you told him his condition was not improving. In actual fact, it was degenerating?"

"Yes."

"You have testified that stress has a detrimental effect on the heart?"

"Most assuredly," the doctor said.

"Thank you, doctor. That's all for the moment," she said.

She brought up Munsen Donald and had him read from his reports, stressing the dates of each incident to obviously point out the correlation with Henry Deutch's doctor visits. Then, just before the trial recessed for the weekend, she called up Sophie Potter, Doctor Bloom's receptionist, who admitted she had given Anna Young a detailed account of Henry Deutch's physical condition.

All Del was able to do was get her to admit she had done so on her own initiative because she thought it was something that would please Anna.

Richards was up for a recross. One question.

"Did it indeed please Anna Young, Miss Potter?"

Sophie hesitated. She looked like a trapped rodent for a moment.

"Yes," she admitted.

Richards smiled.

"No further questions," she said.

"You were brilliant, Del, but she sits there looking like she couldn't care less," Jackie said after they had gotten into his car and started away from the courthouse. Jackie's mother had left in her own car.

"It's not that. She has an incredible ability to focus, extract herself from the fray. Actually, I'm trying to learn how she does it," he said. "And I wasn't that brilliant. Paula Richards was the one who was able to leave the jury with a big point in her favor, not me. Good planning. You want the jury to think more about your arguments than your opponents', especially over a weekend hiatus."

"Mother was a little upset about how you made Father McDermott look bad," Jackie revealed. Then she smiled. "I thought you made some excellent points there."

"I guess we better not go to bingo night," Del said, and laughed. Then he shook his head. "This was where I could do the best. The parts that are coming are all better for the enemy," he said. "Paula Richards will be parading one expert after another to testify and strengthen her contention that Anna Young's actions could be and were deadly. She established motive well and this last bit of testimony supports premeditation, planning, malice aforethought. I've got my work cut out for me, Jackie. Forget we're married this weekend."

"You mean you're not going to go to my parent's brunch

on Sunday? I think Daddy's invited some people just to meet you," she said.

"I don't know."

"What else can you do, Del? You've prepared and prepared, haven't you?"

"You always miss something, Jackie. I want to review some of the newer material. Let's wait and see, okay?" he said to offer a compromise.

She nodded, but he knew she wasn't happy.

The moment they got home, he began what he promised. He shut himself up in his den and began to pore over the files. Public defenders didn't have assistants and investigators. It was truly a David and Goliath situation. Me against the state, he thought, and bore down.

It didn't pop up at him. In fact, he went past it and actually forgot about it. Somehow, maybe magically, it just reappeared in his thoughts and he turned back to reread. For a moment he held his breath for fear it might disappear and be only something he had imagined. But it didn't. The words were there on the lab report:

Traces of potassium, magnesium, zinc, phosphorous, iron, and sulphur dioxide: Primarily sucrose.

Serves me right for not paying attention in chemistry class, he thought, and then he sat back and began to consider why this was important and why, in the end, it would mean Anna Young's acquittal.

Twenty-two

"**M**unsen," Munsen Donald barked into the phone. He wasn't exactly sure why he felt so miserable, but he did. He knew he had good reason not to be unhappy and he had told himself, promised the gods, in fact, that if all was well with Lisa, he would never lose his sense of proportion again. It would take an awful lot for him to get upset, lose his temper, or bathe in self-pity. He hated himself for not adhering to his promise and so soon after he had made it, too.

"Can you meet me in your office in fifteen minutes?" Del asked him. "Oh, this is Del Pearson," he followed.

"I recognized your voice, Mr. Pearson. What's up?"

"I know from our previous discussions that you want things to work out for Anna Young as much as I do," Del said.

Munsen hesitated. This was indeed why he was feeling miserable. He, too, thought he could foresee where Paula Richards was going and how successful she would be in getting there.

"Yeah, so?"

"I think you can help me help her, if you want," Del said.

"How?"

"Now it's fourteen minutes," Del said. "I'm in my car. I took a chance you would agree."

"Okay," Munsen said, smiling. "I'll be in my office in thirteen."

Actually, only ten more minutes had passed before Del entered and found Munsen sitting expectantly behind his small desk.

"This must be good," he said, leaning forward.

"I think it is," Del said. "We talk about equal justice for all in this country, even brag about it, but I'd be the first to admit that money buys a better defense attorney and that has some weight on the scales of so-called blind justice."

"You didn't do so bad in there today for a charity attorney," Munsen said.

"I had some moments, but I don't have the resources to do what Anna Young deserves done in her defense. The state has an army of investigators. Private detectives are expensive and there's just so much I can do on my own."

Munsen smiled.

"Okay, counselor, what do you want me to do and why?" he asked.

Del sat and opened his file.

"I've got this suspicion, but we have to work fast. I'm asking for something to be analyzed tomorrow and if I'm right, I want to bring in my theory with factual support by Monday," he said. "Maybe," he added, "even an arrest."

"Okay. What's the theory?"

"Before I make any accusations, I need some information. I'm on my way to see Deutch's doctor again, to ask him one question, the answer of which I have every reason to believe I already know."

"Okay. And then?"

"This is the report you made concerning the events that occurred and your investigation on the morning you discovered Henry Deutch's dead body. Please reread it and tell me if it's accurate to the word, especially your phone conversation."

Munsen raised his eyebrows and took the report. He read it carefully and nodded.

"Yeah, I'd say so."

"Okay. Take me to see Gerson Smallwood."

"Smallwood? You mean to his house?"

"His drugstore is closed. I drove right past it."

Munsen laughed.

"I don't think he's ever open after six unless someone calls him for an emergency. Not for years, even on weekends."

"Therefore, his house."

"Then what?"

"I'll ask him one question, too. The answer I believe I know as well."

"Then what?"

"Then you have to become the charity investigator," Del said. "But don't worry. I'll be right beside you."

Less than an hour later, armed with the two answers he had anticipated, Del stopped with Munsen for a beer at Kayfields. All of the regulars were there reviewing the trial. When Del entered with Munsen, he was treated like a celebrity.

"You did real good in there today, Mr. Pearson," Roy said. There were a number of seconds to the compliment.

"The district attorney didn't do so badly for herself either," Del replied. "It was just round one."

"Somehow, I think you're going to do well in round two," Dennis Rotterman predicted.

"Who the hell do you think you are?" Charlie Trustman shouted at him, "Anna Young looking into a crystal ball?"

Everyone laughed, even Del. Then he and Munsen went off to the side to talk. They planned their strategy for the next day.

"Even with this information and if I get what I hope to get from the lab tomorrow, I'll still have to do some good bluffing," Del said.

"You a good poker player?"

"Should be. I'm a lawyer. If I'm successful, I'm coming down to join you and your buddies in Kayfields one night."

Munsen laughed.

"You always give this much of yourself to your clients, Mr. Pearson?"

"I like to think I do, but . . ."

Munsen nodded, understanding.

"Anna's got something, a way of winning you over. She's a special woman. Maybe she's not really supernatural or anything, but she's got something," Munsen said. He leaned closer to lower his voice. "I can't talk about her too much. My wife might get the wrong idea. Know what I mean?"

"Exactly," Del said. "Someone, and I think I know who now, called my wife to leave anonymous messages to that effect."

"Yeah. Well you know you're good when the enemy tries to stop you before you start."

"I hope I'm as good as they think and we can end this."

"Funny, in a way Anna will be validated if we do," Munsen said.

"I've been thinking the same thing. Maybe that's what makes me work so hard for her."

Munsen smiled. They finished their beers and then left. Munsen drove Del back to the firehouse where he had left his car. When Del arrived home, Jackie was practically waiting at the door.

"Where did you run off to like that?" she demanded.

"I have a lead I want to follow."

"You went to see her?"

"Not her, but I went to Sandburg," he said. "Why the cross-examination? You get infected in the courtroom today or something?" he kidded.

She shook her head. He could see the tears welling up in her eyes.

"What?"

She shook her head again.

"Another phone call?"

"Yes."

"Saying what?"

"That you were with her. Asking me to think about how closely you two sat in the courtroom. Warning me that she put some sort of spell on you."

"Idiotic, stupid . . ."

"You're wearing that ring she gave you, Del. Why would you do that?" she asked.

"You know," he said, "I actually forgot it was on."

She smirked.

"Really."

"Okay," she said.

"Jackie, listen to me. There's nothing going on except an attempt to provide a good defense. I swear it," he pleaded. He held up his hand and seized the ring with his left forefinger and thumb. "You want this off, it's off," he said.

"What do you want, Del?"

He looked at the ring.

"I don't want it to become a problem for us. It was given to me for protection."

"You believe that stuff she preaches and does?" Jackie asked, incredulous.

"Of course not," Del said. He took the ring off and put it in his pocket. "It's nothing. Really. I love you, Jackie. I'm just trying to do a good job. It meant a lot to me to see you there in court, too," he added.

She softened and he stepped forward and embraced her.

"Besides a couple of dozen or so citizens of Sandburg, you're the only one on my side," he said. "I hope."

"Of course I'm on your side," she said, and they kissed. He kept his arm around her shoulders as they walked toward the bedroom. He paused at his den, glanced at the desk as if he was tempted to return, and then looked at her and smiled.

"Let's just go to bed," he said. "It's been a helluva long day."

"Not just to sleep, I hope," she said. "I hope you saved something for me."

"Bet your life on that verdict," he replied, and kissed her softly on the lips.

Their lovemaking was graceful, gentle, full of quiet exploration, caresses, and kisses that almost resembled the caresses and kisses of two young teenagers discovering the wonder of each other's bodies, each other's building excitement. When he settled in between her legs, he hesitated for a moment to tell her how much he needed and loved her. She reached up to put her hands around his neck and pull his lips closer. They moved with perfect synchronization, their rhythms so simultaneous their moans were in stereo. Each time she came, she pressed her fingers into his shoulders. He felt like an artist, sculpting a sensuous, passionate statue to rival Rodin's *The Kiss*. Jackie's face glowed with pleasure.

For a brief moment, he saw Anna. He blinked and she

was gone, but it was as if she had visited Jackie's body just long enough to make him reach higher and higher, deeper and deeper until his passion consumed him as well and he found relief in his orgasm and subsequent withdrawal. His heart was pounding.

"Are you all right?" she asked him.

"Yeah. I'm just catching my breath."

She turned over and gazed down at him.

"You were wonderful, counselor."

"Hey, I had a lot to work with," he said. She kissed him and lay back.

Before he fell asleep, she nudged him again.

"What?"

"I'm sorry about before."

"It's understandable. Don't worry about whoever is calling. I'll get a trace on the phone if we have to, but I'm hoping to end it all tomorrow."

"How?"

"Let me just work it out first."

She was quiet, but her worry was palpable.

"Del?"

"Yeah?"

"Put the ring back on," she said. "I'm okay with it . . . and who knows?"

"Right," he said. "Who knows?"

Just before noon the next day, Del's cellular vibrated. He had just come from forensics.

"I just found another piece to the puzzle, Mr. Pearson," Munsen said. "How did you do?"

"As expected," Del said.

"Just come down to the station. We'll go up there together," Munsen said.

"It's out of your jurisdiction."

"I'll rely on professional courtesy. Don't worry about it," Munsen said.

Less than an hour later, they were on their way to New Paltz in Munsen's police vehicle.

"If this doesn't turn out well, you could take some heat leaving your post," Del reminded him. "Paula Richards would insist on it."

"More reason to go," Munsen said. "I didn't vote for her."

Del laughed.

"Neither did I," he said.

New Paltz was a college town because of the state university campus, but it was a great deal more with its vintage buildings, cafes, bed-and-breakfast establishments, art houses, and quaint shops within the heart of the famed Hudson Valley. Just to the west of the village were the mountains and cliff faces of the Shawangunks, affectionately known as "the Gunks," which attracted both amateur and seasoned climbers and hikers.

There was considerable traffic, both car and pedestrian, when they drove onto Huguenot Street. Minutes later, Munsen pulled up to Rasklein's Pharmacy. They sat in the car, contemplating it for a moment.

"You're sure she's on duty now?"

"Yeah," Munsen said. "The best way to do this is to come at her hard and fast," he suggested. "She won't notice that my uniform reads Town of Fallsburg. It's intimidating. We've got to make it look like an arrest is imminent."

"Exactly," Del said. "Here's where that poker face comes to play. Ready?"

"Yep."

They got out and entered the drugstore. Dave Rasklein was behind the prescription counter explaining a medication to an elderly lady. He glanced at them and then continued his explanation.

Barbara Deutch was ringing up a cosmetic sale behind the counter on the right. She looked at them furtively and then hurriedly counted out the change for the two middle-age women.

Del nodded toward Dave Rasklein and then he and Munsen stepped up to the drug counter just as the elderly lady finished thanking him and turned away to leave.

"Can I help you?" Dave asked. He was a man in his fifties, with more salt than pepper thin hair, dark brown eyes, and a long thin nose to hover over his slightly thickened lips. His narrow shoulders lifted in a gesture of anticipation as his eyes searched Del's and Munsen's faces for some hint of intent. After all, a uniformed policeman and a man in a suit were hovering at his counter and looking rather serious.

"We're here to speak with a Barbara Deutch," Del said.

"Deutch? Oh. Sure. Barbara," the druggist called to her. He turned back to them. "She still goes by her maiden name, Loukis," he quickly added.

Barbara Loukis was barely five feet tall with rather dull, stringy light brown hair. Her best feature was her hazel eyes, slightly almond shaped. Her nose was a bit too wide and her lips almost masculine in thickness. She had an ample bosom, a narrow waist but wide hips.

Without speaking, she came toward them.

"Is there someplace we can use?" Munsen asked Dave Rasklein.

"Huh? Oh, sure. Come right back here," the druggist suggested, and indicated a door on the left that opened to a storage space filled with sundries, cosmetic supplies, and some stationery goods. There was one wooden chair toward the rear of the room and a single neon light fixture above.

"What's going on?" Barbara demanded.

"These men want a word with you," Dave said.

"Why?" she asked sharply.

"We're investigating a murder," Munsen said dryly. "We were hoping to question you here rather than at the police station."

"Oh, my goodness," Dave said. He looked at Barbara. "This must be in regards to your father-in-law."

Barbara's face reddened, but she held her defiant gaze.

"What do you want from me? I don't know anything about that."

"It would be better if we spoke in private, Mrs. Deutch, " Del said, emphasizing *Deutch* with deliberateness.

With some reluctance she entered the storage room, her arms folded over her bosom in a gesture of continued defiance, even fortification.

"What do you want?" she snapped, turning on them.

Del let a moment pass while they both stared at her and she waited, obviously impatient but unnerved.

"This will be the one and only opportunity we will give you, Mrs. Deutch."

"Opportunity for what?"

"To save your ass," Munsen snapped.

"Why? What the hell are you talking about?"

"New evidence has been discovered," Del said. "Henry Deutch died with residue from the pill he took still under his tongue, enough for an analysis. That was done and that led to an analysis of the pills in the bottle that was labeled nitroglycerin. As we know you know, those pills were placebos, sucrose, and they had been substituted that day for Mr. Deutch's medication."

Del took a deep breath.

"Your husband's fingerprints are on that pill bottle and

that pill bottle was given to Henry Deutch the day before. Your husband claimed he hadn't been to see your father-in-law for almost a week before the death."

"You gave him those placebos to put in that pill bottle," Munsen charged, hovering over her as if he was about to beat her for it.

"You're an accessory to a murder," Del said. "It was pre-meditated. Murder one."

"The death penalty in this state," Munsen added.

"Own up to it now, cooperate with us, and we'll see what we can do with the district attorney to help you. We're about to arrest your husband, but we thought we'd give you this one chance."

"When we turn around and walk out that door," Munsen said, "it's over."

Barbara looked unable to speak. Her eyes were wide, her mouth locked open.

"We have every reason to believe and will soon prove that your husband killed a man named Tony Monato, who, we now know, planted the chicken and the rat to frighten Henry Deutch. You could be held accountable as an accessory for that murder as well."

"Practically guaranteeing you the death penalty," Munsen added.

"Well?" Del quickly demanded.

"It wasn't my idea," she said. The words burst out of her as if they had been burning inside her like some acid from some spoiled food. "I didn't even know what he was going to do with it. He asked me to get him some placebos and I did. That's all I did."

"Yes, but you knew you and he would inherit Henry Deutch's money and property," Del said. "You can't hope to escape by claiming you didn't know what he was going to do with it."

"I told him it wasn't right, but he did it anyway," she added. "How can you blame me for that?"

"You gave him the modus operandi," Del said.

"What do you know about the death of Tony Monato?" Munsen asked before she could catch her breath.

"I didn't know he was going to do that. I don't know the man and I didn't know what they had planned together. Until they did it," she moaned.

"Go on," Munsen urged.

She shrugged.

"He went to one of the antique stores on Huguenot, Becker's, and he found this special old knife he called something."

"An athame?" Del asked.

"Yes, I think that's what he called it."

"Okay," Del said.

"What are you going to do to me?"

"Protect you," Munsen said. "I don't think your husband would appreciate you much now. Where is he?"

"He's home," she said. "Sleeping. We live above the restaurant. He closed it down for good yesterday and said he won't have to get up early ever again."

"How come you're still working?" Munsen asked her.

She looked down.

"He said it would look suspicious if I quit too soon," she admitted.

Del looked to Munsen.

"I'll make a call, get the local gendarmes over there," he said.

Barbara sat on the chair, looking dazed.

"Am I going to go to prison?"

"Just sit tight," Del told her.

He and Munsen stepped out and Munsen turned to him.

"Wolf's prints on the bottle. That was a good one."

"They might be there, but we don't have his prints to compare yet," Del said with a shrug.

"If they're not on the bottle, the district attorney could pursue the idea Anna did that switch with the pills. Without Barbara's testimony, that is, and you wouldn't have been any further along."

"But we just got Barbara's testimony," Del said, smiling.

"Thursday nights about eight," Munsen said, heading for the telephone.

"Huh?"

Munsen turned.

"Our poker game in Kayfields. You qualify," he said.

Twenty-three

Wolf Deutch lay back on the pillow with his hands behind his head and stared up at the ceiling. It was flat white, but it had webs of cracks, some of which looked like road maps. He let his eyes follow one line and then another. He had no idea how long he was doing it. Time didn't really matter very much. He had no schedule dictating his day. Never again would he worry about getting up late and, besides, he liked tracing the lines. He could do this forever.

Wolf was always a big daydreamer. It was as if his thoughts traveled through corridors with large, gaping holes in the walls, and often drifted out. As far back as elementary school, his teachers complained about his lack of concentration, his inability to focus on one thing. Later, he would be diagnosed with ADD, Attention Deficit Disorder. His mother was so upset about it she wanted him taken to see doctors in New York City, but his father referred to his favorite explanation for everything Wolf did that was a disappointment.

"He's just lazy," his father declared. "They have fancy names for a simple problem to give themselves work and make themselves seem important. When I was his age, that sort of thing was cured quickly with a sharp slap of the ruler on the behind."

In the end it was always Wolf's fault, no matter what. As hard as he tried, Wolf couldn't recall a single warm moment with his father. He never demonstrated love or compassion, not even on his birthday. Helping his father off to the great beyond didn't even nick Wolf's conscience. It was time for him to go anyway. He wasn't enjoying a single waking moment. All he did was complain. He belonged with his mother, Wolf thought. If he could, I'm sure he would thank me for it now.

Wolf smiled at the scene: his father's ghost appearing at the foot of his bed.

"Son," he would say, "thanks for getting me out of there, away from those miserable people and all that aggravation. You deserve all that you've inherited. Have a good life and when it's time for you to be here, we'll have a place for you, but please, before you come, get a haircut and buy some clean clothes. Your mother says hello."

"Hello, Mom," he cried, and laughed.

The knocking at the door downstairs startled him and quickly washed the grin off his face. He listened and heard it again, louder. Whoever was there was being very insistent. He tried to think of anyone who might be coming to collect on a debt. They all must've heard by now that he was into some money. The hell with them, he thought. Let them chase me for it.

The knocking continued. It sounded as if they were rattling the door on its hinges. Who the hell . . . can't they see the big sign in the window declaring the restaurant was closed?

He rose slowly and went to the living room which had windows looking down on the front entrance of the restaurant. He saw the two police cars, one from Fallsburg township and the other from New Paltz. Slowly and as quietly as he could, he opened the window and stuck his head out just enough to look down at the front door of the restaurant.

There was no difficulty recognizing Munsen Donald immediately. The man was too big to miss, and that was definitely Anna Young's lawyer, Del Pearson, beside him and a local policeman as well. Wolf's heart thumped as the blood rose to his face. He pulled himself back and then he looked down once more because he thought he had seen someone else and he was terrified at whom he resembled.

Yes, there he was. His father, looking up at him. That ghost. He didn't come to his bed. He came to the front of the restaurant with them, to get him, to punish him. He could practically hear him shouting up.

"Come down here, you lazy bum. You can't even kill me right. You gotta go get a town drunk to hang the chicken and put the rat in my bed! Stupid, of course, he would try to blackmail you. You idiot!"

How could this be happening? What was going on?

He practically lunged for the telephone on the side table and quickly tapped out the drugstore number. Dave Rasklein picked up on the second ring.

"Can I speak to Barbara, please. It's Wolf, Mr. Rasklein."

The pharmacist was quiet for a moment.

"Mr. Rasklein?"

"She's not here," he said.

"What? Why not? She's supposed to be there. She didn't quit, did she?"

They were pounding on the door below.

"She's not here," Rasklein repeated.

"Where is she?"

"She's . . . with the police," he said.

The phone seemed to burn his hand. He just dropped the receiver.

With the police? Why? What did she do?

"What did you do?" he screamed. He turned in a complete circle, trying to decide what he should do.

First, he rushed back to the bedroom and put on a pair of pants. He slipped his feet into a pair of loafers and plucked a shirt off the chair where he had thrown it the night before. He shoved his arms through the sleeves and then pulled open the bottom dresser drawer. Quickly tossing the underwear out and over his shoulder, he reached his model 10 Smith and Wesson .38. He had gotten it with a permit to have for protection in the restaurant, but he liked keeping it upstairs just in case some burglar broke in while he was asleep. He stuck it between his hip and pants and started down the stairs.

They were calling to him now, pounding and calling. He clearly recognized his father's voice, too.

How could his father be here? What did Barbara do? It was all going so well, just as he had planned. Him, the boy with ADD, the boy who was lazy, the failure, had done so well. This was wrong. This wasn't fair.

I did it right. I did it all right. Even the district attorney thought so, he thought. He was in a rage. Why was this happening?

He crouched and scurried behind the bar to go out the opposite side and slip through the kitchen door. The restaurant had a back door. He'd get out and then . . . what? Get away until he found out what was actually happening, he thought. That was the best plan.

Outside, Munsen grew suspicious.

"He knows we're out here," he said. He turned to the local policeman. "Back door to this place?"

"I think so," the patrolman said.

"You cover the front. I'll check it out," Munsen suggested.

The local cop looked more than happy about that. His face was full of visible relief.

"I'll call for some backup too," he suggested, and returned to his vehicle, leaned through the window, and reached for the car phone.

Del looked at Munsen.

"Be careful, will you. I won't have any explanation if something happens to you."

"Anna won't let it," Munsen said, and headed around the corner.

Just before he reached the back of the building, Munsen heard the door open and close. He crouched down and drew his pistol out of the holster. Then he inched his way toward the corner.

Wolf paused outside the door to listen as he planned his next move. He would go through the yard, over the fence behind the supermarket, and drop onto the side street. Then he would walk quickly to the corner, cross and head around to the patch of forest. Best thing was to lay low until he had a chance to gather his wits and know where to go.

Before he stepped forward, he heard Munsen Donald's feet crunch the gravel on the side of the building. He reached for his pistol and cocked it. Then he retreated enough to slap his back against the building and wait.

Munsen came around the corner carefully. At first, he didn't see Wolf because he was so still and completely draped in a shadow cast by a long, low cloud.

"Get away from me," Wolf cried, his pistol up before Munsen had a chance to level his at him.

"Take it easy, Wolf," Munsen said.

"How did you come back?" Wolf demanded.

"What?"

"Why can't you just be dead? It's time for you to be dead," he said. "You're better off dead. You're happier. Get dead again."

"Who do you think I am?" Munsen asked. "Wolf, this is Munsen, Munsen Donald from Sandburg, remember?"

Wolf shook his head.

"Call me lazy now. Go on. Call me lazy," he challenged and waved the pistol.

Munsen felt himself turn to ice. Wolf Deutch's eyes were so glazed it was obvious he was looking inside his imagination and not at him. He certainly didn't hear him. There was only a second to act, maybe not even that. With his pistol cocked, Wolf would surely get off one shot and at this point-blank range, that bullet would rip a whole in me big enough for a small pickup truck, Munsen thought.

Suddenly a sparrow that had made its nest under the eaves of the building sprung out, its wings flapping. Wolf's eyes lifted in surprise and Munsen fell to his right, raising his pistol and emptying one chamber at the same time.

The bullet ripped into Wolf's right shoulder, spinning him around. He fell forward.

The moment Munsen hit the ground, he rolled and got to his feet, rushing at the fallen man. He twisted the pistol out of his hand just as the New Paltz officer rounded the corner of the building, his pistol drawn.

"Call for an ambulance," Munsen snapped.

Del appeared right behind the local patrolman.

"What happened? You all right?"

"Yeah."

He looked down at Wolf and then up at the sparrow's nest. "I'm fine," he said. He smiled. "Thanks to Anna."

Judge Landers clamped his hands together and sat back in his large, soft black leather desk chair to look at Del Pearson and Paula Richards. Wolf Deutch was in the hospital where he had given a semi-bizarre statement about having to kill his father again. One of the forensic detectives had located blood splattered on Wolf's old boots and there was a strong possibility it would be tied through DNA to Tony Monato, another nail in Wolf's coffin. They hadn't yet gotten him to admit to Monato's murder, but with Barbara's testimony, it looked like a lock.

"I can tell you this," Paula Richards said through clenched teeth after the judge had spoken, "I still feel she's somewhat responsible. She brought Henry Deutch to the point where he needed the nitroglycerin tablets and even if they were there, he probably would have dropped dead."

"You might feel that, but I have grave doubts you would get even a simple majority, much less a unanimous jury verdict to that effect, Paula," Judge Landers said. "This trial is over. And you don't have to worry about the Monato murder. Mr. Pearson here has handed it to you on a silver platter," he added.

Del thought the judge was truly enjoying the moment which underscored the feeling Del had always had concerning the judge's opinion of Paula Richards.

Paula pressed her lips together.

"Funny how you and your people missed that business with the placebo."

"Sucrose is sugar. We just thought he had eaten some candy. No one made a big deal over it when the medical examiner didn't," she said defensively.

"One person did . . . Mr. Pearson here."

"Nevertheless, I had a very valid position with this prosecution," Paula Richards asserted.

"Oh, no question, no question. And if it had gone to conclusion, you might have succeeded in having an innocent woman convicted with that brilliant argument."

"I repeat, she's not so innocent," Paula insisted.

"Maybe not. So few of us are anymore," Landers quipped. "So, now that this is behind you, what's the story with the nomination, Paula?" The judge leaned forward. "Care to give us a scoop?"

"I don't know what I'm doing yet," she said, and stood up. She blew some air through her closed lips, glanced at Del and then shrugged. "Of course, being in Congress might be a helluva lot easier than this."

"True," the judge said. "You need only a simple majority to win."

Paula Richards finally smiled.

"Excuse me for saying so, Judge, but you can be one son of a bitch."

"Comes with the territory," Landers said, shrugging as if she had given him a compliment.

He and Del watched the district attorney leave, her shoulders back, her neck stiff.

"She's not a good loser," Landers said, shaking his head.

"She didn't lose. Justice was served," Del said. "The prosecution is supposed to care about that, about truth."

The judge peered at Del over his glasses.

"I like that. An idealist in my courtroom. It's like a breath of fresh air, and just like fresh air, it doesn't last too long in a courtroom."

"Thanks, I think," Del said.

Judge Landers nodded at the door. "She won't win, you know. I've already heard talk about how the opposition is going to make hay of this prosecution." The judge drew an imaginary marquee in the air. "Would you vote for a district attorney who saw someone riding on a broom?"

Del laughed and stood.

Judge Landers nodded.

"You did well for yourself, counselor. Anna Young should be very grateful.

"I can tell you now," Landers continued, "now that it's over, but she got to me the way she fixed those dark eyes on me the whole day in court. It got so I tried not to look at her. It was as if she was forcing me to . . ."

"What?"

"Be a good judge and worry about good defeating evil as much as what's legal and what's not," Landers said. "There, you see what you're doing to me. You're making me an idealist again. Get the hell out of here before I become incompetent," he declared, waving at the door.

Del smiled, shook his hand, and left to face the crowd of reporters waiting on the courthouse steps. This time, he wouldn't be so anxious to flee their cameras and their questions. He even considered the fact that he was getting to enjoy it, enjoy the high profile cases. Perhaps it was time now to move on and chase that Mercedes, make his in-laws happy, be a big fat successful attorney.

Well, maybe not fat, he thought, and strutted to the door.

Anna was at her table, working on someone's dress when he entered her shop. She glanced up at him but continued working.

"I just stopped by on my way through to see how you were doing," he said.

She smiled and paused. Then she turned to him.

"You have a good heart," she said. "Sometimes it will challenge things you feel you have to do and you will struggle. Yours is a world filled more with gray than with black and white," she added. "Just keep the gray as light as you can."

He laughed.

"Now that this is over, what are your plans?" he asked.

She thought a moment and smiled.

"They have not yet been decided."

"You really believe all this is somehow part of a grand design?" he asked, gesturing toward the window as if everything was outside her little shop.

"Let's just say there's a design but we have to discover it," she replied. "Just the way you discover yourself and continue to do so."

He fingered the ring she had given him.

"Keep it on," she suggested.

His smile widened.

"I had no intention of giving it back."

"You earned it anyway," she said. "Thank you for being who you are."

"I could say the same to you."

They stared at each other for a long moment.

"Well, I've got to get going. I have an appointment in Ellenville and just thought I'd take this route so I could stop by to see how you were."

"Thank you for doing so," she said. "Good fortune to you and to your wife," she added.

"Thank you, Anna."

She turned back to her work.

He stood in the doorway a moment and looked back at her, and then he closed the door behind him, took a deep breath, and started for his car. The town looked peaceful, content.

Mostly, it looked safe, he thought.

Epilogue

Fall had always been Del's favorite season in the Catskills, and not only because of the vibrant colors. The air was different. Cooler, crisper, it had the effect of revitalizing him. He thought about beautiful afternoons, wearing his turtleneck sweater, jeans, and sneakers, playing touch football on rich green lawns, taking walks with Jackie, and knocking the juiciest looking wild apple off the branch. And then there was always the geese and duck sightings, the V formations appearing against the sea of blue, their chorus of quacks full of pride, inviting the landlocked, flightless humans to gaze up in awe at their beauty and power as they headed south.

It was enough to help him forget for a while that a long, dreary winter lie in waiting, anxious to pounce with its fingers of ice and its cold breath. It would begin with a rainfall of orange and yellow and brown as the leaves were blown off branches and sent floating to earth. On weekends the rakes came out, the lawn mowers purred, small spirals of smoke emanated from piles and from large cans. Houses

were being fitted for storm windows, snow birds following
the lead of ducks and geese were having their homes win-
terized, the pipes drained, the antifreeze put in toilets.

In earlier years when the Catskills was still a major playground and resort area, the contrast with summer was so
dramatic one would question his or her eyes and ears. In
literally a few days, the famous Labor Day weekend, the
communities went from hustle and bustle, from traffic and
noise, to an almost eerie stillness reminiscent of the film
On the Beach. Store owners who had been forced to put in
eighteen-hour days breathed with relief. Hotel workers bid
their goodbyes and headed to other resort areas for new
work. Young people were preparing and being prepared to
begin a new school year. The traffic and pedestrians disappeared as if some powerful god had snapped his fingers. It
was truly as if the whole area had taken a deep sigh and settled back, anxious to hibernate and restore itself.

Sandburg and most of the other hamlets and villages
now had much less of a dramatic change. The weather differences were there, of course, but without the hordes of
tourists, the bungalow colonies and hotels, there was no
grand exodus. It was as quiet on the day before Labor Day
as it was the day after.

On a particular Sunday in early October, Del impul-
sively made a turn and headed for Sandburg. He hadn't
been there since the trial had ended two months ago and
he had spoken briefly with Anna in her shop. He had been
busy ever since he had joined Sacks, Levits and Aster, the
firm his father-in-law had recommended. In truth, it was
an exciting, growing law firm and the partners had great
respect for him. A junior partnership loomed on the immediate horizon and it was easy to foresee a full partnership in
a short time thereafter. That gold ring of success his father
had pursued so vigorously in vain now looked easily within

Del's reach. He was proud of that, proud of how his parents would feel with every one of his accomplishments.

Jackie and he were talking about building the house on the land his father-in-law had set aside for them. It was a beautiful lot with a full view of the lake. What point was there in refusing it just because it was his father-in-law giving it to them? Why not, Del rationalized, let Jackie's father do something for her, something he really wanted to do? Wouldn't he want to do the same for his daughter some day or his son?

Yet he couldn't deny that he had some pangs of conscience, some rebellion of pride. He didn't want to be known as the "son-in-law." He wanted his own identity, but in truth that seemed clearly to be coming now. It was false pride and unfounded fear to think otherwise. He wasn't arrogant about it; he was simply being realistic.

Even with only the one day in court defending Anna Young, he had gained some fame. Sometimes people kidded him about being the witch's attorney, but more often than not, he participated in really interesting legal discussions concerning the district attorney's case and how to defend against it. There were other examples of similar prosecutions in the country, too, and with every one, his case was made reference to, which caused his name to be written in articles and reports.

And then there was another reason to be proud and optimistic about the future. Two days ago, Jackie had it confirmed. She was finally pregnant. Maybe that was what had motivated his turning toward Sandburg, he thought. Could he give Anna credit for this? Of course he told himself it was silly to do so, even to suggest it. He'd never told Jackie about Anna's rituals and what he had done up in Anna's apartment one afternoon. Wisely, he thought this was one of those things better buried in the memory.

But the thought of it revived all his feelings about Anna Young, the mystery in her eyes, the softness in her smile and her voice, the great calm that had never left her despite the hoopla and the terrible threat of her being convicted of first degree murder and maybe even executed. Even now, when he was in court and particularly annoyed or disturbed by a judge's ruling or a turn of events, he would check his temper and his disappointment by simply recalling Anna's face, Anna's wonderful black diamond eyes. In his memory she floated like some soft caress that would go on forever and ever, or at least as long as he could recall the sound of her voice.

He laughed when he entered Sandburg. There was that mutt, that cross between a police dog and some sort of retriever, comfortably ensconced at the center of Main Street. It lifted its head lazily as he approached, gazed at him with disbelief, and then struggled to its feet and sauntered off to the side where it plopped with an almost audible groan of annoyance to wait for him to go by.

Del drove past Anna's shop. It was dark and looked quite shut up. The building beside it, the one from which Tony Monato had taken those erotic pictures of her, had been torn down and there was just an empty lot now. It made the street look like a mouth with missing teeth, he thought. He stopped, contemplated the shop, and then got out and went to the door. He shaded his eyes and gazed into it.

There was nothing there, no tables, no racks for clothes, nothing.

"She's gone," he heard and turned to see Munsen Donald crossing the street. "I saw you go by Kayfields," he said. "I was just coming out and waved."

"Didn't see you. Sorry. Where is she?"

"Who knows?" Munsen looked at the shop door and shook his head. "I didn't even know she was gone until days after she left. I know it was days, but I don't know the exact day she left."

"How did she leave?"

Munsen pushed his cap back and scratched the front of his head. Then he smiled.

"Okay, here it goes. Benny Sklar says he saw her get on the Greyhound Bus. Tilly Zorankin swears a black limousine drove up and she got in and it went off with her. Dennis Rotterman says he thought he saw her walking out of town with a little suitcase. And then I got Phil Katz whispering to me that Melvin Bedik picked her up and took her off and only he knows where she went. Melvin says Phil's crazy. The bottom line is she's gone."

"What'dya know," Del said, shaking his head. "She didn't even call to say goodbye."

Munsen laughed.

"Maybe because she's not gone," he quipped. Imitating her he added, "I am everywhere." He looked at Del's hand. "I see you're still wearing the ring she gave you."

"Sure. Why fly in the face of the possibilities? The great mathematician Pascal was said to have been an atheist until he turned over in a carriage and survived and then concluded he would believe in God just in case."

Munsen laughed.

"Smart man. You're doing well these days I hear."

"I'm a lawyer. It's embarrassing not to do well," Del said. "So about how long has she been gone?"

"About a week now, give or take a day. But I gotta show you something," Munsen added. "Got a few minutes?"

"Sure."

"Let's take your car."

He went around and got in, telling Del to drive up Church Road. They went to the old cemetery and got out. Munsen led him to Gussie Young's grave.

There at the center was a burst of wild roses, all a deep pink.

"They're called Dog Roses," Munsen said. "The day after I heard Anna was gone, I came up here on a whim. I figured she might have left something, some message for the people here. There wasn't anything but these flowers blooming."

"So?"

"They don't bloom this time of the year, Mr. Pearson. June, late July maybe, but not now. I grew up here. I know a little about it. It's almost like a burst of joy, don't you think?"

Del laughed. Then he nodded.

"Maybe, maybe."

He stepped forward and plucked a petal. The flower had a very sweet aroma.

"Delicious," he said.

"Anna would make tea with it, I bet," Munsen said.

Del thought a moment and then he took out his wallet and put the petal in.

"Just like Pascal . . . just in case," he said.

Munsen laughed. Del started away and Munsen started to turn, but stopped. He touched Del's arm and they both looked back at the tombstone.

A sparrow had landed on it.

It paraded back and forth, its chest out, proud. Its wings fluttered.

The two men looked at each other.

"Naw," Munsen said.

"Maybe," Del said.

The sparrow shot off into the forest and disappeared.

They left in silence, each lost in his own thoughts, each afraid to admit how much he wanted to return to his childhood faiths and the wonder of make-believe when someone as beautiful and soft in their eyes as Anna Young sat them at her feet and began with the most exciting words of all, "Once Upon a Time."

NEATH PORT TALBOT LIBRARY
AND INFORMATION SERVICES

1		25		49		73	
2		26		50		74	
3		27		51		75	
4		28		52		76	
5		29		53		77	
6		30		54		78	
7		31		55		79	
8		32		56		80	
9		33		57		81	
10	.	34		58		82	
11		35		59		83	
12		36		60		84	
13		37		61		85	
14		38		62		86	
15		39		63		87	
16		40		64		88	
17		41		65		89	
18		42		66		90	
19		43		67		91	
20	9/13	44		68		92	
21		45		69		COMMUNITY SERVICES	
22		46		70			
23		47		71		NPT/111	
24		48		72		.	